Refusal

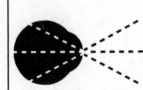

This Large Print Book carries the
Seal of Approval of N.A.V.H.

DICK FRANCIS'S

REFUSAL

FELIX FRANCIS

THORNDIKE PRESS
A part of Gale, Cengage Learning

GALE
CENGAGE Learning·

Detroit • New York • San Francisco • New Haven, Conn • Waterville, Maine • London

Copyright © 2013 by Felix Francis.
Thorndike Press, a part of Gale, Cengage Learning.

Thorndike Press® Large Print Core.
The text of this Large Print edition is unabridged.
Other aspects of the book may vary from the original edition.
Set in 16 pt. Plantin.

LIBRARY OF CONGRESS CATALOGING-IN-PUBLICATION DATA

Francis, Felix.
   Dick Francis's Refusal / by Felix Francis.
     pages cm. — (Thorndike Press Large Print Core)
     ISBN 978-1-4104-6216-9 (hardcover) — ISBN 1-4104-6216-1 (hardcover)
   1. Private investigators—Fiction. 2. Horse racing—England—Fiction.
   3. Murder—Investigation—Fiction. 4. Mystery fiction. 5. Large type books.
   I. Title.
   PR6056.R273D56 2013b
   823'.914—dc23
                                    2013029682

Published in 2013 by arrangement with G. P. Putnam's Sons, a member
of Penguin Group (USA) LLC, a Penguin Random House Company

Printed in the United States of America
1 2 3 4 5 6 7 17 16 15 14 13

For my grandson
Samuel Richard Francis

And with my special thanks,
as always, to Debbie

1

"No," I said. "Not a chance."

"But, Sid, you must."

"Why must I?"

"For the good of racing."

It was a familiar tactic.

"I'm retired," I said. "I told you. I don't do that sort of thing anymore."

Sir Richard Stewart, currently chairman of the British Horseracing Authority, hadn't worked his way up from Saturday-morning shelf stacker to become chief executive of the country's largest supermarket chain by taking no for an answer.

"Come on, Sid," he said with a knowing smile. "Everyone knows that Sid Halley is still the best of the best." Sir Richard playfully punched my arm. "And you know you want to, really."

Did I?

It had been nearly six years since I'd opted out of the private investigator business. Six years in which I had established myself as a moderately successful independent investor, dealing primarily in blue-chip stocks on the major markets but also, with increasing frequency, bankrolling individual inventors who had good ideas but little or no cash.

Six years of mostly stress-free living with no one trying to beat me up, or worse.

"No," I said again with finality. "I don't want to, really, not now, not ever."

I could tell that Sir Richard wasn't happy, not happy at all.

"Sid," he said, drawling the word out for a couple of seconds, "can I tell you something in confidence?"

"Of course."

He leaned forward towards me as if he didn't want to be overheard, which was rather strange considering we were alone in the living room of my Oxfordshire home.

"I am seriously concerned that the whole future of our sport is at risk." He pursed his lips, raised his eyebrows and nodded at me as if emphasizing what he'd just said. "Racing only survives due to its integrity. Oh yeah, sure, everyone has stories of races being fixed or horses getting nobbled, but, overall, racing is very clean. If it wasn't, the public wouldn't have the confidence to bet, and then where would we be?"

I said nothing.

"That's why we at the BHA invest so much time and money in our dope-testing facilities and then punish any wrongdoers so harshly. We don't exactly enjoy taking away people's livelihoods, but we do want to deter others from trying."

I nodded at him. I knew all this.

"So why all the panic?" I asked.

"I am convinced that someone is beating the system — manipulating the results of races. That's why we need you."

"How about the BHA's own security service?" I asked. "Why can't they deal with it?"

"I have urged them to," he said with a sigh. "But they tell me that there's nothing amiss and that I'm mistaken. But I know I'm not."

"How do you know?" I asked.

"I just do," he replied adamantly.

It wasn't exactly convincing, but Sir Richard was a man who had often staked his reputation on his beliefs and he'd rarely been wrong.

"I'm sorry," I said, standing up, "but I still can't help you."

Sir Richard looked up at me. "Can't or won't?"

"Both," I said. "And I probably wouldn't

9

be of any use to you even if I tried. I've lost the investigating knack."

"What nonsense!" said Sir Richard, also standing up. "Have you lost the knack of breathing as well? The Sid Halley I used to know could find out more with his eyes closed than the whole of the Met Police with theirs open."

I looked at him from a distance of about nine inches.

"I am no longer the Sid Halley you used to know."

He stared straight into my eyes for a few seconds, until I turned away.

"That's a real shame," he said with a sigh.

I felt wretched, but there was nothing more I could say.

"I think I'd better go," Sir Richard said, leaning down to pick up his briefcase from the sofa. "I'm clearly wasting my time here."

Now he wasn't only unhappy, he was angry with it.

"I'll show myself out," he mumbled, barely able to maintain the usual pleasantries. He turned to go.

"Sir Richard," I said, putting a hand on his arm to stop him. "I'm very sorry but I no longer do that sort of thing."

"That's what dear Admiral Roland told me last week, but I didn't fully believe him."

He paused and looked again into my eyes. "Sid, I am firmly of the opinion that racing, as we know and love it, is under threat."

He was scared, I thought. Really scared.

"What evidence do you have?" I heard myself ask.

Dammit. No. No. I must not get involved.

Sir Richard opened his briefcase and pulled out a clear plastic folder containing some sheets of paper. "I have made a list of those races where I believe the result has been manipulated in some way."

"But what actual evidence do you have?" I asked.

"Don't you believe me?" Sir Richard snorted, pulling himself up to his full height, which was a good six or seven inches above my head.

"It's not important if I believe you or not," I said, ignoring his indignation. "But I would still need some hard evidence to look at."

"So are you saying you will help after all?" He was suddenly more hopeful.

"No," I said. "I'm not saying that. But I'll have a quick scan of your list, if you like."

He handed me the folder. "Keep it," he said. "I have other copies."

"Who else have you spoken to about this?" I asked.

"What do you mean?"

"Who else, other than the BHA Security Service, have you spoken to about this? Who else has seen your list?"

He seemed surprised by my questions. "A few, I suppose."

"Who?" I asked, pressing him.

"Some of my fellow BHA directors have seen it. And my secretary, of course. She typed it for me." He smiled.

"Anyone else?"

"A few others at my club. The Admiral, for instance. I was trying to get him to approach you on my behalf."

I inwardly sighed but stayed silent.

"Is that a problem?" he asked.

"Perhaps it might be more prudent to keep your concerns to yourself. At least until they've been proven."

"But it seems that no one *is* going to prove them," he said irritably. "Everyone thinks I'm making it all up. Including you."

"I still think it might be better not to broadcast your suspicions. The wrong ears may hear them. If there is indeed something going on, you don't want the perpetrator finding out that you're investigating."

"I'm not bloody investigating, am I?" he retorted angrily. "And talking to a few members of my club is hardly broadcasting."

I decided not to say anything further, but if a decade of being a private investigator had taught me anything, it was that secrecy and surprise were usually the best policy.

And being a member of Sir Richard's club was no guarantee that an individual was an upstanding member of society. For hundreds of years there has been a steady flow of fraudsters, swindlers, thieves and murderers passing through the gates of British prisons, many of whom had been members of London's most prestigious gentlemen's clubs.

"Sid, will you help me?" Sir Richard asked. "For the good of racing."

"I'll look at your list."

"Good."

"But I will not investigate anything," I said quickly. "Like I told you, I've given that up."

"But you will tell me what you think?"

"Yes," I said. "I'll look at the list and I'll tell you what I think."

He nodded as if satisfied. "I'd better be going or I'll miss my train."

"Are you going back to London?" I asked.

He shook his head. "No, to my house near Winchester. There's a direct train from Banbury every hour."

"Do you need a lift to the station?"

"No, thank you." He smiled. "I have a taxi waiting for me."

We went outside into the March sunshine, and I saw him into the taxi. Then I stood and waved at him as he was driven away. Was he imagining things or was there indeed something wrong in British racing? And did I care enough to get involved?

I was still out on the road with my right arm raised when Marina swept down the hill in our Range Rover and turned in through the gates.

"Who was that?" she called, climbing out of the vehicle with a bright green shopping bag.

"Sir Richard Stewart," I said.

"And who's he when he's at home?"

"Chairman of the British Horseracing Authority."

"What did he want?"

"He wants me to investigate some corrupt goings-on in racing."

She stood, facing me stiffly, on the gravel.

"And what did you say?"

"I told him I don't do investigating anymore."

She relaxed a fraction, the telltale rigidity in her neck disappearing as her shoulder muscles eased.

"Good."

"What did you buy?" I asked, changing the subject.

She smiled. "Something for Sassy. I couldn't resist it." She reached into the bag and withdrew a child's pink dress with lines of blue and yellow embroidery on the bodice. "Isn't it sweet? And it was in the sale."

"Lovely," I said.

Sassy was our daughter. Saskia, to be more correct. Sassy by name and sassy by nature. Six years old going on sixteen and growing up far too fast for my liking.

"She can wear it to Annabel's birthday party."

Annabel was Sassy's best friend at school.

"Lovely," I said again.

We went into the kitchen, and Rosie, one of our two red setter bitches, came over and nuzzled up to my leg, hoping for a treat.

"What corrupt goings-on?" Marina asked in a deadpan tone.

"Nothing," I said, waving a hand in dismissal. "Sir Richard has some crazy notion that someone is manipulating results of races. But his own security service says there's nothing wrong, and they're no fools."

"And you told him you weren't interested?"

"Yes," I said. "Don't worry. I have no intention of investigating anything. All I said to him was I'd have a look at a list he brought of the races he believes have been affected."

"And will you?"

"I'll glance through them later."

She wasn't happy. I could tell.

Marina and I had moved out of London when she'd been seven months pregnant with Saskia. It was to be a new beginning — one of rural tranquility.

Marina hadn't quite made an ultimatum, but she had been pretty resolute nevertheless. She'd told me how much she loved me and how she had tried to be positive about my job, but she found she couldn't go on living a life that involved checking for thugs with knuckle-dusters or silenced pistols around every corner. Continuous fear was totally exhausting her, and things would only get worse when the baby arrived.

I had to effectively choose between her and my job.

The choice had been easy.

Once before, when I'd been a jockey, I'd chosen my job over my then wife, and, in hindsight, it had been a mistake.

I couldn't blame Marina. She had been shot, beaten up and repeatedly threatened,

16

every time in a bid to get me to stop what I'd been doing.

It had become common knowledge in criminal circles that beating up Sid Halley was counterproductive. He would simply come after you with increased vigor and determination.

So the lowlifes, which I tended to encounter all too regularly in my occupation, had taken instead to attacking my girl, attempting to use her as a lever against me.

And, in the end, it had worked.

There is only so much that one is prepared to allow in the pursuit of truth and justice. The world, I decided, would have to get on with its business, legal or otherwise, without the intervention of Sid Halley.

So I had become the loving husband and, subsequently, the doting father.

But my former job remained the elephant in the room — always large, always there, difficult to ignore but rarely spoken of.

Only occasionally, like now, did the elephant raise its head a little and send shivers of dread down Marina's spine.

I took the plastic folder with me when I went to collect Sassy from school.

"Don't forget to collect Annabel as well," Marina shouted to me through the kitchen

17

window. "She's here tonight for a sleep-over."

"Bit unusual for midweek, isn't it?"

"Tim and Paula have gone to London for the night. Some livery dinner or something."

"OK, I won't forget."

Collecting my daughter from school was one of the true pleasures of my day. She would bound out to the car, grinning from ear to ear with excitement, and would be so keen to tell me about everything she had been doing that she would almost forget to breathe.

Her school was only a mile away, in the next village, but I was habitually early and often would be sitting, waiting, for ten minutes or more before Sassy appeared. Today I had left home especially early, as I wanted time on my own to look through Sir Richard's lists.

As usual I parked the Range Rover opposite the school gates, and then picked up the plastic folder from the passenger seat.

There were nine races listed on two sheets of paper, but there was precious little reasoning as to why each race was on the list. At first glance, there was nothing remarkable about any of them and nothing that would immediately link them together.

Three of the nine had been hurdle races,

18

and the remaining six were steeplechases. All had been run during the preceding six months, the main months of the jumping season, always on major racing days, but none of them was actually the big race of the day. Only two had been won by the favorite or the second favorite, and all of them had been won at prices of six-to-one or greater.

Nevertheless, I could see nothing particularly noteworthy or unusual about any of them.

So why were they on this list?

Sir Richard Stewart may have been fanciful in his suspicions, but he was not stupid. There had to be a reason why he had put this list together, and he had obviously expected me to notice it. But I couldn't, at first glance. Perhaps watching the video of each race would help.

"Afternoon, Mr. Halley," called a voice.

I looked up from the papers in front of me and over to the school gates on my right.

"Hello, Mrs. Squire," I called back through the open window.

Mrs. Squire was the head teacher, and it was her habit to stand at the school gate at the end of the day as the children departed.

"I understand you're also collecting Annabel Gaucin today."

19

"Yes, that's right."

Mrs. Squire nodded at me and then turned to speak to a group of mothers waiting near the gate, some of them with strollers occupied by future school pupils.

The children spilled out of the building, and there was the usual mad rush across the playground. I climbed out of the Range Rover and crossed the road. Sassy was always one of the first to get to the gate — I put it down to her racing heritage — but Annabel was clearly more ladylike in allowing others to go first, so Sassy and I had to wait a few seconds for her to join us.

"Hello, Daddy," shouted Sassy, waving madly.

I would surely never tire of being called *Daddy.*

"Hello, darling," I shouted back.

Mrs. Squire allowed her through the gate, and she rushed over to me and took my hand, my right hand, my real hand, rather than the plastic-and-steel doppelgänger that existed on my left.

In due course, Mrs. Squire also released Annabel, and she joined us.

"Take Saskia's other hand," I told her, and we crossed the road safely in a line, continually looking both ways. There were almost no cars moving in the village other than

20

those collecting the children from the school, but one could never be too careful.

Saskia was my pride and joy, arriving exactly nine months to the day after my marriage to Marina.

"Wedding-night baby," a friend had once said to me with a wink. "Good job she wasn't early."

I had smiled back at him, knowing that, in fact, it had been a good job she'd been late. Marina had definitely said "I do" with a bun already cooking nicely in the oven.

It had all seemed so easy. We had ceased the birth-control precautions, and — hey presto! — Marina had become pregnant instantly. It made it all the more frustrating that she had been unable to conceive again since Saskia's birth.

We had seen every fertility doctor worth his salt, and they all said there was no medical reason why. Just relax, they said, and it will happen. Well, we had relaxed, but it hadn't happened in six years, and we were beginning to be resigned to the fact that Sassy would be our only child.

However, Marina was still young enough, so we went on trying most nights with enthusiasm.

Marina took the two girls off for a walk

around the village with the dogs while I went into my study and looked at the videos of each of the nine races on the *Racing Post* website.

Something that I hadn't appreciated from the bare written details was that none of the races had been close contests. On each occasion, the winner had come home well in front, largely unchallenged by the others.

Not that this made them unusual. Many steeplechases are won by good jumping around the whole track rather than by a sprint over the last furlong.

So was Sir Richard suspicious because he thought the other runners hadn't been trying?

I looked up the jockeys who had ridden in the races.

Many of the same jockeys had ridden in more than one. But there was no general pattern with, for example, the same jockey winning each time.

I looked again at the typed list. At the end of the factual information about each race someone, presumably Sir Richard, had added a few comments and observations.

After one particular race at Sandown he had written, "Starting price 8/1, Tote paid only £5.60 for the win." After another, at Newbury, he had put, "Winner at 10/1, Tote paid only £7.20."

Many of the others had the same sort of comments. The only thing that seemed to be consistent about each race was that the Tote win payout was much lower than might have been expected compared to the starting price.

The Tote doesn't use odds as a bookmaker would.

If a bookmaker offers you a price of eight-to-one, then if the horse wins, the bookmaker will pay you out eight for every one that you staked, irrespective of how many people made the same bet. And the official starting price is an average of the bookmakers' prices at the time the race starts.

The Tote, however, is short for Totalizator and is a parimutuel system, meaning that the total of all the money staked on all the horses in the race is simply divided by the number of winning tickets to determine the payout, or return. Consequently, the Tote return odds are rarely exactly the same as the starting price, sometimes being greater and sometimes less, but it is very unusual for it to be so much smaller than the starting price, as it had been for all the races on the list.

The only explanation for the low Tote return was that a disproportionately large

amount of money had been bet on the winning horses with the Tote compared to that
bet on the same horses with the bookmakers.

Maybe this was the reason behind Sir
Richard's suspicions.

But it didn't seem that much to get excited
about.

Everyone in racing was well aware that
placing very large bets on the Tote could be
counterproductive as it tended to reduce
the effective odds of the return. You were
simply winning back the money you had
wagered minus the twenty-four percent slice
the Tote keeps back to cover its costs and to
provide itself with a profit.

Why would anyone do that? It was crazy.
Particularly when you could get better odds
with the bookmakers.

But betting on the Tote is far more anonymous than with the bookies, who tend to
recognize a regular client with a bulging
wallet. And the bookmakers are the first to
cry foul if a long-odds and heavily backed
horse romps home by a distance, causing
them to be seriously out of pocket. But the
Tote doesn't care which horse wins. It takes
its twenty-four percent cut, and the only
thing that matters is the total money staked
on all horses. The more staked, the more it

makes. There is no one to complain that disproportionally large bets had been placed on the winner, other than perhaps the other holders of winning tickets who would put it down to their bad luck that the Tote return was less than they might have expected. And, after all, who would complain when they had just backed a winner and made some money? They were far more likely to celebrate.

At the big meetings there are literally hundreds of different Tote terminals, and the busy staff take little or no notice of who is handing them cash. During a whole afternoon, a determined individual could stake many thousands of pounds, if not many tens of thousands, on any given horse without anyone raising an eyebrow.

I looked again at the list.

All of the nine races had been in the latter half of the day's card, and seven had been either the second-to-last or last race of the day.

Plenty of time to get the money on.

And with a substantial betting crowd on a big-race day, the win pool would generally be so large that a big bet would have less of a "diluting" effect, and odds of five- or six-to-one weren't exactly bad.

Especially if, as Sir Richard had implied,

someone knew the outcome of the races beforehand.

2

"Daddy, Daddy, come and play with us."

Sassy and Annabel came running into my office.

"Where's Mommy?" I asked.

"Ironing," said Sassy in an ironic tone. "She said to ask you."

I inwardly laughed. Marina hated ironing.

"Please," Sassy whined.

"OK," I said. "What do you want to play?"

"Catch," said Annabel, excitedly jumping up and down.

No, I thought, not catch. Not with only one real hand.

"How about Ping-Pong?"

"Yes, yes," the girls shouted with enthusiasm.

So we went into the garage, where I'd set up a table, and spent the next half hour with me at one end and the two girls at the other, hitting balls back and forth, but mostly collecting them from the floor or under the table.

"Who'd like an ice cream?" I asked.

Table-tennis bats were quickly abandoned, and we adjourned to the kitchen for scoops of raspberry ripple topped with sprinkles.

"Mr. Halley," Annabel said between mouthfuls.

"Yes, Annabel?"

"What's wrong with your left hand?" She pointed at it with her spoon.

The innocence, I thought, of the six-year-old child.

"He hasn't got one," said Sassy matter-of-factly. "That's made of plastic."

I glanced at Annabel, worried that she might be shocked by the revelation, but she seemed not to be alarmed in the slightest.

"Can I look at it?" she asked.

Reluctantly, I lifted my left hand up onto the kitchen table.

Sassy unbuttoned my shirt cuff and pulled my sleeve up above my elbow. She had great fun explaining to Annabel everything about my myoelectric marvel.

"This is the battery," she said, pointing to a rectangular block, about three inches by one, clipped into the fiberglass forearm. "That's what makes it work."

"What does it do?" Annabel asked.

28

"Come on, Daddy," Sassy said bossily, "open up."

I sent the nerve impulses, and, as if by magic, and accompanied by a barely audible whirring noise, the artificial fingers and thumb uncurled and the plastic hand opened.

"Wow!" said Annabel. "That's cool."

Cool was not a term I would have used.

Sensors in the plastic arm picked up the nerve impulses from my skin and caused tiny hidden motors to move the latex-covered steel digits.

It was certainly clever, but it was not cool.

In fact, it was a bore, and one that I was beginning to increasingly detest. Some days I didn't even put the thing on, but I knew that Marina felt it was better for Saskia to have a "normal-looking" father.

Nowadays, I did everything almost exclusively right-handed.

It hadn't always been that way. Once I'd had two hands, and I had used them to good effect to be champion steeplechase jockey on four occasions. Then a racing fall had put paid to both my career and to the use of my left hand. A poker-wielding, sadistic villain had then finished off what the fall had started, and I'd lost the hand completely. That had been some fourteen years ago, but I'd never got properly used to it, nor would I.

I still had two hands in my dreams.

"Now close it again," Sassy said.

I sent more impulses, and the fingers closed. It may have looked and moved quite like the real thing, but it couldn't *feel*. I couldn't tell when, or how strongly, I was gripping something. Wineglasses could either slip from my grasp or be crushed to fragments, and I would be none the wiser.

"Can I have a go?" Annabel asked.

"Don't be silly," Sassy said to her. "You'd have to have your arm chopped off first." She made a chopping motion with her right hand on her left forearm.

The disappointed look on Annabel's face implied that it might be worth it just to have a go with the plastic arm.

"Go on, now, you two," I said, pulling my sleeve down again to my wrist and rebuttoning the cuff, using the dexterous set of fingers on my right hand. "Off you go into the garden. I've got some work to do."

I stood by the kitchen sink for a while, looking out at them through the window. They were on the lawn, throwing a tennis ball back and forth, the dogs rushing from one to the other, hoping desperately that they would drop it, as they did continually.

30

I smiled.

What joy children brought.

I rang Sir Richard Stewart's home number at five o'clock.

"I've looked at your lists," I said.

"That was quick," he replied. "And what do you think?"

"I can see why you think there may be some betting irregularities, perhaps with large winning bets being placed on the Tote, but I don't see why you think that means the results must have been manipulated. There may have been other large Tote bets that lost."

"But there are patterns," he persisted. "Major racing days, for example."

"Lots of punters go racing only on the big-race days," I said. "Perhaps our Tote big bettor is one of them. And how do you think the results have been fixed?"

"I don't know," he said.

"I presume all the horses were tested."

"Yes, the first three were routinely dope-tested and all were negative."

"How about the others?" I asked.

"There is occasionally some random testing on other runners, but I don't know about those races in particular. But I do know there have been no positive test results on any jumpers so far this year."

"Have you questioned any of the jockeys?" I asked.

"The head of the Security Service approached one or two after I raised my suspicions with him, but nothing came of it. I was accused of being delusional and told that I was making the whole thing up."

"I'm sure that isn't true," I said.

"It is," he replied quickly, the anger clear in his voice. "I know all the staff snigger behind my back and think I'm too old for this job, and that I'm losing my marbles, but, I tell you, I'm not."

He paused, and I said nothing.

"That's why I need you, Sid, to investigate what's going on and to stop it before racing is irreparably damaged."

"Sir Richard, I told you, I don't investigate anything anymore. If your own security service tell you there's nothing going on, then, perhaps, you should listen to them. Peter Medicos is no fool, and he's difficult to shake off if he smells even the slightest whiff of corruption."

Peter Medicos had been the head of the BHA Security Service since retiring from the Lancashire Police as a detective chief superintendent some seven years previously.

"Huh," Sir Richard snorted loudly down

the line. Clearly, he didn't have the same confidence. "I'm hugely disappointed in you, Sid. Why can no one else see what is going on?" He sounded thoroughly frustrated, and not a little frightened. "Well, I'm telling you, *I* intend to find out what's happening. And I'll not bloody rest until I do, with or without your help."

He hung up abruptly, leaving me holding the dead handset.

Was there something going on or had he made the whole thing up?

And did I care?

Yes, perhaps I did.

I went to find Marina, who was in the living room with Sassy and Annabel, watching a Walt Disney cartoon on the television.

"I'm going to see Charles," I said. "I won't be long. I'll be back for supper."

Marina looked up at me from the sofa, and I could tell that she wasn't very pleased. She knew only too well why I wanted to talk to Charles.

"Daddy, Daddy, please be back to read us a story," piped up Sassy.

"All right," I said. "I'll be back by seven-thirty to read you both a story. But you must be in bed."

Suddenly, she wasn't so keen. "But we've

got Annabel staying. Can't I stay up later tonight?" She looked up at me with doleful eyes.

"No," I said firmly. "That's all the more reason to be in bed early. It will give you time to talk to each other as you go to sleep."

She cheered up, but only fractionally. Getting Sassy into bed each night was always a battle of wills, and hers was very strong.

"I'll take my bike," I said to Marina. "I promise I'll be back."

The main reason why Marina and I had looked for a house in West Oxfordshire was to be close to Charles, and we had amazingly found just what we wanted in a village only two miles away from his place at Aynsford.

Admiral Charles Roland, Royal Navy Retired, was like a father to both Marina and me, in spite of not being a blood relative of either of us. He was, in fact, my ex-father-in-law, even though I generally dropped the ex-, and our friendship had not only survived the turbulent breakup of my marriage to his daughter but had become closer with every passing year. He had instantly taken to Marina, and was reveling in the role of honorary grandpa to Saskia, not having any true grandchildren of his own from either of his two daughters.

He was now well past eighty, but you wouldn't know it by looking at him. He was nearly six feet tall, still with a shock of black hair, and his back was as ramrod straight, as it had been when he'd entered Dartmouth as an officer cadet some sixty-five years previously.

He was waiting for me in the drawing room, wearing his favorite burgundy-colored, velvet-and-silk smoking jacket. He was standing in front of the fire, with two tumblers already filled with generous fingers of his best Scotch.

"I thought you might need it," he said, handing me one.

"Why did you think that?"

"It's been a long time since you came here on your own, without either Marina or Saskia." He took a sip of the amber spirit. "And I know you well, Sid, very well. Now, what's the problem?"

Indeed, he did know me well.

Charles's place at Aynsford had always been my sanctuary, my bolt-hole. A place to run to when things weren't going well or when I needed advice from a wise counselor. Such as now.

"Sir Richard Stewart," I said.

"A-ha!" he said, throwing his head back

with a laugh. "I wondered if that was it. He spoke to me about you last week."

"Yes, he told me."

"I presume, therefore, that he also told you of his theory that someone is fixing races."

"Indeed, he did," I said. "Do you believe him?"

Charles lowered himself into a deep, chintz-covered armchair.

"I believe that he believes it," Charles said.

"I don't doubt that," I replied, taking the armchair opposite. "But according to Sir Richard, Peter Medicos thinks he's delusional."

"I have known Richard Stewart for over twenty years and I've never once thought of him as delusional."

"But we're all getting older," I said, "and age does funny things."

"So what do *you* think?" Charles asked. "You can't simply agree with Peter Medicos or you wouldn't be here."

"I've had a look at Sir Richard's list of races and I agree that the Tote returns on them might appear suspicious, but he has no evidence, or even any idea, of how the results could have been manipulated. He's either wrong about that or there's a huge conspiracy going on."

"Conspiracy by whom?" Charles asked.

"I don't know," I said. "But it must include the jockeys."

"Are you going to find out?"

"No," I said decisively, "I'm not. I've given all that up."

"Then why are you here?"

Perhaps he knew me too well.

I sat in silence for a moment and took a mouthful of my whisky.

"Just suppose he's right," I said. "I feel I can't do nothing. I told him about an hour ago that I thought he must be mistaken, but I could hear real anger in his voice, as well as a touch of fear. And I have huge respect for Sir Richard."

"Why don't you have a quiet word with Peter Medicos? Then you'll have heard his opinions directly rather than relying simply on what Richard told you he'd said."

"Now, why didn't I think of that?" I said, laughing. "I'll call him in the morning."

We finished our drinks in relaxed companionship, discussing recent racing news and results.

He saw me out through the glassed-in porch.

"Why aren't you a *Sir*?" I asked. "I would have thought that all admirals were knighted."

"I was only a rear admiral," Charles said. "Not high enough."

"Do rear admirals stay in the rear, then?"

"Absolutely." He smiled broadly. "Back in the sixteenth and seventeenth centuries, a rear admiral was the commander of the fleet reserve, those squadrons kept in the rear until they were needed. But, nowadays, all admirals sit in offices rather than in ships. The last admiral to command at sea was Sandy Woodward during the Falklands War. That was when we had a proper navy. Bloody politicians. They've cut so much that there are now almost as many admirals as there are ships."

He clearly didn't approve of the politicians or the cuts.

I knew. I'd heard it all before, and often.

I cycled hard on the return journey, but still it was a few minutes after seven-thirty when I parked my bicycle in the garage, turned off its lights and rushed into the house.

"I'm back," I called as I climbed the stairs. "Are you ready for that story?"

Fortunately, Marina was also running a little behind schedule, and the girls were still in the bath, splashing about and throwing great handfuls of bubble-bath foam at each other. What fun!

"Come on, you two," Marina shouted above their noise. "Out!"

They were soon wrapped in large, fluffy white towels, and then dressed in multicolored pajamas, before jumping into the twin beds in Sassy's bedroom.

"Give us a story, Daddy," squealed Sassy excitedly, sitting bolt upright in bed. "Tell us about riding in races."

Saskia had been born long after I had retired from riding, but she always wanted to hear about my time as a jockey.

I sat down on the end of her bed.

"Once upon a time," I said, "I rode in the Grand National."

"Did you win? Did you win?" shouted Annabel.

"You'll have to wait and see," I said. "Now, where was I? Oh yes, I was riding in the Grand National. The horse was called Noss Boy, and he was a big bold gray who jumped like he was on springs."

I described how we had raced around the Aintree course on the first circuit, with me bouncing up and down on the corner of the bed as if I was riding.

"Come on, Sid," said Marina, coming in from the bathroom. "It's time these two were asleep."

"Mommy, don't be such a spoilsport,"

Saskia said crossly. "The race isn't finished yet."

"Well, hurry up, then." Marina collected some clothes from the floor and went out.

I bounced faster, jumping Becher's Brook and the Canal Turn in a single bound.

"It's such a long way from the last fence to the finish," I said, panting. "Come on, boy, you can do it. Only a few yards to go. Come on, boy, come on."

I waved my right hand back and forth as if riding a close finish.

"We win!" I shouted, and the girls leaped up and down on the beds in excitement. "Time for sleep, now," I said, calming everything down, "or you'll be too tired for school in the morning."

I tucked them in and gave them both a kiss on their heads. "Night-night." I switched off the main bedroom light but left the door ajar so the room wouldn't be completely dark.

Marina had already gone downstairs, and I followed her down and into the kitchen.

"What's wrong?" I asked.

"What do you mean?"

"You're being very grumpy."

"No, I'm not," she replied sharply.

"You are," I said, going over and taking her in my arms. "What is it?"

"Nothing." She pushed me away.

"I'm not going to investigate anything," I said. "I promised I wouldn't, and I won't."

"So why did you go and see Charles?"

"I wanted to ask his advice about something."

"About what?"

"I asked him what I should do about what that man said to me this afternoon, about his suspicions that someone is manipulating race results." I paused. "I'm not going to investigate them, but I could hardly do nothing, could I?"

She didn't say anything, but I suspected that *nothing* was exactly what she wanted me to do.

"Charles suggested that I speak to the head of racing security and then leave everything to him. I'm going to call him in the morning. And that's all."

She relaxed a little, but there remained a degree of tension between us for the rest of the evening. However I might have tried to reassure her otherwise, Marina was clearly terrified by the prospect of me getting back into investigating. It had become an ogre in her mind, far more fearful in her imagination than it would be in reality.

At least that's what I thought at the time.

■ ■ ■ ■

I called Peter Medicos on his cell phone just after I'd dropped the girls at school the following morning.

"Hello, Sid," he said in his broad Lancastrian accent.

"Do you have a moment?" I asked.

"You'll have to be quick. I'm really pushed, but fire away."

"It's about Sir Richard Stewart."

"Yes, I know," he said. "Terrible, isn't it?"

"What's terrible?" I asked.

"About Sir Richard," he repeated. "Terrible."

I wondered if I was stuck in a parallel universe.

"Peter," I said slowly. "What is it that is terrible about Sir Richard?"

"About him being found dead," he replied, equally slowly. "Isn't that what you're phoning about?"

"Dead!" I said. "But when?"

"This morning," he said. "A couple of hours ago. Found in one of his old cars. Seems he might have killed himself."

3

By midmorning, Sir Richard's apparent suicide had become the number one news item on the radio, but the reports gave only a little more information than Peter Medicos had already told me.

It seemed he had been found by his gardener, sitting in his classic Mark IV Jaguar in a closed garage with the engine running. According to a statement from his distraught son, Sir Richard had been alone at their Hampshire home while Lady Stewart had been visiting her sister in London. He could think of no reason why his father would have taken his own life.

Nor could I.

Sir Richard had sounded a million miles away from committing suicide when he'd hung up on me the previous afternoon.

Well, I'm telling you, I intend to find out what's happening. And I'll not bloody rest until I do, with or without your help.

It did not strike me as the words of someone who would kill himself only a few hours later.

So if it wasn't suicide, what was it?

I knew of several cases where people had died accidentally by starting their cars in enclosed spaces, totally unaware of the rapid and fatal consequences of carbon monoxide buildup. A concentration of less than half of one percent of carbon monoxide in air is enough to kill a full-grown adult, and it will do so without warning.

But almost everyone knows the risks, and surely, as a classic-car collector, Sir Richard would have.

So if it wasn't suicide or an accident, was it murder?

Perhaps it was due to my previous line of work, but I always tended to consider there were suspicious circumstances surrounding any unexplained death unless, and until, it was proved otherwise.

Sir Richard Stewart announces that he believes someone is manipulating the results of horse races and that he intends finding out who, and the next morning he's found dead of an apparent suicide.

Was I the only person who thought it rather too convenient?

I called Peter Medicos again.

"Yes, Sid?" he said, sounding slightly annoyed at being interrupted. "What can I do for you now?"

"Peter, I'm sorry to disturb you again on what I know must be a difficult day, but I never got round to telling you why I rang you earlier."

"About Sir Richard?" he asked.

"Yes," I said. "He came to see me yesterday afternoon saying he was concerned that someone was fixing races."

"Oh, that," he said, irritation clear in his tone. "He'd been banging on about it since Cheltenham."

"Is it true?"

"Not that I'm aware of."

"Did you investigate any of his claims?"

"I had a quiet word with a couple of the senior jockeys, and they reckoned it was all a load of rubbish."

Well, they would say that, I thought, especially if they were involved.

"Do you think his death might have anything to do with it?" I asked.

There was a pause from his end. "In what way?" he said. "Are you suggesting he killed himself because I didn't take his accusations seriously?" He was clearly not pleased.

"Are you positive that he did actually kill himself?" I asked. "Did he leave a note?"

"Sid, I suggest you leave any inquiries to the professionals like the police or the BHA Security Service. Neither of us would appreciate an amateur getting involved."

I resisted the urge to tell him that I was no amateur in the investigating business, and there had been a time when the BHA Security Service had regularly come knocking on my door for help.

"I assure you I have no intention of getting involved," I said. "But I think the questions need to be put. Sir Richard was adamant that something was amiss, and now, with him suddenly dead in unexplained circumstances, someone should look into his suspicions."

"They will," Peter said. "I'll make sure it happens."

"You'll inform the police, then?" I persisted.

"Yes," he said curtly.

Why did I not really believe him?

I spent most of Thursday morning sitting at my desk, trying to concentrate on stock price trends and bond yields but always coming back to Sir Richard and his Mark IV Jaguar.

My phone rang. It was Charles.

"It all sounds very fishy to me," he said

straightaway. "I'd never have put Richard Stewart in the suicide stakes. He was far too courageous."

"Doesn't it take courage to kill yourself?"

"Of course not," Charles replied sharply. "In dire circumstances, it takes courage to stay alive."

And Charles knew a thing or two about courage in dire circumstances. He'd been a nineteen-year-old midshipman on HMS *Amethyst* during the ship's run down the Yangtze under fire from the Chinese communists when thirty-one of his shipmates had been killed.

"So what do you think?" I asked him.

"Murder," he said unequivocally. "Has to be."

"You've been watching too much television," I said with a laugh, but something in me did tend to agree with him.

"Look at the facts," Charles said. "I don't believe it could have been suicide, and someone with Richard's knowledge of cars wouldn't die accidentally of inhaling exhaust fumes. So it has to be murder."

"We don't yet know all the facts," I said. "And we're only assuming carbon monoxide poisoning was the cause of death. It might have been due to natural causes."

"He seemed as fit as a fiddle when I saw

him last week."

As he had been the previous afternoon, but heart attacks can strike down even the healthiest-looking of individuals.

"Do you know if he had any coronary trouble?"

"Sid," Charles said in a condescending tone, "we both know it was murder, so why don't you get on and investigate it."

He made it sound so simple.

"I'm sure the police will do that," I said.

I could hear him sigh down the line in frustration. "Once upon a time, a long time ago, just after you'd stopped race riding, you needed a great kick up the backside to get you moving again. I fear it's time someone gave you another one."

"Charles!" I replied in an anguished tone.

"I'm sorry," he said, not sounding it, "but it's true."

"It is not," I said defensively. "I have chosen quite deliberately to stop investigating, and I am very happy doing what I do now."

"And what is that, exactly?" he asked.

"You know perfectly well what I do."

"Moving money round and round," he snorted. "That's not a proper job."

I didn't want to argue with him, not that it would have done any good. The Admiral's views and opinions could be as difficult to redirect as the aircraft carriers he had once commanded.

"I'll pass on our thoughts to the police," I said calmly. "And Peter Medicos told me that he'd look into Sir Richard's suspicions."

"Isn't that the man who thought he was delusional?"

"Yes," I said.

"Then I won't hold my breath."

No, I thought, nor would I.

I went back to my financial dealings and wondered if Charles was right.

Was this a proper job?

It certainly was gainful employment. Over the past six years, I had made far more money sitting at a desk than I had scrambling about in wet ditches or snooping through other people's dustbins. But I hadn't actually *done* anything or *made* anything. I had simply correctly predicted when certain stocks or bonds would go up or down and had bought or sold them accordingly.

Rather like backing horses at the races and then waiting for others to do the work needed for them to win.

My thoughts were once again interrupted by the telephone.

"Hello," I said.

"Is that Mr. Halley?" said a voice with a strong Northern Irish accent. "Mr. Sid Halley?" He emphasized the *Ha* in Halley.

"Yes," I said.

"Mr. Halley," he repeated, "I need you to do something for me."

"Who is this?" I asked.

"Never you mind," he said with a degree of menace. "I need you to investigate something, do you hear?"

"I'm sorry. I no longer investigate anything."

I hung up.

The phone rang almost immediately.

"Mr. Halley," said the same voice. "I'm not asking, I'm telling you. You will investigate. Do I make myself plain?" There was real threat in his tone.

"Who is this?" I asked again, this time angrily. "How dare you call me like this?"

"How dare I?" he said, almost with a laugh in his voice. "I tell you, Mr. Halley, I dare lots of things. And you *will* do as I say, I promise you."

"I will not," I said quickly and hung up again.

I immediately dialed 1471 to get the phone number of whoever had called but was informed that the caller had withheld it. I wasn't surprised.

I sat looking at the phone on my desk, expecting it to ring again, but it didn't.

The calls had quite disturbed me.

It certainly wasn't the only time someone had told me over the telephone that I would do as they said, far from it, but it was the first occasion that they had wanted me to *start* investigating something. In the past it had always been a threat to stop me doing so.

I tried to go back to what I'd been doing, but my mind wasn't on it. Instead, I went to find Marina.

Marina van der Meer, as she had been before we married, was a research biologist who had worked for Cancer Research UK. She had given up her job when we moved out of London only a month before Saskia was born, but now, with our baby at school, Marina worked part-time from home, editing and background-checking scholarly scientific papers prior to publication.

As usual, she was sitting at the kitchen table, tapping away on her computer, surrounded by several heavy volumes of texts on cellular biology.

"Do you know what the central dogma is?" she asked as I walked in.

"Is it to do with religion?"

"No," she said. "The central dogma of molecular biology."

"Haven't a clue," I said.

"Nor, it seems, has the author of this useless paper." She sighed and stretched her arms upward.

"So what is it?" I asked. "This dogma thing?"

"It's one of the guiding principles of life. It states that genetic information in a nucleic acid can be perpetuated or transferred, but the transfer of information into a protein is irreversible."

I rather wished I hadn't asked, so I said nothing.

"Who was on the phone?" Marina said, changing the subject but continuing to concentrate on her computer screen.

"Charles was first, then someone I don't know."

"What did Charles want?"

"You know that man who came here yesterday afternoon?"

"The man from the racing authority?"

"Yes, him," I said. "Well, he was found dead this morning."

She spun around in her chair and looked up at me, worry lines etched across her forehead.

"Was it anything to do with what he came

to see you about?"

"I don't know," I said. "But I doubt it. It appears he may have committed suicide."

"Oh, how awful."

"He was a friend of Charles. They're members of the same club."

"Poor Charles," Marina said.

Poor Sir Richard, I thought.

"What did Charles want you to do?" Marina asked.

"Nothing," I lied. "He just wanted to talk about it."

"I suppose the police should be told that he was here yesterday, and also what you talked about."

"Hmm, perhaps you're right. Maybe I'll call them."

And should I also tell them, I wondered, about the Northern Irish voice that had threatened me over the telephone?

"What's for lunch?" I asked.

"What would you like?" Marina said. "I've got some Thai chicken curry soup in the fridge."

"Lovely."

We sat together at the table and had the soup with some hot French bread.

"Oh, a letter came for you," Marina said, holding it out to me.

It was from Queen Mary's Hospital in

Roehampton, I could tell from the return address on the envelope.

"It will be a reminder for my appointment next Tuesday," I said. "For my annual checkup and service." I held up my left hand, the plastic one.

Marina went back to her computer and her editing, so I took the letter with me along to my office and opened it there.

It was indeed a reminder for my appointment but there was something else with it. A letter from a Dr. Harold Bryant.

Dear Mr. Halley,
I am aware that it is some time since you lost your left hand due to a combination of a horse-racing fall, and a further trauma, and I have been apprised of your use over the past fourteen years of a myoelectric prosthesis by Mr. Alan Stephenson, formerly of the Roehampton Rehabilitation Centre.

You may be aware from reports in the press that Queen Mary's Hospital has embarked on a program of total hand and wrist transplantation, and I believe that you may be a suitable candidate for such a procedure.

If you might be interested in finding out any more, then I would be most happy to meet with you on your visit to the hospital next Tuesday.

Yours sincerely,
Harold Bryant, FRCS
Head of the Transplant Team

I sat at my desk, looking at the letter, continually reading and rereading the same words: *total hand and wrist transplantation.*

I looked up hand transplants on the Internet and spent the next two hours watching videos posted on YouTube of people who'd had them. Some of the results were amazing and there was even a film of a man playing a piano with two new hands, albeit using only a finger or two from each one.

What did I want?

I had become accustomed to using one hand for almost everything, but some actions were entirely beyond me. I had long given up shoelaces and exclusively wore slip-ons, but putting on socks, knotting ties and buttoning up trousers remained the bane of my life. Did I want to go through all the agony of surgery just so I could dress myself more easily?

And what about the antirejection drugs I would need to take for the rest of my life? Was I ready for that?

Maybe I was.

I hated my prosthesis, the steel-and-plastic "wonder" that occupied the space below my left forearm. It was top-of-the-range, the best artificial hand money could buy, but *artificial* it remained, cold to the touch and unfeeling in every respect. I couldn't use it to pick up coins or hold a fork.

So engrossed was I with my research into transplants that I lost all sense of time.

"Are you going to collect Sassy or am I?" Marina said, standing in my office doorway, looking purposefully at her watch.

"Oh God. Sorry," I said. "I'm on my way."

I rushed out to the Range Rover, spun the wheels on the gravel drive and made it to the school as the children began spilling out of the buildings.

"Hello, Mr. Halley," said Mrs. Squire, the head teacher, as I rushed from the car to the gate. "What are you doing here?"

I looked at her quizzically. "I'm collecting Saskia."

"But Saskia's already gone." Mrs. Squire looked worried.

"Gone?" I said, a sense of foreboding rising in my chest. "Gone where?"

"She left half an hour ago with your sister and brother-in-law."

Now my pulse rate shot up and adrenaline

flooded through my body.

I didn't have a sister, or a brother-in-law.

4

"I am so sorry." Mrs. Squire was in tears. "They had a letter from you asking me to let Saskia out of school early today for a family party. It was to be a surprise for Mrs. Halley, so I mustn't ring."

We were in her office in the main school building.

"Do you have the letter?" I asked. My mouth was dry.

"No. They took it with them."

"I'm calling the police," I said, taking my phone out of my pocket, but it rang in my hand before I had a chance to dial.

"Mr. Halley," said the voice with the Northern Irish accent. "Now will you do as I say?"

"Where's my daughter?" I screamed at him.

"Why, she's at home," he said with a laugh. "Where all little girls should be at this time of day."

"At home?" I said, confused.

"Yes," he said. "Home with her mother."

I put my hand over the microphone. "Mrs. Squire. Ring my house." I gave her the number, and she used her office phone to make the call.

"Mrs. Halley," she said, "it's Mrs. Squire from the school. I have your husband here."

She handed me the receiver across her desk.

"Sid," said Marina in a highly agitated tone, "what is going on? Saskia's just walked in on her own. Where are you?"

"Stay inside and lock all the doors," I said.

"But . . ."

"Do it now!" I said. "And don't answer the door. I'm on my way back."

I handed the phone back to Mrs. Squire. "Saskia's at home," I said to her.

I could see the relief flood right through her as she slumped down into her chair.

"Thank God," she said.

God had nothing to do with it, I thought.

I lifted my cell back to my ear but the line was dead.

"What about the police?" Mrs. Squire asked.

"I'll call them from home," I said. "I need to get back there. How long will you be staying here?"

"Another hour at least," she said.

"I'll call you."

I ran out to the car and burned rubber all the way down the lane to our house, sending gravel up in a spray as I braked in the driveway.

"What the hell is going on?" Marina asked as I walked in, her eyes wide in fright.

"I don't know," I said. "Someone else collected Saskia from school and brought her home."

"Who?" she demanded.

"I don't know," I said again.

"And how come the bloody school let her go?"

"Whoever collected her said they were my sister and brother-in-law. They claimed they had a letter from me. They showed it to Mrs. Squire."

"My God!" Marina almost sagged at the knees.

"Where is Sassy now?" I asked.

"In her room," Marina said. "She's in tears. I was so cross with her. I thought she'd walked home on her own."

I ran up the stairs to Saskia's room and Marina followed.

Our little girl was curled up on her bed, hugging her pillow. I went and sat on the end of the bed and stroked her back.

"I'm sorry, Daddy," she said without lifting her head.

"It's all right, darling," I said. "Tell us what happened."

"Mrs. Squire told me I had to go with those people."

"Did you know who they were?" I asked gently.

"No," she said quietly.

"What have we told you?" Marina shouted angrily. "Never go anywhere with strangers."

Saskia burst into tears again. "But they said you'd asked them to collect me."

"It's all right, darling," I said, giving her a hug. "Mommy's not really cross." I stared daggers at Marina over Saskia's head.

"Mrs. Squire told me," Saskia said between sobs.

"Did Mrs. Squire ask if you knew the people?"

"No," Saskia said. "She came into our classroom and told me I was leaving early today, so I went with her to the people."

"Now, darling," I said, "this is important. Can you remember what the people said to you? And how many people were there?"

"There was a man and a lady. The lady said how lovely it was to see me again. I thought it was a silly thing to say as I didn't know who she was, but, you know, all sorts of people say that to me because they have seen me before, but when I was small, and I don't remember."

"Did she sound funny?" I asked.

"What sort of funny?"

"Did she have an accent?"

Saskia looked at me and leaned her head to one side as if thinking.

"I don't know," she said.

"How about the man?" I asked. "Did he say anything?"

"He told me to get out of the car."

"Where was the car?" I asked.

"On the road."

"Outside this house?"

"Yes," she said. "Just down the hill a bit."

Slowly, Saskia told us everything that had happened between the time Mrs. Squire came to fetch her and her arriving home. The man and woman hadn't said anything else to her, but he had driven around for half an hour or so before dropping Saskia outside. We asked her if she could describe the couple, but all she could really say was that they were white and quite old, almost as old as Mommy and Daddy, and the lady was wearing blue jeans with red-and-white sneakers.

"I'm sorry, Mommy," she said.

"That's all right, darling," said Marina, giving her a hug and a kiss. "But don't do it again."

We left Saskia, lying curled up on her bed, and went downstairs.

"What the hell's going on, Sid?" Marina snapped at me again. "Why did you ask if the woman had an accent?"

"I just thought she might have."

"Why?"

I'd have to tell her, I thought, but she wouldn't like it. And she didn't.

"Why didn't you tell me this at lunchtime?" she demanded.

"I didn't think it was that important," I said. "I've had all sorts of nutters call me over the years. I thought he was another one of those."

"But they took Sassy," she said in exasperation. "We must call the police."

I looked at my watch. It was nearly half an hour since I had left Mrs. Squire at the school.

"What if they take another little girl," Marina said with determination, "and then they don't take her home."

"You're right," I said. "I'll call them, and also Mrs. Squire."

In fact, I tried Mrs. Squire first, to check that she hadn't already called the boys in blue, but she hadn't.

"Saskia is fine," I said to her. "But we are going to have to call the police."

"I understand," Mrs. Squire said wearily. "I'll wait here until I hear from them."

The police arrived in the shape of Detective Chief Inspector Watkinson of the Thames Valley Constabulary, along with a detective sergeant, who was immediately dispatched by his boss to go and interview Mrs. Squire at the school.

"Abduction of a child is a very serious offense," said the D.C.I., "punishable by anything up to life imprisonment."

There was, however, not a great sense of urgency in his demeanor because, as he pointed out, the victim of the abduction, Miss Saskia Halley, had been returned unharmed and unmolested to her home within half an hour.

"Are you sure it wasn't the parents of one of her friends?" the chief inspector asked as we all sat around the kitchen table. "Perhaps they thought they were doing you a favor."

"I'm certain," I said. I told the policeman about my calls from the Irishman, and his bushy eyebrows rose a notch or two.

"Do you have any idea who it was?" he asked.

"None," I replied. "But surely you can find out from telephone records."

"I doubt it," he said. "Most villains these days use untraceable, pay-as-you-go cell phones that they buy with cash. They regularly throw away the SIM card and replace it with another one they buy at any phone shop for a couple of pounds. We might be able to find out roughly where the calls were made from but not who made them."

That might be a start, I thought.

"Could I ask your daughter a few questions?" asked D.C.I. Watkinson. "I had hoped to bring a female constable with me, but there wasn't one available. But I will send for one if you want me to."

"It will be fine," said Marina, "as long as I'm with her."

"Of course."

Saskia sat on Marina's lap and repeated everything she had told us while the chief inspector made notes in his black notebook.

"What color was the car?" he asked quietly.

"Blue," she said without a hesitation.

"Light blue or dark blue?"

"Dark blue."

"And did it have back doors?"

"Yes," Saskia said. "And it smelled of dogs, like Daddy's car."

"Was it a Range Rover like your daddy's?"

"No," she said, smiling. "It was small like our old car."

The chief inspector looked at me.

"We had a Volkswagen Golf before the Range Rover."

"Was the car the same as Daddy's old one?" he asked, turning back to Saskia.

She lifted her shoulders and held her hands out sideways.

"That means she doesn't know," said Marina.

The chief inspector smiled. "I have two kids of my own, boy and a girl, older now, but they used to do that all the time, especially when I asked which of them had broken something. It didn't always mean they didn't know, just that they weren't telling."

"I think Saskia would say if she knew," Marina said, defending her little girl. "She's not really into cars."

"Was the door handle to get out the same?" he asked.

Saskia again leaned her head to one side and screwed up her mouth as she tried to remember. "I think so," she said eventually. "And the car had a big dent in the side."

He wrote something down in his notebook. "Call me if she remembers anything else." He handed me his business card with the direct number to his office. "We'll run a search for dark blue VW Golfs. There can't be that many with dents."

The sergeant returned at that point, and the chief inspector went outside to talk to him. Presently, they both came back in.

"Mrs. Squire, the head teacher, has managed to give us a basic description of the couple," said the sergeant. "They were in their thirties or forties, white, and the man was on the short side with a slim build. He had short dark hair, and the woman had mid-length light brown. Unfortunately, Mrs. Squire was more concerned about how the school looked — it seems one of the children had recently thrown up in one of the corridors. She thinks she might know them again. We'll get her to do an e-fit later at the station." His tone indicated that he didn't hold out much hope of it being any use.

"Did they speak with an Irish accent?" I asked.

"Not that Mrs. Squire had noticed."

"Could your caller have been putting on the accent?" asked the chief inspector. "To disguise his own voice?"

I suppose it was possible. "I'll ask him when he phones again."

"*If* he phones again."

"He'll phone again," I said with certainty. "He hasn't told me yet what he wants me to investigate."

"Don't you think calling the police will have frightened him off?"

"No," I said, "I don't."

"But why bring Sassy home if he wanted to have a hold over you?" Marina said. "Why not keep her?"

"He just wants me to know what he *can* do. It's a threat. Nothing more."

"It's more to me," said D.C.I. Watkinson.

"And me," said Marina.

The man rang again that night, at a quarter to midnight, on the house landline, as Marina and I were getting ready for bed. I picked up the receiver on the bedside telephone.

"So, Mr. Halley," he said in his strong Belfast accent, "will you now do as I say?"

"Is that accent put on or are you really Northern Irish?" I replied, ignoring his question.

"I'm an Ulsterman," he said. "And proud of it."

"Well, I'm a Welshman and also proud of it, but I don't go round kidnapping little girls."

"Kidnapping? Don't be daft. I only gave

68

the wee lass a ride home."

"I called the police." I said.

"I don't doubt it."

"And they'll trace this call."

"D'you think I came up the Lagan in a bubble?" He laughed.

"What do you want?" I asked.

"Like I told you, I need you to investigate."

"And like I told you," I said, "I don't do that anymore."

"I think you'll be making an exception."

"I think I won't."

"Now, listen to me, Mr. Halley," he said, all laughter having gone from his voice. "I've shown you what I can do, so I have. Do you want your wee lass returned to you next time in a box?"

"Bugger off," I said and slammed the receiver back in its cradle.

Marina had been listening.

"What the hell did you do that for?" she screamed at me.

"Shhh! You'll wake Sassy. I know what I'm doing."

"Do you? It's our daughter's life we're talking about."

"Trust me," I said, taking her hands in mine. "There is only one way to treat a bully and that is to bully him back. If we roll over

69

under his threats and do as he says, we'll never be free of him."

The phone rang again.

"Ignore it," I said, but Marina had already grabbed the receiver.

"Listen to me, you bastard," she shouted into it. "Leave our daughter alone. Leave us all alone."

"Ah, Mrs. Halley." I could hear him quite clearly in spite of Marina having the phone pressed to her ear. "Tell your husband to see sense. I only need him to do one job for me."

"What job?" Marina asked, pushing away my hand as I tried to take the phone from her.

"I need him to investigate Sir Richard Stewart's allegations of race fixing."

I sat on the edge of the bed with my mouth hanging open in surprise.

I reached over and took the phone from Marina.

"What did you say?" I asked.

"You will investigate Stewart's claims and find them groundless."

"And are they groundless?"

"You will find them so."

That hadn't been what I'd asked, but it was answer enough.

"Sorry," I said. "My investigating days are over."

I hung up.

"Are you mad!" Marina shouted at me. "You must do as he says."

"I must not," I said decisively. "He's asking me to investigate, but he also tells me what I will find out. If Sid Halley says there's nothing going on, then people will believe that nothing is going on. But there clearly is or he wouldn't be so keen to get me to say otherwise. He wants a whitewash. So where would that leave my credibility, and where would it leave racing?"

"What's more important? Bloody racing or your own daughter?"

I was certain that Saskia would ultimately be in more danger, not less, if I did what the man demanded, but Marina could only see the short-term consequences.

"First, you don't want me to investigate anything, and now you think I'm mad not to."

"I don't know what I want." Marina sat down on the side of the bed and buried her head in her hands. "I'm just frightened."

I went and sat next to her and put my right arm around her shoulders.

"Trust me," I said again. "I know what is

71

best. I will protect you and Sassy. I promise."

And, I thought, I would start investigating.

I would find out who was doing this to us, and stop him.

Both Marina and I took Saskia to school on Friday morning, Marina having spent the night in the other bed in Saskia's bedroom and with the landing light switched on, but there had been no further interruptions, telephonic or otherwise.

Marina didn't want Saskia to go to school at all. In fact, she was all for locking ourselves in the house and getting the police to mount guards at the doors.

"We can't live like that," I'd said. "We have to go on as normal."

"Normal!" Marina had shouted at me. "Sid, it's not normal to have your child kidnapped."

It had been the police who had been the deciding factor. D.C.I. Watkinson had called at seven-thirty to say he would meet us at the school. He would have a team of officers there to interview other parents and to reassure them that their children were safe.

I, personally, thought that the police presence would have the opposite effect, and so it proved, with many mums taking their children straight back home again.

"Did you trace the call?" I asked the chief inspector. Marina had insisted that I give the police permission to listen in and trace our calls.

"Ah, not exactly," he admitted. "It appears that our friend used several reroutings through a number of different SIM cards, some of which were overseas."

"D'you think I came up the Lagan in a bubble?" I said quietly to myself.

"What did you say?" asked the chief inspector.

"D'you think I came up the Lagan in a bubble?" I repeated louder. "It's what the man said when I told him the police were tracing the call."

"And what does it mean?"

"It basically means *Do you think I was born yesterday?* The Lagan is the river that runs through Belfast. Our friend, as you call him, is smarter than we take him for."

"He's not that smart," said the chief inspector, "not if what I hear is true."

"And what do you hear?"

"I hear that the more someone tries to tell Sid Halley what to do, the more he does the opposite." He smiled. "The more you warn him off, the harder he comes after you."

"And where did you hear that?" I asked.

"On the police grapevine."

"What else does the police grapevine say about me?"

"That you're not opposed to taking the law into your own hands."

"Hand," I said, smiling. "I've only got one."

He smiled back at me. "Yeah. I've also heard you sometimes use that false one as a club."

"Don't believe everything you hear," I said, laughing, although I knew it to be true. "But I might club our friend if I find him." I made a clubbing motion with my left forearm.

"Yeah, like I said, it wasn't very smart of him to involve Sid Halley when he didn't need to. Bit like poking a hornets' nest with a stick. Bloody stupid."

"Have you spoken to the police investigating Sir Richard Stewart's death?" I asked, changing the subject.

"Only briefly, earlier this morning," said the chief inspector. "They seem pretty convinced it was suicide."

"Well, for what it's worth, my father-in-law thinks it was murder, and I tend to agree with him."

"On what evidence?"

"Not much. My father-in-law was a naval admiral, but he was also a friend of Richard Stewart, and he doesn't believe he was the type to kill himself."

"Is there a type?"

"Maybe not," I said. "But don't you think it's rather suspicious that Sir Richard comes to see me on Wednesday morning about race fixing, then he's found dead on Thursday, the very day some Irish nutter kidnaps my daughter, demanding that I investigate the self-same race fixing?"

"Mmm, I see what you mean. It does look slightly odd."

"Slightly odd!" I said ironically. "I think it looks extremely odd. So what are you going to do about it?"

"Maybe I'll have another word with the Hampshire force," he said, clearly not believing that the opinions of an elderly retired sailor and an ex-jockey were that important. "Meanwhile, will you do what our friend demands?"

"Yes and no," I said. "Yes, I'll investigate the race-fixing allegations but, no, I won't file a whitewashed report. Instead, I'll find out who is doing what to whom and stop them."

"If you find the people who abducted your daughter, let *me* deal with them," he said, suddenly more serious. "The law doesn't take kindly to interference from members of the public."

At least he hadn't called me an amateur as Peter Medicos had done.

"I thought you said that warning me off was counterproductive."

"I mean it," he said, pointing a finger at my chest.

So did I. If I found the man responsible for abducting Saskia, I'd like to club him good and proper.

5

Where did I start to find the man with a Northern Irish accent?

He'd said he was an Ulsterman and proud of it.

I looked up the population of Ulster — just over two million. Assuming half of those were female and a quarter were children, I reckoned I had about seven hundred and fifty thousand men to choose from.

I thought back to the voice on the phone. I was pretty sure it hadn't been a very young man or someone in his dotage. That would cut the numbers down a bit, but I could still be looking at a potential pool of half a million.

Perhaps I needed to start at the other end.

I retrieved the folder of Sir Richard's papers from the drawer in which I had placed them. If I could discover there had indeed been race fixing and, if so, who had been responsible, then I might be able to trace it back to an Irish connection.

I looked again at each of the suspect races and made a detailed list of the jockeys and trainers involved. Two jockeys had ridden in all of the nine races, with one other having had a ride in seven.

That, I decided, was where I would start.

I used my computer to look up the racing fixtures for the coming weekend.

Jump racing in England is mostly a winter sport, with the major steeplechase and hurdle races taking place each year between November and April. The Cheltenham Festival, the highlight of the jumping calendar, had been held the previous week, and the Grand National was another four weeks away, after which the steeplechase season would wind down for another year.

Not that jump racing finished altogether. Many of the smaller tracks continued to stage jump meetings throughout the summer months, while most of the bigger ones, Cheltenham excepted, concentrated on the flat code until the late autumn.

During June and July, many steeplechase horses, including the real stars of the sport, were rested and put out in paddocks to eat the fresh grass and stretch their legs.

The jockeys, however, don't enjoy such luxuries, spending the same time driving all

over the country to ride the juvenile, begin-
ner and novice horses that made up many
of the fields, the horses that might just possibly become the stars of tomorrow. Rides
gained on novices in the summer could occasionally turn into championship rides in
future winters.

But that was all several weeks away yet.

The *Racing Post* website showed me that
there were due to be three steeplechases and
four hurdle races on a card at Newbury the
following day, and the two jockeys who had
ridden in all the nine suspect races would
both be in action, together with another
who had ridden in four of them.

"I'm going to the races tomorrow," I said,
walking into the kitchen to make myself a
cup of instant coffee.

Marina looked horrified. "But what about
Sassy and me?"

"You can come if you want."

"Sid," she said, putting her hands on her
hips, "what about our safety? Have you
forgotten there's a maniac out there who
abducts children?"

"Of course I haven't," I said. "But sitting
in here behind closed doors isn't going to
find out who it is. You'll be safe enough at
the races with all the people round or you
can stay here and lock yourself in."

She stared at me across the kitchen, and I couldn't read what she was thinking. "Are you mad?" she said. "Of course we're coming with you. I'm not staying here on my own, with or without locked doors."

"Great," I said. "We'll leave at eleven."

The three of us went to Newbury in the Range Rover, with Sassy sitting in the center of the backseat on her booster.

There had been no further communication from "our friend" since the two late-night calls on Thursday, and the lack of contact was beginning to worry me slightly. What was he planning? I didn't think for a second that he'd given up on his quest.

Consequently, I was extra vigilant as I turned through the gates and into the racetrack parking lot. I was pretty sure we would be safe inside the enclosures simply because it would be difficult to make a rapid getaway from there with a kidnapped child, but in the parking lot was another matter.

I followed the directions of the attendants and parked in a growing line of cars on the grass. We waited for the group of four young men in the adjacent car to climb out and get themselves ready, and then the three of us joined them, seeking safety in numbers, as we walked together towards the racetrack entrance.

"Aren't you Sid Halley?" one of the men said to me. "The jockey?"

"I used to be him," I said, smiling, "but now he's too old."

"Happens to us all, mate," the man said. "I used to run marathons, but look at me now." He grabbed his substantial stomach and guffawed loudly.

But I didn't feel like laughing.

Latterly, and for the first time I had begun to feel my age. I no longer bounded out of bed each morning, and I could no longer shrug off late nights and hangovers.

My more sedentary and deskbound life-style of recent years had also taken their toll on my fitness, and I was now regularly beaten in a sprint by my six-year-old and her friends. Indeed, going for a run around the village had become a chore rather than a joy.

I was nearing my forty-seventh birthday, and the flecks of gray hair, which had first appeared at my temples about ten years previously, had started to spread right across my head. Soon I would have to admit that it was the dark bits that were the real flecks in an otherwise solid gray landscape. But at least I still had my hair. Some of my former jockey colleagues were long past the comb-over stage and looked even older than I did.

On top of everything else, the years of racing falls were beginning to catch up with me, and my ankles were regularly sore and aching from arthritis. It didn't bode particularly well for the future.

I wondered if Dr. Harold Bryant at Roehampton also did complete foot and ankle transplants.

"So, Sid, what's going to win the big race?" asked my marathon friend with the bulging stomach. "You must know, being an insider."

Being solicited for tips was the bane of any jockey's life. Jockeys notoriously make bad tipsters. In my case, when I was riding, I was invariably overoptimistic about my own chances and would tell everyone to back me.

Early on in my career, I had expected to win every race I'd ridden in. I soon began to realize that I was more disappointed when I lost than I was pleased when I won. Experience soon changed that attitude, and a good job too. Otherwise, it might have been the quick road to depression and suicide. "To tell you the truth, mate," I said, turning towards him, "I don't even know what's running."

"You're just saying that to protect the price." He placed his finger knowingly down the side of his nose and winked at me.

I didn't bother to deny it. He wouldn't have believed me anyway.

The seven of us made it to the racetrack entrance in easygoing companionship, safe from molestation or abduction, and the four guys peeled off to the nearest bar while Marina, Saskia and I made a direct line towards the Weighing Room. There was still well over an hour to go before the first race, and there were things I had to do.

"You two can go for a wander round," I said to Marina. "There are some people I need to talk to."

Marina had Saskia firmly by the hand. "We'll stick with you," she said, the stress of the past two days etched deeply on her face.

"It's all right," I said to her calmly. "You will be safe in the racetrack enclosures."

The look she gave me implied that she didn't agree. "I'd still rather stick with you. But I'll give you the space you need to talk to people." She didn't like it. She didn't want me to investigate at all, but she knew we had no choice in the matter.

"Mommy, can I go and see the horses?" Sassy said, pulling hard at her mother's arm.

"No," Marina said firmly. "Stay here with

Daddy."

"Please!" Sassy squealed, pulling harder so that her body was almost at forty-five degrees to the vertical.

Marina smiled at me wryly. "What do you think?"

"Stick with other people. You'll be fine."

Marina allowed herself to be dragged slowly away towards the horses in the pre-parade ring, but she didn't look very happy.

"Be back here well before the first," I shouted after her.

I had come to Newbury to speak to Jimmy Guernsey and Angus Drummond specifically, the two jockeys that had ridden in all nine of Sir Richard Stewart's suspect races, and also to Tony Molson, who had ridden in four of them, but there was much more to the day than that.

I hadn't been to the races for nearly two years, not since the Grand National before last when the brewery that sponsored the race had held a reunion for all living National-winning jockeys. And I couldn't remember how long it had been before that. Without my investigating work, I had found it meaningless to do so.

I still longed to be one of those daring young men in their bright-colored silks, hurtling over fences at thirty miles an hour and risking life and limb on a daily basis. But I had risked a limb once too often, and, since then, I found no great pleasure in watching others still do what I hungered for.

So I had stopped going racing altogether. It had been less painful.

"Hello, Sid," said one trainer that I used to ride for, placing his hand on my shoulder. "Long time no see."

"Hello, Paul," I replied, smiling at him.

"Sid," called another trainer, hurrying past, "have you got yer saddle? I need a jock in the fourth. Mine's ill."

"Don't tempt me," I said, laughing.

I looked up in the race program to see which jockey it was. Dammit, I thought. It was Tony Molson, one of those I'd come specifically to speak to.

I spent the next five to ten minutes or so greeting old friends and slipping back into racing life like a hand into a well-worn glove. It all fit snugly around me, and the pain of not being directly involved seemed to have eased a little. I resolved not to be away from my love for so long again.

All the while I kept a lookout for either Jimmy Guernsey or Angus Drummond and, presently, I saw them both walking in together from the direction of the parking lot, chatting amicably. I wanted to speak to them separately rather than together, so I allowed them to walk past me into the Weighing Room and the jockeys' changing room beyond. According to the race program, Jimmy had a ride in the second race while Angus's first engagement was in the third.

"Sid, me old mucker. How's the world treating you?" I was slapped on the back and turned to find Paddy O'Fitch, a fellow ex-jockey and a walking racing encyclopedia and, before last Thursday, the only man I'd known who spoke with a broad Belfast accent. "I thought you must be dead."

"Not yet, Paddy, not quite," I said, smiling. "And how are you keeping?"

"Well, I think," he said. "My bloody doctor keeps going on about me drinking too much Guinness. But as I tells him, if I drinks less of the black stuff, then I eats more, and that puts me cholesterol right up like a rocket. Can't bloody win, can I?"

I had been secretly hoping that Paddy might be at Newbury. Not that Paddy was his real name. He had been born plain Harold Fitch in Liverpool, but he was more Irish than the Irish, and he loved everything green — except, that was, his beer, which he liked black with a white head.

"Can I buy you a drink?" I asked him.

He looked around in a guilty manner, perhaps checking for his "bloody doctor."

"I shouldn't," he said. "If I get started before the horses have even gone out for the first, then I'll be paralytic before the end of the day. How about later?"

"After the fourth?" I said. "In the Champagne Bar."

"Do they serve Guinness?"

"I'm sure they will for you," I said. "Otherwise, we'll go elsewhere."

"Right y'are," he said. "After the fourth." He looked at his watch. He didn't look too happy. "Can you make it after the third? I'm not sure I can wait until after the fourth."

He could always have gone earlier and bought himself a pint, but then I wouldn't have had the pleasure of his sober, sharp mind.

"OK," I said. "After the third. But don't drink anything before then."

"Me? Drink? Whatever gave you dat idea?"

"See you after the third, then," I said. "In the Champagne Bar."

"Right y'are, Sid. But what is it that you'll be wanting?"

"Why should I be wanting anything?" I asked.

"Don't be daft, of course you'll be wanting something. No one buys me drink just for the fun of it."

I laughed. "See you after the third."

He walked away from me, steadily, upright and in a straight line. I wondered how long it would last. After his riding years, Paddy O'Fitch had made his living by writing brief histories of racing and selling them in the racetrack parking lots. The business had flourished and developed into a multimillion-pound enterprise, which Paddy had then sold to an international media consortium for a fortune. Without the business to run, Paddy had become bored and was now seemingly intent on drinking away all the proceeds from the sale. But he seemed happy enough, and I could think of worse ways of spending one's retirement. He was also the most knowledgeable man on a racetrack of anything and everything that was happening. At least he was when he was sober.

With the help of the official standing guard over the jockeys' changing room door, I managed to collar Angus Drummond on his own outside the Weighing Room between the first and second races.

"Angus," I said, "do you remember riding Leaping Gold at Sandown in February? On the day of the Mercia Gold Cup?"

"Yeah," he said, "sure do. Novice chase, weren't it?"

Angus Drummond may have had a Scottish-sounding name, after his Scottish grandfather, but he was a West Country lad through and through, with an accent to match.

"Yes," I said. "Second-last race of the day."

"What about it?"

"Can you remember why Leaping Gold ran so badly? He started favorite but finished seventh, a long way back."

"He hit the third fence," Angus said confidently, "good and proper. Knocked the stuffing right out of him. Wouldn't bloody go after that."

"How about Enterprise in the two-and-a-half-mile novice hurdle at Ascot the week after?" I asked.

"What's this?" he asked. "Twenty questions?" He laughed.

"I've got a client who is looking to buy a decent horse, and he wanted me to check up on those runs before he parts with any money."

"Oh," he said. "Well, you can tell your client that I knows how to ride them if he's looking for a good jockey."

"But you didn't ride Enterprise very well at Ascot, did you?"

"What d'yer mean?" The laughter had suddenly disappeared from his voice.

"You went off too fast at the start, and the horse ran out of puff well before the finish. You were tailed off and pulled up before the last hurdle."

"The horse didn't stay," Angus said aggressively, sticking out his jaw.

"The horse wasn't given the chance to stay," I said, purposely trying to provoke a response. "I'm surprised the stewards didn't have you in to explain your riding."

"They did," he said sheepishly. As I had known they had. "But they agreed that it wasn't my fault as the horse had run away with me at the start."

Indeed, it had. I'd watched the video. But Angus Drummond was an experienced professional jockey, and horses shouldn't run away in such hands. So had the horse been allowed to run away on purpose?

I decided against asking Angus that question.

For the time being anyway.

Paddy was waiting for me at a high cocktail table in the Champagne Bar after the third race, and he was quite surprised to discover that I was not on my own.

"Paddy," I said, "this is Marina, my wife, and Saskia, our daughter."

He wiped the palms of his hands on his trousers, then offered one to Marina. "Lovely to meet you, Mrs. Halley," he said, showing a nervousness I found quite amusing.

"And you," Marina said, shaking the offered hand and doing a good job of disguising her shock at hearing another Belfast accent.

"Would you like a Guinness?" I asked Paddy.

"Well, yes, I would, to be sure," he said. "But they don't serve Guinness in here, so I took the liberty of fetching one, like, from the Long Bar under the grandstand. I was sure you'd pay me back." He lifted a plastic pint beaker, half full of the black stuff, from the table.

"Is it your first?" I asked in mock accusation.

"To be sure, it is," he said, smiling and holding the beaker to his lips to take a hefty swig.

I was pretty "to be sure" that it wasn't, but there was not much I could do about it.

I collected a glass of champagne for Marina and two Cokes for Saskia and me. The girls moved away to the next table while I leaned closer to Paddy to speak directly into his ear.

"Now, tell me, Paddy, who else speaks with a broad Belfast accent at the track? Someone who fixes things? Someone who's used to throwing his weight around and getting his own way?"

"Bejesus!" Paddy said, moving back a step or two. "Are you mad? Do you want to get yourself killed now?"

I was absolutely stunned by his reaction to my question. He went quite pale, and I thought he might faint. I looked around me for a glass of water to give him, but instead he took another large gulp of his Guinness and steadied himself against the side of the cocktail table.

"Now, why would you be asking me such a question? What have I ever done to you?"

"Paddy," I said sharply. "Pull yourself together."

"No," he said, still wide-eyed. "You pull yourself together. If I'm thinking it is who you might be after, you've got to be crazy. Either that or just plain bloody stupid."

"Who is it?" I said directly into his ear.

"Do you not know?"

"Paddy, I wouldn't be asking if I knew."

"Sid, you've been away too long."

"All right, maybe I have, but who is it?"

"I'll not be telling you," he said with fear now in his wide eyes. "I'll not be the one to tell you."

"Write it down, then," I said, passing over a pen and my race program.

He looked around him as if checking that no one was looking over his shoulder. Finally, when he was satisfied that none of the other bar patrons were watching, he wrote two words in capital letters on the edge of the program: BILLY MCCUSKER.

"And who's he?" I asked, none the wiser.

Paddy took another look over his shoulder to check for eavesdroppers.

"He's vicious," Paddy whispered. "Don't mess with him."

I wasn't sure I had any choice in the matter.

"But who is he?"

"New kid on the block," Paddy said. "Now in his early forties. Grew up in West Belfast during the Troubles. His father ran a big construction firm and was murdered by the IRA for doing building work for the British Army. By the time young Billy was twenty, he was commanding a breakaway, hard-line Protestant group called the Shankill Road Volunteers, and his sole aim was to kill Roman Catholics who he believed lived in the wrong place. He also didn't like Protestants who had anything to do with the Catholics. No proof, of course, but there's little doubt that McCusker is responsible for over a dozen murders as well as scores of punishment beatings."

"Nice," I said.

"Not really," Paddy said. "He was jailed for life in 1996 for the particularly gruesome murder of a young Protestant teenager whose only mistake was fathering a child with his Catholic girlfriend, but Billy was soon released under the terms of the Northern Ireland Peace Agreement. Not that he's a reformed character or anything. He's been involved in racketeering and extortion ever since. And he still hates all Roman Catholics, who he blames for killing his da."

"So when did he come over to the mainland?"

Paddy looked around once more and was satisfied that there was still no one else listening. "About six years ago. It seems the Shankill Road Volunteers fell out with another Protestant paramilitary group over money, and a turf war ensued. Billy's side lost, so he and his mates were run out of West Belfast in a hurry. Word is, they had to leave so quickly that they were left with only the clothes they were wearing at the time. They transferred to Manchester, but they hadn't left so fast that they forgot to bring their nastiness with them."

"So how did McCusker get into racing?" I asked.

"He quickly got involved with a Manchester-based bookmaking outfit, inappropriately named Honest Joe Bullen. Perhaps Billy bought Honest Joe out or maybe he took possession by force. Either way, he now controls the business, and it has expanded rapidly since then by buying up other independent betting shops in and around Manchester and Liverpool."

"Or bullying them into submission," I said.

"Far more likely," Paddy agreed.

"How does a convicted terrorist get a bookmaker's license anyway?" I asked.

"Perhaps it was some deal over the peace agreement, sectarian convictions struck from the record or something, or maybe it's not him who holds the license. I don't know, but, no matter, Billy McCusker definitely calls the shots at Honest Joe's, and he's not making any friends, to be sure."

"But why are *you* so frightened of him?" I asked.

"Because I'm a Roman Catholic. *In nom-*

ine Patris, et Filii," he said, suddenly crossing himself, *"et Spiritus Sancti."* Paddy finished his sign by pointing one of his slender fingers at my chest. "And you should be frightened of him too. Everyone should. Word on the street is, he eats Catholic babies for breakfast. Like I tells you, don't mess with Billy McCusker."

I wasn't.

But was he the one messing with me?

6

Marina, Saskia and I waited outside the Weighing Room after the last race, and I caught Jimmy Guernsey as he emerged to go home.

"Well done, Jimmy," I said as I stepped into stride alongside him, with Marina and Saskia hurrying along behind. "Good win in the last."

"Huh, thanks, Sid," he replied almost in a monotone. "I should have won the two-mile chase as well if that bloody horse Podcast could jump. Stupid lump of dog meat. Tripped over the sodding last with the race at his mercy."

"Nice, easy fall, though," I said, remembering back to how Jimmy had rolled over twice on the turf and then jumped up quickly. Fortunately, for him, there had been no following horse to land on his outstretched left palm with a razor-sharp horseshoe to slice through muscle, bone and sinew, as there had been in my career-ending last race.

"My pride was hurt more than my body," he agreed. "What brings you here, then? Haven't seen much of you lately."

"Actually, I came to speak to you."

"Really." He seemed surprised. "Never heard of the telephone?"

"Much better in person," I said.

"What about?"

"Red Rosette."

"What about him?"

"His run at Sandown last month," I said. "In the novice chase. Same day as the Mercia Gold Cup."

He shook his head slightly. "Can't remember. I ride lots of horses. I know he didn't win. I'd have remembered that."

"No," I said, "he didn't win. Made a hash of the last fence. You asked him to take an extra stride, but there wasn't room. He got in too close and plowed his way through. Do you remember now?"

"Yeah, I believe I do. Silly mistake of mine. I thought he was too tired to stand off, and I misjudged the distance."

"Yeah," I echoed. "And how about Martian Man in the novice hurdle here at Newbury on the same day as the Hennessy? Was that a silly mistake as well?"

Jimmy stopped walking.

"What are you implying?" he asked, not looking at me.

"I'm not implying anything," I said, although it was clear I was. "I just wondered if you had a theory of why a horse that on all his previous runs had been a front-runner with no noteworthy sprint finish had been held up for so long at the back of the field on this occasion that he'd never had a chance to overhaul the leaders in the straight."

"I did nothing wrong," he declared.

"Didn't you?" I asked pointedly.

"Leave me alone," he said, setting off again at an even faster pace.

I walked a few steps after him but then stopped and called out to him instead. "Is that what you said to Billy McCusker?"

There was an almost imperceptible break in his stride, only for a split second, but I'd noticed. He recovered quickly and walked away towards the racetrack exit without looking back.

"Who is Billy McCusker?" Marina asked.

"I think he may be the man on the telephone with the Northern Irish accent."

"Call the police," Marina demanded.

"I will," I said, "when I'm sure it's him."

We were sitting in our Range Rover, having safely negotiated the return trip across the parking lot.

"But who is he anyway?"

"A former Belfast paramilitary thug who's now a bookmaker in Manchester."

It wasn't the answer that Marina had wanted or expected.

"My God!" she said. "That's all we need. A bloody terrorist after us."

"Mommy!" Sassy shouted from the backseat. "That's a naughty word."

"Shush, darling," I said.

But it wasn't Marina's use of the naughty word *bloody* that I found disturbing, it was the word *terrorist.* I was about to start the engine when I suddenly had visions of booby traps and car bombs.

"What on earth are you doing?" Marina asked in irritation as I slipped out of the driver's seat and went to look under the Range Rover's hood. I also checked all around the vehicle, and underneath it as well, but there was nothing out of the ordinary, at least nothing I could see.

"Just checking," I said with a smile as I climbed back in, but there remained a certain degree of unease in my mind when I did finally push the start button.

Nothing happened. Of course nothing

happened, nothing other than the twin-turbo V6 3.0-liter diesel engine coming smoothly to life.

I silently rebuked myself for being so melodramatic. The situation was tense enough already.

Nevertheless, I spent almost as much time watching the rearview mirror as I did the road on the fifty or so miles up the A34 to home, but, if a car had followed us, I couldn't spot it.

I was also careful when we arrived back at the house, leaving Marina and Saskia in the locked car while I checked for unwanted guests lurking in the undergrowth.

"We can't go on living like this," Marina said in desperation when we were all safely inside and I'd relocked all the doors. "I can't get you to search the garden every time I need to put the dogs out."

"No," I agreed, "but the dogs will bark if they hear anything."

"But what are *you* going to do about it?" she asked.

"What can I do?"

"Get the police to stop this McCusker man terrorizing our lives. They can arrest him for kidnapping Sassy from school, for a start. Go and call them now." It was not a request but a demand.

"OK," I said, "I will."

I went into my office and Marina followed. I called the number on the chief inspector's business card.

"Detective Chief Inspector Watkinson, please," I said to the person who answered.

"He's off duty," came the reply.

"Could you please ask him to ring Sid Halley?"

"Oh, hello, Mr. Halley. This is Detective Sergeant Lynch. I came with the chief inspector to your house on Thursday afternoon. Can I help?"

"I may know the identity of the man on the phone, the one with the Northern Irish accent."

"Who is it?" D.S. Lynch asked.

"A man called Billy McCusker, from West Belfast."

"You say you think he may be the one?" said the sergeant. "Or he may not be?"

"I can't be certain."

"I can't arrest a man for kidnapping if you only think he may be responsible, now can I? What evidence do you have?"

What did I have? Only Paddy O'Fitch's Guinness-fueled rambling and a brief break in Jimmy Guernsey's stride when I'd called out the name Billy McCusker. Even I could see it didn't amount to much.

"Not much," I conceded, "but surely it's a name worth pursuing?"

"I will make a note of it and discuss it with the chief inspector on Monday."

"What about us?" I interjected strongly. "My family and I feel that we are living under a threat from this man, and the police aren't taking our security seriously. He's taken my daughter once from her school, and I have absolutely no intention of letting him take her again. We need some police protection."

Marina was nodding in approval alongside me.

"I will also discuss that with the chief inspector."

"What about over the weekend?" I said.

"Mr. Halley, I'm sorry but we simply don't have the manpower to provide you with a personal bodyguard. I advise you to keep all your doors locked and call me again if this man McCusker contacts you. The chief inspector will be sure to call you on Monday."

I felt I was being fobbed off and my genuine concerns for our safety were being underestimated or dismissed. But I was not surprised. I'd had lots of dealings with the police over the years, and it was always my belief that they were much happier investigating serious crimes than they were trying to prevent them in the first place — look at the number of violent crimes committed by those out on bail, awaiting trial for previous violent offenses.

"Well?" said Marina, who'd only been listening to my side of the conversation.

"The sergeant said he'll discuss it with Chief Inspector Watkinson, and they'll let us know on Monday."

"Monday!" she screamed. "We might all be dead by Monday."

"Marina, my love, calm down," I said, trying my best to soothe her anxiety. "If necessary, I will have to do what this man asks — at least until Monday."

I spent most of the evening at my computer in my office researching the Troubles in Northern Ireland in general and Billy Mc-Cusker in particular.

I was surprised to find that far more British soldiers were killed in Northern Ireland during the Troubles than have died in both Iraq and Afghanistan put together. More than seven hundred British servicemen lost their lives as a result of Irish terrorist action between 1969 and 2001, but none of those deaths could be laid at the door of Billy Mc-Cusker.

According to Paddy, Billy had left the security forces well alone and had concentrated on killing members of the minority Catholic community.

Even though there was a mass of information on the Troubles, there were only two short references I could find to any Billy McCusker. The first was a brief account in official court papers of the outcome of a trial for murder at Belfast Crown Court, where McCusker had been convicted of killing one Darren Paisley by nailing him to a wooden floor in a disused factory and leaving him there to die of thirst. According to the report, McCusker claimed to have informed Paisley's father where to find his son, but Paisley Senior denied ever having received such a message.

There was a small picture accompanying the report, a police mug shot of McCusker taken soon after he'd been arrested. I studied the image intently. It was nearly twenty years since it was taken, but the features were very distinctive — high cheekbones and a low, protruding brow that gave his eyes a deep, sunken appearance.

The second mention was in a list of prisoners released from the Maze prison under the terms of the Good Friday Peace Agreement. Billy McCusker had walked free after serving just two and a half years of a life sentence by somehow convincing the government of the day that his murder of a fellow Protestant was a sectarian offense.

Other than that, there was nothing else. I searched through the online archives for Northern Irish newspapers from the *Belfast Telegraph* to the *Carrickfergus Advertiser,* but there was not a single mention of anyone called Billy McCusker. He had obviously been very proficient at keeping his name out of the media.

Honest Joe Bullen appeared several times in the Manchester and Liverpool dailies, especially in reports of betting-shop take-overs, but there were no references to Billy McCusker as being the owner of the company.

Could Paddy O'Fitch have been wrong?

I doubted it. Paddy was a walking encyclopedia when it came to racing matters, and his fear of McCusker had been genuine and unquestionable.

The phone on my desk started to ring.

I looked at my watch. It was a quarter to midnight — just as before.

"What do you want?" I said, answering.

"Ah, Mr. Halley," said the now familiar voice. "How good of you to answer your phone. Did you have a good day at New-

106

bury races?"

"That's none of your business," I said.

"Oh, I think it is," he said in his condescendingly humorous tone. "Everything about you is now my business."

"And how about the other way round?" I said. "Are *you* also my business?"

There was a slight pause. "Mr. Halley," he said, all humor having disappeared, "you will find out that I will very much be your business if you don't do as I tell you."

"Why would I do what a kidnapper and a murderer says?"

"Who says I'm a murderer?"

"I'm sure Darren Paisley's father would, for one."

There was a much longer pause from the other end of the line. I wondered if it had been wise to declare my hand so early. Once upon a time, I'd managed to defeat another particularly nasty villain only because he had underestimated me as a foe. There would be no chance of that now.

"I will send you a report. Sign it."

"I will not," I said. "I only sign reports I write myself."

"Make it easy on yourself. Sign the report now and save yourself a lot of grief. You'll sign it eventually."

"On the contrary," I said, "you can save

yourself a lot of grief by leaving me alone and going back to West Belfast."

"I'm warning you, Mr. Halley," he said.

"And I'm warning you too, Mr. Mc-Cusker."

I hung up. There was little point in carrying on what would quickly descend into name-calling.

I sat at my desk looking at the telephone and, sure enough, it rang again.

"Now, listen to me, you bastard," I said, picking it up, but it wasn't him. Another voice, an English voice, cut through what I was saying.

"Mr. Halley, this is Detective Sergeant Lynch."

"Who?"

"Detective Sergeant Lynch," he repeated. "I was listening in to your call."

I'd forgotten about that.

"If the man calls again, try and get him to confirm that he is indeed Billy McCusker. Then we can issue a warrant for his arrest."

"Don't you have enough already?" I asked. "He didn't deny it."

"He probably wouldn't deny it even if you were wrong. To throw us off on a tangent."

"Get off the line, then, in case he calls again."

I sat at my desk, watching the phone, for

well over an hour, but without it ringing, before going quietly up the stairs to bed.

Marina was asleep in Saskia's room again, so I lay in our bed alone with the lights out, thinking about what I should do next.

The chief inspector had said that involving Sid Halley was comparable to our friend poking a hornets' nest with a stick. I now felt that I had well and truly poked a hornets' nest of my own.

I thought about Darren Paisley, lying nailed to a floor for days on end until he died of thirst. It made me shiver.

Perhaps it wasn't so much poking a hornets' nest as putting my hand into a bag of vipers — my real hand, that is.

Chief Inspector Watkinson called at eleven o'clock on Monday morning.

"How the search going for the blue Golf with a dent?" I asked.

"Not well," he said. "It seems that dark blue is the favorite color for Golfs, and there are tens of thousands of the damn things still running around on British roads."

"Are any of them registered to a Billy Mc-Cusker?" I asked.

"Not that we can find. And I can hardly describe your actions as wise, telling him that you knew who he was."

"What would you have me do?" I asked him. "Roll over and capitulate?"

"No," he said. "But it might have been safer to keep that knowledge to yourself."

"I hoped that by telling him I know his name, it might actually make my family and me a little safer. Surely he wouldn't be stupid enough to harm us if the police would then immediately be aware of who'd done it."

"I have spent an hour this morning discussing Billy McCusker with my police colleagues from the Northern Ireland Police Service and I wouldn't bank on that. He may have been convicted of only one murder, but he is known to have committed many more, along with all sorts of other criminal activity. However, it seems that recently he has been extraordinarily adept at avoiding prosecution."

"Did you also speak to the police in Manchester?" I asked.

"As a matter of fact, I did," he said. "But, so far, McCusker seems to have kept himself out of the Manchester courts. Not that there aren't plenty of rumors flying round — you know, extortion and money laundering, that sort of thing." He sounded almost blasé about it.

"So will you give us some protection?"

"I'll ensure that your village is regularly patrolled. I can't do more than that. I can't even keep the tap on your telephone after midnight tonight without renewing the order, and I don't think my superintendent's budget will allow it."

"What does McCusker have to do before you'll put an armed policeman at our door?"

"Mr. Halley," said the chief inspector, "I have no reason to believe that you or your family are in any imminent danger."

"Did you listen to the call he made last night?" I asked almost in disbelief. "He as good as told me that he would give me more grief unless I signed his report."

"So why don't you sign the report and then tell the racing authorities it was signed under duress and that it should be ignored?"

"That would surely amount to the same as not signing it in the first place, at least in his eyes. And, anyway, I have my pride, you know."

"Pride before a fall?" said the chief inspector. "Maybe it's time to be pragmatic and do what he asks."

"You can't seriously believe that Mc-Cusker would go away just because I signed his stupid report," I said. "I've come across people like him before and, trust me, it's not a matter of getting this damn thing

111

signed or not, it's more about getting the better of Sid Halley."

"You flatter yourself."

"You may think so, but I've been in this situation all too often in my life. That's why I gave up the investigating business. I'm not the police, and too many of the people I have encountered have taken out their frustrations on me personally. I have the scars to prove it. I even met a man who believed that murdering me would give him a certain status in prison as the man who had killed Sid Halley."

"But he didn't kill you."

"No, not quite." But I could remember how frighteningly close he had come to doing so. And it had been the growing realization that there were so many gangsters standing in line to be the one to kill Sid Halley that had made my decision to stop investigating so easy. Consequently, I had broadcast to the world that Sid Halley had retired from chasing villains and that henceforth they had nothing further to fear provided my family and I were left alone.

Clearly, that announcement had not fully registered with Billy McCusker.

Now I had little choice but to fight back. And fight back I would.

7

On Tuesday morning, much to Marina's dismay, I caught the train from Banbury to London for the annual checkup and service on my myoelectric hand.

"You should stay here and look after Sassy and me," Marina had said crossly over breakfast.

"Sassy will be fine at school," I'd replied. "They've employed a security guard to ensure no child can leave the premises unless personally collected by a parent or guardian. It took me several minutes yesterday afternoon to convince him that I was indeed Saskia's dad because I didn't have any ID on me, and I'm sure he thought I was too old."

Marina still hadn't liked it. "But what about me?"

"Why don't you come to London with me? You could do some shopping while I go to the hospital."

Marina would have normally jumped at the chance to have a day's shopping in London, so it was a measure of her disquiet that she opted instead to go spend the day with Paula Gaucin, Annabel's mother and Marina's best friend, who lived almost next door to the school in the next village.

"I can then be close by in case Sassy needs me," she'd said, even though both of us knew that Saskia was the least worried of the three of us. She had gone off happily to school, as she always did, seemingly not affected one jot by her unauthorized lift home the previous week.

I took a taxi from Paddington station to Roehampton Lane and walked into the now familiar Queen Mary's Hospital building and along the corridor to the prosthesis service department.

My current left arm was the third I'd had in fourteen years and a replacement for the previous one, which I'd damaged beyond repair due to using it as a crowbar to extricate myself from some handcuffs. The brainiacs at Queen Mary's had not been amused, and I'd been sad to see it go. That particular arm had saved my life.

There was no doubt that the mechanical engineering involved in making an artificial hand that moved with my thoughts and motor-nerve impulses was pure genius, but the medics had yet to discover a way of giving the fingers any sensory function. Hence I reckoned that it was little more use to me than an old-fashioned hook made famous by the captain of the same name in *Peter Pan.*

Now I eased my truncated left forearm out of the tightly fitting fiberglass shell and handed the false bit of me over to one of the technicians. He plugged a computer lead into a small socket alongside the battery compartment.

"Everything seems to be in order," he said, studying his computer screen. "All the motors are working fine." I found it slightly eerie to watch as my now disembodied left hand opened and closed by itself as it lay on the technician's workbench. "Do you have any difficulty operating it?"

"I suppose not," I said. "But, to be honest, I hardly use it anymore. I wear it more for show, like a piece of clothing."

"A very expensive piece of clothing," he said.

Didn't I know it! The insurers had refused point-blank to cough up for the damage to my previous hand on the grounds that use as a crowbar was not in their list of insured perils, and it could hardly be described as fair wear and tear. So I'd had to pay for the new one.

"I don't suppose you can make it feel?" I asked the technician.

"Sorry," he replied. "I hear that there's some research going on in the States to add pressure sensors to the fingers that connect via electrodes to the patient's brain. But it's in the early stages. No sign of it here yet."

"Shame," I said.

"I'll give this a proper internal clean and lubrication. It'll take about twenty minutes. You can wait outside, if you like." He made it clear that he didn't really want me looking over his shoulder, watching him work. I'd seen it all before anyway.

"I've an appointment to see Dr. Harold Bryant," I said.

"Ah, Harry the Hands," the technician said with a smile. "Got his sights on you, has he?"

"Sights?" I said.

"For one of his hand transplants. Dead keen, he is. And he's good too. Great results so far. Early days, of course, but I don't think he'll be putting me out of a job just yet." He laughed.

I wasn't at all sure it was a laughing matter.

116

"How many transplants has he done?" I asked.

"Only one," replied the technician. "At least he's only done one here. But he did some before that as part of a transplant team in America — in Kentucky, I think."

One transplant didn't sound to me to be quite enough.

Did I really want to be Harry the Hands' second guinea pig?

"I'll have this finished by time you've seen Harry — that's if you still need it."

I left the technician laughing again at his own little joke, walked down the corridor to the outpatient department and straight into a consulting room to meet Dr. Harry Bryant, Fellow of the Royal College of Surgeons, aka Harry the Hands, who had been waiting for me, his sights at the ready.

"Mr. Halley," he said in a surprisingly soft voice for such a big man, "how wonderful to meet you at last." He stood up from behind his desk and leaned forward to shake my right hand with a firm grip. "Please, do sit down."

I sat in the chair across the desk from him.

"Now," he said, leaning back, "tell me why you want a new hand."

Harry the Hands and I spoke for almost an

hour, but, somehow, the discussion did not proceed in the manner that I'd been expecting.

Either he was being very clever or I was being rather dim, or maybe it was because what he was offering was precisely what I craved, but far from him having to convince me to be his guinea pig number two, I found myself being the one who was selling *me* to *him* as a possible candidate.

"When are we talking about?" I asked. "How soon?"

"We need to do some tests first, to look at your remaining forearm to ensure that you are suitable, and then it's up to fate — we have to wait for a suitable donor."

Donor. It was the first time he'd used the word.

Donor.

There was suddenly more of a psychological dimension to the whole thing. It was far beyond simply replacing what I'd lost; it was having someone else's hand attached in its place.

"There are no guarantees," Harry said. "During my time in the United States, we had some problems with rejection, and not only physical rejection of the hand by the body's immune system. There was also a case of emotional rejection when the recipient couldn't come to terms with having a new limb that wasn't his to start with."

"What did you do?" I asked.

"The transplanted hand had to be removed."

"So the transplant is reversible?"

"You should not enter into this procedure with that state of mind. Yes, we can remove the hand again, and it has occasionally been necessary. But there is every likelihood that such a removal would not leave your arm as it is now."

"In what way?" I asked.

"Amputation would likely have to be above where your arm finishes now, maybe even above the elbow."

"Oh," I said.

"But we should look at the positives as well. My experience has also shown me how successful hand and wrist transplantation can be. There are patients who had the operation more than ten years ago who now live perfectly normal lives."

"I know," I said. "I've watched the videos on YouTube."

I walked out of Queen Mary's Hospital with a new spring in my step. Suddenly, the prospect of dispensing with the steel and plastic and having a living, feeling left hand

119

again had filled me with great excitement.

After my meeting with Harry, I had been taken away by one of his team who had conducted the tests. Blood was drawn and X-rays taken; measurements of my right hand were made — to try to match for size and color — and I was asked to fill out a lengthy psychological evaluation questionnaire.

I looked down at my freshly serviced prosthesis.

"Your days are numbered," I said to it out loud and received a rather strange look from a woman who was waiting with me for the bus to Hammersmith. I smiled at her and she moved away a few steps.

So absorbed had I been with the whole concept of the transplant that I had quite forgotten my ongoing troubles with Billy McCusker, at least I had until my cell rang while I was sitting on the bus.

"Mr. Halley," said the now familiar voice, "have you received the report?"

"No," I replied. I'd left home before the mailman had been. "But it would make no difference if I had. I won't sign it, and I won't play along with your silly game."

"It's not a game, Mr. Halley."

"Well, whatever it is, I'm not playing."

I disconnected the call.

What had that policeman said? *Maybe it's time to be pragmatic and do what he asks.*

Not bloody likely.

Marina picked me up from Banbury station at three, and we drove together to collect Saskia from school.

"Had a good day?" Marina asked. "Did your hand pass its checkup?"

"Yes," I said, "my hand was fine. And it was a very good day." I paused. "I met a surgeon who does hand transplants."

"What did he want?"

"He wants to give me a new hand."

"What?" Marina exclaimed, almost driving into a stationary bus. "You can't be serious."

"I'm very serious," I said. "He told me he could give me a working, feeling hand again."

"But surely it's been too long since you lost yours."

"Apparently not," I said. "In fact, he prefers to have patients who have had no hand for some years."

"But when?"

"They would need to do some tests first to make sure my arm is suitable, and also for tissue typing, then it would be a matter of waiting for a suitable donor."

121

"My God!" Marina said. "How macabre."

"Harry Bryant, that's the surgeon, said that it will be very important to think of the hand as mine and not as still belonging to someone who has died."

"It's all a bit strange though, don't you think, wishing for someone to die."

I thought back to what Harry the Hands had said to me as I'd been leaving his office. "We'll sort out all the tests and then you'll just have to wait and hope for rain."

"Why rain?" I'd asked him.

"There are always more donors when it rains."

"Why?"

"Motorcyclists," he'd said. "Far more motorcyclists are killed in the wet."

Even the memory of the conversation made me shiver.

I agreed with Marina. It was a very strange mind-set indeed to be hoping for others to die so I could have their bits.

Sassy came bounding down the path to the gate but had to wait her turn to be released by the school security guard.

"Hello, darling," I said as she jumped up into the Range Rover. "What have you learned today?"

"Nothing," Sassy said with conviction,

"but Annabel and I played hopscotch at lunchtime and, Mommy, I won."

"Well done, darling," Marina said.

I smiled broadly as I drove the couple of miles and turned in through the gates of home.

"Where are the dogs?" I said, the smile suddenly disappearing from my face.

"I left them in the kennel," Marina said with certainty, but we were looking at the kennel, and the gate was now wide open. "I know I did. And I came back to check on them round two o'clock. They were there then."

"Wait here," I said, parking the Range Rover on the drive, "I'll go and have a look." I got out of the car. "Lock the doors."

Both Marina and Saskia looked at me with big, frightened eyes.

I walked over to the kennel. It was a small, red-brick building in the corner of the garden with a fenced-off run that included a patch of grass. I had built it soon after we moved in so that we could leave the dogs alone for the day without them having to be cooped up inside the house. The kennel gave them the chance to be under cover if it rained but also to lie in the sun on nice days.

"Here, girls," I called out, but neither of our two setters appeared. "Mandy, Rosie, where are you?"

I went into the kennel, through the open gate, but there were no dogs hiding in there. I hadn't expected them to be. The two would always rush to the kennel gate whenever we came home, standing up on their hind legs with their front paws on the rail, their tails wagging enthusiastically. It would have been very unlike either of them to hide from us.

I walked over to the house with a degree of trepidation, but I could see no sign of a forced entry. Nevertheless, I was very wary as I went inside and searched thoroughly both upstairs and down. I had mental visions of pet rabbits boiling in saucepans or bloodied horse heads lying between satin sheets, but there was nothing.

I went back into the garden and searched everywhere, including amongst the deep undergrowth in the shrubbery.

Nothing.

The dogs weren't anywhere on our property.

I went back to the Range Rover.

"What is going on, Sid?" Marina asked with alarm. "Where are the dogs?"

"I don't know," I said.

"Has someone taken them?" Sassy asked.

"They may have got out and run away."

Sassy pulled a very sad face. "Why would they run away?" she said. "Don't they like living with us?"

"Of course they do, darling," said Marina. "Don't worry. We'll find them."

I wished I shared Marina's confidence but decided not to say so.

"Can we go and look for them?" Sassy asked miserably. "I want Rosie and Mandy back now." She started to cry, and Marina tried to comfort her.

I think we all felt like crying. Rosie and Mandy were almost as much a part of our family as Saskia, and I had little doubt as to who was responsible for their disappearance.

Billy McCusker was right. This was no game. It was war.

"Dog theft is all too common, I'm afraid. Did you have a padlock on your kennel?"

"It's not theft," I said. "It's kidnapping."

"Dognapping, you mean. Have you received a ransom note?" D.S. Lynch wasn't being very helpful. "And how do you know for sure that their disappearance is due to Billy McCusker?"

"I just do," I said.

I could remember Sir Richard Stewart saying the exact same words in the exact same frustrated tone during his visit to my house the previous week when I had questioned his conviction that race results were being manipulated.

I didn't question it anymore.

"So what are you going to do about our dogs?" I asked.

"There's nothing I can do," said D.S. Lynch.

"How about sending a detective round to fingerprint the kennel or organizing a search party?"

"Mr. Halley, even if I knew for sure that the dogs had been taken rather than wandering off on their own, I couldn't allocate any manpower to finding them. Dogs are considered property. In the eyes of the law, the theft of a domestic animal is no more serious an offense than the taking of, say, a bicycle or a garden table, and I'd hardly send a posse out in search of those, now would I?"

"I thought they once hanged horse thieves in the American West."

"Maybe they did, and stealing sheep used to be a capital offense here too, but we've thankfully moved on in the past two hundred years."

"But the dogs are part of our family."

"They may be," he said, "but they *are* just dogs."

Just dogs!

Not to us, they weren't. To us, they were like children.

"So what should I do?" I asked.

"Contact your local dog warden. Any dogs that are found should be handed in to him. Were they wearing tags?"

"Yes," I said. "On their collars. They're also microchipped."

"Then you should contact the microchip service provider and tell them the dogs are missing and check that their records are up to date. Other than that, all you can do is wait."

Wait for Billy McCusker to call, I thought. And then what? A ransom demand? Sign more papers? Absolve him of his sins? Curl up and die?

I was desperate to fight back, but how could I if I couldn't see my enemy?

It was definitely time to look for him.

8

Marina took Saskia out in the Range Rover to try to find the dogs while I sat in the house waiting for the inevitable call from Billy McCusker.

I collected the mail from the basket under the letterbox in the front door. The so-called report was amongst the bills and the junk mail, a slim brown envelope with no markings other than my name and address printed on a white stick-on label.

I was careful not to touch the surfaces of the envelope, holding it only by the edges. I didn't for a moment think there would be any fingerprints on the paper — none, that was, other than the mailman's — but one could only hope that McCusker had been careless.

I slit open the envelope using a carving knife and poured out the contents onto the kitchen table.

There was only one sheet of ubiquitous

white copy paper, with one brief computer-printed paragraph under the heading *A Report into Sir Richard Stewart's Allegations by Sid Halley.*

I was approached by Sir Richard Stewart concerning his belief that the results of certain races were suspicious and that irregular betting patterns existed on those races. I have studied the races in detail, and I have interviewed some of the jockeys that rode in the races concerned. I am satisfied that the betting patterns for the races were not exceptional or unusual, and I am content that no evidence exists which supports the beliefs held by Sir Richard.

There was a space beneath the paragraph for my signature and the date.

It was laughable. The man was more of a fool than I had thought.

For a start, a genuine Sid Halley report would have been prepared on proper headed, printed notepaper and would have included detailed notes of all the interviews conducted, with records of *with whom, where* and *when,* not to mention a detailed breakdown of each of the original allegations, race by race, with a thorough and reasoned conclusion drawn from expressed evidence.

There was no way I was putting my name to this garbage, true or false. I had standards to live up to.

Marina and Saskia returned about eight o'clock without the dogs. Not that I'd imagined for a moment that they'd find them. In fact, I feared that our girls might never be found.

McCusker was a killer. He'd been convicted of one gruesome murder and he'd clearly been responsible for many others. Dispatching a couple of dogs would not have severely pricked his conscience. He'd have probably enjoyed it.

Little Saskia was inconsolable, weeping buckets into Marina's shoulder as she carried her into the kitchen.

"Bedtime," Marina said to me, and she took Saskia upstairs to her room.

I looked again at the sheet of paper and its printed paragraph.

I have interviewed some of the jockeys that rode in all the races concerned.

Indeed, I had, on Saturday at Newbury. But how did McCusker know that?

Had he been watching my movements or had either Jimmy Guernsey or Angus Drummond reported back?

I went through to my office and looked again at the detailed lists I had made of all the jockeys and trainers of the more than one hundred horses that had run in Sir Richard's suspicious races.

In all, there were thirty-six different jockeys who had taken part in the nine races. A third had ridden in only one of them, eight more had ridden in two, while the other sixteen had gone to post in three or more, including Angus Drummond and Jimmy Guernsey, who'd had mounts in all nine.

I decided to concentrate first on those who had ridden three or more times. Other than Guernsey and Drummond, I knew most of them fairly well, all except a couple of the younger ones who had only recently entered the sport.

I used the *Directory of the Turf* website to look up all their private addresses. Of the sixteen, eleven lived within a six-mile radius of Lambourn, the Berkshire village that was a major center for racehorse training, especially steeplechasing. Maybe I could visit some of those in a single day, but I'd have to choose a day when there were no local jump meetings and hope they were at home.

I looked up the fixtures, but, as I'd feared,

there were no days in the coming week without any jump racing at all. However, there was one with only a single meeting at Wetherby and that was in two days' time, on Thursday. Most of the southern jockeys, those who lived around Lambourn, would be unlikely to travel so far north for mid-week racing.

Next I turned to my list of the horses' trainers, but that was interrupted by Marina who came downstairs from trying to settle Saskia.

"Sid," Marina demanded, "what the hell is going on? Where are the dogs?"

"You know what's going on," I said. "And I have no idea where the dogs are."

"But you know who took them."

"I think I know," I said. "At least I think I know who arranged it. The same man who arranged for Sassy to be collected from school last Thursday. The same man who's been calling us and demanding that I sign a report that's a complete load of rubbish. The man with the Northern Irish accent."

"Billy McCusker?" she said. "The terrorist?"

"Yes."

"What does he want from us?" It was a rhetorical question. Marina knew what he wanted. "Can't you just sign his bloody report and be rid of him?"

"Signing his report won't get rid of a man like that," I said.

"Then, for God's sake, how *do* we get rid of him?" Marina shouted.

"Shhh, you'll disturb Sassy," I said, but Marina didn't seem to care. She was frightened, and angry, and I was the only one around to lash out at.

"Do what he bloody wants, can't you," she screamed at me. "I love those dogs." She started to cry. I stood up and went to put my arm around her, but she pushed me away. "Just do what he wants," she sobbed.

Did I have any choice?

"OK," I said. "I'll sign his bloody report, but it won't be the end of it, you'll see."

As if on cue, the telephone on my desk started ringing.

"Aren't you going to answer it?" Marina asked as we both stood there, looking down at it.

I picked up the handset. "Hello," I said tentatively.

"Is this the Halley residence?" It was a voice I didn't recognize, and one that was definitely not Northern Irish.

"Yes," I said with some relief.

"My name is Philip York," he said. "I'm a veterinarian, and I've been treating a dog of yours. It has your name and telephone number on its collar tag."

"Yes," I said excitedly. "We've lost two dogs. They went missing this afternoon."

"Well, I only have one of them here," said Philip York, "and I'm afraid the news is not good."

"Oh?"

"No," he said. "She was found running loose on the freeway and she has obviously been hit by at least one vehicle."

"Oh," I said again, trying to hold back my emotions. "How is she?"

"Not good," he said. "Not good at all. I'm really only calling to let you know that I'm putting her down."

"No," I said instinctively. "There must be something you can do?"

"Mr. Halley, I'm sorry but there's no alternative." He spoke with authority. "Her back is broken."

Marina was in tears again alongside me. She may have been only listening to one side of the conversation, but she knew exactly what was being discussed.

"Which dog is it?" I asked, this time unsuccessfully keeping the grief out of my voice.

"It says Mandy on the tag."

"Where was she found?" I asked.

"On the freeway," he said again.

"Which freeway?"

"The M6," he said.

"The M6? Whereabouts?"

"Just north of Stafford. My practice is in Creswell, junction 14. The police brought your dog in here about twenty minutes ago."

The clock on my desk showed it was half past nine.

"But I live in Oxfordshire, near Banbury," I said.

"Banbury is eighty miles from here," he said. "My wife's parents live there. When did you say your dogs went missing?"

"This afternoon. My wife checked on them at about two, so sometime between two and three-thirty."

There was a pause in the conversation as we both absorbed the significance.

"So Mandy didn't just wander off, then," said the veterinarian.

"No," I agreed.

"Have you informed the police?"

"Yes, but they're not very helpful. Dogs, it seems, are nothing more than mere property in the eyes of the law. Like a garden table, I was told." I paused again, almost overcome with sorrow at the loss of such a dear friend. "The law is an ass."

"I'm sorry," the veterinarian said. He

135

would know only too well how dogs were much more than just "property" to their owners.

"Do you know if there was any sign of the other one?" I asked.

"The police didn't say anything to me about there being a second dog. Perhaps you should give them a call."

"Yes," I said, "I will."

"What do you want me to do with the body? I can dispose of it fairly easily here unless . . ." He tailed off.

"Can I collect her tomorrow?" I asked.

"Of course." He gave me his address and I wrote it down. "I'm so sorry."

"Thank you," I said. "And thank you for calling me and letting me know."

"Right," he said. "I'd better get on. I'll see you tomorrow."

"Tomorrow, then," I said. "Oh, hold on, don't go. One last thing."

"Yes?" he said.

I was near to tears. "Please give Mandy a last stroke from us, you know, before . . ."

"Of course," he said. "She's sleeping — heavily sedated already. She won't feel or know anything."

I suppose it was a comfort, but not much.

I stood, hugging Marina, as great bouts of grief caused her whole body to shake.

Mandy had been a member of our family for the past six years, since she'd been a two-month-old little bundle of red-haired joy we had excitedly collected from the breeder.

"Let's look on the bright side," I said. "Rosie may be loose as well. All we have to do is to find her."

"How?"

"Let's start by calling the Staffordshire Police," I said.

"Staffordshire?"

"Mandy was wandering on the M6 north of Stafford," I said. The M6, I thought, was the route from our house to Manchester.

The Staffordshire Police, far from being sympathetic over our loss, were angry with us for allowing our dog to wander on the freeway where it could have caused a major traffic accident.

I tried to point out that it wasn't our fault but to no avail. Informing them that there might be a second dog loose did nothing to improve their humor. In fact, quite the reverse.

"What time does it get light tomorrow?" Marina asked when I hung up.

"Around six."

"Then we'll leave here by five." It wasn't a question. It was an instruction.

■ ■ ■ ■

Billy McCusker called again at a quarter to midnight.

"You bastard," I said, picking up the phone by the bed.

"Now, now, Mr. Halley, mind your language."

"You've gone too far this time," I said.

"You English, you're so sentimental about your animals. Why don't you do as you're asked, and I'll go away."

Did I believe him?

"Where are my dogs?"

He ignored my question. "Did you get the report?"

"Yes."

"Good." He sounded pleased and so sure of himself. "You will sign it and send it to the head of the BHA Security Service."

"And if I don't?"

"Oh, Mr. Halley, I think you will. Your wife has such a beautiful face. It would be a shame to put that in danger, so it would."

"Bastard," I said again.

"Do as you're told, Mr. Halley."

He hung up.

I sat on the edge of the bed, wondering how I had got into this mess and, more to the point, how I was going to get out of it.

Would signing his damn report make any real difference? Maybe not. So why was I so fixated about not doing so? Pride, I suppose. But Chief Inspector Watkinson had referred to pride as coming before a fall. Be pragmatic, he'd told me.

Be pragmatic, I now told myself, and save Marina's beauty.

I went downstairs to my office and signed the paper.

9

Almost five hours after starting to search, I tried to tell Marina that we were wasting our time, but without much success. She was determined to stay as long as it took to find our Rosie.

We had left home in the dark, just before five o'clock, with Saskia wrapped in a blanket on the backseat. I'd been asleep for barely four hours, but I was wide awake and eager as we approached junction 14 on the M6 just as the sun began peeping up over the eastern horizon.

Where did we begin?

The previous evening, the police had told me that Mandy had been found about half a mile short of the junction on the northbound carriageway, so there seemed as good a place as any. But stopping on the hard shoulder was surely for emergencies only.

I decided this was an emergency and pulled over.

The freeway was already busy with a continuous stream of early-rising truck drivers tearing along the inside lane at breakneck speed. One didn't realize how fast the traffic moved on a freeway until you were standing only a couple of feet away from it, much as one didn't appreciate the pace of a steeplechase until you stood right next to a fence as the horses jumped by.

It had sounded so easy when Marina and I had discussed it on the way here. We would both shout Rosie's name in turn, and out she would appear from the undergrowth.

Sadly, it wasn't quite like that.

The incessant noise of the trucks as they thundered by meant that we could hardly hear what we were shouting at each other as we stood side by side behind the car.

"This is hopeless," I bellowed in Marina's ear. She nodded. "Let's get off the freeway."

We climbed back into the Range Rover and made an exit at junction 14.

At that point, the M6 freeway was built through land that had been used extensively for mineral extraction. There were several large disused gravel pits now filled with water, and cutting through the whole area were the West Coast Main Line railway tracks between Birmingham and Crewe.

It began to dawn on me what a Herculean task it was to search for our missing dog in such a large space even if we could assume that she had been released at the same spot as Mandy.

But Marina was not to be deterred, and I found myself driving time and again up tracks into the old gravel works until barred by chain-link fencing or padlocked gates. Marina then took to standing on the passenger seat with her head up through the sunroof as I drove, shouting for Rosie at the top of her voice, with Saskia and me adding more decibels through the open side windows. But our voices wouldn't carry far. The continuous roar of the traffic on the nearby freeway was all encompassing, drowning out any other sound. We wouldn't have heard a dog barking in response to our calls if she had been more than a stone's throw away.

I took the Range Rover back under the freeway and approached it from the other side and into a country park created around some of the water-filled gravel pits.

Again Marina and Saskia shouted for Rosie and again there was no response, save from a couple of locals out walking their own dogs.

"Haven't seen a loose Irish setter anywhere?" I asked, going up to one of them.

"Sorry, mate," he replied, holding his own golden retriever tightly by its collar. "When was it lost?"

"Yesterday afternoon," I said.

He shook his head. "Crazy dogs, red setters. Always running off. Not as bad, mind you, as Afghan hounds. They'll never come back."

I made a mental note never to get an Afghan hound.

"Come on," I said to Marina. "We're wasting our time."

"Just a bit longer," she said imploringly. "We must try for a bit longer."

We found Rosie on what I had decided would be our very last excursion up a dirt track. One moment, I was working out how I would tell Marina and Sassy that we had to go home now and, the next, our dear little Rosie came bounding up to the car, her tail wagging intensely, as if it was nothing out of the ordinary to meet us eighty miles away from home.

Marina and Saskia wept buckets, and I shed more than a tear or two myself, as we each gave her the biggest hugs.

Just dogs? Ha! What nonsense.

Marina danced around and around with joy beside the car as Saskia and I poured water and dog biscuits into bowls for Rosie to gobble down. Her normal feed time was five o'clock in the afternoon, and she hadn't been given anything yesterday.

"Now we have to find Mandy," Sassy said chirpily.

Marina and I looked at each other.

"Sassy, darling," Marina said, "I'm afraid Mandy won't be coming home." Marina did her best to tell Saskia everything in as kind a way as possible, but our little girl was confused and completely distraught.

"But why, Mommy?" she kept howling. "Why did someone take her? Why is Mandy not coming home? Why? Why? Why?" Even Rosie licking Sassy's face could not console her in her grief.

I asked myself if this nightmare was somehow my fault. Had it been me who had caused all this hurt by not agreeing sooner to do what McCusker wanted?

I felt wretched.

But it wasn't me who had kidnapped the dogs. It wasn't me who had let them loose to run and be hit on the freeway. I had been happy in my life of stocks and shares, bonds and gilts. It had been McCusker who had been the unwelcome visitor. I hadn't been searching for him. He had turned up unannounced and unwanted.

No. The fault lay firmly at his door, not at mine.

But how could I make him pay?

We went to Philip York's veterinary practice just after midday.

Marina and I had discussed what was best — in particular, what was best for Saskia. My first instinct had been to bring Mandy's body home for burial, but, on reflection, I wasn't sure that was the best course. We needed to move on, perhaps with the help of a new puppy, and dwelling on the past with a grave in the garden as a continuous reminder would be counter-productive.

Philip York understood entirely.

"I can dispose of the remains," he said quietly and only to me. "No problem."

"How, exactly?" I asked. I didn't want Mandy lying on some garbage dump being picked at by the crows.

"Cremation," he said. "There's a service that will collect. They're very good."

"Fine," I said.

None of us even saw Mandy.

Philip York gave Rosie a quick check over and declared her fit and well, and we departed, with him refusing my offer of payment. "I receive an annual retainer for doing police work," he said, "and I'll charge

them for the disposal since they brought
her in."

"How about Rosie?" I asked.

"There's no fee for telling you that your
dog is fine," he said, smiling. We shook
hands warmly. "I remember watching you
ride. Shame about your accident." He
glanced down fleetingly at my left hand, as
everyone did. "When I was younger, I used
to be one of the veterinary surgeons at Haydock. I still love my racing, especially over
the jumps, but this practice is now so
demanding that I hardly ever have the time."

"Never complain that you're busy," I said.

"No," he agreed.

We took Rosie home to Oxfordshire, where
she seemed confused and lost without her
elder sister, alternately lying in her bed and
then pacing around the house and garden
as if searching. How I wished she could talk
and tell us what had happened.

Marina had earlier called Mrs. Squire, the
head teacher, to say that Saskia wouldn't be
in today, but at end-of-school time she took
our sad little girl over to the Gaucin household to play with Annabel. I wasn't sure
whether it was mostly for Saskia's benefit or
for Marina's. She too was also desperately
down over the loss of Mandy and was in

need of some cheering up by Paula.

One of the disadvantages of marrying a foreign national was that family members were usually so far away. Marina could have done with a good cry on her mother's shoulder, but Mr. and Mrs. van der Meer, Marina's parents, were in Fryslân, a northern province of the Netherlands, and even though they visited us fairly often, they were hardly down the road when needed for a good weep.

After Marina and Saskia had gone, I sat alone in my office, staring at the signed report that still sat on my desk. Without enthusiasm, I took an envelope from a drawer and wrote out the address: Peter Medicos, Head of Racing Security, The British Horseracing Authority, 75 High Holborn, London, WC1V 6LS.

I folded the paper and sealed it in the envelope, but not without first making a photocopy. I then stuck a first-class stamp on the top right-hand corner.

I sat looking at it.

Was I doing the right thing?

No, was the simple answer, I was not doing the right thing. But did I have any choice in the matter? McCusker had threatened to disfigure Marina's face, and I believed that threat to be genuine. If there

was one thing I had learned about Billy Mc-
Cusker, it was that he had no conscience
whatsoever over inflicting pain and injury
on other people. He seemed devoid of mor-
als, and that made him a very dangerous
enemy, indeed.

The mail was collected from the box on
the village green at four o'clock.

At five minutes to four, I carried the
envelope out of the house and put it in the
bright red mailbox, hesitating only for a moment before popping it through the slot.

What was done was done, I told myself
and went back inside.

Rosie came up to me and looked up with
her doleful eyes as if to say *Where's Mandy?*
I stroked her head, and then she wandered
back to her bed in the hallway.

We would both have to learn to live in a
new environment.

On Thursday morning, having checked the
Racing Post to see which jockeys were
riding that day at Wetherby, I left home early
and drove south towards the village of Lambourn to visit some of those who weren't.

I had debated with myself all the previous
evening over what to do.

Maybe I should just return to my stocks
and shares, to financing bright but broke

entrepreneurs, and leave Billy McCusker free to terrorize some other poor soul. But would he leave me alone as well?

Now he had forced me into signing such nonsense once, would he not do so again?

Surely it wouldn't do any harm to go talk to a few of the other jockeys who had ridden in the suspect races.

Marina hadn't been happy about it, but she wasn't happy about much at the moment.

"I think I'll go and visit my parents for a few days," she'd said over supper. "I'll take Saskia with me. Her school breaks up for Easter on Friday. We'll go on Saturday morning and be back for Annabel's birthday party on Wednesday afternoon. I feel I need some time away from here."

Away from me? I'd wondered.

"Great idea," I'd said, trying to sound positive.

"I'll book the flights to Groningen. Papa can pick us up from there."

My first visit was to Robert Price. He was one of the top ten or so of steeplechase jockeys and had been for at least the past eight years.

According to the *Directory of the Turf,* he lived in a farm cottage outside Lambourn village on Hungerford Road.

"Hello?" said a young woman in her mid-twenties who answered the door. "Can I help you?"

"I'm looking for Robert Price," I said. "I thought he lived here."

"He does," said the woman. "I'm his girl-friend."

"Sid Halley," I said, extending my right hand. "I also used to be a jockey."

"I know exactly who you are," she said, glancing down at my left arm. "I'm Judy. Judy Hammond." She shook my hand. "You used to ride for my father."

"Brian Hammond?"

"Yes," she said. "You sometimes used to come to Dad's yard to ride out. It was very exciting for us to have the champion jockey riding at our place."

"You're kidding me," I said.

"No, it's true. I even bunked off school one day so I could watch you ride. Magic, it was." She blushed.

I also was embarrassed but pleased as well. It had been so long now since my riding had been anything like magic that it was nice to be remembered as I had been, when I'd been complete with two hands, when I'd had a full set of fingers that could feel the reins.

"Is Robert about?" I asked, changing the subject.

"He's been schooling the novices at Dad's place, but he should be back soon. You can come in and wait, if you like."

"Thanks," I said, stepping into the cottage. "Does he ride much for your father?"

"All the time. Bob's been the stable jockey for years."

I wondered how that went down in the Hammond household. Stable jockey cohabiting with the trainer's much younger daughter had, in my experience, never been very popular with the trainer's wife — something about family sleeping with the servants.

"Do you fancy a coffee?" Judy asked over her shoulder. "I'm making one for myself."

"Lovely," I said, following her into the kitchen. "Nice place."

"We're working on it," she said, smiling. "I've lived here with Bob for two years now." She poured boiling water from a kettle into two mugs. "Milk?"

"Yes, thanks. No sugar."

She passed over the steaming mug, and we sat opposite each other at the kitchen table.

I was to the point of regretting not having gone somewhere else first and then come back later when I heard the front door being opened.

"Hiya, babe," called a male voice from the hallway. "Whose car is . . ." He tailed off as he walked into the kitchen. "Sid Halley. Blow me down. Good to see you, Sid. Must be ages." His body language was not as welcoming as his words.

"Hi, Robert," I replied, staring him directly in the eyes. He quickly looked away. Too quickly, I thought.

"What brings you to our humble abode?" he said with a laugh, sitting down at the end of the table. He was doing his best to make light of everything, but I knew differently. Something was troubling him greatly, and my presence was fanning the flames.

"Is Maine Visit one of Judy's father's horses?" I asked. Robert said nothing. "And how about Tender Whisper and Lobsterpot?" They were the three horses he had ridden in the suspect races.

Maine Visit had been second in a handicap hurdle at Newbury on Hennessy Gold Cup day and, in my opinion, should have finished much closer to the winner than the seven lengths it stated in the official result.

"Yup," he said eventually, all laughter now having faded. "All three."

"Do you know an Irishman called Billy

McCusker?"

The color drained out of his face as if a light had been switched off.

"What is it?" Judy shouted, clearly distressed by the reaction. "Bob, darling, are you all right?" She stood up and fetched him a glass of water. "Here, drink this."

He drank down the liquid, and a little color returned to his face.

"I'm fine," he said, not sounding it. "I'm fine, really."

"What happened there?" Judy demanded loudly. "And who the hell is Billy McCusker?"

I thought for a moment that Robert was going to have another turn, but he drank more of the water and steadied himself.

"Someone that both Robert and I know," I said. "Don't we, Bob?"

He nodded slightly, his head hanging down in his hands with his elbows on the table.

"I think you'd better leave," Judy said to me, all schoolgirl hero worship having clearly evaporated. She stood next to me with her hands on her hips.

"OK," I said, getting up and walking into the hallway. "But tell Robert to call me. We may be on the same side."

"And what side is that?" she asked belligerently.

"The side of the angels," I said.

I just didn't fancy meeting with them anytime soon.

10

I managed to see only one other jockey on my list before it was time to go home to collect Saskia from school.

I caught David Potter at his home in Upper Lambourn as he was preparing to go play golf. I pulled my Range Rover into the driveway right behind his Jaguar.

David had been a journeyman jockey for most of the previous twenty years, riding steadily here and there without ever being directly connected to any one stable. He was good, though, and he'd had more than his share of winners, but somehow had never broken into the really big time. We'd ridden against each other fairly often when he'd been a fresh-faced youngster, but we'd never been friends. Nowadays, according to the data on the *Racing Post* website, David was riding less and less frequently, sometimes only two or three times a week. Not enough, I thought, to be making a decent living but, obviously enough, to run a Jaguar.

"Bloody hell, Sid," he shouted at me, coming out of the house with his golf bag over his shoulder. "Move your sodding car, can't you? I'm going to be late for my tee time."

"Sure," I said, "just as soon as you've answered some questions."

"What questions?"

"What do you know of a man called Billy McCusker?"

"Never heard of him," David said confidently as he loaded the clubs into the trunk of his car.

"He's Irish," I said, "from West Belfast." That struck a chord. Now I had David's full attention. "And he has a telling way with threats and violence."

David stood for a few seconds, looking at me, as if deciding what to do.

"You'd better come inside," he said.

David never did make it to his game of golf.

His elderly widowed mother had been the lever in his case. First, the threats. Then someone had broken all her downstairs windows in the middle of the night. The poor woman had apparently been so traumatized by the experience that she'd spent the following week in a psychiatric hospital.

156

"What else could I do?" David said. "It was only one race, and I didn't think I had any chance of winning it anyway. But then there was a second race, then a third and a fourth. Now I live in dread of the phone ringing."

"Four races?" I said. "I've only got you down for three."

We sat at his kitchen table and compared notes while Joyce, David's wife, fussed around us, continuously cleaning and polishing.

The fourth race was not on Sir Richard Stewart's list. It had been a three-and-a-half-mile stayers' hurdle at Sandown the previous January.

"It was really strange," David said. "None of the jockeys seemed to want to win. I remember, as we were coming round the bottom bend towards the second last, Jimmy Guernsey was in front, and he kept looking round to see if anything else was coming. It was actually quite funny."

"So what happened?" I asked.

"Jimmy won it. When he couldn't see anything coming to take over, he sat down and rode out a strong finish all on his own. Won by ten lengths or more."

"Can we look it up on the Internet?" I asked.

David fetched a laptop computer, and we logged on to the *Racing Post* website and checked the official result.

There had been twelve runners, and Jimmy Guernsey had indeed won, by fifteen lengths, on a horse called Le Champagne, at a starting price of five-to-one.

"That distance was flattering," David said. "Believe me, no one else was trying."

I did believe him.

According to the website, the win Tote return for Le Champagne was ten pounds and twenty pence, equivalent to a price of over nine-to-one. No wonder the race wasn't on Sir Richard's list. He'd been looking for races with a Tote return well below the starting price, not well above it.

I looked at the detailed notes on the race. Three of the twelve runners hadn't made it to the finish line. One of them had fallen at the last flight of hurdles in the back straight on the second circuit and had brought down the other two.

Being "brought down" was the absolute worst way to lose a race, jumping soundly, then tripping over another horse that was already lying on the floor. It was always unexpected and occurred without warning. I could remember all too well some of the crashing falls I'd had due to being brought down.

"Perhaps the designated winner was one of those three," David said. "When Jimmy saw that it was no longer in the race, he decided to go on and win it."

"But, hold on," I said, "that would mean that Jimmy knew beforehand which horse was meant to win."

"So it would," David said slowly, taking in the implications. "All I was told was to make sure I didn't."

"Who told you?"

"The Irishman. On the phone, the night before."

He pushed his chair back noisily on the stone-tiled kitchen floor, leaned back and put his hands on his head.

"So what are you going to do now?" he asked.

"In what way?"

"Are you going to the Security Service?"

"Should I?"

"I'll deny everything," he said.

"Then why tell me?"

"I don't know." He sat forward. "Perhaps you just caught me unawares."

"There's no possibility, then, that you'll complete a signed statement for me?"

"You must be bloody joking," he said with

a laugh.

"But surely you'd like to be rid of this man?"

"I certainly would," David replied. "But not at the cost of my jockey's license, which I'd be bound to lose if I admitted I'd stopped horses in four races, even if there were extenuating circumstances. You know what they're like at the BHA. Two-year ban, minimum. And they never forgive or forget."

He was right. We both knew it.

"Sid, I'm getting on now. I've probably only got a couple of seasons left in me, if that. And I want to go into training after I retire from riding, and I'll need a license for that too. I have no intention of throwing it all away."

Then he shouldn't have stopped the horses, I thought, but he wasn't the only one who had done things he didn't want to as a result of threats from Billy McCusker. I was a member of that club as well.

Marina and Saskia left early on Saturday morning, booking a taxi to take them to Birmingham Airport.

"But I'll take you," I'd said when Marina told me.

"Sid, leave it. Sassy is still very upset about Mandy, and it would be better if we just leave quietly in a taxi."

Better for whom?

I wandered around the house after they'd gone, missing them already and feeling miserable. I knew Marina blamed me for the dogs being taken in the first place. She hadn't exactly said so, but I knew. She believed that if I'd agreed straightaway to McCusker's demands, none of it would have happened and Mandy would still be alive.

She might be right. But surely that didn't make it my fault?

I rang the Admiral.

"Do you fancy a visitor to watch the racing on the television?" I asked.

"Just one?"

"Yes. I'm on my own for the day. I need cheering up."

"Then come for lunch first," he said.

"I don't want to be any trouble."

"It's no trouble. Mrs. Cross will conjure up something, I'm sure."

Mrs. Cross had been Charles's housekeeper for as long as I'd known him, which was close to thirty years, ever since his daughter, Jenny, had fallen irrationally in love with a young up-and-coming jockey — me.

"That will be lovely," I said. "I'll see you

at one o'clock."

I spent the rest of the morning catching up on paperwork — paying bills and answering e-mails.

A letter from Queen Mary's Hospital arrived in the mail around eleven, and I spent some time sitting at my desk looking at it unopened. It would be the results of the tests they had done on Tuesday.

What did I want it to say?

Would I be pleased or would I be disappointed if I had, or hadn't, been considered suitable for a transplant?

Come on, I said to myself, stop being such a coward. Open the damn thing.

I slit open the envelope and extracted the single sheet of paper inside. It was a letter from Harry the Hands.

Dear Mr. Halley,
It was very good to see you on Tuesday.

My team and I have looked at your medical test results and we have evaluated your psychological questionnaire in great detail.

I am very happy to inform you that we consider you an excellent candidate for a total hand and wrist transplant.

I would be most grateful if you could make another appointment to come and see me at the hospital as soon as possible to make all the necessary preoperative arrangements.

Yours sincerely,
Harold Bryant, FRCS
Head of the Transplant Team

Wow, I thought. This might actually happen, and soon.

"Where's Marina?" Charles asked over lunch.

"Gone home to her mother," I said flippantly. "And she's taken Saskia with her."

Charles looked up at me from his smoked salmon. "Permanently?"

"No," I said. "At least I hope not."

"Trouble?" Charles asked, never being one to beat about the bush.

"Some," I said.

"Anything to do with Richard Stewart?"

I nodded. "Bloody man. Why didn't he keep his suspicions to himself?" That was a good point, I thought. How had Billy McCusker known that Sir Richard had suspicions in the first place? Was it through someone at his club? Surely not. Then how?

"So you now believe him?" Charles asked somewhat smugly.

"Yes," I said. "Absolutely."

163

I told Charles everything — the calls, the threats, Saskia being collected from school by strangers, our trip to Newbury races to see Jimmy Guernsey and Angus Drummond, the taking of the dogs, Mandy's death, my trip to Lambourn to see the other jockeys, the lot. I even told him about the ridiculous report I'd been sent and me having signed it.

"That is trouble, indeed," he said. "What do the police say?"

"They're investigating the abduction of Sassy from school, but I don't think it has a very high priority. This McCusker fellow knew what he was doing by returning her home before we even knew she had gone. I think the police believe she was offered a lift home by a friend as a favor. Someone who is now too scared to say so."

"How about the dogs?" Charles asked.

"Ha," I said. "Don't make me laugh. They have as much interest in the taking of the dogs as in the theft of a bicycle. In fact, probably less. They told me so themselves."

"But that's ridiculous." The Admiral was angry on my behalf.

"In the eyes of the police, dogs are just belongings."

"What nonsense," he said.

We ate our salmon in silence for a while.

164

"So what are you going to do about this McCusker man?" Charles asked, taking a sip of an excellent Chablis.

"I don't know," I said. "I take his threats very seriously. I've done what he wanted. Now perhaps he'll go away and leave me to live my life in peace."

"And are you going to just sit back and let him get away with it?"

"What else do you suggest I do?" I asked. "I've been trying to think of a way of defeating him, but can I really risk Marina's beauty or Saskia's life to gain revenge over the death of a dog?"

"Then why did you go and see Robert Price and David Potter even though you'd already signed and mailed the report?"

It was a good question.

"Perhaps I have an insatiable appetite for the truth."

We watched the televised racing from the all-weather track at Kempton Park, and also from Meydan Racecourse in Dubai, but without much enthusiasm.

"Flat racing never excites me as much as jumping," Charles said. "I think it's because the horses seem to race for only a year or two. You don't have time to get to know them like the jumpers."

On the screen I could see Peter Medicos, the BHA head of racing security. He was standing in the parade ring at Kempton in his trademark tweed suit and battered trilby, watching the horses. I wondered what he made of the single-sheet, signed report that would have arrived on his desk on Thursday morning.

Many years ago, whenever I'd submitted an inquiry report to the racing authorities, it had come with a covering letter, reasoned arguments, detailed analysis and rational conclusions, as well as a full breakdown of where I'd been and what I'd done, together with appendices of interview transcripts and any further evidence on which I had based my conclusions.

So he must have been surprised by my most recent offering. Part of me wanted him to realize it was a fake. Perhaps I should tell him so.

"So when are Marina and Saskia back?" Charles asked.

"Wednesday," I said. "They land at noon. Saskia's going straight to a birthday party for one of her classmates."

"So what are you going to do for the next four days?"

"You make it sound as if I can't look after myself."

"You could always stay here with me," Charles said. "I'd enjoy the company." He sounded rather dejected.

"Charles, are you lonely?"

"I suppose I am a bit," he said. "What with Jill and Jenny now both living abroad, and you and Marina having such busy lives . . . Oh, I don't know. So many of my friends are dropping off the perch that I seem to spend all my time at bloody funerals. I suppose it'll be my turn soon."

"Nonsense," I said. "You've got years in you yet."

"Have I? I'm not really sure I want them." He sighed. "I used to love going to London to stay in my club for a few days, you know, to have lunch and dinner with chums, to relax over a glass of port, chew the cud, solve the world's problems, that sort of thing. It was like old times in the wardroom. But this last time there were only a few people in the club that I even recognized. Even Jack, the old barman, has retired. These days, the place is full of young city types with their cell phones always going off in the dining room." He sounded disgusted by such behavior. "With Richard Stewart now gone as well, I don't think I'll be staying there anymore."

"I didn't realize you knew Sir Richard so

well," I said.

"I didn't, really. I only ever saw him in the club, but, over the years, we grew to become friends. I will certainly miss him." He sighed again.

"Come on, Charles," I said. "You're meant to be cheering me up, remember, not depressing me."

"More wine," he said with a smile. "That's what we need." And he went to fetch another bottle of Chablis from the fridge.

We watched the World Cup race live on the television from Dubai, where the victorious American-bred colt, owned by an Irish millionaire and ridden by a French jockey, was hailed as a great English success because he was trained in Newmarket by an Italian immigrant. Such was the global nature of Thoroughbred horseracing.

"What do you think about me having a new hand?" I asked Charles.

"Why? Has that one stopped working?" He looked down at my prosthesis.

"No," I said. "I meant a new real hand. One that feels. A transplant."

"I don't understand."

"I've been offered the chance of having a hand and wrist transplant," I said. "Apparently, they've been quite successful in the

United States."

"But where does the hand come from?"

"From a donor. As with any transplant, there has to be a donor."

"You mean from a dead person?"

"Of course," I said with a laugh. "They're hardly likely to chop the hand off someone still alive just so I can have it."

Charles pulled a face. "I'm not sure I like the sound of that."

"Where do you think hearts come from for heart transplants or kidneys?"

"Yes," he said. "But they come from . . . inside. No one could look at a heart and say, 'That looks like old Fred's heart,' but they could with a hand. You'd even have someone else's fingerprints." He shivered. "I wish I hadn't told you now."

"Are you seriously going to agree to this?"

"Charles," I said firmly, "have you the slightest idea what it's like to have only one hand? I can't do up buttons without a desperate struggle. I can't hold open a newspaper or tie a knot or do any of the millions of other things that you need two hands to achieve, like tearing a sheet of bathroom tissue off the roll. Do you, in fact, notice that dear Mrs. Cross cuts all my food into bite-sized portions because I can't use both a knife and a fork at the same time? I can't even clap."

"And would a hand transplant allow you to do all those things?"

"Yes," I said, "it would."

"Well," he said, "perhaps you'd better have one, then."

Yes, I thought, perhaps I better had.

11

On Sunday I went to the races at Uttoxeter, and I took the Admiral with me.

I hadn't spent Saturday night at his house, as he'd wanted, because I'd had to get home to feed Rosie.

"You could always bring her here with you," Charles had said. "It's been quite a few years now since I've had a dog in this house."

"Maybe that's what you need to stop you being lonely," I'd replied, but he had shaken his head.

"I'm now too old to go for long walks, and that's what a dog needs."

Indeed, it was.

In the last light of the day, I'd taken Rosie up to the fields behind our house after I returned from Aynsford.

It had only been a few days, but she seemed to be adjusting well to the absence of Mandy, although she followed me around the house rather than lying in her bed in the hallway as she had always done before.

She had bounded excitedly through the fields of winter wheat that the recent fine weather had encouraged to grow as tall as she, and it had made me smile to watch her as she jumped up with each stride to check that I was still there, only her head showing above the stalks. It had looked like she was swimming in a sea of green.

My mind, however, had kept returning to the one big question that had been circling around my consciousness for the past week: Should I try to do something about Billy McCusker?

The moral answer was yes. But what was an acceptable cost?

I'd been battered many times in my life, mostly by racing falls, but there had also been a fair share of occasions when beatings had been inflicted by my fellow human beings.

Steeplechase jockeys get hurt, and often. It is a fact of racing life. If you can't deal with it, then it's simple, don't become a steeplechase jockey. But I'd also been beaten up, shot, stabbed and half flayed alive.

Some might say I was mad, but all those other injuries were a price worth paying for doing what I believed to be right, and I hadn't exactly foreseen that I'd get shot or stabbed. But now, with Billy McCusker, I knew only too well what the consequences would be — he'd told me.

In a race, no jockey expects his mount to fall, flinging him to the turf from a height of over six feet while traveling forward at thirty miles an hour. Falls invariably hurt, and sometimes they hurt really badly, with broken bones and dislocated shoulders. Nevertheless, jockeys go out to race day after day, knowing that the probability is such that they will, on average, go crashing down to the grass at half a mile a minute every twelve to fourteen rides.

But they can never be sure that a given ride will end in a fall. Every jockey assumes that he'll always get around safely in spite of the odds stacked up against him.

Taking on Billy McCusker would be like knowing that my horse would definitely have a crashing, bone-breaking fall at the very first fence.

Would I then be so keen to line up at the start?

Uttoxeter racetrack on that sunny Easter Sunday was full to overflowing, with the local populace being reinforced by folk from the cities of Stoke, Derby and Lichfield, all eager for a day out at the races.

"Are we here for anything in particular?" Charles asked as we walked from the car to the enclosures.

"What do you mean?" I asked.

"I just wondered if you had plans to talk to any more jockeys."

"Maybe," I said.

Charles smiled. "You can't change, you know, Sid. Not inside. Once a detective, always a detective. You might tell me you're not going to do anything about this man, but I know you better than that."

Was he right?

"I do want to have another word with Angus Drummond," I said. "He's got three rides here this afternoon, and it's so much easier than driving all the way down to Tiverton to see him at home."

I had also decided that it would be a good time to talk to Angus because Jimmy Guernsey was a hundred and fifty miles away, riding four horses on the card at Fontwell Park.

It was a calculated move but one potentially fraught with danger.

I was pretty sure that Jimmy Guernsey must be on the McCusker team as he had obviously known which horse was due to win at Sandown in the fourth race that David Potter had described. And possibly Robert Price too. But maybe, like David, Angus Drummond was more of a victim than a villain.

If I were wrong, he would be sure to report back to McCusker that I was still asking questions, with all the consequences that that would bring. But if I were right, I'd have another potential ally in the war.

Perhaps what I had in mind was to convince a large enough number of the jockeys to agree that if I did a deal with the BHA so that they would receive immunity from prosecution and every other sanction, they would then give evidence against McCusker and Guernsey, and that would be enough to get the two warned off from racing for life.

It wasn't going to be easy. David Potter had made that abundantly clear. He had been even more frightened of Billy McCusker than he was of the BHA Security Service and he was absolutely terrified of them.

As if on cue, Charles and I found ourselves walking through the entrance at the same time as Peter Medicos.

"Hello, Sid," he said.

"Hi, Peter," I replied. "Do you know my father-in-law?"

"Admiral," Peter said by way of greeting, raising his trilby slightly. "How are things at Aynsford?"

"Fine, thank you," said Charles.

There weren't many regulars on British racetracks that Peter Medicos didn't know. It was said he had a fantastic memory for faces, and clearly for much more.

"I didn't realize you lot worked on Sundays," I said. "Are you here chasing anyone in particular?"

"I work seven days a week, Sid," Peter said with a smile. "No respite for the righteous. I was at Kempton yesterday, and I'm always on the lookout for wrongdoing and mischief making. But I also have a weekend cottage near here, so I've a soft spot for Uttoxeter."

"Have there been any developments regarding Sir Richard Stewart's death?" I asked.

"The police seem pretty sure it was suicide."

I could sense that Charles was about to interject, so I looked at him and fractionally shook my head. He quickly got the message. In my opinion, Peter Medicos knew too much about us already, and I saw no reason why he should also know that my father-in-law had been a friend of Sir Richard's for more than twenty years.

"And thank you for that sheet of paper you sent me last week about his bizarre suspicions. It confirmed what I'd been thinking. Not that I was expecting it, mind you, so don't go thinking you can apply to us for a fee."

"I won't," I said.

I wanted so much to tell him to ignore the paper, to state that it was all lies and that Sir Richard had been right all along, but doing so would have resulted in too many other questions, most of which I didn't want to have to answer.

Not yet anyway.

Talking to Angus Drummond was going to be more difficult than I had imagined because he took elaborate steps to avoid me, hiding for most of the afternoon in the jockeys' changing room. When he did come out to ride, he sprinted across from the Weighing Room to the paddock without giving me any chance to snag him.

I could see this wasn't going to work. He would, no doubt, sprint to his car at the end of the day and then he'd be gone. He was a thirty-one-year-old, race-fit jockey while I was now pushing forty-seven and rather more portly around the waist than I had been in my riding days. In a simple Le

Mans–style run to the cars and drive away, Angus would win with ease.

So I decided to cheat.

His last ride of the day was in the sixth race, the second last on the card, and, sure enough, he sprinted out of the Weighing Room to the paddock before it and sprinted back in afterwards, not giving me a chance for a single word.

I then hung around outside the door for him to reappear after changing.

As he emerged he saw me and made a dash for the exit, rushing past me without glancing at my face. Little did he realize he was wasting his breath. He was going nowhere fast, not in his car anyway.

I hurried out to the parking lot in his wake to find him standing, frustrated, next to his BMW.

"It's not punctured," I said. "Just flat."

"Did you do this?" he shouted at me, pointing at his offside front tire.

"Yes," I said. "But I have a pump that will reinflate it."

"Are you bloody crazy? What sort of idiot lets the air out of other people's tires?"

"What sort of idiot," I countered, "stops horses?"

"I don't know what you're talking about," he said, but his body language gave me another answer. He was scared.

"Oh yes, Angus," I said, "I think you do."

"Jimmy says I shouldn't talk to you. He says you'll cause trouble."

"Then Jimmy is a fool. I might just be the only friend you've got."

That surprised him. "Friend?"

"Yes," I said. "A friend. And all you need to do is tell me why."

He looked around him as if trying to find a way to escape. "You wouldn't understand," he said.

"Try me," I replied. "I've been threatened too, you know."

Angus Drummond looked at me afresh. "I didn't have any choice," he said. "He said he'd burn down my parents' farm."

"The Irishman?"

Now he looked at me in total surprise, but then he nodded. "He torched a barn full of hay and threatened to burn down the rest of the farm if I didn't play ball. What else could I do?"

The last race was over, and the crowd surged out to the parking lots, everyone intent on beating the rush but being part of it.

"I'll fetch the pump," I said. "You stay here."

He nodded at me in a resigned manner.

I went over to the Range Rover, opened the trunk and lifted the floor tray to retrieve the battery-operated air pump from the compartment beneath.

"What's going on?" asked Charles, walking up to the car.

"I'm helping Angus Drummond with a flat tire," I said.

"Puncture?"

"No. Someone let the air out."

Charles raised a questioning eyebrow in my direction, and I laughed.

"I'll wait for you here, then," he said, climbing into the front seat of the Range Rover.

The pump made light work of reinflating the tire, and, while it did, Angus told me more of his disagreeable encounters with Billy McCusker, not that he'd known him by name.

"At first, I told him to get stuffed," Angus said. "He wasn't the first cold caller to try and get me to stop a horse, and I gave him short shrift, just like the others. But he said I'd regret it if I didn't cooperate. I asked him what he meant, but he said to wait and see. The following night the Dutch barn full of our whole year's hay crop went up in flames. It burned for three days and lit up the night sky for miles. Broke my mother's

180

180

heart after all the work we'd done cutting and baling the stuff.

"At first, we thought it must have been an accident — you have to be so careful with hay to make sure it's properly dry as it can naturally create a lot of heat deep down in a bale and spontaneously combust. We thought that was what must have happened, but then the Irishman rings me and says that he set it alight, and the rest of the farm would go the same way if I didn't do as he wanted."

"Do your parents know about the calls from the Irishman?"

"No, of course not. He said he'd surely burn the farm if I told anyone, even them." He suddenly looked rather worried that he'd told me.

"How about the police?" I asked.

"They came and looked at the remains of the barn, all twisted metal from the heat, but I didn't tell them about the calls. I was too scared. They didn't say it was arson, or anything, and Dad made a claim on the insurance."

"And you stopped the horse?"

"Yeah," he said slowly, "I did. But then he rings again and says he wants another one stopped. And another. And so on." He looked miserable.

181

I disconnected the pump from his car's lighter socket and wrapped the cable around it. "Good as new," I said with a smile, giving the tire a kick.

"What are you going to do about it?" Angus asked. "Are you going to the Security Service?"

"No," I said, "not yet. I'll tell no one for now, and don't you tell anyone that you've told me."

"Are you mad? Of course I won't."

"And, specifically, don't tell Jimmy Guernsey."

"Jimmy?" he said, surprised again. "Why would I tell Jimmy?"

"Doesn't he tell you which horse to stop?"

"No. I get my instructions direct from the Irishman."

"So why did Jimmy tell you not to speak to me?"

"I'm not sure," Angus said. "When we saw you at Newbury last week, he just said to me that Sid Halley was always trouble and that I should stay away and keep my mouth shut."

"Do you know if Jimmy was stopping horses as well?" I asked.

"I reckoned he might be. He rode in all of the races when I stopped one, and he didn't win any of them either, which, according to the form, he should have. But I didn't dare ask him."

It was incredible, I thought.

McCusker had terrorized so many jockeys that he'd been dictating the running of whole races and none of them had dared talk to one another about it for fear of retribution, either from the racing authorities or from having a family farm burned down or having an elderly widowed mother sent bonkers by nighttime attacks on her house or any number of other horrific consequences.

It was wicked. But how could I stop it? More to the point, how could I stop it without bringing down the wrath of Mc-Cusker on myself and my family — or on anyone else, for that matter?

I drove the Admiral back to Aynsford mostly in silence while I was thinking, but, eventually, his inquisitive nature got the better of him.

"So what did he say?"

"He told me that McCusker burned down a barn at his parents' farm and threatened to do the same to the rest of it unless he stopped the horses."

"My God," said Charles. "You must go to the police."

"Must I?" I said. "What good will that do?"

"They'd be able to arrest McCusker."

"Would they?" I asked. "On what evidence? Angus didn't know his name until I told him just now. For him it was simply a telephone call from some Irishman. And even if they did arrest him, then what? They're hardly going to send him to prison for very long for burning a few tons of hay. He'd be straight out on bail anyway, and then how would I protect the Drummond farm, to say nothing of Marina and Saskia? This man needs to be stopped for good, not just for a few hours of police questioning."

"So how are you going to do that?" Charles asked.

"I'm working on it."

I went on working on it for the last few miles to Aynsford but came up with precious few sensible ideas.

Murdering Billy McCusker seemed to be the only satisfactory long-term solution. There would then be no chance of him ever carrying out his threats, not unless he came back to haunt us. However, there was one major drawback to this strategy — I didn't intend spending the next twenty years or so of my life in one of Her Majesty's prisons. I had other plans.

Perhaps, I thought next, I could convince someone else to kill him, but conspiracy to murder carries the same jail sentence as actually committing it. And I didn't even know where to find the potential victim, let alone a hired assassin.

"Do you want to come in?" Charles asked as I pulled into his driveway.

"Thanks, Charles, but I'd better be getting home. Rosie's been on her own in the kennel all afternoon and she needs feeding."

"I hope you've put a lock on it," he said.

"I sure have. A nice big, shiny padlock. And a man came on Friday morning to weld a top onto the sides so that it's now a complete cage."

Charles thankfully resisted the temptation to quote the proverb about stable doors and bolting horses.

On Monday morning I went to see Tony Molson, the jockey who'd been ill on the day of the Newbury races.

Tony was about thirty and moderately successful, riding mainly at the Midlands tracks for a number of small-time local trainers who didn't have enough horses to warrant having a stable jockey of their own. He'd started out as a flat apprentice in

Newmarket but had switched to steeple-chasing early on after he'd grown too heavy. I'd retired long before he started, but I'd seen quite a bit of him over the years, and he had ridden in four of Sir Richard Stewart's suspect races.

He lived north of Banbury, in Chipping Warden, and it took me some time to find his house. It was tucked away on one of the lanes behind the church, and I had been expecting Rose Cottage to be old and quaint, maybe with a thatched roof, and certainly with some roses growing in the front garden.

However, that was not the case.

Rose Cottage was, in fact, a modern, box-like property that had been built in the grounds of a much larger home that abutted the churchyard, and its front garden was given over entirely to a concrete parking area.

There was one car parked in the space: a dark blue, four-door VW Golf with a big dent in its side.

Now, was that just a coincidence, or what?

12

I rang Tony Molson's doorbell, and I also banged on his front door for good measure.

A dog started barking loudly somewhere in the house, and, presently, Tony opened the door a fraction. He tried to close it again as soon as he saw who it was, but I was too quick for him, promptly putting one of my size-eights between the door and the jamb.

"Go away," Tony shouted, pushing hard on the door but to no effect.

"Did you know that the maximum penalty for kidnap is life in prison?"

"I don't know what you're talking about," he shouted.

"Oh yes, Tony, I think you do," I said calmly. "And the headmistress at Saskia's school says she would recognize you."

"Go away," he shouted again, this time with rising panic in his voice.

"Tony, if I go away now, I'll come back with the police. They've been looking for your car for ten days." He went on pushing the door, bending the wood. "Or else we could talk, just you and me."

"I don't want to talk to you," he said.

"Then you're a fool," I replied. "The police will break down this door, and you won't be back here to fix it for years. Is that what you want?" I paused. "Or would you rather help me stop the Irishman who dumped you in this mess in the first place?"

I was guessing, but it was a reasonable guess.

"Did he send you?" Tony asked.

"No, of course he didn't. He doesn't know I'm here."

"Are you sure about that? He seems to know everything about us."

"What *does* he know about you?" I asked.

Tony didn't reply, but he gradually eased the pressure on the door and then opened it wide. He looked terrible, as if he hadn't slept for a week.

"Are you OK?" I asked.

"No," he said, dejected. "But you'd better come in."

A young woman in her mid-thirties was sitting on the sofa in the living room and, if anything, she looked worse than Tony, with huge black circles under her eyes. She was wearing blue jeans and red-and-white sneakers just as Saskia had described, and she looked frightened. Tony invited me to sit down in one of the empty armchairs facing her.

"Margaret, my love," he said, "this is Sid Halley, Saskia's father."

If anything, she suddenly looked even more frightened.

"I'm so sorry," she said. "We didn't hurt her, I promise. We both love children." Tears streamed down her face. "We took her home as soon as we could. We really are sorry, aren't we, Tony?" She was pleading with me, and she looked up at her husband for support.

"Yes," he said, moving to put an arm around his wife's shoulders. "We're both very sorry, but we had no choice."

They were both tragic and pathetic.

"Of course you had a choice," I said angrily. "And you chose to abduct a six-year-old little girl." I could remember all too clearly the blind panic I'd felt when Saskia had been missing from school that afternoon. "And how about my dogs?" I went on. "Did you take them too?"

"Dogs?" Tony said with what seemed to be genuine surprise. "We've done nothing with any dogs."

I was inclined to believe him.

"Are you going to call the police?" Margaret asked.

"I should," I said. "But, first, tell me why you feel you had no choice."

"The Irishman," Tony said.

"What about him?"

"He threatened us."

"How?"

"He somehow found out that I was married before Tony," Margaret said quietly.

"So?" I said. "I've also been married twice. Millions of us have."

"But Margaret was never divorced," Tony said.

Bigamy.

"Is that all?" I said with incredulity. "Surely a bit of bigamy is not enough to turn you into kidnappers."

"No," Tony said pitifully, shaking his head, "it's worse than that. Much worse." He looked unhappily at his wife. "Margaret, we'll have to tell him." She said nothing but gently rocked her body back and forth. Then she nodded slightly in agreement.

"We have two sons," Tony said. "Lovely boys. Jason and Simon. They're twins. They'll be thirteen next month." He paused for a moment and wiped a tear from his cheek. "Only they're not actually my boys." Margaret began sobbing. "Although I'm the only father they've ever known, they aren't biologically mine. They belong to Margaret's first husband."

I still couldn't see the problem.

"I helped Margaret run away with them after a French court gave custody to their father."

So Saskia wasn't the first child they'd kidnapped.

"Why a French court?" I asked.

"Margaret married a Frenchman," Tony said.

Gradually, with my continuous encouragement, the whole story came out. Margaret had been an impressionable art student of eighteen who'd gone to study in Paris, where she'd become infatuated with Pierre Beaudin, the thirty-five-year-old son of a rich Parisian businessman. She'd become pregnant with the twins and, for some reason, had married Beaudin. It seems that he'd been sleeping with a whole raft of teenage girls, of whom Margaret had simply been the next in line. Why he'd married her, was anyone's guess. Perhaps he'd done it for the children. However, he'd soon reverted to his former ways, bedding a string of new young women, and by the time Margaret had been due to deliver the babies she had filed for divorce and also for the custody

191

of the twins.

But within a day of the birth in a Paris suburb, a French judge had announced that since they had been born in France and were therefore undeniably French, the twins had to remain in France with their French father while the courts considered the divorce.

"Pierre's father fixed it," Margaret said quietly. "I knew all he wanted was the twins, they were his only grandchildren, and he had friends in high places. I also knew I'd never see my lovely boys ever again if I came home and left them in France, but how could I stay — Pierre had thrown me out on the street."

"So that night," Tony said, "I took Margaret and the children from the clinic in Montparnasse and drove them to Ostend in Belgium. From there we took the ferry to Dover. We hid the babies on the floor of the car, behind the front seats, when we drove through passport control."

"But then what?" I said.

"Margaret and I were married the next day, even though she wasn't yet divorced, and then we registered the births of the boys as ours, in England."

"But how did you know each other?" I asked. "And well enough to get married so quickly?"

"We were childhood sweethearts," Tony said. "All the way through school. I'd been devastated when Margaret went to Paris. But she turned back to me when she needed help." He smiled warmly at her.

He must love her very much, I thought, to have forgiven her for going away and marrying almost the first Frenchman she came across and then to take her back with two of his children.

"Tony helped me disappear," Margaret said, holding his hand. "New husband. New name. New life."

"So how did the Irishman find out?"

"We've no idea. We thought only four people other than us had ever known the truth," Tony said. "Margaret's mum and dad, her sister and the nurse at the Montparnasse clinic who helped us remove the twins from the secure nursery."

"Are they all still alive?" I asked.

"The family are," Tony said. "I don't know about the nurse."

"Was there any contact with the nurse after you took the babies?"

"We wrote to each other a few times," Margaret said. "She told me about the almighty scene that occurred when Monsieur Beaudin Senior arrived at the clinic to find the children had already gone. He threatened to sue everyone until they were found."

"So the nurse knew your new married name?" I said. "And your address?"

"I suppose she must have to send the letters."

"How about your parents and sister?" I asked.

"Mum and Dad would never tell anyone," Margaret said with certainty. "We never ever talk about it in case the boys might overhear. They have no idea."

"How about your sister?"

"I'm sure she wouldn't say." She sounded as if she was trying to convince herself more than me. "Although she can be rather indiscreet, especially if she's been drinking."

"Where does your sister live?" I asked.

"Manchester."

Could that be just another coincidence?

"When did the Irishman first call?"

"About two and a half years ago," Tony said. "Right out of the blue."

Two and a half years ago was well before any of the races that Sir Richard Stewart had believed were suspicious.

"What did he say, exactly?" I asked.

"He said that he knew our secret and he would inform the French authorities unless

I did as he wanted. I couldn't believe it. We thought we'd been so careful."

"So how many times have you stopped a horse for him?"

Tony looked at me in some surprise. "How do you know about that?"

"That's why I came here," I said. "I wanted to talk to you about stopping horses, and you didn't turn up at Newbury last week when you were meant to."

"I cried off sick."

"I know, but were you actually sick?" I asked.

"No," he admitted. "I was too frightened to go. It was too soon after . . ." He tailed off. Too soon after kidnapping my daughter, I thought. "I was afraid the police might be looking for me."

If Tony had been at Newbury that day, I would have spoken to him outside the Weighing Room about the horses and I would never have seen his blue car or the dent in its side.

"So," I repeated, "how many have you stopped?"

"Dozens," Tony said gloomily. "Most didn't have a chance anyway, but maybe five or six could have won if I'd let them try."

Even I was shocked.

"How many dozens?"

"I don't know," he said. "Lots. I haven't kept count. I get a call giving me the name of a horse that mustn't win. Sometimes one a week, sometimes two. There were four at this year's Cheltenham Festival alone, not that any of them would have probably won even if I'd wanted them to.

"Two of them fell, and I can assure you I didn't do that on purpose, especially not when one was at the first hurdle in the Supreme Novices' when I was out in front with twenty horses all behind me. Kicked to hell and back, I was, and I've still got the bruises. I may be bad, but I'm not crazy with it."

He smiled wryly.

"Is this still going on?" I asked.

"Sure is," he said. "I'm due to ride a horse called Ackerman at Towcester tomorrow in the two-and-a-half-mile chase. I can tell you now he won't win, not unless all the others fall over, and then I'll be in trouble."

"When did you get the call?"

"This morning. Just before you came."

I passed much of Monday afternoon with Tony, going through race results for the past two and a half years, trying to make some sort of list of those horses on which he had been told to lose, trying to spot a pattern.

196

The four races on Sir Richard Stewart's list were all there, but Tony didn't remember them as being anything out of the ordinary, if stopping horses could ever be described as not being out of the ordinary.

I looked particularly at the win Tote returns, on the lookout for more races where the return was appreciably lower than the winner's starting price might suggest.

There were a couple of strong possibilities, but they didn't follow the previous pattern of being at the southern racetracks nearer to London. One had been at Haydock Park and the other at Aintree, both of them the second-to-last race of the afternoon on a big race Saturday the previous autumn — and both Haydock Park and Aintree were deep in the Honest Joe Bullen bookmaking territory around Manchester and Liverpool.

But there were masses of other races where the Tote returns were as one would expect. Clearly Tony had not only ridden in "super-fixed" races where McCusker had intimidated all but one of the jockeys into stopping their horses, he'd ridden in others where it may have been only Tony's mount that wasn't trying.

But that information, by itself, would have been incredibly valuable to a bookmaker. If he knew for sure that a given horse wouldn't win, he could offer higher odds on that horse in the certain knowledge that he'd never have to pay out. And higher odds would encourage more punters to bet.

It almost seemed to me that McCusker had used his information about the Molson children to control Tony's riding over a two-and-a-half-year period but had moved up a gear to the super-fixed races only last October. Perhaps he had found it so easy to get Tony to ride as he wanted that he'd simply expanded his franchise until he controlled every rider in the race.

Then, far from being satisfied by only taking bets, he had then started placing them using cash on the Tote so there would be no damning record of unusual betting practices likely to alert the authorities, as there would have been on the Internet exchanges.

It was a win-win situation.

No wonder Sir Richard Stewart had been so frightened. He'd had good reason to be. If what I suspected were true, it would indeed undermine the whole integrity of British racing.

13

On Tuesday I went to watch Tony Molson ride Ackerman in the two-and-a-half-mile handicap chase at Towcester races, but not before I had spent most of the morning catching up on other things. This investigating business was playing merry hell with my "day job" of keeping up with share prices.

Also on Tuesday morning I had a difficult telephone call with Marina from her parents' home in Fryslân.

"Please, Sid," she pleaded, "stop whatever it is you are doing to annoy this man."

"I've done what he wanted," I said. "Perhaps now he'll leave us alone."

Or perhaps he won't, I thought.

I was sure that McCusker didn't need me to *do* anything to annoy him, just *being* Sid Halley was enough.

Marina didn't understand. She was a scientist, used to rational thought and logical analysis. Billy McCusker didn't employ either. All his actions were determined by emotion and greed. He wanted to be the big cheese in racing, the boss, the controller, and everything he did was directed towards that aim. He was like an unstoppable bulldozer pushing logic, the law and good sense aside with its blade.

"I'm so frightened," Marina said. "I want to come home, but I'm not sure I can."

"It'll be all right," I said, trying to sound reassuring. "I'll stay with you all the time. We'll do everything together, and we will keep Saskia safe too."

"OK," she said nervously.

"I'll be there tomorrow morning to pick you up from the airport. I promise."

Towcester racetrack in Northamptonshire had always been one of my favorites when I'd been a jockey.

It was a track where sound tactics were as important as a fast horse. The fences were inviting to jump, but the real test of stamina was the last mile to the finish, which was uphill all the way to the wire. Many a race had been lost at Towcester by not leaving enough fuel in the horse's tank for the stiff climb home.

Ackerman took the lead straight from the start in the two-and-a-half-mile handicap chase, the first race of the afternoon. He led the field of ten past the grandstands for the first time at a good pace, rounded the sharp right-hand corner and galloped away from the crowd towards the open ditch.

I thought Tony was taking them along too fast.

I had looked up Ackerman's form. He was a seven-year-old bay gelding and had run a total of twenty-one times over fences, winning only twice and being placed on six other occasions. Nevertheless, he had started this race as favorite at four-to-one.

His two wins had come the previous season, and, on both occasions, he had started slowly and had only taken the lead coming to the last fence, then ridden out in the run to victory.

Tony was riding a completely different type of race today, continuing to make all the running, as the ten of them swept downhill towards the water jump at the lowest point on the course.

I knew what he was doing. He was running the "finish" out of his horse, and, sure enough, four of the others came past him easily in the climb to the final turn.

At the second-last fence, Ackerman was still fourth, but he was laboring with tiredness, swaying slightly from side to side, and clearly not responding to Tony's furious urging for more speed.

Even though one of the three in front of him fell at the final obstacle, there was no chance that Ackerman would ever catch the winner, who pulled away along the home stretch to win by ten lengths. I thought it unlikely that Ackerman would have won anyway, but Tony's tactics had absolutely guaranteed that he wouldn't. However, third was not a complete disgrace, and no one could have accused Tony of not riding the horse out during the closing stages to gain the best possible position. The damage had been done long before they had turned into the final straight.

I walked over to the unsaddling enclosure to watch the first three horses come in and stood close by the position reserved for the third.

"I think we'll go back to Plan A next time," the trainer said quite forcefully to Tony as the latter dismounted and removed his saddle. "Like I said, he definitely prefers to be held up for a late run."

"You might be right," Tony replied, "but it was worth a try."

The trainer didn't particularly look like he thought it had been worth the try, and I could already read in his expression that he might be employing a different jockey next time.

Tony walked right past me on his way to the Weighing Room. His face was expressionless, and, if he saw me at all, he made no sign of recognition, simply staring straight ahead with a tightlipped mouth.

He must have known that he was throwing away his career, one way or the other.

"Hello, Sid," said a voice behind me with a Belfast accent.

I turned around, smiling. "Hello, Paddy, fancy a Guinness?"

"I thought you'd never ask, me old mucker."

We moved to the bar in the base of the grandstand, and I bought a pint of the black stuff for him and a half of lager for me.

I'd hoped that Paddy O'Fitch might be at Towcester. He lived in the small market town of Brackley, ten or so miles down the road.

"So, Paddy," I said as we moved away from the bar to a cocktail table, "what else can you tell me about Billy McCusker?"

Paddy made a face as if he'd swallowed a wasp. He looked all around him to check no one was listening.

"Bejesus, be quiet, will you!" he said in a forced whisper. "I now wish I'd told you nothing. I've been having nightmares about it ever since." He looked all around once more. "And the word is dat you're asking questions among the jocks about him."

"Who told you that?" I asked, surprised.

"It's a dangerous game, to be sure."

"Come on, Paddy, who told you I've been asking questions?"

"No one," he said, smiling.

I realized I had fallen into one of his little traps. I had done nothing more than confirm to him what he'd assumed, that I had indeed been asking questions of the jockeys. Stupid, I thought, and I can't afford to be stupid. The Sid Halley of old would surely not have made such a mistake.

And what worried me most was that Paddy now knew something that he wouldn't be able to resist telling others.

It was in his nature, to be sure.

I left Paddy in the bar lining up another pint of Guinness while I went outside to watch the racing. Tony Molson was riding again in the third race, for a different trainer, and I watched as he cantered his horse to the far end of the straight for the start of the two-mile novice hurdle, one of thirteen runners.

This time, Tony rode a picture-perfect

race, holding up his horse in third place until the field turned into the finishing straight for the final time. Then he asked his mount for two mighty leaps over the last two flights of hurdles before releasing him to storm up the hill to the winning post, passing the other two horses to win by a neck.

Tony was a good jockey, there was no doubt of it. I suppose that was why he was still engaged by trainers to ride their horses. But for how long would they put up with him occasionally not riding to their instructions to win but to somebody else's to lose?

Robert Price had also been riding in the third race, and I made a beeline to intercept him as he was walking back to the Weighing Room with his saddle over his arm.

"Hi, Robert," I said, coming alongside. He jumped as if he'd been poked with an electric cattle prod. "I'm still waiting for your call and I'm getting impatient."

He didn't say anything, he just looked around him as if he was searching for help. He obviously found none, so put his head down and walked faster.

So did I.

"Have you told Judy yet?" I asked, trying to keep up.

"Told her what?" he mumbled back.

"About Billy McCusker."

"Leave me alone." He started to run.

"Why do you know him, Robert?" I shouted after him, but he didn't stop or look back. He skipped up the few steps into the Weighing Room and disappeared into the jockeys' changing area, his sanctuary, where I could no longer follow.

I watched the rest of the races from the steps at the front of the main grandstand. At Towcester, the steeplechase course is on the outside of the loop, closest to the enclosures, and the grandstands are built nearer to the track than on any other racecourse in the country. The two combine to give the spectators an inclusive feel for the racing, with the thudding of the horses' hooves on the turf clearly audible over the buzz of the crowd.

It was enough to make any man's heart beat faster and mine was no exception, as I helped cheer home the short-head winner of the three-mile chase. Perhaps for the first time I was content to stand and watch without suffering pangs from not being directly involved in the action.

I must be getting old, I thought.

Race riding, especially over the jumps, was a young man's sport, and, increasingly, a young woman's one too. While the flat boys regularly went on into their late forties or even into their fifties, jump jocks, beaten up by regular falls, were finished long before that.

Now, for me, it was as if a curtain had been lifted from my eyes.

At last, during that day at Towcester, I found I could watch and enjoy others doing what I had ached for so long still to be doing myself. Gone, finally, was the sense of injustice that my riding career had been so unfairly cut short, something that had intruded almost daily into my thinking and driven me away from the races.

So it was with a happy heart and a renewed spring in my step that I went out to my car after the last race.

Many of the crowd had already gone home as the fine, sunny afternoon was rapidly deteriorating into a rather gloomy evening with the prospect of heavy rain from the ever-building dark clouds, and I could feel the first drops of it falling on my head as I hurried along.

I didn't get there.

Two large men in black anoraks were waiting for me, crouched down behind the car parked next to mine. As I reached for the door handle of the Range Rover, I was grabbed around the neck by one of the men. The second one punched me in the solar plexus with such force that all the breath was driven out of me and my legs buckled at the knees, only my head in the stranglehold stopping me from going down altogether.

Not again, I thought, as I hovered around the edges of consciousness. Not another bloody beating.

I tried to say something, to call out for help, but there was no air in my lungs with which to shout.

The second man hit me again, this time lower, in the groin.

"Stop asking jockeys questions," said the first man right into my ear.

He released his grip, and I slithered to the grass, clutching myself between the legs. The second man then gave me a kick in the face by way of a leaving present before both of them melted away into the shadows.

The whole thing had taken only a few seconds.

No one had come to my aid. It had all happened so fast that no one would have had a chance to stop it even if they'd seen what was going on.

I lay on the ground, curled up, trying to breathe, as the rain started in earnest, great drops of it splashing off the cars around me.

I dragged myself up so that I was kneeling but still bent double, with my forehead resting on the wet turf and with a degree of panic rising in my throat. I was winded. My diaphragm had gone into spasm, making it impossible for me to fill my lungs.

It had happened to me several times before after falls and I knew that all I had to do was to wait calmly for the muscle to stop cramping and to start working again. But I fervently wished it would hurry up and do so because, in the meantime, I wasn't breathing, and the lack of oxygen reaching my brain was making my view of the world increasingly grayer than it was in reality.

My ability to inhale returned suddenly with a rush, and I gulped down lungfuls of welcome, damp air while my vision returned to full color. Only then did I notice the stream of bright red blood droplets falling from the end of my nose onto the vivid green grass.

I felt awful.

I ran my tongue gingerly around my teeth but couldn't detect any sharp edges that shouldn't have been there. That was a relief, at least. Next I carefully moved my right hand up to my nose, but that too seemed to be intact. The blood, I discovered, was coming from a cut on my left cheek just under the eye where the man's boot had split the skin.

My face didn't seem to hurt very much, but that was perhaps due to the combination of the fire burning in my belly and, even worse, lower down. And to add insult to injury, I was getting thoroughly soaked and rather cold.

I slowly hauled myself to my feet, but, even though it was a slight improvement, I was still doubled over by the pain in my groin.

"Are you all right?" said a voice from somewhere above my head.

"No, not really," I croaked back.

I looked up to find the owner of the car that I was leaning against, his ignition key in his hand.

"Are you drunk?" he asked in a tone that implied that he didn't much like drunks.

"No," I said, "I was attacked."

"Attacked?" he repeated. "Do you mean mugged?"

Did I? Nothing had been stolen. My wallet and cell phone were still in my pockets.

"Nothing was taken," I said. Other than my self-respect, I thought. I forced myself to stand up straight. "I'll be fine now, thank you."

"But you're bleeding," he said.

"Yes, but it'll stop."

"I say, aren't you Sid Halley?" He almost laughed. "I used to love watching you ride. Pure genius on horseback."

A fan was all I needed. I hoped he wouldn't ask for my autograph.

"I'll be fine now," I repeated, hoping he would get into his car and go.

"Didn't you lose your arm?" he asked, looking down at my hands.

"Please," I said, "could you just go now?"

"I'm only trying to help," he replied, somewhat affronted.

"Yes, I know," I said, "and thank you. But I'll be fine now."

"Was it two men," he asked, "in black anoraks and leather gloves?"

"Yes," I said, looking up at him again with more interest.

"Thought so," he said. "I knew they were up to no good when I saw them running."

But surely everyone had been running. It was raining.

"Where?" I asked.

"They were running back in as everyone else was leaving. They barged past me. And they were laughing."

"Could you describe them?" I asked. "Or identify them again?"

All of a sudden, he looked unsure. He could see the blood still oozing from my face. "I don't want to get involved."

He was suddenly very eager to depart. He opened his car door and started to get in.

"Did you see which way they went after passing you?" I asked him, holding the door open against his pull.

"No," he said, pulling harder.

"Were they talking to each other?"

He stopped pulling the door and looked up at me. "Yes," he said. "As a matter of fact, they were. Joking around."

"Did they have Irish accents?" I asked.

He nodded. "Yes, they did."

I'd thought so, but I hadn't been sure, not from just four words.

Now it was confirmed.

Neither of the two men had had the high cheekbones and low brow of McCusker's police mug shot, so it hadn't been their boss. But I was pretty sure that the two men were other members of the Shankill Road Volunteers, now relocated to Manchester.

14

I sat in my Range Rover in the Towcester racetrack parking lot for over half an hour, leaning on the steering wheel without moving, waiting patiently for the pain in my guts and genitals to subside to the point that I could operate properly once more.

I was well used to this feeling, but it was not one I relished.

Regularly during my riding career, after a heavy fall, I had sat on a bench in a jockeys' changing room while the pain in my battered body had gradually subsided to a level where I could begin to change out of my racing silks and go home to nurse my bruises in a hot bath.

Eventually, I sat up straight and looked at myself in the rearview mirror, but I wasn't particularly enchanted by the sight. I had an inch-long cut beneath my left eye with blood smears all over the rest of my face and down my shirt, which was still wet from the rain.

But at least I had stopped bleeding. It wasn't a deep wound, more of a superficial scratch, and I dabbed at it carefully with a tissue before deciding that it didn't need any stitches. I didn't fancy spending the next four hours in the emergency room, and the medics would have asked too many questions. I also needed to get home. Rosie was in the kennel, and she would be wondering when her dinner was coming.

I started the Range Rover and drove to the exit.

Most people had gone, but there was still a lone traffic policeman directing the last few cars through the arched parking lot gateway. I wondered briefly if I should stop to report the attack to him, but the perpetrators would be long gone by now, and it would simply mean a long and tedious explanation to the Northamptonshire Police of all that had occurred.

I decided that I'd tell D.C.I. Watkinson or D.S. Lynch when I next spoke to them, so I accepted the traffic cop's invitation to pull out onto the main road and drove home.

I collected Marina and Saskia from Birmingham Airport at eleven o'clock on Wednesday morning with a real shiner.

I hadn't enjoyed a particularly restful night, and, once or twice, I had even begun to wonder if not going to a hospital had been a wise decision.

It was my guts that were the main problem. Once upon a time, my stomach had been used as a target by a petty villain who, much to both his surprise and mine, had actually pulled the trigger of his .38 caliber revolver.

The resulting damage had left me with an alimentary canal that didn't cope very well with any disruption to normality, and a direct punch from a burly Northern Irish ex-terrorist was certainly not normal.

Consequently, I spent much of the nocturnal hours sitting on the toilet.

I used the time to think.

Stop asking jockeys questions, one of the men had said.

How had McCusker known that I was asking questions?

Because someone must have told him.

But who?

I thought back to my encounter with Robert Price after the third race and the way he had looked around as if searching for help. Had he been looking for the two men in the black anoraks? If so, he must have known they were there. Could he have been the one to inform McCusker that I wasn't simply getting on with my life of stocks and shares?

Marina was quite shocked by the damage to my face, which looked much worse the morning after than it had at the time. The cut had turned an ugly burgundy color with a background of bruising that was darkening to black by the minute. In addition, my eyeball was bloodshot, with streaks of red running across the white on both sides of the iris.

"What happened?" she asked calmly, trying not to alarm Saskia, who was just glad to see her daddy again, black eye or not.

"I walked into a door," I said. I didn't expect her to believe me.

"How about the other guy?" she asked.

"Two of them," I said. "And, sadly, they're still standing."

"What are you talking about?" Saskia asked, looking up at us.

"Nothing, darling," I said. "Daddy's had a little accident with his eye."

I picked her up and winced with pain from my bruised abdomen. Marina watched and tightened her lips in annoyance. "I thought you weren't going to do this anymore."

"I'm not," I said.

She looked as if she wished she'd stayed

in Fryslân with her parents.

"What time is Annabel's party?" I asked, trying to defuse the situation.

"Three-thirty."

"Come on, then. Let's get you home."

McCusker called again at a quarter to midnight on the house phone just as Marina and I were going to sleep.

"Did you get my message, Mr. Halley?" he asked.

"Sod off," I replied sleepily and put the phone down.

It rang again almost immediately, but I ignored it.

"Answer it, for God's sake," Marina shouted at me on the sixth ring. "It'll wake Saskia."

I picked it up.

"Mr. Halley, you should learn some manners," said the now familiar Irish brogue.

"So should you," I replied. "Beating people up in racetrack parking lots is hardly polite."

"Come now, Mr. Halley," he said. "From what I gather, those boys hardly touched you. If they'd given you a proper beating, you'd not be able to walk. Kneecaps are notoriously difficult things to fix."

He talked about it in such a casual man-

217

ner, as if violence was an everyday occurrence. As it probably was in his world.

But I knew that it was also a thinly veiled threat.

"I've done what you asked," I said. "Now leave me alone."

"I will, to be sure," he said. "For now."

"Forever," I said firmly.

"Mr. Halley, you are in no position to call the shots, d'you hear me?" There was distinct menace in his voice, exacerbated by his continuing use of my name and his peculiar pronunciation of it. "It'll be me, not you, who decides when you might be of use to me again."

I said nothing.

"In the meantime," he went on, all menace having suddenly disappeared from his tone, "take note of the message."

"And if I don't?"

"That would be very unwise, Mr. Halley."

"Are you threatening me?" I asked.

"No," he said. "But let's just say that I'm advising you." He hung up, leaving me sitting on the edge of the bed with the dead receiver still in my hand.

"Will he leave us alone now?" Marina asked.

"I hope so," I said.

But I doubted it.

■ ■ ■ ■

I lay awake in the dark, trying to decide what I should do next.

A twinge from my kneecaps told me to do absolutely nothing, and that was probably the most sensible course. But it went against everything I stood for in my life.

I hated the thought that McCusker could do so much damage to my beloved racing, but I hated even more the fact that I knew exactly what he was doing and I still couldn't prevent it.

Or could I?

Questioning the jockeys and trying to produce a united front that could go to the racing authorities clearly wasn't going to work because I had no idea which of them was likely to tell McCusker that I'd been asking. I certainly had no intention of reapproaching Robert Price or Jimmy Guernsey, both of whom I now had to assume were McCusker's men.

So was there anything else I could do?

I thought about sending an anonymous note to Peter Medicos, rubbishing the bogus report that I had sent him the previous week. But would he take any notice? Had he not told me at Uttoxeter on Sunday that my single sheet had confirmed what he himself had been thinking all along? Surely he would go on believing it.

Sir Richard Stewart had been the last of the "old guard," those who had moved the policing and security of racing away from the self-electing Jockey Club, first to the Horseracing Regulatory Authority, and then finally to the more accountable British Horseracing Authority.

A new breed of racing supremo had developed within the new structure. Gone were the titled, wealthy, landowning elite of the old Jockey Club, replaced by career sports administrators and businessmen.

The change had been quite dramatic over the previous six or seven years, and it had left me without an ear to the top table. Now, with Sir Richard gone, I knew none of the current board of directors personally. There was no one I could approach to pass on a warning in strict confidence, and Sid Halley's standing in the sport was not as it had been only a decade before.

Maybe I should just sit back and hope that someone else spotted what was going on. Then Billy McCusker would be *their* problem and not mine. Not unless he then came back to me to write another whitewashed report. But what damage would he have done to racing in the meantime? Would the betting public's confidence have been shattered forever?

And what should I do about the Molsons? There was no doubt they had been the couple that had collected Saskia from school. They had admitted it all to me. And the police were still looking for their dark blue Volkswagen Golf with its dent in the side. But did I actually want them to be found? Did I want to bring their world tumbling down around their ears by having their twins returned to France after thirteen years? But how could I stop the police searching for the car without telling them that I'd found out who'd been responsible?

So many questions and so few answers.

In the end, I drifted off into a restless sleep, only to be awakened seemingly immediately by my alarm clock.

On Thursday, Marina, Saskia and I did everything together as a family.

It was a beautiful day, and, as the schools were still on their Easter break, the three of us, plus Rosie, went for a long walk over the hill to Aynsford for lunch with Charles.

Both Saskia and Rosie were slowly coming to terms with the fact that Mandy wasn't coming back, and Sassy had even stopped asking me where she was buried.

The Admiral came out to meet us as we walked down his extensive driveway.

"I could see you coming down the path on the hill," he said, holding his arms open wide in welcome. "What a wonderful day for March. We're even lunching in the garden." He smiled and took Saskia by the hand as we went through to the patio out the back.

Neither Marina nor I had said anything about my black eye, and Charles knew better than to ask, while Mrs. Cross just looked concerned but said nothing.

Mrs. Cross had conjured up a feast in spite of the short notice I had given that we were coming. Cold meats and salad for the adults, fish fingers and fries for Saskia and a dog bowl of meaty chunks with gravy for Rosie.

"I hope it's all right," she said to me. "I've no idea how long that tin of dog food has been in the pantry. We haven't had a dog in this house for years, but I've never liked to throw it away."

"I'm sure it'll be fine," I said. "Rosie won't eat it if it's off."

Rosie scarfed it all down in twenty seconds flat as Mrs. Cross and I watched. She laughed. "Nothing wrong with that, then."

The rest of us enjoyed a more sedate lunch, sitting around the garden table under a sunshade.

"This weather will surely help Invoice in the Ludorum at Sandown," Charles said as he served himself some ham from the platter. "He loves firm going."

Invoice was the favorite for the Victor Ludorum Steeplechase on Saturday, having won two previous races in the series for novice chasers.

"That rain on Tuesday night won't have helped," I said, remembering back to the drenching I'd had in the parking lot at Towcester races.

"Not enough," Charles said, shaking his head. "They've been watering the course at Sandown for weeks, but it's still rock hard. The water drains away so fast."

"You seem to know a lot about it," I said.

Marina looked at me sharply as if to tell me not to be so rude.

"John Chesterfield, he's a director at Sandown, he told me on the telephone last evening."

"I didn't realize you were so well connected," I said sarcastically, and received another disapproving stare from Marina.

"He's a member of my club," Charles said rather pretentiously. "In fact, he's the chairman of the membership committee. We were discussing something else, and he mentioned to me the state of the course."

"My mother sent her love to you, Charles," Marina said, changing the subject.

"Thank you, my dear," Charles replied. "Please send mine to her when you next speak."

"Thank you, Charles, I will," Marina said, giving him a lovely, bright smile. I was watching her. It was the first time I'd seen her smile in quite a while. It was like the sun coming out.

After lunch, Marina and Saskia went off with Mrs. Cross to see the chickens that she kept in what had once been a walled vegetable garden.

"Any news?" Charles asked me.

"What sort of news?"

"About this Irish terrorist man?"

"I got beaten up by a couple of his thugs on Tuesday," I said. "And warned off from asking any more questions of jockeys."

Charles wasn't shocked; he wasn't even particularly surprised. He just nodded his head in acceptance.

I could remember once, many years ago, when Charles had been complicit in furthering violence towards me from some of his houseguests. At the time he'd had some good reasons, and Charles was a military man. Appropriately directed violence in the military was not only permitted, it was encouraged and trained for.

"And are you?" he said.

"Am I what?"

"Warned off from asking questions of jockeys?"

We both watched as Marina and Saskia walked up the garden towards us hand in hand, laughing in the sunshine. They were my life now and nothing was more important to me than their well-being.

"What do *you* think?" I said in a resigned tone.

"Mmm." Charles hummed in agreement. "I see your problem. But *I* could always fire off a few warning shots myself, you know, tell a few people what's going on. I could mention it to John Chesterfield for a start, next time I see him at the club. Thanks to you, I know quite a lot of influential people in racing. I could quietly spread the word."

"I don't know," I said, pondering. "It may not be such a good idea. I don't want word getting back to him that my ex-father-in-law is asking the questions he's banned me from asking."

"Do you want this man stopped or not?" Charles asked.

"I do, but not at any cost. You don't know what he's like."

"Oh, I think I do," Charles said. "I've known my share of bullies and dictators. Mao Tse-tung, for a start."

"I didn't realize you'd met him personally," I said.

"I didn't, but I met a few of his buddies, and they were enough to show me the sort of man he was." He screwed his face up in disgust. "You can't appease them, you know. You have to stand up and fight. Winston Churchill was right."

"Charles, we're not talking about World War Two here."

"Aren't we?" he replied. "If someone had stood up to Hitler sooner, there might not have been a war at all."

Marina and Saskia rejoined us, and the topic was dropped.

"Mommy, Mommy," said Sassy, "can we play sardines now?"

Sardines was Saskia's current favorite game. It was like hide-and-seek, but each finder had to then hide with the original hider, until only one person was left looking.

"No, darling, not now," Marina said. "We must be getting back home. These lovely March and April days are fine while the

226

sun's out, but they get cold very quickly when it starts to go down. Charles, thank you for a lovely lunch."

"Anytime, my dear," Charles said, giving her a kiss.

"Bye-bye, Grandpa," Sassy said.

"Bye-bye, my darling," Charles replied, leaning down to give her a kiss as well. "Come and see me again soon."

"I will," Sassy piped up, waving madly at him as we left.

The three of us, plus Rosie, walked back over the hill towards home. Rosie chased some butterflies back and forth amongst the clover and the early buttercups, and Saskia walked between Marina and me, holding our hands to be continually swung backwards and forwards.

It was as happy a time as I could remember.

Such a shame that it didn't last.

15

Judy Hammond called me on Good Friday morning as Marina and I were finishing breakfast.

"I'm at my wits' end," she said. "Bob has been a different person since you came here. He's so scared, he'll hardly set foot out of the house. He's meant to be at Dad's open day today, but he won't go. What have you done to him?" She was angry with me. "And who the hell is this man Billy McCusker? Bob won't tell me."

I thought she was crying.

"Judy," I said. "I can't help you, not unless Robert is prepared to talk to me."

What was I saying! Was I mad? Did I not value my kneecaps?

I thought I'd decided against having anything further to do with Robert Price. If, as I suspected, he was McCusker's man, everything I spoke to him about would surely be reported back to his boss.

Perhaps what Charles had said was true: *Once a detective, always a detective.*

Maybe I couldn't give it up.

Maybe, inside, I didn't want to.

"He won't talk to you," Judy said with certainty. "He won't even talk to me."

"Ask him anyway," I said. "Tell him it'll be in strict confidence. And also tell him that if he doesn't, it won't be long before the police will be knocking at his door."

"The police!" she shouted with a tremble of fear in her voice. "Oh my God!"

"Yes, the police," I repeated. I wasn't entirely sure it was true, but it was clearly having the required effect. "And tell Robert not to talk to anyone else, and especially not to Billy McCusker."

"What the hell is going on?" she asked.

"Ask Robert."

What the hell was going on? It was a good question.

"I've had the results of the tests," I said to Marina as she was sitting at the kitchen table, tapping away at her computer. "The letter came when you were away."

"What tests?" she asked, still concentrating on her screen.

"The transplant tests."

She stopped her typing and turned to look

229

at me. "And?"

"I passed," I said, smiling. "They seem to think that I'm an excellent candidate."

She was silent for a few moments as she absorbed the enormity of what I'd said.

"Are you absolutely sure it's what you want?"

"No," I said, "I'm not absolutely sure. But I know I hate what I've got." I held up my left forearm and its plastic attachment. "Anything would be better than this thing."

"There's a risk with any surgery," Marina said.

"I know there is, but I'm pretty healthy, and I'm not decrepit just yet. I wouldn't think twice about it if I needed surgery for anything else."

"How about the drugs? You'll have to take them for the rest of your life to prevent rejection. What are the side effects?"

I'd almost forgotten that I was married to someone with a doctorate in molecular biology.

"Dr. Bryant told me that the drugs are getting better all the time and any side effects are generally slight. Some people don't have any at all."

"How slight?" she asked. "And how many people do have substantial side effects? And what are they?"

"I don't know," I said, feeling like a miscreant schoolboy who hadn't done his homework.

"Well, I think you should ask."

"Let's do it now."

I called Harry the Hands, using the direct number printed at the top of his letter, and was quite surprised to find him in his office.

"I didn't really think you'd be there on Good Friday."

"I'm on call, and accidents don't stop happening just because it's a bank holiday. I've been in the operating room much of the night, trying to save the hand of a young farmer who foolishly got it stuck in an electric chain hoist."

"And did you save it?" I asked.

"Of course. Well, I think so. Time will tell." I could hear him yawning. "Now, Sid, how can I help?"

"My wife has some questions for you."

"Fire away."

I let Marina talk with him, using the speakerphone so I could hear both sides of the conversation. Every time Marina raised some argument against, Harry was able to counter with a convincing response.

As I listened, I realized how desperately I wanted Harry to win each point. I suppose it was an indicator of how much I yearned for the transplant.

"OK, then," said Marina eventually, "it's Sid's call."

"Are you sure you're happy?" I said to her.

"Yes, if you are."

"OK," I said. "Harry, let's get going."

"Not quite so fast," he replied through the speaker. "We have to do some paperwork first, and you will also need another assessment with an independent psychiatrist, but I think that will be a formality. Perhaps you could come to see me at the hospital sometime next week?"

"Sure," I said. "How about Monday?"

Did I sound too eager?

"That's Easter Monday, and I won't be on call," he said. "How about two o'clock on Wednesday? I'll need to get a psychiatrist, and mornings never seem to be a good time for shrinks."

"Wednesday at two is fine by me," I said. "How quickly after that is it all likely to happen?"

"Well," he said, "that depends on how long it takes to find the donor. It could be a week or it might be a year or even more. Nobody knows. We will need a telephone number at which you can always be contacted, day or night, the moment a suitable hand does become available."

And in the meantime, I thought, hope for rain and careless motorcyclists.

Judy Hammond called again at six o'clock.

"Bob still won't tell me what is going on, but he has agreed to talk to you," she said. "But not on the telephone. He doesn't trust it. Can you come over to our place?"

Did I trust Robert Price any more than he trusted the telephone?

"No," I said. "I can't, not tonight. Tell him to go and use a pay phone if he thinks his is bugged."

"How about yours?" she said.

The police had long stopped listening in to my telephone calls. Did I think anyone else had taken over?

"I'll take the chance if he will."

"I'll talk to him," she said. "But I've had to threaten to leave him to get him this far."

"I'm sorry," I said.

"Yeah," she said wistfully, "so am I. And I'm not sure things can ever be the same again."

She was blaming me. I could hear it in her voice. But she needed to look closer to home to find the real culprit.

"And, Judy," I said firmly, "I don't want to speak to him if he's been in contact with Billy McCusker."

"He hasn't," Judy replied confidently.

"How do you know?"

"Because he's even more afraid of Billy McCusker than he is of you, or of the police."

And so he should be, I thought. "Then get him to call me."

"I'll try," Judy said.

Robert Price called me an hour later from a public-phone box in Wantage.

"I don't trust the phones," he said, "not with all that hacking stuff. You go to a phone box and call me back at this number." He gave me the number of the box he was in.

"Robert," I said, "you're being overdramatic."

"If you want me to answer any questions, you'll have to go and phone me from somewhere else other than your home."

"OK," I said. "Wait there. I'll call you in ten minutes."

Much to Marina's irritation, I drove the Range Rover over to Aynsford to use Charles's phone.

"What do you want?" Robert asked aggressively, answering at the first ring. "Why don't you just leave me alone?"

"Happily," I said, "but not if you're fixing races."

"Who says I am?"

"Come on, Robert," I said. "We both know you are, so stop playing around. Was it McCusker's idea?"

"Oh God," he said. "What a mess."

"So help me sort it out. Tell me about Maine Visit in the handicap hurdle at Newbury on Hennessy day." It was the first of the three horses that he'd ridden in Sir Richard's suspect races.

"What about him?" he asked. "I just made sure he didn't win. He didn't have much chance anyway."

I realized that that was what they all said, as if, in some way, it diminished their guilt. Even if it wasn't true.

"Was that the first horse you ever stopped for him?"

"No," he said without elaboration.

"So what was?"

There was a long pause.

"Robert?"

"Summer Nights," he said.

I could hardly believe it. Summer Nights was the best horse in Brian Hammond's yard, probably his best horse ever. Winner of one Cheltenham Gold Cup as well as two King George VI chases, Summer Nights was a true star in the world of steeplechasing.

"When?" I asked.

He sighed audibly down the line.

"In the Newton Gold Cup at Ascot two years ago."

"He must surely have started favorite," I said.

"He did. Odds-on in a field of only four."

"So what happened?" I asked.

"We plowed through the last open ditch on the way up from Swinley Bottom, and I immediately pulled him up and jumped off as if he was hurt."

I vaguely remembered seeing it on the television at the time.

"But why did you plow through the fence? Summer Nights is the best jumper there is."

"I asked him for a big stride, far too big. Poor old Summer didn't know what to do. Confused, he was, but he did as I asked. He tried to clear it, but it was too far even for him, and it was much further than I'd realized. I was shit scared that I'd really hurt him, but he was fine."

"Didn't anyone suspect?"

"No. Summer and I were close up but still at the back of the field, and we were racing directly towards the TV cameras at that point. All anyone saw was Summer plowing through the fence from head-on. No one saw that I'd stood him so far off. And, anyway, everyone was more concerned that he was hurt."

"But why?" I asked.

There was another long pause.

"It's complicated," he said.

"Tell me anyway."

"I met McCusker about three or four years ago. He approached me, asking for information. At first, I told him to get lost, but . . ." He paused again. "He offered me money. All he wanted was to know if any of the horses in the Hammond yard were slightly off-color or particularly well — you know, that sort of thing."

"You knew he was a bookmaker?"

"Yes. Of course."

For a jockey to communicate such insider information to a bookmaker — or to anyone else, for that matter — was strictly against the Rules of Racing, and Robert Price knew that too. The penalty was disqualification from the sport for up to five years.

"How much did he pay you?" I asked.

"A couple of hundred each time — not much. But I desperately needed the money. I'd just bought my cottage, and I had a nasty fall at Wincanton. Broke my leg. Sidelined for four months, all through the winter, and I was having real trouble paying the mortgage."

As McCusker would have probably

worked out.

"Are you still selling information to him?"

"He's a right bastard, let me tell you. He's screwed me good and proper."

"How?" I asked with encouragement.

"Bloody fixed me, didn't he? After the first few times, when he sent me the cash, he said he didn't like putting banknotes in the mail so he wanted to hand them over in person. He set up a meeting in a multistory parking lot in Oxford. He handed over a brown envelope of cash, and he insisted I count it there and then. I must be bloody naïve or something. Next thing I know, one of those memory-card things arrives at my place with a video on it of me taking the money. All in bloody Technicolor. You could see him handing over an envelope, then me counting the cash — all in tenners, it was — and then I stuff the bulging envelope into my coat pocket, shake his hand and walk off out of the picture. You could see everything, except, of course, McCusker's back is towards the camera all the time so it doesn't show *his* face, only mine — and in glorious close-up."

"So what happened next?" I asked.

"He told me he wanted me to stop Summer Nights in the Newton the following Saturday or he would send the video to the

BHA. I told him it was ridiculous. I couldn't stop old Summer because there was such a small field, and the other runners weren't up to much. But he told me to find a way. *Fall off, if you have to,* he said, *but make sure you don't win.*" He paused. "Bloody desperate, I was, in the race, I can tell you. Summer is so sure-footed, he didn't even stumble or peck or anything, and I couldn't just roll off the side for no reason, now could I? He was traveling so well, and I was getting desperate. That's when I decided to stand him off the open ditch."

"Have you stopped him any other times?" I asked.

"No. But I live in fear of McCusker asking again."

"How many horses have you stopped altogether?"

"A few. Too many." Robert sounded thoroughly miserable. "Sid, I'm going to lose my license, aren't I?"

Probably, I thought.

How often, I wondered, did just a tiny little bit of temptation turn into a runaway train, spiraling out of control towards destruction? Quite a number if Billy McCusker was involved.

"Why did you tell McCusker that I was asking you questions?"

"Because I was scared," he said.

I hadn't been entirely sure it had been him, but now I was.

"How did you tell him?" I asked.

"What do you mean?"

"How did you tell McCusker that I was asking you questions? Did you phone him, or what?"

"Yeah, I phoned him."

"So what's his number?"

He didn't want to tell me, but I wasn't completely against using threatening tactics myself.

"I'm sure Judy Hammond would love to hear that her father's stable jockey is stopping his horses from winning," I said menacingly. "Or that the health of the star horse in his yard was placed in jeopardy by being deliberately stood too far off a fence."

"She wouldn't believe you," Robert said.

"Oh, I think she might," I replied. "I rode for her father too, you know. And, anyway, are you prepared to take the risk?"

"Bastard," he said with feeling.

"What's McCusker's number?" I asked again.

He told me.

It was a cell number beginning 07. I scribbled it down on the notepad on Charles's desk, hoping that McCusker hadn't changed it. It was the first piece in the jigsaw of me getting to him rather than the other way around.

"How often do you call him?"

"Never," he said. "Well, almost never. Not now. But he gave me that number right at the beginning so I could phone him with any information. I still had the number in my contacts list, so I called it after you'd been at my cottage last week."

"And McCusker himself answered?"

"He sure did. After only one ring."

The following day, Invoice won the Victor Ludorum Chase at Sandown by four lengths without so much as breaking into a sweat, taking the lead coming up to the last fence and striding away to the winning post un-challenged.

I watched it on the television with Saskia in the living room.

"Did you ever win that race, Daddy?" she asked.

"No, darling," I said. "But I won lots of other races at that racetrack."

"Can I learn to ride?" Sassy asked.

"Of course, darling," I said. "I'll talk to Mommy about it."

But I knew that Mommy wasn't very keen on the idea. I'd suggested two or three times

241

over the years that we might buy a pony for Saskia, but it had always come to nothing. Marina was desperately worried that Saskia would get hurt as I had.

Mommy had always been "risk-averse." I supposed it was something to do with her work in researching cancers.

In contrast, Daddy had always been "risk-inclined," kicking horses hard into fences when it would have been much safer to take a slight, steadying pull.

Who dares, wins — and all that stuff.

As true for jockeys as for the Special Air Service.

16

On Wednesday morning Saskia went back to school after the Easter break, and I took the train from Banbury to London for my two o'clock appointment with Harry the Hands at Queen Mary's Hospital, and also with the psychiatrist, one Dr. Tristram Spakeman, a bow-tied eccentric who seemed to me to have caught a touch of madness from his patients.

"Do you ever worry about dying?" he asked me by way of introduction.

"Yes," I said, "all the time. But I'm not obsessive about it."

He hummed and made some notes in a spiral-bound notebook. Perhaps he thought that he should be the one deciding if I was obsessed or not.

"Would you describe yourself as a normal person?" he asked.

What should I say? I didn't think I was that normal, but, then again, I was hardly abnormal either.

"Pretty normal," I said. "I have two eyes and two ears, which is normal, but only one hand, which isn't." And, thankfully, my black eye from the Towcester racetrack parking lot had almost completely faded away.

"Does it worry you that you only have one hand?"

"No," I said. "*Worry* is too strong a word. I'd say it frustrates me."

"Are you easily frustrated?"

I felt like saying that I was frustrated by his questions but decided against it.

"Quite easily, I suppose."

"Do my questions frustrate you?"

Wow!

"A bit."

"Yes," he said, "I'd think they would frustrate me too. But they have to be asked." He smiled at me in a slightly unnerving way. "Now, Sid . . . is it all right if I call you Sid?"

"You can call me what you like," I said. I looked down at his business card in my hand. "Shall I call you Tristram?"

"I've been called worse," he said, smiling again. "Now, Sid, tell me about your parents."

"Now, Tristram," I replied, mocking him

slightly, "what have my parents got to do with me having a hand transplant?"

"I'm trying to get to know you better," he said, "so I can make a reasoned analysis of your mental state."

"My mental state is fine," I said, "and my parents had little to do with it. My father was killed in an accident before I was born, and my mother died of cancer when I was sixteen."

"Do you miss them?" he asked.

"I don't miss my father because I never knew him. But, yes, I suppose I do miss my mother. I wish she could have been alive to see my daughter."

"Did you cry when she died?"

"Buckets," I said. "But I got over it, like everyone who loses their mother."

"Some people never get over it," the doctor said. "A lot of depression is grief-related."

"But I'm not depressed," I said.

"No." He made another note in his book.

He went on asking me questions for nearly an hour, and I began to like him more as the time progressed. He had me talking about all sorts of things I wouldn't have imagined: dreams, hopes for the future, fears, even what I thought about when I was driving the car.

245

Seemingly, the only topics we didn't discuss were race fixing and Billy McCusker.

"Right," the doctor said at length. "That will do."

"Have I passed?" I asked.

"It is not a matter of passing or failing," he said. "But I presume you mean is there any reason why you should not have a transplant."

"And is there?"

"No," he said, "none at all. I think you are psychologically sound in your outlook, and I think you are a suitable candidate for a transplant."

"Great," I said.

"But be careful. I detect from our discussion that you can be rather impulsive at times, sometimes acting without thinking through all the consequences. But, to counter that, you do seem to know what you want."

He was good, I thought. Very good.

Harry Bryant was delighted and set about explaining to me all the various bits of paperwork we needed to complete.

"The final consent forms will have to be signed just before the operation," he said, "when we have the donor hand available.

But you need to confirm that you understand now what the limitations are and that we can give you no guarantees as to the future dexterity of the transplanted hand."

He gave me a number of documents to read and then invited me to sign each of them in the space provided.

"Covering your back?" I said.

"Absolutely," he said with a laugh. "I trained in America, don't forget. They'll sue you for anything. We had one patient who threatened legal action over the fact that his new fingernails grew at a different rate to the ones on his other hand."

"Faster or slower?" I asked.

He laughed. "I've no idea."

I filled in the last of the documents, the one that recorded all my contact details.

"Right," he said, collecting all the papers together. "That's it. You're now officially on the transplant waiting list. If you are ever away from these telephone numbers, you must phone us with instructions of how to contact you. If you go abroad, you will come off the list while you're away."

"Why?" I asked.

"We need you in the operating room within a maximum of six hours," he said. "If a suitable hand became available and you were farther away than that, the transplant might not be viable."

"What would happen to the hand?"

"If it was appropriate for someone else, either here or in Europe, then they might be offered it, but most likely it would stay with the donor."

"And be buried?"

"Yes," he said. "Or cremated."

"I'd really hate that to happen," I said. "I think I'd better stay within six hours of the hospital."

And hope for rain.

I walked out through the hospital gates in a state of great anticipation and excitement, wondering if the next time I passed through them I would be on my way to having a new hand — to a new life as a complete human being.

The cell phone rang in my pocket. It was Marina.

"Hello, my darling," I said happily as I answered it.

"Sid, Sid." Marina was in a panic. I could hear her hyperventilating.

"What is it?" I shouted down the phone, all happiness instantly banished and with the adrenaline level in my blood shooting up to maximum.

"The police are here."

"Where?"

"At Sassy's school. Together with two women from social services."

"Why?" I asked helplessly.

"They say they've come to take Sassy into care."

"What?" I suddenly couldn't feel my legs.

"They say they're taking Saskia into care," Marina repeated. Then I could hear her screaming at someone, "Leave her alone!"

"But they surely can't take her into care just like that."

"They can and they are," Marina said in tears. "And they also say they're going to arrest you for sexually abusing her."

I wasn't quite sure how I got myself from Roehampton to Marylebone station and onto a train to Banbury. Afterwards, I couldn't recall a single moment of the journey.

Everything was racing in my head.

How could I be accused of sexually abusing my own daughter. It didn't make any sense.

I sat on the train as it pulled out of Marylebone, wondering what I should do. Who should I call?

Once upon a time, I'd have phoned my tame Whitehall mandarin, Archie Kirk, but, sadly, not only had he retired from his job but also from his life.

A lawyer. That's what I needed.

The only lawyer I knew was a local solicitor in Banbury who had done all the legal work when Marina and I had bought our house, and I hardly knew him very well. But he would have to do, especially as I still had his direct phone number on my contacts list.

"Jeremy Duncombe," he said, answering on the second ring.

"Hello, Jeremy," I said, "this is Sid Halley. Do you remember me? You did the searches on my house some time ago."

"Of course I remember," he said. "Nice place in Nutwell."

"That's right." I paused. "Jeremy, I've got rather a problem and I need some advice."

"OK," he said. "Shoot."

Suddenly, it didn't seem very easy to explain that I was about to be arrested by the police for child abuse even if the accusation was completely untrue. No smoke without fire, I could hear myself saying.

"It seems that, for some reason that I don't understand, the police want to question me."

"What about?" he asked.

"Well," I said, "I know this sounds crazy,

250

but they seem to think I've been molesting my daughter."

I couldn't bring myself to use the term *child sex abuse*, but there was still a distinct silence from the other end, and the man opposite me on the train looked at me with contempt.

"And have you?" Jeremy said.

"No, of course not."

"Are you with the police at the moment?" he asked.

"No, I'm on a train from London to Banbury. My wife called me and told me that the police were looking for me and why."

"What are your intentions?"

"I'm going straight to Banbury police station to put an end to all this nonsense, but I thought I ought to contact a lawyer first, and you are the only one I know."

"I'm not really the right person," Jeremy said. "I usually deal only with house conveyance and the occasional will. You need a solicitor that specializes in crime."

"So how do I find one in the next hour?"

"There are two in our practice, but I'm certain that they'll both be at the Banbury Magistrates' Court this afternoon."

"It's next door to the police station," I said. "Can you contact one of them and tell them to meet me there in an hour's time."

"I'll try," he said without much confidence. "But I wouldn't bank on them being there. They've each got a full caseload at the court and it sits late on Wednesdays."

I hung up and smiled at the man opposite me. He didn't smile back.

Great, I thought. What next?

The phone rang in my hand. Number withheld.

"Hello, Mr. Halley," said Billy McCusker. "Are you well?"

"What do you care?" I said.

"I thought I told you to stop asking questions of jockeys."

Goose bumps rose up on my arm, and the hairs on the back of my neck stood up. How did he know I'd been asking more questions?

"I haven't been," I said.

"Oh, I think you have, Mr. Halley," he said. "And now you will pay for it."

"What do you mean?" I asked.

"Such a sweet little girl," he said. "I hope she doesn't fare too badly in a children's home."

"You bastard," I shouted, but he'd already gone. The phone was dead.

I looked up to see most of the people in the carriage were now looking in my direction. I smiled at them all, and some even turned away.

How could McCusker do it?

Not only was he able to determine which horse won a race or force a frightened couple into kidnapping a child, but now he was seemingly able to direct social services to take Saskia into care and also to have me arrested.

How far did his deadly tentacles reach?

I called Robert Price.

"I thought I told you not to contact Mc-Cusker," I said forcibly into the phone while at the same time trying not to be too loud. My fellow travelers were paying me too much notice as it was.

"I didn't," he said. "I swear to you, I didn't."

Then how did McCusker know? Had Robert been right all along when he claimed his phone was being bugged? Was my phone tapped as well? Had McCusker just listened in on our little exchange?

I tried to remember what had been said between Robert and me on Friday evening and on which phones. How much of our conversation had McCusker listened to? And, in particular, was he aware that I had his phone number?

Next I tried to call Marina, but there was no reply from our house, and her cell went straight to voice mail.

Who else should I speak to? I might not have the chance for very much longer.

Whenever I'd been in trouble, or had been hurt, I'd always sought sanctuary at Aynsford with Charles, and now was no exception.

"But that's preposterous," he said when I told him of my latest woe.

"I know that and you know that," I said, "but other people will still believe it."

"Of course they won't."

"Oh yes they will," I said. "Once upon a time, being labeled a prostitute was the worst one could be called. But, nowadays, a whore is positively respectable compared to a pedophile or a child abuser. Just the whiff of an association with someone of that type is enough to damn you in the eyes of the public."

"So what are you going to do about it?" Charles asked.

"I'm on my way to Banbury police station, where I hope I can sort it all out. But I need a solicitor. And quickly."

"I have a barrister friend, a QC. Member of my club. I'll give him a call. See if he can fix anything."

I was grateful, but even Queen's Counsels tried to steer well clear of child abusers. It wasn't good for their image or their careers.

I never did get to Banbury police station.

Three police officers, two in uniform and one not, were waiting for me on the platform when I alighted from the train.

I had wondered about the man sitting opposite me who had taken his cell phone along to the train's lavatory as we'd passed through High Wycombe and I now saw him smiling smugly as the two uniformed officers took me firmly by the arms.

"Mr. Halley," said the plainclothes man standing in front of me, "I am Detective Sergeant Fleet, and I am arresting you on suspicion of the abuse of a child in contravention of the Sexual Offences Act of 2003. You do not have to say anything, but it may harm your defense if you do not mention, when questioned, something that you later rely on in court. Anything you do say may be given in evidence."

I said nothing but allowed myself to be escorted out of the railway station and into a waiting police car.

They took me not to Banbury but to Oxford police station, where I was checked into custody by a burly sergeant in a white shirt who made it very clear from the start that he didn't like "kiddie fiddlers," as he called them.

I had to empty my pockets and hand over my cell phone, my wallet and my belt, which were carefully placed each in its own see-through plastic bag that was then sealed with a signed label. Next someone took my photograph, head-on and in profile, and then a DNA sample was scraped, none too gently, from the inside of my cheek.

There was a moment of amusement, at least on my part, when one of the custody staff tried to take the fingerprints of my left hand. No one had asked me if I had a prosthesis, so I hadn't told them, especially as their brief pat-down search hadn't discovered it.

Not that the custody sergeant was laughing.

"Take it off," he ordered brusquely.

"Why?" I asked.

"Because I say so."

I could tell that arguing with him was not going to make any difference, so I carefully extricated my left forearm from its tightly gripping fiberglass sleeve and handed the hand to him, palm uppermost. He looked at it in disgust and then placed it in another of his plastic bags.

"I'd like to see my solicitor," I said.

"All in good time," the sergeant replied unpleasantly.

"And I'd like to speak with Detective Chief Inspector Watkinson."

"He'll no doubt speak to you when he's ready," replied the sergeant, making a note of what I'd said. He turned to his staff. "Take this scum to cell five."

"Hold on a minute," I said. "Don't I get to make a phone call?"

"All in good time," he repeated. "Cell five."

Two of the custody staff frog-marched me through a metal gate and down a cream-painted corridor to cell number 5, where I was unceremoniously thrust through the entrance. The door was immediately clanged shut behind me.

I suppose I couldn't blame them.

I don't like pedophiles either, and, whatever the law may say to the contrary, in the eyes of the police all people arrested are guilty until proven innocent, and, even then, they'd still have their doubts, especially if those arrested are suspected child abusers.

I sat down on the concrete bed with its thin blue-plastic-covered mattress and pondered how things could change in my life so rapidly. Within two hours I had gone from a state of great anticipation and excitement to one of utter despair and hopelessness.

I could tell that sorting out this mess would take a lot more than a brief word with D.C.I. Watkinson and a laugh at the gullibility of social services. It was probably going to require court appearances, together with the associated, unwelcome press coverage.

And how long was I going to be cooped up in this damn cell?

I reckoned there wouldn't be much chance of me getting from here to the Queen Mary's operating room in the next six hours if a suitable donor hand became available.

Good job, it wasn't raining.

17

I was allowed to make my one phone call about two hours later, after repeated requests. I knew my rights, I told them, and I was entitled to let someone know where I was.

I called Charles from the custody sergeant's desk, using his phone.

"Where are you?" Charles asked.

"Oxford police station," I said. "Did you speak to your QC friend?"

"Yes. He's arranged for a solicitor, but she's currently looking for you at Banbury."

"Good. Ask her to come to Oxford. And, Charles, please call Marina and tell her where I am and that I'm fine."

"That's enough," said the custody sergeant, taking his phone from my hand. "Take him back to his cell."

"I need to speak to Detective Chief Inspector Watkinson," I said.

"All in good time," the sergeant said once

more. "Back to his cell."

The frog-march procedure was repeated.

"When will I be interviewed?" I asked one of my manhandlers.

"All in good time," he also replied.

It must be policespeak for *Not yet.*

I was interviewed by a detective superintendent at nine o'clock in the evening, four and a half hours after I'd been arrested and an hour after the arrival in Oxford of Maggie Jennings, the solicitor arranged by Charles's QC friend, not that I'd been allowed to meet with her until five minutes before the interview.

"I'm sorry for the delay, Mr. Halley," said the superintendent, not sounding it. "We have been conducting a search of your premises."

"There is nothing to find," I said.

"I would like to have a private conversation with my client," Maggie Jennings interjected loudly.

"Interview suspended at" — the superintendent looked at the clock on the wall — "twenty-one-oh-two." He switched off the recording machine and left the room, followed by his sidekick, leaving Maggie Jennings and me alone. I wondered if the room was bugged but decided against asking.

"Mr. Halley, I thought I told you not to say anything other than 'No comment' to direct questions." Maggie Jennings was quite angry with me.

"Sid," I said to her. "Please, call me Sid. And why shouldn't I say something? I have nothing to hide. I've done nothing wrong."

"Mr. Halley . . . Sid," she said, "you are facing very serious allegations, and the police will take what you say and twist its meaning to make it look bad for you. Trust me, it is much better to say nothing."

I couldn't see how. Surely only guilty men would stay silent.

Maggie went over to the door and knocked on it. It immediately reopened, and the superintendent and sidekick returned to their seats.

The recorder was switched back on.

"Interview resumed at twenty-one-oh-five," said the detective. "Superintendent Ingram, Detective Sergeant Fleet, the accused, Mr. Halley, and Ms. Jennings, the accused's solicitor, being present.

"Now, Mr. Halley," he went on, "if there's nothing to find at your premises, tell us where should we look instead for all your pictures of little girls."

261

"No comment."

"You do have pictures of little girls, don't you?"

"No comment," I said again, biting my tongue.

What I wanted to say was that of course I had pictures of little girls, thousands of them. Six years of pictures of Saskia, from the moment of her birth right up until yesterday afternoon in the garden: pictures of her at home and at school, at Charles's place or on holidays at the beach in Holland, at Christmas dinners and at birthday parties, pictures of her anywhere and everywhere. I habitually had my phone at the ready, with its built-in, multi-megapixel camera. What father didn't? There was nothing wrong or sinister about it.

"Do you know a little girl called Annabel Gaucin?" he asked.

I looked sideways at my solicitor. Ever so slightly, she shook her head.

"No comment," I said.

"She's only six years old." There was contempt in his voice. "Mr. Halley, why is there a photograph of Annabel Gaucin naked on your cell phone?"

"No comment."

"A photograph of her standing naked in *your* house?"

"No comment."

If he'd seen the photo, he knew damn well that Annabel had been standing in the bath next to Saskia, and both of them had been covered in bubble-bath foam. Apart from their smiling faces sticking out amongst the bubbles, hardly a square inch of bare skin had been visible on either of them. And how did they know the photo was of Annabel anyway?

I was beginning to understand what Maggie had meant about the police twisting everything to make it look bad.

It didn't seem to make any difference if I answered their questions or not, and I didn't like it. It made me squirm in my seat.

The interview continued in much the same manner for the next hour, with me saying "No comment" to every direct question put to me by the superintendent. D.S. Fleet sat silently throughout, watching me. I had heard him say nothing since reciting the arrest caution at Banbury railway station.

I requested another private conversation with Maggie Jennings, where I again voiced my objections to not answering the superintendent's questions.

"I know what I'm doing," Maggie said. "You don't have to prove your innocence."

"But I want to," I replied. "I am innocent."

"I know what I am doing," she repeated. "Trust me."

I wasn't entirely sure that Maggie believed in my innocence. Perhaps the questions about the photo of Annabel had shocked her. But, at the time, it had never crossed my mind that anyone could ever think that it was anything other than what it was, a proud father taking a snap of his six-year-old daughter harmlessly playing in the bath with her best friend. Marina had been in the picture as well, and it had been her idea to take it.

So I went on replying "No comment" to every question I was asked, and, eventually, like me, the superintendent got fed up with it.

"Interview terminated at . . . twenty-two eighteen," he said, stopping the recording. He then stood up and walked straight out of the room without a further word.

"What happens now?" I asked Detective Sergeant Fleet, the silent sidekick, but, as before, he said nothing. He just looked at me as if I was a piece of dog shit that he'd picked up on his shoe and then he followed his boss out the door, closing it behind him.

"They'll definitely keep you here overnight," Maggie said, "and probably question you again in the morning. They will be already searching your house and checking through your computer memory for any other indecent images."

"The photo of Annabel is not indecent," I said. "It shows her standing in the bath with my daughter, and they are both covered from head to toe in bubble-bath foam. My wife is in the photo as well. There's nothing remotely sexual about it." But it was true that, at the time, I'd had a thought that I probably shouldn't have taken it. And I wouldn't have done without Marina's insistence.

"They'll keep you here anyway," she said. "They can hold you for thirty-six hours, unless they apply to a magistrate for an extension."

"An extension?" I asked.

"In total, they could hold you for up to ninety-six hours before they must either charge you or release you."

"Ninety-six hours! That's four days."

"That would be in an extreme case," Maggie said, trying to be reassuring. "If they find no further images, and the one they have you say looks so innocent, then you will be released sometime tomorrow, maybe on police bail to reappear at a police station at a future date when they have completed their inquiries. Unless, of course, they have statements from other people that are incriminating."

From whom? I thought. McCusker must have terrorized someone into making a complaint about me in the first place. Who knows what else he might have set up?

Maggie went over and knocked on the door. "I'll see you in the morning."

"Where are you staying?"

"My office has fixed a hotel. Don't worry about me. I'll be fine. The police will let me know if and when you are to be interviewed again tomorrow. In the meantime, say nothing to any of them about your case. And be warned, there is no such thing as a 'friendly, off-the-record chat' with a custody officer."

The door opened and two of those selfsame custody officers came in as Maggie departed.

In keeping with my instructions, I said nothing to them as I was frog-marched once again back to cell number 5. There seemed little chance of anything "friendly" towards me from this lot anyway. Even the meal waiting for me in the cell was stone-cold and had clearly been left there for ages. It was a dark brown stew of indeterminate content, and the gravy had congealed on the plastic plate to a texture akin to wall-paper paste.

With four days of this diet, I thought, I'd soon be back to my riding weight.

"How do you explain these?" asked the superintendent the following morning.

He threw a brown envelope onto the table in the interview room, and I could see all too clearly the top few of the thick wad of photographs that had spilled out of the end. The images were of young children in sexual situations, and they were enough to make any normal person sick.

"No comment," I replied once more.

"This envelope was found in your shed," he said, "hidden under a stack of old gardening gloves."

I could hear the blood racing through my ears, my mouth went completely dry and my throat felt like it was closing up.

I'd never seen the envelope or the photographs before. They had to have been planted there by McCusker, or by one of his chums, but I didn't think the superintendent would believe me even if I'd been allowed by Ms. Jennings to say so.

Suddenly, the stakes had been raised considerably, and I could feel myself plunging headlong into oblivion, unable to stop, like the *Titanic* steaming full-speed ahead into an iceberg, followed by a one-way trip to the abyss.

Whoa, I said to myself. Calm down. Take a few deep breaths.

I forced myself to slowly take a drink of water from the glass in front of me.

"I would like to speak to Detective Chief Inspector Watkinson or to Detective Sergeant Lynch."

It wasn't the first time I'd asked, but, as before, the superintendent took no notice.

"There are fifty-eight highly indecent images of children in this envelope," he said, sorting through some of them on the table in front of me. "Some of them showing children in sexual situations with adults, not that you can see the adults' faces of course. Let me tell you, Mr. Halley, there's enough here to get you a nice long stretch in the slammer. And you know what happens to people like you when they get inside." He drew a finger across his throat.

"Please do not intimidate my client," said Maggie Jennings.

The policeman glared at her in a manner that suggested that he'd have quite liked to intimidate her as well.

"I will answer your questions," I said to him, "but only if you allow Detective Chief

Inspector Watkinson and Detective Sergeant Lynch to be present."

Maggie Jennings looked at me in amazement and again asked for a private conference with her client.

"Are you sure that is wise?" she asked when we were alone.

"I'm fed up with being accused of something I haven't done and then not defending myself. Those photographs have been planted in my garden shed. I've never seen them before nor want to see them again. It may not be wise to answer his questions, but it can't be any worse than saying 'No comment' all the time. It sounds as if I've something to hide, which I haven't. Even I'm beginning to doubt my innocence as I listen to myself."

"OK," Maggie said, shaking her head in disagreement. "You're the client."

But instead of continuing with the interview, I was taken forcibly back to cell number 5 and left there all alone for ages and ages.

To say it was frustrating would have been a major understatement.

I was used to being in control and knowing what was going on. But here I was totally isolated, not even aware what was happening to my family.

Were Marina and Sassy somewhere together? Or was my little Saskia frighteningly alone in some unfamiliar children's home as McCusker had insinuated?

Not knowing was the worst bit.

These days, we are all so used to having cell phones and the Internet immediately at hand that we feel completely at a loss without them. It's as if we are addicted to the contact with the world at large and are unable to cope with even a few hours of digital isolation.

I clenched and unclenched the fingers of my right hand as if flexing them back and forth would take away their urge to be texting on my phone or typing on my computer keyboard.

Meanwhile, the fingers on my left hand remained stubbornly unresponsive to any stimulation whatsoever — not least because they were still lying some fifteen yards away from me in the custody sergeant's desk drawer.

The time dragged by interminably, and I went on worrying about Marina and Saskia. I considered that it was my role to look after them, a role that I was currently failing to fulfill in spectacular fashion. I wasn't even able to look after myself.

There was no clock in the cell. As a

general rule, I used the time readout on my cell phone instead of a wristwatch. So I tried to estimate how long a minute was. Then five minutes. Then ten. But I had no way of knowing if I was right.

For the second time today, I could feel the panic rising in my throat.

Calm down, I told myself again, calm down. More deep breaths, not that deep breaths were very pleasant. Police cell blocks, I had discovered, had an all-pervasive smell: a mixture of stale sweat, urine and vomit overlaid with the pungent aroma of ammonia disinfectant.

I had to do something to keep my brain active so I started to do mental calculations about my surroundings that did not involve the passing of time. How big was my cell? How many cubic meters of air were there in it? If a lungful of air was five liters, how many different lungfuls of stinking air were there in the cell? And so on.

I knew I was being silly, but such had become my state of mind that anything was better than climbing the cell walls, and I felt pretty close to that.

I must remember, next time I'm arrested, to have a book with me to read, not that this lot would have let me keep it.

■ ■ ■ ■

The custody staff came for me, in the end, and I was frog-marched back to the interview room and sat down forcibly on the chair by the table.

I looked up at the clock on the wall. It showed the time was ten minutes to noon. I had been back in my cell for just over two hours. It had felt like five times as long. How did anyone cope with years of solitary confinement? I reckoned I'd go mad in a week.

Maggie Jennings came in, followed by the superintendent, his detective sergeant sidekick, and then by D.C.I. Watkinson, who took a seat slightly behind the other officers. There was no sign of D.S. Lynch, but one couldn't expect everything. D.C.I. Watkinson would have to be enough.

The superintendent went through the procedure for starting the recording, stating the date, the time and those present in the room.

If I'd thought the presence of D.C.I. Watkinson was going to make everything fine, then I'd been sorely mistaken. If anything, the demeanor of the superintendent had hardened, as if he hadn't liked being dictated to by one of his prisoners.

"Right, Mr. Halley," he said. "Let's start again. Do you know a little girl called Annabel Gaucin?"

"Yes," I said. "She is a school friend of my daughter."

"Has she ever been in your house?"

"Yes," I said. "She has stayed over on several occasions. And before you bother to ask, yes, I took a photograph of her about two weeks ago with my daughter in the bath. My wife is in the shot as well, and the photo is not sexual in any way."

"Wouldn't you say that taking a photograph of two naked six-year-old girls was sexual?"

"No," I said, "I wouldn't. They were completely covered in bubble-bath foam. What is remotely sexual about that?"

"Marilyn Monroe thought bubble bath was sexy. She was often filmed in a bath full of bubbles precisely for that very reason."

"That's different," I said. "And anyway, the one I took is certainly not indecent."

"A jury will be the judge of that."

Oh God, I thought. A trial? With a jury? Surely they would understand that the photograph was just an innocent family snap. But how about the other ones, those in the brown envelope found in my garden

273

shed. There was no way that they could be described as innocent family snaps.

"Mr. Halley," the superintendent went on, "have you ever inappropriately touched Annabel Gaucin?"

"No," I said indignantly, "I have not. I haven't touched any little girls except my own daughter, of course."

"Have you ever touched your daughter's genitals or her anus?"

I didn't like the way these questions were going. Perhaps "No comment" would have been better after all.

"I often changed her diapers when she was a baby," I said, "like all good fathers. And I bathe her occasionally when my wife is away or busy. But, no, absolutely not, I have never ever touched her in any sexual way. I wouldn't."

"Have *you* ever been naked in your daughter's presence?"

I thought back to when little Sassy regularly used to climb into bed with Marina and me in the mornings. I'd been naked then.

"Probably when she was a baby," I said. "My wife and I think nothing of walking round our bedroom undressed. Saskia would sometimes be there."

"When was the last time you were naked

in your daughter's presence?"

"I don't know," I said.

"Last year? Last month? Last week?"

"Much longer ago that that," I said, sweating slightly. "Years. Probably not since she's been at school."

"Have you ever been naked in the presence of any other child?" he asked.

"No," I said with certainty.

"Are you the adult in any of these pictures?" He picked up the brown envelope.

"Absolutely not," I said. "And I have never seen those photographs before. I believe that they were planted in my shed by the same man who has been threatening me on the telephone, the same man who had my daughter kidnapped from school."

I looked at D.C.I. Watkinson in expectation that he would back up my claims, but he sat there tight-lipped, saying nothing. He'd obviously had his orders to sit still and stay silent.

I turned back to the superintendent. "Have you even talked to Detective Chief Inspector Watkinson about Billy Mc-Cusker?" I asked.

"That is not relevant to this case."

"Yes, it damn well is," I said angrily. "Mc-Cusker phoned me yesterday on the train only a few minutes before I was arrested to say that I would pay for not doing as he wanted, and he also said he hoped my little girl wouldn't fare too badly in a children's home. So don't tell me he's not relevant to this case. It has everything to do with Billy McCusker."

"Billy McCusker didn't take the photograph of the two little girls standing naked in the bath."

He seemed obsessed with it.

"Look," I said, trying to sound as rational as possible, "have you actually seen the picture? If so, you know as well as I do that that it's just an innocent family snapshot, which, on its own, would not have resulted in any arrest or even a raised eyebrow." But, I thought, it had been like icing on Mc-Cusker's cake. Even he couldn't have imagined his good luck.

"So why was I arrested?" I went on. "And before anyone had seen that picture on my phone anyway? Someone must have made a complaint against me. Who was it?"

The superintendent said nothing.

"It wasn't Annabel Gaucin or her parents who complained, was it?" I said, working up quite a head of steam. "So who was it? Someone with an Irish accent?"

Again there was no response.

"I'm telling you, Superintendent Ingram,

this whole thing is a complete setup. Billy McCusker, or one of his cronies, hid those photos in my shed where they knew you'd find them. Then they called you and made a complaint against me. Have you even tested the photographs for fingerprints? You certainly won't find mine on them."

"Interview suspended at twelve twenty-two," said Superintendent Ingram suddenly, pushing the buttons on the recording machine.

The three policemen stood up in unison and turned towards the door.

"How much longer am I going to be held here?" I asked with a degree of anger in my voice. "I would like to go home and look after my family."

The superintendent didn't even pause in his movement.

"Chief Inspector Watkinson," I called out to him, "you must realize what is going on. Can't you do something?"

He briefly turned and looked at me with sorrow in his eyes, but still he said nothing. My only hope was that he'd speak to Ingram outside.

The door closed behind the three of them, leaving me alone in the room with Maggie Jennings.

"What now?" I asked her.

She seemed as surprised as I was that the interview had been stopped so abruptly. "I'm not quite sure. He might want to talk to you again, or they may think they have enough evidence to charge you with the possession of indecent images. Or else they'll release you on police bail, pending further inquiries."

"What does police bail mean, exactly?"

"It means you are released, but you have to report to a police station on a given date and time. It's used a lot, especially when the police don't have enough evidence to charge and they want more time to investigate. There are often conditions attached, and you may have to surrender your passport to stop you from running away to somewhere abroad."

Somewhere abroad sounded rather attractive to me at that moment.

"How about if I'm charged?"

"Then you'll be kept here at the police station until you're taken before a magistrate. That would most likely be tomorrow morning."

"Then what?"

"The magistrate would probably grant you bail."

I didn't much like her use of the word *probably.*

18

I was released on bail at four o'clock that afternoon. But, as expected, there were conditions.

Not only did I have to surrender my passport but I was forbidden from knowingly coming within two miles of Annabel Gaucin, and also from being anywhere alone with my daughter.

"But that's crazy," I said to the custody sergeant who read out the conditions. "I *live* within two miles of Annabel Gaucin."

"Then you'll have to live somewhere else," he replied unhelpfully. "You can always refuse to accept the conditions, but you'll then go before a magistrate who may remand you in custody. It's your choice. The conditions have been requested by social services, and they know best."

I privately thought that, in this case, social services clearly didn't know best, but there was nothing I could do about it.

Once again, I signed a paper with which I didn't agree.

Charles came to collect me in his aging Mercedes. I'd asked him to use his spare key to our house and bring with him my passport from the top drawer of the desk, which I then solemnly handed over to the custody sergeant in exchange for my false arm, my belt, my wallet, and my liberty.

They kept my phone as potential evidence.

Charles and I walked out of the police station straight into a barrage of reporters and photographers, all shouting questions at me and firing off their multiple flashguns. There was even a TV crew, with a camera and microphone pressed close to my face.

I was taken completely by surprise and almost ducked back into the police station, but I knew I wouldn't get much sanctuary there. It had probably been one of the custody staff that had tipped off the press in the first place.

So Charles and I suffered the discomfiture of the paparazzi scuttling along beside us, snapping away, as we walked the fifty yards or so to his car.

"Get in," Charles shouted at me over the roof as he unlocked the Mercedes, but closing the doors wasn't that easy, as the photographers kept trying to pull them open again to get a better shot.

In the end, Charles pulled away from the curb with the doors still open.

"Mind out," I shouted at him as he drove straight towards the TV crew. "For God's sake, don't run them over or we'll both be back in clink."

Fortunately, the crew had the good sense to scamper to one side as the car accelerated away.

"Bloody hell," Charles said with a laugh. "Just like running the gauntlet of the PLA."

"The PLA?" I asked.

"People's Liberation Army," he said. "The Chinese. Down the Yangtze. Only, this lot weren't firing live rounds."

It had felt like it, though, and I was sure that the film and photographs they had taken would end up on tonight's TV news bulletins and in the pages of tomorrow's national dailies.

"Why didn't you warn me?" I asked. "You must have seen them on the way in."

"Sorry. I didn't notice," Charles said. "And I probably wouldn't have realized they were waiting for you anyway."

Why would he?

"Are we being followed?"

Charles looked in the rearview mirror. "I

don't think so, but I'll make a few turns to be sure."

We spent the next ten minutes or so snaking through Oxford's one-way system until Charles was satisfied that no one was following, and then he set the nose of the Mercedes on a northwesterly heading towards Aynsford.

"How was it in the police station?" Charles asked.

"Dreadful," I said. "I was treated like a pervert."

At least Charles didn't ask me if I *was* one.

"What's all this about not being able to live in your own house?"

I had tried to explain the conditions to him in the brief telephone call that I'd been allowed to make from the custody sergeant's phone. I'd only called Charles because I was unable to contact Marina either at home or on her cell, and the sergeant hadn't been pleased by the delay.

"Thanks to bloody social services, I can't go within two miles of Annabel Gaucin, and she lives only a mile from us."

"Where, exactly?" Charles asked.

"In Eastlake. Next to the school."

"You'd better come home with me, then," Charles said. "My house is at least three miles from Eastlake School."

"Can I borrow your phone to try Marina?" I asked.

"I don't own a cell phone," he replied. "I've never liked the damn things. You can call her when we get to Aynsford."

How did anyone manage these days without a cell phone? I had now been separated from mine for a mere twenty-four hours and I felt bereft and entirely lost without it. I thought about asking Charles to stop at a phone box but decided that when we got to Aynsford would be soon enough. I couldn't think that Marina was going to be pleased about things anyway.

"How are they?" I asked.

"Marina was pretty angry."

"With me?"

"With everyone, I think, though with social services mostly. But I haven't spoken to her since last night, when you called. Saskia was being cared for by social workers, and Marina was still trying to find out where she was."

I bet Marina was pretty angry. So was I, and mostly because I had been unable to establish from the police who had made the initial complaint against me and for what.

I'd been bailed only on suspicion of making and possessing indecent images of children. There had been no further mention of any actual abuse.

"Why, then," I had asked the custody sergeant, "is there a condition not to go near Annabel Gaucin, or be alone with my daughter?"

"Social services can't be too careful," he'd said in reply.

I personally thought the conditions had been imposed just to be bloody-minded, but it was no good me saying so. He'd have probably laughed.

I called Marina's phone as soon as I arrived at Aynsford.

"Where are you?" she shouted, sounding stressed.

"At Charles's place. Where are *you*?"

"At some dreadful children's home outside Oxford."

"Do you have Sassy?"

"They say I can take her soon. Why aren't you at home?"

I tried to explain that I'd only been released because I'd agreed to various conditions, but she didn't really understand. She was concentrating too much on getting Saskia back.

"Come straight to Aynsford when you've got her," I said. "We'll talk here."

■ ■ ■ ■

Marina was in tears when she and Saskia eventually made it to Charles's house soon after seven o'clock, tears of anger, relief and tiredness all rolled into one.

I went out to meet them in the driveway. Marina ran towards me and began thumping me hard on the chest with her fists, but I grabbed her and held her tight as she sobbed into my shoulder.

"Oh, Sid," she moaned, "what is happening to us?"

If only I knew.

Charles came out and took Saskia by the hand.

"What's wrong with Mommy and Daddy, Grandpa?" she said.

"Nothing's wrong, darling," he said. "Come on inside. I'm sure Mrs. Cross will have some biscuits for you."

The six-year-old and the octogenarian went into the house hand in hand while Marina and I stayed where we were on the gravel.

"Sid," Marina said, calming down and pulling away from me, "tell me honestly, have you anything to do with those photos the police found in our shed? I need to

285

know the truth."

"My darling," I said, "I swear to you I'd never seen them before the police showed them to me. Someone planted them in the shed for the cops to find. I absolutely promise you I have nothing to do with them. I cross my heart." I crossed my heart with my forefinger.

"And hope to die?" Marina said with a wan smile.

"That too." I smiled back at her. "I think the police must believe it as well or they would have surely charged me."

And, I thought, social services wouldn't have let Sassy back into our care.

"So are you now free?" Marina asked.

"I'm out on police bail. I'm technically still under arrest, but I don't need to be held in custody while they make more inquiries. But I will have to report back to the police station in a couple of weeks."

"So can we go home now?"

"Come on inside," I said, "it's cold out here."

We went in and sat at the kitchen table while I explained to her in detail what had happened and the reasons why I couldn't go home.

"But surely no one could believe that you would do anything to Annabel," Marina said. "And I was there all the time. Why didn't they ask me?"

"Perhaps they still will," I said, stroking her hand. "But what I can't work out is how the police knew Annabel's name."

"That was probably my fault," Marina said. "While the police were searching our house, one of them asked me about a photo of two little girls covered in soap bubbles that had been found on your phone. I laughed and told them it was our daughter and her best friend playing around in our bath, but then they asked me for the name and address of the other little girl. I didn't think there was anything wrong in giving it to them." She suddenly looked worried again.

"It's fine," I said, stroking her hand again. "It was only an innocent snap of the girls having fun."

But the police had thought differently and that had almost been enough to get me charged with making indecent images of children.

"Just because *I* can't go home doesn't mean that you and Sassy can't. I don't mind staying here on my own."

"Not bloody likely," Marina said, making me laugh. "Not with that dreadful Irishman still on the loose." She shivered. "We're staying right here with you — that's if Charles will have us." She turned to him.

"Of course, my dear," Charles said with a broad smile.

"It may be for some time," I said by way of warning. "At least for the next week or two."

"No problem," he said, still smiling. "Stay as long as you like. But I may not have enough food to feed you all, even for tonight. I know dear Mrs. Cross is capable of most miracles in the kitchen, but I fear that, on this occasion, I have not a single loaf or fish for her to work with."

He held his hands wide with his palms uppermost, and I smiled at the biblical reference. I also marveled at his steadfastness and unflappability in a crisis and supposed that it stemmed from many years of command in the Royal Navy.

"I have a fridge full of food at home," Marina said. "I'll simply go and fetch it. I've got to go and feed Rosie anyway. She must be wondering what's happened to us all."

And so it was decided.

Marina would drive the two miles to our house to collect food, Rosie, changes of clothes and our toiletry bags.

"I'll come with you," Charles said, "just in case."

"Just in case of what?" she said, looking worried.

"The press were waiting outside the police station earlier, and, now that I think of it, there may have been someone outside your house when I went to collect Sid's passport. I'd hate you to get caught up with them on your own."

"The press?"

"Photographers and a TV crew," I said. "They were waiting for us outside Oxford police station. I think Charles is right. In fact, I think he should drive you in his car. You can sit in the back and put a blanket over your head if there is anyone there."

"Isn't that rather over-the-top?" Marina said.

"Trust me, having camera lenses thrust right in your face isn't funny. If there's no one, all will be fine, but . . . Let's not take unnecessary chances."

Who was being "risk-averse" now, I thought.

Off they went in the Mercedes while I played sardines with Saskia, nominally under the supervision of Mrs. Cross to ensure we were never left alone together, although, of course, we were, as Mrs. Cross stayed firmly in the kitchen throughout, refusing to enter into the game. Sardines with just two people didn't make sense and hence reverted to hide-and-seek.

At least Sassy didn't seem to be too perturbed by her experiences at the hands of social services. They had obviously been more kind to her than the police had been to me.

Marina and Charles were away nearly an hour, some of which I spent in Charles's drawing room watching the television news while Mrs. Cross rustled up some baked beans on toast for Saskia's supper.

Sid Halley's arrest for child sex abuse was the second story after the lead item about unemployment and the state of the economy. The reporter didn't seem to know many actual facts, other than I'd been arrested and then released on bail without charge, but it didn't stop him speculating about the reasons for my arrest. It all sounded pretty slanderous to me but was, no doubt, couched in words that would escape the wrath of the law like *allegedly* and *supposedly*.

The film of Charles and me walking from Oxford police station to the car was shown prominently not once but twice, and it made for uncomfortable viewing.

If I'd been charged, under English law,

the TV company wouldn't have been able to show the images or make their speculations. The lid of *sub judice* would have come down with a clang to prevent it.

So an innocent man, released on bail pending further inquiries, can have his reputation torn to shreds more effectively than someone who admits his wrongdoing and is charged.

It was strange how British justice worked.

"The press *were* at the house," Charles said, carrying a box of groceries into his kitchen. "A couple of photographers and a TV crew. Marina hid under the rug. There was also a policeman standing guard at the gate."

That would make the neighbors talk, I thought, except they would already be talking if they'd watched the news.

"I think it was a bloody cheek," Marina said. "He came in with us and insisted on us showing him everything we were removing from the house. What on earth has it got to do with the police what I've got in my fridge?"

Nothing, I thought.

Not unless there were more indecent pictures of young girls hidden amongst the lamb chops and the pots of yogurt.

■ ■ ■ ■

That night, lying awake in an unfamiliar bed, Marina told me how awful it had been when she had arrived at Saskia's school to find her once more being taken away by strangers.

"I thought she was being kidnapped again," she said. "I was so frightened." I held her hand tightly under the bedclothes.

"Then I saw a policeman who was there as well. He told me they were going to arrest you for sexually abusing her. Of course, I didn't believe him, but he assured me it was true. He had the paperwork to prove it. I have to admit that I then lost my cool a bit. There was lots of shouting."

"I'm not surprised," I said, trying my best to be comforting. "It must have been horrible."

"It was," she said, "especially with all the other mothers watching. The policeman had to physically restrain me as the social service women took Sassy to their car and drove her away. He even threatened me with arrest if I didn't calm down. But it's not nice watching your baby being taken away from you."

I squeezed her hand again, and we lay in

the darkness for a while not speaking.

"Sid, what is going on?" Marina said finally. "Why won't this man leave us alone?"

"I don't know," I said. "But it has to be about more than that damn report. I've signed that, and still he won't leave us alone. I think it's now about control of me, and I am bloody determined that I will not be dictated to about how I work and to whom I speak. But what I don't understand is that in getting at me in this way, he's also harming my usefulness to him in the future."

"How do you mean?"

"Well, he was so keen to get me to sign that report and send it in to the BHA because, I assume, if Sid Halley said there was nothing amiss going on, then it was safe for the BHA to assume that there was, indeed, nothing amiss going on. My reputation for incorruptibility was such that I was once told that 'OK'd by Halley' was racing slang for *honest* and *reliable.*"

"So?"

"With all this publicity, McCusker will only succeed in getting me labeled as a child abuser, and my word won't be worth tuppence in the eyes of the BHA — or anyone else, for that matter. Then I'll be of no further use to him. 'OK'd by Halley' will mean something completely different, and nothing complimentary."

"Can't you stop him?" she asked. "Use some of your legendary underhand tactics to rid us of him permanently?"

Blimey, I thought, that was a bit of a turnaround.

"I could always try murdering him."

"What a great idea," she said with a laugh.

"But I'll have to find him first."

"I'm sure you could do that if you tried hard enough."

"I do have his cell phone number."

"Do you, indeed?" Marina said. "That should help."

"I hope so. I'll get started on it in the morning."

"Good boy," Marina said, cuddling up to me under the bedclothes. "No one messes with our daughter and gets away with it."

19

First thing on Friday morning, I sat in Charles's study and used his landline to start pulling in favors from a couple of police acquaintances that I'd helped get out of difficult situations in the past, both of whom were still serving officers.

"Sid, I can't," one of them said when I told him what I wanted. "Especially not with your ugly mug splashed all over today's front pages."

"Sure you can, Terry," I replied. "Look it up on the police computer and tell me what it says. Computers these days know everything about everybody, and, if they don't, you'll have to contact MI5. I know you have friends there from your time in antiterrorism."

"But it's against the law."

"Come off it! For how long has Terry Glenn been worried about keeping within the law? And, if I remember correctly, it was also against the law for me to get you off the hook during the Stephenson gun-smuggling affair, but I managed it."

"But that was nearly fifteen years ago."

"So you owe me for the last fifteen years of your career. What rank are you now? Inspector? On a good salary? With a guaranteed, cost-of-living-adjusted pension? Must be worth at least one little favor for me in return."

"I'll see what I can do," he said reluctantly.

"Yeah, Terry, you do that."

Next, I rang the other, a detective serving in the Greater Manchester force, whom I'd known since I'd investigated a stable-lad drug ring for the Jockey Club twelve years previously.

"Hello, Sid," he said. "It's been a long time."

I could detect the worried undertones in his voice as if he was expecting bad news.

"Norman," I said, "I need a favor."

"I was afraid of that," he said in reply.

"It's not much," I said. "I want a copy of everything you have on one Billy McCusker of your parish."

"You must be bloody joking," Norman said. "I can't give you that information."

"Why not?"

"Well, for a start, it's against the law. But

also, have you any idea how much there is of it? We have boxes full of stuff about Billy McCusker."

"Then why haven't you locked him up and thrown away the key?"

"It's not from lack of trying, I can assure you. Somehow he manages to keep one step ahead of us all the time, as if we have a spy in our midst."

"A mole," I said. "Probably someone Mc-Cusker controls, using threats."

"You're most likely right."

"How about if I promised to serve his head to you on a platter — that's you, personally? Would you let me at least have a look at the files?"

"I told you, it's against the law."

"Yeah," I said, "but could you fix it?"

"No, I couldn't."

"Then send me a summary. I need to know where he lives, what he drives, where he works and who he associates with. It would also be good to know what you thought of his acquisition of Honest Joe Bullen's betting shops and whether you have opposed Billy McCusker holding a bookmaker's license."

"So not very much, then," Norman said mockingly.

"No, not much, and I'm sure you can fix

it," I said, not rising to his bait.

"Come on, Sid, give me a break. If I'm found out helping you, I'll lose my job for sure. I'm due to retire next year and I need my pension."

"Don't give me all that sob-story stuff," I said. "I'm not asking you to kill him. I just need some information on his where-abouts."

"I can't," he whined, "especially with all this in the papers today about you and little girls."

"It's all lies," I said. "I'm being framed by Billy Bloody McCusker."

"Why?"

"I'm not sure, but I intend to find out. And you are going to help."

"I can't," he said again.

"Yes, you can, Norman. And you owe me big-time, remember?"

Both he and I were well aware that without my timely intervention with a young drug-crazed and knife-brandishing thug in a disused warehouse in Salford, Detective Inspector Norman Whitby would have been pushing up the daisies for the past twelve years.

Not that I actually enjoyed calling in favors like this. It wasn't as if I had done what I'd done only to have something in return at a later date. But now I needed help like I'd never needed it before.

"How's it going?" Marina asked, coming into the study.

"So-so," I said. "How was Sassy at school?"

Saskia had been determined to go in spite of Marina wanting to keep her away and Saskia had won the argument easily.

"Fine. She didn't turn a hair. Not quite so good for me, though."

"In what way?"

"Oh, only the other mothers making snide comments and such. You know what people are like. And I was really upset when Paula treated me as if I wasn't there."

"You can't blame her," I said. "It's not every day that the police tell you that your daughter may have been indecently photographed by your best friend's husband. Just ignoring you seems to be quite mild."

"I would have liked her to ask me about it directly."

"Would you if it had been Saskia and Tim?"

"I suppose you're right." She came around behind me and ran her fingers through my hair. "You're always right."

I wished I were.

I hoped I was right going after McCusker.

The safer option may have been to adopt the ostrich pose of head in the sand. But I wasn't like that, and I couldn't live like it.

Suddenly, it felt good to be doing again what I'd craved to do for so long. Charles had indeed been correct — *Once a detective, always a detective* — and now I had the unequivocal support of Marina.

"But you must stay safe," I said to her. "This man thinks nothing of using violence for the slightest reason. No more walking alone along dark alleys."

"Or through racetrack parking lots," Marina said, stroking my face next to my left eye. "It will be just like old times."

One of the major problems of losing one's cell phone is that you lose your contacts list with it — all those precious telephone numbers on which we rely gone forever, or, in my case, gone until the police saw fit to return my phone.

I had even preempted such a loss by backing up my contacts list on my laptop, but such sensible foresight had been totally undone by the fact that the police had taken my computer as well.

Hence I had to rely on an old, nonelectronic, handwritten address book that Marina had collected from my desk.

I flipped through the pages, trying to find inspiration from the names, and ended up in the *B*s.

Barnes. Chico Barnes.

Many years ago, Chico and I had been colleagues at the Hunt Radnor Associates detective agency, and we had been in a few scrapes together, not least when we were almost flayed alive by some particularly nasty villains who were manipulating horse-owning syndicates.

We'd been a good team, and I'd been massively disappointed when Chico had decided to retire from investigating to concentrate on his day job, teaching PE and judo to what he always referred to as "a bunch of juvenile delinquents" at a North London high school.

I'd also heard that he had married and settled down to family life. Perhaps a wife had rounded some of his rough edges. Or maybe not.

Boy, could I do with his help now.

I called the number in the address book, wondering if, after so long, it would even be current.

"Hello," said a female voice.

"Is that Mrs. Barnes?" I asked.

"Yes," she said tentatively as if expecting the call to be from someone selling something she probably didn't want.

"Is Mr. Barnes there, Mr. Chico Barnes?"

"No," she said. "He doesn't live here anymore."

"Oh," I said. "Do you have a telephone number for him?"

She reeled off a cell number so fast that I had to ask her to repeat it.

"Thank you," I said.

I rang the new number.

"Hello," said the familiar cockney voice.

"Chico, it's Sid."

"Bugger me! Sid Halley! It's been so quiet, I thought you must be dead."

That's also what Paddy O'Fitch had said. Had I seriously been that lifeless over the past six years? Maybe I had.

"How's the teaching?" I asked.

"Bloody dreadful," Chico said. "I'm getting too old for this judo lark."

"You and me both," I agreed.

"Yeah, but at least you're not trying to throw classes of overweight adolescents over your shoulders every day. I'm sure they weren't all this heavy when I started."

I laughed. "Get the school canteen to serve them fewer fries."

"So what can I do you for?" Chico asked.

"I was wondering how you were," I said, "catching up and all that."

302

"Don't bloody piss on me, you liar. You're after something."

"Why couldn't I just be curious as to your present circumstances? Why do you assume that I must be after something?"

"Because I knows you too well, Sid Halley. So what is it?"

"It might be dangerous," I said.

"Going into my school each day can be effin' dangerous, let me tell you. We've had three stabbings this year already, and one of them was of a member of staff."

"How about your family?" I asked. "They might disapprove."

"My family disapprove of most things I do. The wife and I are separated, pending a divorce."

"Kids?"

"Nah, that's been the trouble. I wanted, she couldn't, end of story."

"So are you willing to help?" I said, hardly daring to believe it.

"Are you sure you've not grown too old for all that stuff?"

"I've got no choice, mate. Have you seen the papers? I'm being stitched up as a bloody pedophile. If I don't fight back, I'm a dead man walking anyway."

"Yeah," Chico said. "I saw something about you on breakfast TV."

"You, watching breakfast television? I don't believe it."

During the years we had worked together, he'd been out early pounding the streets every morning in his determination to be fit.

"Times have changed," he said with a laugh. "I've grown soft and flabby in my old age." He was about eight years younger than I, although no one knew for certain how old he really was as he'd been abandoned as a toddler on the steps of a police station in a stroller.

"Does that mean you'd be no use to me?"

"I'm not *that* soft and flabby," he said. "What do you need?"

"I think I might need a bloody army," I said.

"That bad?"

"Worse."

"Are you paying? Or do we have a sponsor?"

"Me, I'm afraid."

"That was always your trouble," he said. "You need to get someone else to pay."

"So will you help . . . for peanuts?"

"Sure," he said. "I could do with some excitement."

I spent the next twenty minutes or so telling him about some of my woes.

"This McCusker chappie definitely needs taking out," Chico said.

"You're so right," I agreed.

"Look, I've got to go now and teach a class of little 'ooligans. I'll call you later and we'll work out a plan."

Talking to Chico had raised my spirits. To be working with him again would be fabulous. As Marina had said, it would be just like old times.

Next I called the number printed on Detective Chief Inspector Watkinson's business card and was pleasantly surprised to get straight through to the man himself.

"Thanks a lot for all your help yesterday," I said sarcastically. "You could have backed me up a bit."

"I did," he said. "Why do you think you're out on bail and not remanded to custody? But I shouldn't be talking to you."

"I need to know who made the complaint against me in the first place," I said.

"I just told you that I shouldn't be talking to you."

"But you are," I said. "So who was it?"

"I don't know."

"Can't you find out?" I asked in my best pleading voice. "You know as well as I do that this is all a load of nonsense and that

Billy McCusker is behind it."

"Has he called you again?"

"No," I said. "Thanks to you, I can't live in my own house. And you still have my cell phone, so he has no way of calling me."

It was one of the few advantages of the situation.

"So who was it that complained?" I asked again, bringing him back to the reason for my call. "I need something to use to fight back against him."

"You should leave that to us," he said.

"But you've been far too busy arresting me instead of him. If I leave it to you, nothing will happen, and we both know it. You have to work within a system that McCusker is well used to exploiting for his own ends. I don't."

"OK," he said. "I'll see what I can find out. But you must remain within the law."

"Of course," I replied.

The law of natural justice.

Friday afternoon dragged on interminably, and I couldn't even go to collect Saskia from school as that would knowingly be placing myself within two miles of Annabel Gaucin.

I may have been out of cell number 5 at Oxford police station, but I still felt like a

306

prisoner, albeit in the more comfortable surroundings of Aynsford. But at least there were no more reports about me on the lunchtime television news.

Perhaps, I thought, the story would now fade away to nothing and life would return to normal.

Fat chance.

Sassy came home from school and helped lift me out of my depression, as she danced around Charles's study, showing me a little doll she'd made in a craft class.

"She's lovely, darling," I said. "Does she have a name?"

"Mandy," Sassy said poignantly. Then she rushed out of the study to take the doll to see Grandpa.

"How was it at the school today?" I asked Marina.

"Pretty awful," she said. "One of the mothers, of a girl in the year ahead, shouted to her daughter to stay away from Saskia in case she caught something nasty. I ask you, what sort of a person does that?"

"Ignore them," I said.

"I try, but it's difficult."

I gave her a reassuring hug.

"How about you?" Marina said. "Had any luck with the McCusker hunt?"

"Not much, but I've put out a few feelers

for information. Are you sure you're happy about this?"

"Absolutely," she said with passion. "I hate him, hate him, hate him. He kidnapped Saskia, he took and killed Mandy and then he made me question my own husband's involvement with pornographic photos of children." She paused. "I want rid of this man. All I ask is that we keep safe. Don't do anything if it puts us in danger."

"I won't," I said. "I promise."

But did I really mean it? Could I keep that promise even if I wanted to? Had I not put us in potential danger already simply by asking for the information from Norman Whitby?

I remembered the talk about a mole in the detective ranks of the Greater Manchester Police. What if Norman inadvertently informed McCusker of my inquiries by mentioning them to the wrong person? I thought that it was unlikely, but could I be totally sure?

And what if Norman Whitby was himself McCusker's mole?

It didn't bear thinking about.

The telephone interrupted my dismal thoughts and, coincidentally, it was Norman Whitby on the line, calling back.

"I've got some stuff for you," he said,

barely audibly. "Do you have an e-mail address?"

"Your Thames Valley colleagues have confiscated my computer. Can't you read it to me?"

"No," he said, again almost in a whisper. "I'm in the office."

"Mail it, then," I said, and I gave him Charles's address. "It's safer than e-mailing. There's no record."

"I'll have to print it out." He clearly wasn't very happy.

"And, Norman," I said, "send it first class. I need it tomorrow."

"I'll try," he said quickly and hung up.

If he was the mole, he was a very good actor.

"So what's the plan?" Chico asked, calling back around five o'clock.

"Do you fancy a trip to Manchester?"

"Manchester?"

"I want to see what my enemy looks like."

"When?"

"When are you free?" I asked.

"Anytime you like. Exams start here on Monday, and they run on for weeks, and there's no PE 'cos they all take place in the gym."

"Don't you have any playing fields?"

"We used to, but the bloody council sold them for housing. And we aren't allowed to use the playground for PE even though they all kick soccer balls around it during the lunch hour. Health and Safety rules, apparently, because the playground's made of concrete. It's effin' crazy."

Their loss, I thought, was my gain.

"But don't you have to look after the kids anyway?"

"I'll get out of that, all right. I'll tell them my granny's dying up in the north of Scotland and I've got to go and see her. It's no problem. I've done it before."

"How many Scottish grannies have you got?" I asked, laughing.

"As many as I need."

I hoped he wouldn't use up too many of them.

20

In for a penny, in for a pound.

Late on Friday afternoon I used Charles's ancient computer to send an e-mail to Peter Medicos at the BHA, stating that I wished now to disassociate myself from the report I had sent to him previously regarding Sir Richard Stewart's concerns about race fixing. That I had been wrong, and that further investigation had shown me Sir Richard had indeed been correct in his assertion that someone was manipulating the results of races. And that I recommended that the BHA Security Service should investigate the matter further with reference to the bookmakers trading as Honest Joe Bullen of Manchester.

"Are you sure that's wise?" Charles asked when I told him.

"I don't know," I said, "but it surely must be better for us if Billy McCusker is being distracted by a BHA inquiry into his bookmaking operation."

I purposely hadn't gone quite as far as to mention McCusker by name or to detail the jockeys I had spoken to. Peter Medicos would find out about them all in good time. And the last thing I wanted was for the likes of Jimmy Guernsey to tell McCusker that the Security Service had come directly to him as a result of a tip-off from me.

The package of information from Norman Whitby arrived Saturday midmorning in the mail.

There wasn't as much as I had hoped for, but it would do. The most important thing included in it was McCusker's home address and home phone number — Norman having scribbled alongside: *This is very ex-directory so don't let on how you got it.*

I knew from the Belfast Crown Court report that Billy McCusker was now forty-two years old, but the information from Norman showed that his birthday was, appropriately, the last day of October — Halloween.

From Norman's brief details of McCusker's suspected dealings in a thriving Manchester extortion racket, I suspected that our Billy was one person who didn't need to dress up in a creepy costume on his birthday to scare others. He did it on a daily basis throughout the rest of the year, probably while wearing a business suit and tie.

There had been six arrests of McCusker in the preceding five years. Five times had been on suspicion of obtaining money by menacing and once of inflicting grievous bodily harm with a baseball bat, but only one of those arrests had resulted in subsequent charges. And even on that occasion, any chance of court proceedings had quickly evaporated due to the prospective witnesses for the prosecution suddenly failing to remember what they'd previously reported to the police.

Convenient collective amnesia had set in, no doubt assisted by threats of violence from the defendant or his mates. Getting McCusker convicted of anything was going to be a struggle, let alone something that would send him away for a lengthy stretch.

Perhaps his murder was, indeed, the only viable solution, but Norman Whitby's package also contained information about three of Billy McCusker's close associates — his muscle — two of whom I was pretty sure I'd met in the parking lot at Towcester races. To murder the boss, one might have to dispose of the hired help first, and, somehow, I wasn't too enamored with the odds.

Next I called Terry Glenn again at the Metropolitan Police.

"Hello, Terry," I said when he answered his cell. "Any luck?"

He wasn't pleased to hear from me. "No, Sid. No luck as yet."

"Have you even tried?" I asked, knowing full well that he hadn't.

"Telephone records are highly confidential," he said. "Have you any idea how much shit I'd be in if I was caught giving you that information? Especially since the phone-hacking scandal and all that trouble over selling information by police to the media."

"Have you any idea how much shit you'd have been in if I hadn't bailed you out by getting rid of that handgun from your house before it was searched by Internal Affairs? You'd have gone down for that, Terry, and you know it. Loss of career, loss of liberty, maybe even a loss of life. You know what happens to coppers when they go inside, don't you?"

"But that was all years ago."

"Maybe it was," I said, "but you still owe me. And I have another number for you."

I gave him McCusker's home number from Norman Whitby's package to add to the cell one I'd given him the previous day. "All calls for the past six months will do.

Plus any texts on the cell."

He sighed. "OK, I'll do it for you, but then we're even. No more requests."

"OK," I said, "it's a deal. Print them out and send them." I gave him Charles's address.

"I'll do it on Monday," he said with resignation.

"No, Terry, do it now. You've still got time to catch the Saturday mail."

Around noon, Chico arrived by taxi from Banbury railway station to lift my mood.

It was well over ten years since we had last seen each other, and, as he'd said, he'd put on the odd pound here and there, as had I. There were a few flecks of gray in his tight curly hair, but, overall he looked exactly the same as I remembered him. And his mind was as sharp and rough-edged as it had always been.

"You've aged well," I said, standing in the hallway to greet him.

"I'll be forty this year," he said, "or maybe next."

"You don't look it."

"Shut up, will you. What is this? I haven't come all this way fishing for bleedin' compliments." But his smile showed me that he was still pretty proud of his youthful appearance. "Got to keep my looks, though, haven't I, me old china, now I'm back in the bird-chasing stakes."

"Yes," I said. "I'm sorry to hear about your marriage."

"Don't be," he said. "Better off out of it for both of us, I reckon. How about yours? Right posh bird, by all accounts. Dutch, isn't she?"

"*Ja, maar niet zo posh,*" Marina said with a laugh, coming into the hall from the kitchen. "You must be Chico?"

"Blimey, Sid," Chico said with his eyes firmly on Marina's bosom, "you done well."

Marina blushed.

"Yes," I agreed, "but she has a mean right hook if crossed, so watch it."

Marina pulled a face at me, but we both knew it was true.

"So when do we set off north?" Chico said. "I've not come here to make bleedin' chitchat."

"All in good time," I heard myself say, echoing the police-speak for *Not yet.* "We have to make plans first."

Mrs. Cross made sandwiches for our lunch while Charles, Marina, Chico and I convened in the drawing room as a Council of War.

Even though I'd told them all bits of the

story, I went through things again from the beginning, from the arrival at our house of Sir Richard Stewart right up until my release on bail from Oxford police station.

I explained to them about Sir Richard's suspicions and how he had tried so hard to get me to look into them and how I had refused to do so and the fear and anger that that decision had caused him.

I then told them about the circumstances of Sir Richard's sudden death the following morning and why Charles didn't believe the police view that it was suicide. And also about my telephone calls from the man with a Northern Irish accent, demanding that I should investigate the very concerns that Sir Richard had raised and to make sure I found that nothing was wrong.

I relived the horror of discovering that Saskia had been kidnapped from school, followed by the relief that she had been released unharmed. And the anger that remained that someone could do such a thing.

I described my day at Newbury races and the Guinness-assisted discussion with Paddy O'Fitch, who gave me not only the name of Billy McCusker but also the news of the Shankill Road Volunteers' mass exodus to Manchester. I also recalled for them my less-than-friendly encounter with the jockey

Jimmy Guernsey that had confirmed for me both his and McCusker's involvement in Sir Richard's race fixing.

I told them about how our two dogs had been taken and then let loose a hundred miles away on the M6 freeway, only for Mandy to be killed by the passing traffic. And I revealed my discovery that several top jockeys had been terrorized into stopping horses because of threats or actions against their families.

I raised a few eyebrows, not least Marina's, when I divulged the fact that I knew it had been a jockey, Tony Molson, and his wife, Margaret, who had kidnapped Saskia from her school, but that they had done so under great duress from McCusker.

I explained how I had been to Towcester races to watch Tony Molson stop the horse Ackerman in the two-and-a-half-mile chase and how I had been beaten up for my troubles in the racetrack parking lot by a pair of McCusker's heavies.

And, in conclusion, I described the ignominy and humiliation of being arrested on suspicion of child abuse and of still being treated by the police as if I was a sexual deviant, all thanks, I was sure, to a McCusker-generated complaint.

All in all, it had been an eventful three

weeks, and that was without even mentioning anything about my prospective hand transplant.

"Wow," said Chico when I'd finished my monologue. He'd been sitting quietly, listening, occasionally opening and closing his Swiss Army penknife as if it had been an aid to concentration on my story.

All put together, even I'd been amazed how quickly Billy McCusker had infected our lives like a hybrid flu virus, one for which there appeared to be no simple cure.

"So what's the plan?" Charles said.

"Under normal circumstances, I would make a complaint of my own to the police, but, in this case, I believe that would have about as much effect as peeing on a bonfire. I have a contact in the Greater Manchester force, and he believes they have a mole in their midst. And McCusker is well versed in using the system to stay out of its clutches. This one, I fear, is down to us."

"I don't fancy a full-frontal attack," Chico said, "not with those bleedin' Volunteers running all over the place. I bet they haven't decommissioned their arms. We're going to need to be real sneaky."

I laughed. "We're going to have to be more than sneaky. This man has no conscience and no qualms. He's a killer who knows nothing but violence."

I decided against telling them about Darren Paisley's grisly end, nailed to a floor and dying of thirst.

"Please, please be careful," Marina said, looking at me. "Nothing is worth us losing you."

Were there things worth dying for?

Plenty of people in history had died for causes they believed in. They still did. During the world wars, there had never been a shortage of volunteers for missions from which no one was expected to return, to say nothing of the men and women of the military intelligence units who willingly parachuted into Nazi-occupied France and whose life expectancy was measured in weeks rather than months.

There were loads of examples of people who had freely forfeited their own lives to save those of people they loved.

But had it been worth it?

I remember what my dying mother had told me when I'd been sixteen: *Fleeting and fragile, life is your most cherished possession. Make of it what you can, but protect it with all your might.*

It had been the most awful of times, and I would then have happily given up my own life to make her well again from the cancer that was destroying her body from within.

But even if it had been possible, what good would that have done? She had lived solely to look after me. I was her pride and joy. If I had died instead of her, then her life would have had no purpose.

"I have no intention of dying anytime soon," I said to Marina, and hoped I wasn't tempting fate in the process.

"Me neither," said Chico with a laugh. "I've met a nice little blonde number who needs my body totally intact and full of vim and vigor."

A body totally intact, I mused.

Was it raining?

The Council of War came up with no great master plan for success but rather a whole raft of further questions that needed answering first.

It was decided that Chico and I would go to Manchester to carry out a reconnaissance on McCusker, his home and local area, to get the feel for the enemy and the battle-ground, while Marina, Saskia and Rosie would remain at Charles's place in Aynsford under his protection. As he said, he may be eighty-three, but he still knew how to load and fire the shotgun he had used for nearly fifty years to kill vermin on his land.

I would contact D.C.I. Watkinson again to try to determine who had made a complaint against me, and I'd also try to start lining up the miscreant jockeys in a solid coalition to face the BHA and the police. Not that I thought there was any realistic chance of that.

The meeting broke up at a quarter to three, as Charles had an appointment to see the chairman of the Aynsford Parish Council and Chico wanted to call his little blonde number to explain away his absence for the next few days.

"Why didn't you tell me that you knew who'd kidnapped Saskia?" Marina asked rather irritably when we were left alone. "And, more to the point, why haven't you told the police?"

I explained to her the circumstances.

"How could I tell the police?" I said.

"They should have thought of that before they took her." She was clearly not moved by the possible fate of the Molsons' own boys. "Do you remember how frightened we were? I think we should report them. Otherwise, they might do it again to some other little girl."

"I think the chances of that are zero."

"How about if this awful man McCusker tells them to?"

"I'll just have to make sure he doesn't."

Marina went to collect Saskia from a lunch-time birthday party at McDonald's in Stratford. She hadn't wanted her to go in the first place, but our little daughter was proving to be a highly proficient negotiator in getting her own way.

"OK," Marina had said, in the end, giving in. "But thank God it's not being organized by one of those horrible mothers from her school."

I was pleased. The party was for a girl who'd been at the same playgroup as Sassy, and I thought it was important that she didn't become isolated from her friends, as so easily could have happened under the present circumstances.

"The press have gone from outside the house," Marina said when she arrived back with Saskia, "and the police too. I went past to have a look."

Thankfully, I was now yesterday's news, and the media juggernaut had moved on to camp on some other poor soul's doorstep.

Saskia and Chico hit it off instantly, and it wasn't long before the six-year-old was bossing around the almost-forty, playing endless games of hide-and-seek or making him help her in the building of a make-believe hospital from the furniture in Charles's drawing room.

"I wish I'd had kids," he said to me, taking a breather from moving the armchairs.

"It's not too late," I said.

"I don't fancy getting married again," he said. "Tied me down too much."

"You don't have to be married to have kids . . . not these days."

"But is that fair on the kids? Don't they need the stability?"

I was surprised to hear him say that; after all, he'd hardly had a stable childhood of his own, ever shifting from one children's home to another as each in turn had got fed up with his strange antics, particularly his fondness for climbing up drainpipes to the roof. He'd told me all about it years ago when we'd had a particularly long and boring wait at a racetrack stakeout.

Perhaps the very fact that Chico had been denied such stability himself was why he thought any kids of his should have it.

He went back to playing with Saskia, reveling in being a sick patient for her to cure, while I took Marina off in the Range Rover to see the Molsons.

21

"Why are we doing this?" Marina demanded as we came into the village of Chipping Warden. "We should be going straight to the police."

"What good would that do?" I asked.

She turned slightly in her seat to face me. "It would ensure that those who kidnapped our daughter got their just desserts."

"Would they be *just* deserts?" I asked. "McCusker is the real villain here, not Tony and Margaret Molson. They are only the pawns."

I could tell that Marina didn't agree, and she wasn't happy.

"I tell you what," I said. "If you still want to go to the police after we've met them, I won't stop you. I can't say fairer than that. But let's meet them first."

Tony answered the door at the first ring of the doorbell. He knew we were coming. I'd called him earlier.

"Hello, Mrs. Halley," he said, offering his right hand to Marina. She declined to shake it.

As before, Tony led the way through into the living room.

Margaret was already there with the twins.

"Jason, Simon, this is Mr. and Mrs. Halley," said Tony. "Mr. Halley is a friend of mine. He used to be a jockey too."

I shook hands with both the boys, marveling at how identical they were in every way. They were even dressed identically. Tony had said they would be thirteen next birthday, but they were tall, almost as tall as their mother, and already an inch or so taller than Tony. They would clearly not be following him into racing, not as jockeys anyway.

"Simon," Margaret said to one of them. "Please go and put the kettle on."

I presumed it was Simon who went out to the kitchen, although how his mother had known it wasn't Jason was anyone's guess. I suppose there must be some differences, but I couldn't spot them.

"Jason," Tony said, "go and help your brother. And both of you wait in the kitchen until we come through. We have things to talk about here first, alone." Jason did as he was told and followed Simon. Tony went over to make sure the door was closed behind them.

"Mrs. Halley," said Margaret, "would you like to sit down?"

"I prefer to stand," Marina replied. Things, I thought, were not going very well.

"Why did you kidnap my daughter?" Marina said loudly.

"Shhh!" said Tony, putting up his hands. "The boys will hear you."

"Perhaps they should," Marina said. "Then they'd know what their parents are really like."

I was beginning to regret having brought her here.

"I understand your anger," Tony said to her. "I would be angry too. And we are dreadfully sorry for the pain we've caused you. But we didn't harm your lovely little girl. We wouldn't. And we tried very hard to be nice and not to frighten her."

"You frightened me," Marina said.

And they'd frightened me, I thought.

"We are so sorry," Margaret said. "We were frightened too. And we felt we had no choice. Please don't be angry."

"We are ready to go with you to the police and tell them everything," Tony said. "Right now, if you want. We will have to take our chances with the French authorities. We may lose our boys, but so be it. It's up to you."

There was a long silence before Marina waved her hand in a dismissive manner. I wasn't sure whether she was dismissing the notion of going to the police or dismissing the Molsons to the severity of the law and to the loss of their sons.

"There would be conditions for our silence," I said, and received no negative vibes from Marina. "I need your help to defeat this man. Tony, you will sign a statement, detailing all the horses you have stopped."

Tony didn't look very happy. "I'll lose my jockey's license."

"Only if I give the statement to the BHA," I said. "And you'll lose a lot more than just your license if we go to the police right now."

"So why do you want a statement?" he asked.

"Two reasons," I said. "First, I want a hold over you, to ensure you never go near my daughter again. And, second, it will be the first brick in my wall of evidence against which I hope one day to crush the Irishman. And you will also let me know every time he contacts you to stop a horse."

Tony went on looking miserable. "He called this morning. I've got to stop one at

Uttoxeter tomorrow. Black Peppercorn in the first."

"Does it have a chance?"

"Yeah, a good chance. It'll probably start as the favorite."

"Then win, if you can," I said.

"Are you crazy? The Irishman will contact the French authorities."

"No, he won't," I said confidently. "He may be angry with you, but he won't do anything. He will still want to use you in the future. If he tells the French about the boys, he'll have lost control over you forever. So call his bluff."

He didn't look very sure.

"Tony," I said in my most commanding tone, "you will try and win on Black Peppercorn. And, if you don't, it won't bode well for you at any future inquiry by the BHA. Do I make myself clear?"

He looked even more miserable than before.

He was being squeezed from both sides, but if my experience was anything to go by, he would surely be more scared of Billy Mc-Cusker than he would be of me and the British Horseracing Authority.

I reckoned that the chances of Black Peppercorn winning tomorrow were very slight, almost nonexistent.

■ ■ ■ ■

"How can this bloody man McCusker get away with it?" Marina said as I drove her back to Aynsford. "Surely he should be in prison."

"Indeed, he should," I said.

How did he get away with it? It was a very good question.

It seemed to me that the bigger the crime, the easier it was to escape the clutches of the law.

Perhaps it was that if the offense was large enough, people found it difficult to believe what was happening. Or maybe it was simply a combination of belief, barefaced boldness and balls.

If I were to commit a crime, I was certain that I'd be found out, and I no doubt would be. But McCusker believed he was invincible and that was partly what made him so. Whatever situation he might be in, he would have absolute faith that there was a route to safety and freedom and that he'd find it even if it involved corrupting the entire law-enforcement multitude lined up against him.

Al Capone had ruled Chicago in the 1920s with impunity because he believed that it was *he* who was the "untouchable," not the agents of the FBI. He corrupted police and politicians alike, and he was not averse to nobbling juries as well. He was responsible for numerous murders, many at his own hands, but he was never tried for a single one. And, perversely, it was not his involvement in bootlegging, prostitution and gambling that was his downfall but his failure to pay income tax on the illegal profits from such activity.

I wondered if McCusker paid his taxes, both on the bookmaking profits and also on his other, less salubrious activities.

"So what do we do to get him in prison?" Marina said.

"We could start by checking his tax returns."

"What?"

"Nothing," I said. "I was just thinking out loud."

I drove on in silence for a while.

"Do you really think you and Chico can do something about him?" Marina asked as we approached Aynsford. "I'm getting cold feet about the whole thing."

"Let us go to Manchester and have a look first," I said. "Check out his home and the betting shops. Ask a few questions. It should give us a feel for how we stand. We've done that sort of thing before."

"But that was a long time ago. When you were a lot younger."

"I'm not *that* old," I said mockingly in my defense, "and Chico is still pretty fit. And our brains are as good as they always were, probably better."

"I'm still frightened," Marina said.

Secretly, so was I.

Chico and I left Aynsford at eleven o'clock on Sunday morning, aiming the Range Rover northwards towards Manchester.

We didn't take overnight bags, Chico having convinced me that if this were going to be more than a one-day trip, we would sleep as we were, in the car. My protestations that I was now too old for that sort of thing were dismissed with derision.

"Come on, Sid," Chico had said, "we used to do it all the time."

"Maybe we did," I'd replied, "but these days my aching bones need soft mattresses."

"You're the one that's gone soft," he'd replied.

He had such a way with words, so I'd agreed to his plan while secretly hoping we would be back at Aynsford that night.

Chico had been itching to depart from first light, but I wanted to go via Uttoxeter to watch the two o'clock race.

"Blimey," he said cheerfully as we turned into the rapidly filling parking lot, "I haven't been to the races in years. Not since I stopped working with you. I've watched it on telly, mind you, occasionally in the local betting shop. But I don't suppose much has changed."

"There's a little less formality these days," I said. "And I sense that a lot more young people go to the races."

"You just think that because you're getting so old," he said with a smile.

"Sod off."

"So what are we looking for, exactly?" he asked.

"I want to watch Tony Molson ride a horse called Black Peppercorn in the first."

"Will it win?"

"I doubt it. Tony has been told by McCusker to make sure it doesn't, but I've told him to win if he can."

"Should be interesting, then," Chico said with a laugh. "What do you want me to do?"

"Hang round the betting ring and look at the prices on the boards. Make a note of any bookmakers offering larger-than-expected odds on Black Peppercorn, not that I really expect there to be any. Other than that, keep your eyes and ears open, usual stuff."

"Right you are."

"And unless I call you, we'll leave after the second race. Call me if you need anything." I gave him the number of the new, cheap, cameraless, pay-as-you-go phone I'd bought in Banbury the previous afternoon on the way to the Molsons'.

"Here, use this to get in." I held out a twenty-pound note to him.

"I don't need your cash," he said, slightly affronted.

"Take it anyway. Use it to make a bet, if you want."

He took the money and drifted off towards the entrance as I hung around in the parking lot for a minute or two to let him go through first. We had always worked on the principle that the less we were seen together at a racetrack, the better. One never knew who was watching.

"Halley!" a voice shouted over my left shoulder. "Sid Halley!"

I turned to see Peter Medicos, complete in his tweed suit plus trilby, hurrying towards me through the ranks of parked cars. Dammit! I could have done without that.

"Hello, Peter," I said as he approached.

"Halley," he said, slightly out of breath,

"I've been trying to call you." There had been no courteous lifting of the trilby today.

"I've not been at home," I said. "I'm staying with my father-in-law."

"That would explain it," he said. "Now, what's this business about you being a child abuser?"

I knew that after all the publicity, coming to Uttoxeter races wasn't going to be easy, but I'd hardly expected to be confronted by the head of racing security in the parking lot before I'd even gone into the enclosures.

"It's a mistake, that's all," I said, trying to be dismissive.

"We can't afford to have racing's good name tainted."

I sensed for a moment that he was about to ask me to remove myself altogether, but perhaps he thought better of it.

"And what's all this nonsense about disassociating yourself from that report you sent me? I picked up your e-mail this morning."

"Just what I said. The report is wrong. I now believe that Sir Richard was absolutely correct in his assertion that someone is manipulating results."

"On what evidence?" he asked.

"I've had some private discussions."

"With whom?"

"I'm afraid I can't tell you that," I said. "I

spoke to people in confidence."

"What nonsense," he said. "You must tell me."

"I will not," I said with determination. "But, as you rightly declare, you can't afford to have racing's name tainted. So I suggest that you start your own inquiries into the matter beginning with Honest Joe Bullen, the bookmakers from Manchester."

"I must insist that you tell me who you've been speaking to and what they have said."

"You can insist all you like, Peter," I replied. "But I won't tell you."

"You know that I can make you persona non grata on all racetracks?"

"I think you'd be a fool to do that," I said. "And many would agree with me. I too have racing's good name at heart, and lots of people know it."

He was far from pleased but there was little he could do, short of having me bodily thrown off the premises.

He stomped off in a huff towards the entrance.

Oh dear, I thought. It hadn't been in my plan to make an enemy of Peter Medicos. In fact, I would surely need him as an ally.

Much to my surprise, Black Peppercorn won the first race by a length, cheered home enthusiastically by the crowd as the favorite, at a starting price of seven-to-two.

I watched as the horse returned to the unsaddling area for the winner. Tony Molson looked even more worried than when he'd stopped Ackerman at Towcester.

I went to stand so that he would have to go past me to get back to the Weighing Room.

"Tell me what the Irishman says," I said quietly as he passed me.

He gave me a look of abject horror at what he'd done.

For me, it was only a minor victory. But I reckoned anything that would shift Mc-Cusker out of his comfort zone was valuable.

I wandered back towards the parking lot, fed up with the barrage of stares and whispered comments.

"Isn't that the pedophile Sid Halley?" I heard one woman say to the man she was with. "I think it's disgraceful allowing him in here."

I wanted to tell her that I wasn't a pedophile and that I hadn't done anything wrong, but it wouldn't have helped. She almost certainly wouldn't have believed me.

Was it a trait only of the British to always think the worst of everyone? To accept every accusation without question and to condemn even before the evidence had been presented?

I suppose I shouldn't really blame her. There was news value in the arrest of a suspected pedophile but very little in the subsequent release without charge.

What worried me most was that it was so easy to gain a false reputation but so extremely difficult to shed it again, if and when the grounds of an arrest were found to be false. People mostly went on believing the worst of their fellow man even in the face of compelling evidence to the contrary and that was because proving something *didn't* happen was usually impossible.

I waited for Chico in the Range Rover, wondering if my life could ever return to where it had been before.

In the twenty-first century, accusing someone of being a pedophile was most damning, far worse than being labeled a murderer or even a rapist. Even when untrue, it left a stain on one's character that was difficult to eradicate.

Chico appeared, full of smiles, which helped to drive away the demons in my mind.

"Bloody marvelous, that was," he said, climbing in. "Nice little earner."

"Explain," I said.

"That nag, Black Peppercorn — you know, the one we was watching." I nodded. "Being offered at four-to-one by one of the bookies while the others all had it at threes or seven-to-two at best. I watched him take loads of money from the punters, but he still didn't reduce his odds. In fact, at one point he went out to fives. That was when I invested that twenty note you gave me." He grinned and tapped his pocket. "I was first in line to get paid out. The poor guy looked sick, and he didn't have enough cash in his bag for all those with winning tickets, not even half enough." Chico laughed. "It nearly came to fisticuffs, let me tell you. The cops are still in there trying to keep the sides apart."

"Which bookmaker?" I asked.

"It had Barry Montagu of Liverpool on the board. I took a couple of snaps."

He leaned over and showed me the pictures on his phone, one before the race with the board clearly showing Black Peppercorn offered at five-to-one, and the second one showing irate punters surrounding the beleaguered bookie, waiting to get paid out.

"Bloody funny, it was, and he was getting no sympathy from the other bookies. They all thought he was bonkers for offering such large odds in the first place. Served him right to get stung. They were all smiles. One of them had tears flowing down his cheeks, he thought it was so funny."

No such thing as honor amongst thieves.

Chico chuckled to himself all the way to the M6, where I turned north towards Manchester.

"So where are we going first?" he asked.

"Well," I said, "according to the information we received from Norman Whitby, McCusker lives in the suburb of Didsbury, south of the city center. I think we should start there."

"Looking for what, exactly?"

"The lie of the land. Rumors. Chat in the pubs and bars. Local word on McCusker and the Shankill Road mob. That sort of thing. But nothing too obvious. We need to keep a low profile."

"Do we have any idea what this geezer looks like? I'd hate to sidle up to him in a pub and ask the wrong question."

I pulled a copy of the police mug shot out of my pocket and handed it to him.

"It's nearly twenty years old," I said. "But age will not change the shape of his cheekbones, nor that protruding brow."

"Ugly brute," Chico said, studying the

picture. "I think I'd know those eyes any-where."

"It's the others that are the worry," I said. "The Volunteers, and we have no idea how many of them there are. I've met two in the parking lot at Towcester and I'd be happy not to cross paths with them again, thank you very much. Best to steer clear of anyone with an Irish accent."

"Do you have any idea how many Irish-men there are in Manchester?"

"No," I said. "Do you?"

"Thousands of them," he said. "Maybe as many as a hundred thousand."

"How come you're suddenly such an ex-pert?"

"I looked it up on Charles's computer yesterday evening when you and your mis-sus went to see the kidnappers and when I wasn't playing doctors and nurses with your kid."

I gave him a sideways glance. "I wouldn't go round telling people you were playing doctors and nurses with a six-year-old girl, if I were you. You'll end up in the same boat as me."

"Yeah," he said, "you're right. Sorry. But you know what I mean."

"Tell me about the Irish in Manchester," I said, changing the subject back.

"According to the Internet, lots of them came over during the potato famine of the nineteenth century," he said. "And, as far as I can tell, the rest followed their beloved George Best over more than a hundred years later. And those that don't actually live in Manchester fly over to support the soccer team. A love of Manchester United is probably the only thing that Irish Catholics and Protestants agree on."

"And are they playing at home today?" I asked.

"Tomorrow night," Chico said. "Grudge match against Manchester City. The place will be awash with Irishmen."

22

Chico and I decided to split up and each visit a few of the more than twenty pubs in the bedroom suburb of Didsbury. However, we decided to give a wide berth to those closest to McCusker's home just in case he was out for a pint at his local pub.

We had driven slowly, but not too slowly, past the address that Norman Whitby had given me. Somehow it was nerve jangling to be so close to McCusker, and Chico clearly shared my anxiety as he furiously opened and closed his Swiss Army penknife.

If his house was anything to go by, Billy McCusker had done quite well since his empty-handed flight across the Irish Sea six years previously. It was a mock-Georgian, red-brick mansion with imposing white pillars on each side of the front door, mostly hidden away behind high wrought-iron gates and a chain-link fence topped with razor wire.

"Seems he's not very keen on visitors," Chico said. "But that fence wouldn't keep out anyone determined enough. It's no good putting the razors along the top of the fence like that. It needs to be standing away from it to be any good."

"So you could climb it?" I asked.

"Piece of piss, mate. I've climbed lots of fences like that. Do you want me to do it now?"

"Maybe later," I said, deciding against asking him which other fences he'd climbed and why.

I dropped Chico outside the Bell Inn near East Didsbury station for him to work northwards along the line of pubs on Wilmslow Road, while I parked the Range Rover near the Didsbury Medical Centre and started working the same line south towards him, starting at the White Hart.

I used a cover story that I was thinking of buying a property in the area to talk to the locals, especially about if there was any crime in the district.

There were plenty of the usual gripes about local youths running wild and terrorizing the neighborhood with drugs or racing cars up and down residential streets, but little about any real mobsters.

"How about within the Irish community?"

I asked the barman behind the bar at the White Hart.

"I try and steer clear of them," he said without any warmth. "I mind my own business."

"Does that imply that there is something going on?" I asked, leaning forward to keep my voice down and to encourage him to answer.

"I couldn't say," he said.

"Couldn't or won't?"

"Couldn't *and* won't," he said, then he went off to the far end of the bar to serve one of his sparse Sunday-night clientele.

"Does the name Billy McCusker mean anything to you?" I asked him quietly when he finally came back.

"I think you'd better leave," he said.

"Is that a threat?" I asked.

"Look upon it as a friendly warning."

"How friendly?" I asked, pushing my luck.

"I mind my own business, nothing more. I suggest you do likewise. Now leave."

I finished my Diet Coke and left

Twice he had said to me that he minded his own business. I wondered if by that he meant not the usual sense of not gossiping about others but that he literally minded his own business by paying protection money to keep it safe.

Along with drug dealing, protection rackets were one of the great scourges of inner-city life the world over. *Insurance,* some of the gangsters termed it, or *surety,* against getting your premises trashed or set on fire. The courts called it *extortion* or *demanding money with menaces,* but, whatever it was called, it was all basically the same thing: *Hand over a share of your hard-earned cash or we'll smash up your pub, shop, restaurant or whatever and put you out of business.*

I walked down the road and went into a second pub, The Chequers, which was completely empty of customers save for two men leaning on the bar, chatting to the pub owner.

I bought myself half a pint of lager and again trotted out my story to them about wanting to buy a property in the local area.

"Try West Didsbury," said one of the men. "It's far nicer than here in the east."

"Why's that?" I asked him.

"Nicer houses," he said, "and nicer people."

"Not so much crime neither," said the second man.

"Is there much crime round here?" I asked, looking concerned.

"Far too much," said the second man. "Drug dealing, mostly, with the addicts breaking into cars and houses to get cash for their next fix. If you ask me, they should be strung up."

Fortunately, I thought, no one *was* asking him.

"Any organized crime?" I asked.

"The drug dealing's pretty organized," said the first man, missing the point.

"How about the Irish community?" I asked. "Are any of them into drugs?"

"We don't see much of them round here," he said.

"I wish," said the pub owner miserably from behind the bar.

The conversation, as always, turned to the big match the following evening between the Manchester rivals.

"I reckon United will get beat," said one who was clearly a City fan.

"No chance," said the other.

Their soccer rivalry quickly broke up their drinking session, and, one after the other, they departed, leaving me alone with the owner.

"Very quiet tonight," I said.

"Too bloody quiet," he said. "Always is on Sundays, but this is worse than I've ever known. It needs to pick up in the summer — that is, if we get a summer. Nothing but bloody rain last year. Another one like that and I'll go bust."

"Shame you can't pay for protection against the weather," I said. The pub owner gave me a sideways stare. "Tell me about your Irish trouble."

"Nothing to tell."

"I'm not a copper," I said, "just a fellow sufferer."

"I don't care if you're the bloody Queen of Sheba, mate, I'm not telling you anything. I think it's time you went."

"OK, I'm going," I said, draining the rest of my lager. "But does the name Billy Mc-Cusker mean anything to you?"

"No," he said, but a tightening around his eyes told me that it did.

"How about the Shankill Road Volunteers?"

"Never heard of them." I could tell he was lying by the tiny beads of sweat that had suddenly appeared on his brow.

"How much do you pay?" I asked.

"I don't know what you're talking about."

"Does he collect from all the pubs in Manchester?" I asked.

The owner stood there, looking at me for a moment in silence, as if deciding.

"Does he?" I repeated.

"Someone does," he said. "All those that are still in business. All those not burned down or smashed up. All those with an owner not in the hospital or the cemetery." He spoke with all the pent-up venom of one who'd had no choice in the matter for too long.

"McCusker?"

He nodded ever so slightly, as if the small size of the movement would somehow diminish the betrayal.

"Have you been to the police?"

He laughed. "You must be bloody joking. My friend Bert Goring from the Carpenters Arms, he did that, and now he's six feet under, at least what's left of him is. They torched his pub with him in it. Barricaded the doors so he couldn't get out."

"So you pay?"

He nodded again. "A couple of grand a month. Almost half my profit. I put it down on my tax return as insurance expenses."

"I'm here to stop McCusker," I said.

"You and whose army?" he said, mocking me. "You don't have a chance. He's got the local cops wrapped round his little finger. And it wouldn't make much difference to me anyway. It might even make things worse. Better the Devil you know, eh?"

"But surely you'd like to be rid of him?"

"Another would simply pop up in his place, just as McCusker did after the previous guy got run out of town. There's always going to be somebody." He sounded resigned to it. "I've been in this wretched business for twenty years now and I've never not had to pay someone for protection. It comes with the territory. What makes me angry is how they claim they are doing us a favor. It's enough to make you sick."

"So I can't count on your help, then?"

"No, you can't," he said categorically. "I'd rather be alive and poor, thank you very much. Now, it's time you went, I've said too much to you already."

I went outside and called Chico, who answered at the fourth ring.

"How are you doing?" I asked.

"I'm still in the Bell," he said, "chatting up a nice, cuddly redhead."

"You're meant to be working, remember?"

"I am," he said. "This particular redhead is a cleaner, and, amongst others, she cleans the big house with the razor-wire fence."

"How on earth did you find that out?"

"I just came in here and said loudly that this must be a pretty awful place if people needed to protect their houses with fences like those round a prison camp, and she just said straight out that it was mostly for show. I'd better get back to her. How about you?"

"Never mind me. Get back to your redhead and find out what you can. I'll call you again in half an hour."

I marveled at how he did it. He'd always been able to chat up six birds successfully in the time I took to fail with one, and a stint as a married man had clearly not cost him his touch.

I wandered farther down Wilmslow Road past a parade of shops and the Fortune Cookie Chinese restaurant, with its name written bright in red neon lights.

The next pub I went into was much fuller than the previous two, not least because of two giant TV screens showing the final round of the Masters golf, live from Augusta, all the way across the Atlantic.

I ordered a diet cola and sat down on a barstool to watch.

"On your own?" asked the girl behind the bar, placing my drink down in front of me.

"Yes," I said. "I'm up here house hunting."

"You should talk to Shane Duffy over there." She pointed at the back of a well-built man facing away from me in a group watching the golf. "He works for an estate agent."

"Right," I said. "Thank you. I will."

"Hey, Shane," she shouted across the

crowded room, "I've got a customer for you."

Shane turned around to face me.

I'd last seen him twelve days previously in the parking lot at Towcester races just before he'd kicked me in the face with his boot.

I think I recognized him fractionally before he did me and that gave me a few seconds' start.

I came out of the pub door like a greyhound leaving the traps and turned north up Wilmslow Road, hurrying back towards the parade of shops and the Chinese restaurant.

I didn't like to look back in case the lightness of my face gave me away. The street lighting was minimal, and I was wearing dark trousers and a black windproof jacket. Perhaps he hadn't seen which way I'd gone, so I moved quickly but silently, staying as much as possible in the shadows of the roadside trees.

I went straight into the Fortune Cookie restaurant, closing the door firmly behind me.

"Table for one, sir?" said a young Chinese man in almost perfect English.

"Thank you," I said, "but can I just use your bathroom first."

I could tell he didn't like it. Probably too many people simply wanted to use their facilities and then leave. "Downstairs," he said reluctantly.

I went down as he'd directed and came face-to-face with a large, angry dog that - looked to me like a Rottweiler. It snarled at me in an unfriendly manner and barked twice, loudly.

I nearly went straight back up to take my chances with Shane Duffy, but, thankfully, I could see that the dog was secured to a ring in the floor under the stairs. Nevertheless, I flattened myself against the opposite wall as I edged passed it to the gentlemen's, hoping that the ring and the dog's heavy chain collar would both hold against its pull.

I waited in the lavatory cubicle for what must have been only a few minutes, but it seemed like much longer. No one came in or even tried to.

I emerged slowly, and the dog barked at me again, curling its upper lip and revealing a line of very sharp canine teeth.

What was such a vicious-looking animal doing in a Chinese restaurant?

Its barking couldn't have been that good for business. And, surely, stir-fried dog wasn't on the menu.

I came back up the stairs into the main

part of the restaurant very gingerly, checking the faces of the sparse clientele to ensure that Shane Duffy wasn't one of them, sitting there patiently, waiting for me to reappear.

He wasn't.

"Was that a table for one?" asked the young Chinese man in a slightly sarcastic manner.

"Yes, I think so. Did anyone come in after me asking if I was here?"

"No, sir," he said. "Were you expecting anyone?"

"Did anyone come in at all after me? Someone who didn't stay?"

"No, sir," he said again. "How about a table by the window?"

"No thanks. I'll have a booth." I pointed at the one I wanted.

I sat facing the door and called Chico.

"I need you, right now," I said to him.

"Where are you?"

"Holed up in a Chinese restaurant with one of the bad guys outside looking for me."

"Bad guys?" he asked.

"One of the men who beat me up in the parking lot at Towcester," I said. "I came across him in a bar."

"Oh," said Chico. "So much for our low profile."

"Yeah," I said, "but I really need you here, and pronto. I daren't go outside in case he's waiting for me."

"OK," he said. "The cuddly redhead's boyfriend has turned up anyway and he hasn't taken kindly to my interest in her. It's time to move on, so I'll come and rescue you. Where's the car?"

"Parked near the local medical center. But the key is in my pocket."

"That's careless," Chico said, rubbing in the fact that I was clearly out of practice at this investigating lark. In the past, we had always left a spare car key hidden in the underside of a wheel well in a magnetic box so we could both access it.

"I wasn't expecting to have to do a quick getaway."

"*Always expect the unexpected,* that's what you used to say."

"Sod off," I said.

"What's the name of the restaurant?"

"The Fortune Cookie. It's north of you on Wilmslow Road, on the left. The name is lit up in bright red neon. You can't miss it."

"I'm on my way."

"Be careful," I said. "And don't come and sit with me when you get here."

"I wasn't born yesterday, you know. See you in a bit."

Chico had been an investigator for years before I'd started at the detective agency. He had taught me much of what I knew about the business, and he'd probably forgotten far more than I'd ever known.

The young Chinese man came over with a menu in a red padded folder, which he placed on the table.

"Can I get you something to drink?" he asked.

"Just some tap water, thank you. And I'm afraid I won't be eating after all. I'm just waiting now for a friend to come and collect me."

The young man wasn't particularly pleased.

"You'll have to pay a cover charge," he said. "For the water and the use of our facilities."

"OK," I said. "If it helps feed that dog of yours. I presume it has a purpose?"

"It's a guard dog," he said. "We let it loose in the restaurant at night to deter thieves."

And "insurance" bagmen, I thought. Those who collect the protection monies.

"Do you have much trouble?" I asked.

"Who are you?" he demanded.

"A fellow sufferer. One who's fighting back."

"Don't look for help from me," he said.

"I'm a translator by training. I'm only running this place because my father and mother are now too frightened."

"Didn't they pay?" I asked.

"Why should they?" he said angrily. "They worked hard all their lives for their own benefit, not for someone else to come and demand half their profit for doing nothing."

Why should they, indeed, I thought. Except the alternative was to be frightened out of their own business.

"What happened?"

"Three men attacked my father in the alley out back and then ransacked the place, breaking everything. Two years ago now, but he has hardly set foot outside their flat since. And the restaurant used to be thriving, but now . . ." He spread his arms out. "Look at it. Not enough customers to pay the rates, let alone anyone else. We'll be gone soon."

Be pragmatic, that's what D.C.I. Watkinson had said.

The pub owners obviously held the same view and paid up.

Chico suddenly appeared in the restaurant's doorway.

"Please, would you give this to that man," I said to the young translator, handing him my car key and nodding in Chico's direction.

He did as I asked without questioning why I didn't do it myself.

"He said to call him in two minutes."

"Thanks," I said. "How much do I owe you for the cover charge?"

"Nothing," he said.

I called Chico.

"There's definitely someone waiting outside there, all right," he said. "I spotted him, standing in a doorway on the other side of the road. He was talking on his cell. He's probably calling up reinforcements, so I think it's high time to leave. Where's the bleedin' Range Rover?"

I did my best to describe where I'd left it while Chico told me the plan of escape.

"Push the lock and unlock buttons together on the key," I said. "The lights will flash."

"OK," he said. "I'll find it. I'll call you. And when I say go, run like merry hell."

I waited for what seemed like an age with my eyes firmly fixed on the door, hoping that Shane Duffy and his friends wouldn't come in before Chico made it back.

The phone vibrated in my hand.

"Yes?" I said.

"I'm stopped just down the road," Chico

said. "The reinforcements have arrived. There are three of them altogether. They've been standing across the road, talking in a huddle, but they've now moved, and I can't see them anymore. Get out the back and do it now. Turn right, if you can, and I'll find you."

I stood up from the booth and moved quickly towards the passage to the kitchen just as Shane Duffy and one of his mates came bursting through the front door, brushing the young Chinese man aside. They had baseball bats swinging in their hands, although I didn't think they were looking for a game.

I ran, pushing past two startled chefs and out through the kitchen door into the narrow alleyway behind the restaurant.

The third man was already there. I could see him clearly in the glow from the light on the wall next to the restaurant's back door. And he was also holding a baseball bat.

Bugger.

What had McCusker said when I'd complained to him about being beaten up by his goons in the racetrack parking lot?

Those boys hardly touched you. If they'd given you a proper beating, you'd not be able to walk. Kneecaps are notoriously difficult things to fix.

I feared I was in for a proper beating, and any minute now.

I had turned right, as Chico had asked, but that was only because there was just a solid wall to my left. The alley only went right, and it was blocked by the other man I'd encountered at Towcester, the one who had held my head in a stranglehold, the one who had told me into my ear to stop asking jockeys questions.

I could tell that he knew I'd recognized him. He smiled at me and swung his bat in a great circle around his head.

I walked briskly straight towards him, which seemed to unnerve him slightly, but I knew I had a fraction more chance against one man than retreating into the hands of the other two, who chose that moment to appear through the door some ten yards behind me.

I was like the meat caught in the middle of a baseball-bat sandwich.

And I was scared, very scared indeed.

23

I continued to advance towards the single man if only because it was the way to the end of the alley, and anything was better than the two-to-one odds behind me.

The whole thing seemed to be happening in slow motion.

As I neared him, the man swung his bat at my head, but I was easily able to sway out of its way. However, the two men behind me were closing in alarmingly quickly.

Two things then came to my rescue.

First, the Range Rover appeared across the end of the alleyway, and, second, the Rottweiler was let loose from the Fortune Cookie's back door.

Chico put his hand firmly on the horn, and the man in front of me was distracted, half turning to see what was causing all the noise behind him.

I took my chance, stepping swiftly forward and hitting the man hard on the side of the head with my left arm, my plastic-and-steel wonder, my ever-ready club. He went down in a heap, and I sprinted past him.

Chico had the rear passenger door wide open, and I leaped in, slamming it shut in the same movement, but Chico didn't drive off instantly. Instead, he sat watching the scene in the alley. And he was laughing.

I sat up and looked back.

The man I'd hit was still down on the ground, holding his head, while the other two were fighting off the angry Rottweiler, which was trying hard to bite chunks of flesh out of their legs.

In truth, it was funny, but I was still keen to move on.

"Come on," I said, "let's get going. That was far too close for comfort."

"Now what?" Chico said, driving away.

Now what indeed? I thought. My plan had only extended as far as coming to Manchester and waiting for some inspiration as to what to do next. And the plan hadn't included showing our hand and having the enemy know that we were in their neighborhood.

It had been dark at the end of the alley, but had they seen Chico well enough to identify him again? And had they noticed the make and color of the car? Were they, even now, searching the local streets for us?

Part of me wanted to get out of their patch immediately and go straight back home to Oxfordshire, to Marina and Saskia. But was that what McCusker would expect us to do?

"I think we should go and watch the action at McCusker's house," Chico said.

"What if those goons recognize the Range Rover?"

"It was dark, and they were otherwise engaged. Let's take the chance."

Chico started the car and drove the mile or so to McCusker's mock-Georgian mansion, where he parked in the middle of a line of other vehicles on the opposite side of the road about thirty yards from the wrought-iron security gates.

We sat in the dark for quite a time, watching nothing happen other than the sporadic passing of vehicles along the residential road.

"I'm going for a walk," Chico said, opening the door.

"Is that wise?" I asked.

"Probably not," he said with a huge grin. "But I'm bored just sittin' here."

He slipped away into the shadows while I swapped position from the backseat into the driver's, ready for a quick getaway.

Still nothing appeared to be happening. Were we wasting our time? I thought it was time to go, but I daren't call Chico. The last thing he'd want just now was his phone going off in his pocket.

I squinted through the windshield towards the house and was horrified to see a shadowy figure go up and over the fence at the end farthest from the gates. It had to be Chico.

What on earth was he doing? Was he mad? Surely McCusker would have motion-sensor security lights or even cameras.

I opened the Range Rover window and listened out for a sounding alarm or a shout of discovery, ready to rev the engine and smash down the gates if necessary.

But the night remained quiet, the only sound in my ears being the rushing of my blood and the thump-thump of my own heart.

"Come on, Chico," I said to myself silently. "Get out now."

Suddenly, as I was staring at them, the gates began to open. I slithered down in the seat so I was not so visible, but no car came out. Rather, one of the vehicles coming down the road towards me, a large Toyota Land Cruiser, turned in through the opening. It was impossible to see who was inside due to a combination of poor street lighting and heavily tinted glass.

I watched as the gates closed behind the Toyota and feared for Chico. Was that Mc-Cusker coming home or was it his three goons returning to report a failure to beat up Sid Halley at the Fortune Cookie restaurant? Either way, I didn't think it was good news for my man, currently hiding behind enemy lines.

All I could do was sit and wait.

As the hands ticked around slowly on the Range Rover clock, I became more and more concerned. Five minutes passed, then ten.

What if Chico had been captured? Should I not launch some rescue mission? Or call the local police?

Another five minutes went by. It felt like twenty.

My phone suddenly emitted a beep to tell me that a text message had arrived. I grabbed at it.

The text was just two words long. *Stay put,* it said.

I stayed put, and the clock on the dash ticked around for another fifteen agonizing minutes.

The gates began to open again, and the Toyota drove out. As before, I was unable to see who, or how many, were inside.

Should I follow? But Chico had said to stay put, so I did.

I watched as the gates began to close automatically once more. When there was barely a foot of opening remaining, Chico popped out like a champagne cork and came running over to the Range Rover.

"Go," he said as he climbed in.

The engine was already running, and I wasted no time in engaging drive.

"Where to?" I asked, pulling out.

"Follow that Toyota," he said, panting with excitement and adrenaline. "God, I'm getting too old for this lark." He grinned at me. "Best fun I've had in a long time."

"What did you find out?"

"Not much," Chico said. "But keep an eye on that Toyota. McCusker's three heavies are in it. Wouldn't it be nice if they had a nasty car crash?"

"That's exactly what I was thinking."

I sped up, went through a traffic light that had turned red just a fraction beforehand and hoped that there wasn't a police car behind me.

We followed the Toyota out of Didsbury, south on the A34, then onto the M56. I hung back behind a couple of cars, and I was confident they couldn't spot us in the dark.

I wasn't sure when it dawned on me that they weren't on some local errand. Maybe it was as they turned south onto the M6 near Knutsford.

"Do you think they're on their way to Oxfordshire?" I asked Chico with concern.

"I fear they might be," he replied.

"Why fear?"

"Because I saw one of them load a jerry can into the trunk."

Oh God! I thought of what Angus Drummond had said about his parents' Dutch barn full of fresh hay going up in smoke. Was the same on the agenda for my house?

"What shall we do?" I asked Chico.

"We could call the police," he said. "Or the fire department. But it's still over a hundred miles to Banbury. Let's just wait a while and make sure we know where they're goin'."

I drove on behind them down the M6 past Stafford, past junction 14 and the place where Mandy, our beloved red setter, had been killed on the freeway. I had little doubt that the person who had let her go amongst the speeding traffic was in the vehicle two cars in front of me.

"So what else did you see?" I asked, finally.

"Well," he said, turning to me slightly in his seat, "I goes over the fence really easy and then waits for quite a while on the far side just in case there's an alarm I haven't spotted, one that I might have tripped, sending a silent message to the cops. But nothin' happens, and there are no sirens in the distance, so I goes forward towards the house and works my way round the back, round to the only window with lights and no curtains drawn."

He was almost panting with the excitement.

"It is a study, and it's definitely McCusker who's sittin' at the desk. You can't mistake those eyes — just like in that photo you've got, except he's older and fatter now than he was. I took a snap."

Chico held his camera so I could see the photo he'd taken of McCusker through the study window. "It's not that great because I couldn't risk getting too close."

"It's brilliant," I said, glancing down briefly at the image of my enemy.

"So there I am, happy as can be, sittin' behind a bush near the window, watchin' McCusker shoutin' at someone on the phone, when I hears the bleedin' front gate open. Bugger me, I thinks, there must be a silent alarm after all, and the cops have arrived. So I works my way farther down the garden, lookin' for another way out. But no one comes round the corner with a flashlight or anythin', so I gradually goes back towards the window."

The car in front pulled off at a junction leaving us right behind the Toyota. I eased back gradually, allowing a couple of other cars to overtake me.

"There are now four of them in the study, and McCusker ain't too pleased — I can tell from his body language even though I can't hear his rantin'. Then the four of them go out, and McCusker turns off the light. So I makes my way round the house until I can see the driveway. That's when I sees them takin' a jerry can from the garage and puttin' it in the car."

"Was there anything else that they put in there with it?" I asked.

"Like what?"

"Suitcases or holdalls?"

He shook his head. "Not that I saw."

So this excursion south was not planned to last very long, not long enough to warrant an overnight stay in a hotel.

The Toyota ahead suddenly indicated and left the freeway at the Hilton Park services just north of Birmingham. I eased back a little and followed them down the slip road.

369

They went through to the gas station at the far end, stopping next to one of the pumps. I slowed the Range Rover to a halt in the shadows, and we watched as they filled not only the Land Cruiser but also the jerry can.

Fortunately, I had filled up earlier that afternoon and still had plenty of miles in the tank, easily enough to get home.

Chico took pictures with his phone, but we were too far away for them to be much good.

"These guys are not very bright," Chico said. "The CCTV will capture them fillin' that can. If they use it to torch your place, the cops are bound to find the tapes."

It wasn't much of a comfort.

"Especially if we points them in the right direction."

The refueling stop complete, the Toyota set off again southwards on the M6, with us in fairly close pursuit.

"Right," I said to Chico. "It's less than an hour now to my house. What are we going to do?"

"Can't you phone your tame coppers and tell them what's goin' down?"

I'd also thought of that.

The only number I had for Norman Whitby was his office phone at the Greater

Manchester police headquarters, and the last thing I was going to do was to tell anyone in that organization that I was currently following Billy McCusker's hired goons down the M6. With a mole in the police camp, it might be tantamount to telling the man himself.

I wondered about Terry Glenn at the Met.

I'd just done a deal to say I'd ask him for no more favors, but this was an emergency. And anyway, did I care?

I tried the number of his cell, but all I got was voice mail. I left a message, but I didn't hold out much hope that he'd return the call, not tonight, maybe not ever.

That just left D.C.I. Watkinson and D.S. Lynch, and I wasn't sure how much they would help after all the hoo-ha about the indecent images even if I could contact them at eleven o'clock on a Sunday evening.

"Hello," said an annoying telecom electronic voice when I tried their number. "No one can take your call at present. Please leave a message."

I did as asked and left a message, asking them to call back urgently, but it would likely not be listened to until the following morning, and, by then, it would probably be too late.

24

The Toyota turned off the M40 at the Banbury junction, by which time I was almost in panic mode.

I had called Charles and warned him, even though I was pretty sure that McCusker wouldn't have known his address, not unless Norman Whitby really was the mole in the Greater Manchester Police.

Chico and I had discussed running the Land Cruiser off the road, preferably head-on into a tree or a concrete bridge, but it was traveling at a steady seventy-five miles per hour, and neither of us felt very comfortable at the probability of causing deaths, not even when the individuals concerned were so unpleasant.

As the Toyota slowed down for the roundabout over the freeway, I was beginning to have second thoughts. Perhaps running them off the road would have been the best strategy, but now it was too late.

To my great surprise, the Toyota didn't turn right towards my house in the village of Nutwell but left onto Daventry Road.

"Oh my God!" I said. "It's not my place they're going to burn down. It's the Molsons' in Chipping Warden."

"Who?" asked Chico.

"Tony Molson," I said. "He rode Black Peppercorn to win at Uttoxeter this afternoon after he'd been categorically told by McCusker to lose. I reckon he's going to make an example of Tony to send a message to the others."

I thought back to what the owner of The Chequers Inn had said to me earlier about his friend who had tried to stand up to McCusker. *They torched his pub with him in it. Barricaded the doors so he couldn't get out.*

I feared for Tony and Margaret, and especially for the Molson boys, Jason and Simon. They were the innocent bystanders in this affair.

Four lives. Four deaths. Barricaded into their burning home. Was I now so squeamish about running the Toyota off the road?

But it was much too late. Chipping Warden was just five miles from the freeway junction, and we were halfway there already.

"Call the fire department," I said to Chico. "Tell them there's a fire at Rose Cottage, in Mill Lane, behind the church in Chipping Warden. Use my phone." I tossed it to him. "It's pay-as-you-go. Give a false name."

He did as I asked, giving his name to the operator as William McCusker, which I thought was quite entertaining under the circumstances.

I hung back from the Toyota, not wanting to spook the occupants, and they had already disappeared down Mill Lane behind the church when we pulled into the center of Chipping Warden.

I turned off the headlights and pulled into Hogg End, parking on the grass verge in front of a line of thatched cottages. Chico and I got out, being careful to close the doors quietly behind us.

"This way," I whispered.

There was just enough light from the meager village streetlights for us to negotiate our way silently through the churchyard.

"Where are the bloody fire department," I whispered.

"They'll be comin'," Chico replied. "Now, where's this house?"

"As far as I remember, it's just the other side of the church. It's a modern, red-brick box in a tiny garden."

We crept along the side of the church and

peered around the corner.

There was not much to see except darkness.

There were no lights on in Rose Cottage and not a sign of the Toyota Land Cruiser.

Had I been mistaken?

Had McCusker's chums, in fact, driven straight through the village of Chipping Warden and onwards towards Daventry?

In the far distance I could hear the faint sound of a siren. The fire department was on its way from Banbury. Would it be a wasted journey?

Chico grabbed my coat and pointed.

A pair of dark figures, silhouetted against a more distant streetlight, could be seen at the edge of the property, bending down, about thirty yards in front of us.

The siren was getting louder.

Come on, I thought. Come on, hurry up.

The figures disappeared rapidly into the shadows, and there was no way of telling if they'd come behind the house or had gone around the front.

Suddenly, there was a great whoosh of flames emanating from just where we had seen the two men, and, to our left, we saw the Toyota Land Cruiser take off at speed from behind the house and towards the main road.

The flames seemed to run right around and encircle the whole property, leaping up to the roofline and lighting up the night sky like a giant bonfire. And the searing heat caused Chico and me to cower back around the corner of the church.

"That's gasoline," Chico said. "I can smell it. Effin' stupid. Only a bloody fool sets a fire with gasoline. It's far too explosive."

Maybe, I thought, but it made for a spectacular sight.

"Stay or go?" Chico asked.

I didn't really want to go without knowing if the Molson family would be all right, but, equally, I didn't really want to get tangled up in another police investigation, being accused of setting fire to the place myself.

The cavalry arrived with great clamor and flashing of blue lights, the firefighters spilling out of the truck and running out hoses to the hydrants.

"Come on," Chico said, "nothing more to do here. Let's go and check your house."

"Good idea," I said.

We ran back through the churchyard to the Range Rover, dodging the gravestones.

"No lights," Chico said as I started the motor. "Too many witnesses." He pointed at a number of the local residents in dressing gowns and slippers who had emerged from their beds to see what was causing the noise. "We don't want one of them copyin' down our license plate as we drive away, now do we?"

There was plenty of light from the flames to see our way back to the main road, where I switched on the headlights and turned towards Banbury and Nutwell beyond. The thought that the occupants of the Toyota might be planning to use any remaining contents of the jerry can to do the same to my house encouraged my rather heavy-footed approach to the Range Rover's gas pedal.

I knowingly broke my bail conditions by going within two miles of Annabel Gaucin. In fact, I drove right past her house on the way to mine.

"Stop short," Chico instructed. "Let me have a quick look first."

I switched off the headlights and rolled to a halt about fifty yards up the hill from my front gate.

"It's down there," I said to Chico, "second house on the left. The one with gates to the side."

"Give me five minutes," he said, quietly opening the passenger door and drifting away into the night. Better, I thought, to leave him to it rather than to follow. He seemed to me to have night-vision eyes and a degree of stealth that I could only dream about.

I was still tempted to call the fire department again just in case. It had taken them ten minutes or so to get to the Molsons' after Chico's call, and, judging by the speed and ferocity of the flames, it was just as well that they'd had a nine-minute start over the actual fire.

I stepped out of the Range Rover and stood next to it, listening out for any unusual sounds. There were none, and, presently, Chico returned, walking along the road.

"There's no one here," he said.

I breathed a huge sigh of relief. "How about Aynsford?"

"Let's go check."

All was quiet at Charles's house with, unsurprisingly at one o'clock in the morning, no lights showing in the windows.

I pulled the Range Rover slowly into the driveway, turning off the engine and lights as soon as possible to reduce the chance of waking the occupants.

Was it really only fourteen hours since Chico and I had left here for Uttoxeter races? It felt more like a week.

I crunched gingerly across the gravel and tried the door. It was locked. So much for me trying to be as quiet as possible. I was about to ring the doorbell when I saw what looked like a ghostly apparition coming straight towards me.

Charles, in striped pajamas and dressing gown, was advancing through the glass porch with his shotgun raised at the ready.

"Charles," I shouted quickly, "it's me, Sid. And Chico."

"Are you alone?" he shouted back.

"Yes."

The shotgun wavered, and then my scary double-O view of the ends of the barrels disappeared as he lowered them towards the floor.

He unlocked the door, and he was shaking.

"Come and sit down," I said, taking the shotgun out of his hands.

"Yes," he said. "Sorry."

I broke open the gun and removed the cartridges, thankful that his trembling fingers hadn't pulled the trigger by mistake.

I should have called him before we arrived, but I'd been afraid of waking him. I should have known that, as a military man, he'd have been on sentry duty, standing guard over Marina, Saskia and his house. And sleeping on sentry duty had once been a capital offense.

We went through into his kitchen, and I laid the shotgun down on the table while I fetched Charles a glass of water.

"I've been so worried since you called," Charles said. "I didn't tell Marina because I didn't want her insisting we go to your place."

"Our house is fine," I said. "We checked."

I gave him a quick rundown on what had happened since our departure without actually mentioning the fire at the Molson household. For some reason, I thought it was better to leave out that information. Charles was jumpy enough.

"Do you think they've gone back to Manchester?" he asked.

"I hope so."

The phone rang in my pocket.

"Hello," I said, answering it warily.

"Is that William McCusker?" asked a crackly female voice.

"Who is this?" I asked back.

"A fire was reported by a William Mc-Cusker on this telephone," came the reply. "A fire in Chipping Warden."

I hung up and immediately switched it off.

Chico had been listening to the exchange.

"Take the SIM card out," he said.

I opened the back of the phone, removed the little rectangle and gave it to him. He took a pair of scissors from the worktop and cut through the SIM in three places.

"You'll have to get a new one tomorrow," Chico said. "This one's now history. We'll just have to hope they didn't trace the position of the phone before they called it."

"I doubt it. This phone's hardly cutting-edge when it comes to GPS."

"They can still do it by triangulation of the signal, not that there's much of that here."

"What's going on?" Charles asked, somewhat bemused. "What was that little thing anyway?"

"It's called a SIM card," I said. "It's what makes a cell phone work — gives it its number. We're just making the number redundant so McCusker can't call it."

He accepted the explanation without question and made his way rather unsteadily up the stairs to bed.

"Charles, are you all right?" I asked with concern as I watched him from the hall.

"Fine," he said. "Just tired. It's been a long day, and I'd forgotten how exhausting a six-year-old can be. I've been up and down these stairs at least a dozen times, searching for her, all day long." He shook his head.

Saskia and her games of sardines, I thought with a smile.

"Good night," I said.

He lifted a hand in reply and disappeared towards his bedroom, his movement evident by the creaking of the old landing floor-boards.

I, however, still had things to do, and I went through to Charles's study to use his computer to look for any news on the Molson fire.

I decided that living at Aynsford for any length of time would quickly drive me crazy. Either Charles's computer or the Internet connection, or both, were so slow that I almost had time to make myself a cup of tea between entering a web address and the page appearing on the screen.

But the slowness didn't change the fact that there was no news anywhere on the Net of a fire in Chipping Warden. It was probably too soon.

Short of trying the Molsons' number direct, which might have taken a bit of explaining if anyone actually answered at one-thirty a.m., I would have to wait until the morning.

"Do we need to mount a guard?" Chico

asked when I went back to give him the news of no news.

"What do you think?" I said.

"I think they would have been here by now if they were coming. I reckon we're safe."

"Me too," I said, yawning. "I'm off to bed."

"I'll stay up a while longer," he said, "just to be sure."

I left him in the kitchen, making himself a cup of strong coffee, while I went up the stairs to the guest room, grateful not to be spending the night with Chico in the Range Rover.

Dodging the creakiest bits of the floor so as to be as quiet as possible, I went along the landing to the bathroom to undress and also to ease my left forearm out of the prosthesis, grimacing at the pain that always accompanied the procedure. It was like taking off a tight-fitting shoe without undoing the laces first. At least the impact with the man's head in the alley didn't appear to have caused any damage to its interior workings, not that I really cared if it had. I firmly believed that my prosthesis's days were numbered. Soon I'd have a real, feeling hand that didn't need to be removed every night before I went to bed.

I slid in next to Marina, trying my best not to wake her, but she stirred and turned sleepily towards me, reaching out and cupping my manhood in her warm hands. It caused shudders to go down my legs.

"Mmm," she murmured, "that's nice."

Indeed it was, and we snuggled together. It wasn't long before I had aroused her to full awareness, and she had done more than the same for me.

With all our recent troubles, sex had been well down our agenda — in fact, it had been so far down that it had fallen off the bottom. Marina and I had argued regularly, and there had been a simmering, minor hostility between us ever since that first visit by Sir Richard Stewart.

Now all of that was forgotten as we rediscovered each other's bodies, giving and receiving pleasure in equal measure and bringing each other to a simultaneous, heart-thumping climax.

"Wow," I said. "That was good."

"It certainly was," Marina said. "And I needed it." She snuggled up close to me. "I wasn't expecting you back tonight."

"Would you have preferred it if I wasn't?"

"Don't be silly," she said with a laugh. "Of course not."

We lay together with our arms entwined,

drifting off into contented sleep.

I was awake in an instant as if a noise had disturbed me. It was still pitch-black, so I slowly turned over and touched the top of my bedside clock, lighting up the digital figures, which showed the time as 5:27.

I had been asleep for less than four hours.

I lay in the darkness, straining to hear any unfamiliar or unwelcome sound. There was nothing other than the gentle breathing of Marina next to me, and that was hardly unfamiliar or unwelcome.

Had I dreamed it?

I rolled out of bed, put on my dressing gown and padded as silently as I could across the landing and down the stairs in my bare feet. In spite of the early hour and the near-complete darkness outside, there was just enough light in the house for me to see my way, light from the alarm keypad near the front door, from the cordless phone charger on the hall table and from the digital-clock readout on the electric stove in the kitchen.

I looked down at Rosie, fast asleep in her bed in front of the AGA. I smiled. She was clearly not much use as a guard dog.

All seemed quiet as I peered through the kitchen window for a few moments, searching for any movement outside. There was none that I could see, so I relaxed and went back into the hall, where I was suddenly attacked.

I felt myself being pushed back and then thrown to the ground, landing on my back and hip with a breath-expelling thump onto Charles's antique Persian carpet.

I knew that throw. It was a basic judo move.

"Chico," I said urgently with what little air I could muster. "It's me, Sid, for God's sake."

"Well, why didn't you bleedin' say so?" came back his cockney twang from the darkness. "I reckons you was an intruder, like. You should be upstairs in your slumbers, mate."

"I thought I heard a noise," I said, rolling over and trying to get myself up.

"Here," Chico said, holding out a hand, "let me help."

"Thanks," I said, taking it. It must be a sign of getting old, I thought, that I needed help getting up from the floor. I put it down to only having one available hand to push with.

"Didn't you hear anything?" I asked, rubbing a fast-developing bruise on my right hip.

"Only me droppin' a bleedin' coffee cup," he said sheepishly, "when I nodded off."

"Oh," I said, "that's all right, then. Come on. Let's both go up to bed. No one's going to come now. And it'll be light soon."

"Yeah, I reckon you're right."

We went upstairs together, with him climbing on up to a second level, to the rooms in the eaves that had once been the domain of the domestic servants, while I went and again slid between the sheets with Marina.

This time, she remained sleeping, her rhythmic breathing untroubled by my nocturnal excursion. I smiled in the dark, doing my best to ignore my aching hip, and slowly drifted back to sleep.

25

There was absolutely nothing on the early-morning radio news about a fire in Chipping Warden — no report of the Molson family being burned to death and no account of any gasoline-fueled arson.

In one way, I was hugely relieved. I was sure it would have been the headline story if one of the country's top twenty or so steeplechase jockeys had met his end in such a manner.

I dressed and went down to the study to check once more on the computer and found only one minor reference on a local-news website. It reported that a fire engine had responded to an emergency call soon after midnight and had dealt with a minor blaze near the church at Chipping Warden. It gave no other details and no mention of it being set deliberately or, indeed, of any damage to property.

In fact, it was all rather strange. The fire

that Chico and I had seen could surely not be described as a minor blaze. When we had last seen them, the flames had been so fierce that I had feared for the lives of the occupants of Rose Cottage in spite of the presence of the firemen.

I called the Molsons' number using Charles's phone.

"Tony Molson," said the voice that answered.

"Tony, it's Sid, Sid Halley."

"I'm not talking to you," he said angrily. "Bloody mad, you are. Nearly got us burned alive, you did. I should never have won that race. Now, sod off and leave me alone."

"It was me that called the fire department," I said, hoping that by saying so I wasn't jumping straight into my own firestorm. "How do you think they got there so fast?"

"According to the cops, someone called William McCusker phoned them. I nearly jumped out of my skin when they told me that. They asked me if I knew anyone of that name, but, of course, I said I didn't."

"It wasn't him, it was me," I said again, although, actually, it had been Chico. "I gave them the name William McCusker in order to try and incriminate him."

"So you're telling me that you knew about

the fire before it started. That's what the senior fire officer told me. He reckoned that whoever called them out must have been the person who'd started it. Otherwise, how would they have known?" There was another pause. "Did you start it, Sid?"

"No, of course I didn't," I said. "Billy McCusker's men started it, as you must know. But what I don't understand is how your house wasn't destroyed, the flames looked so intense."

"So you were here last night?" he asked with accusation.

"Yes," I said, "I was. I followed three of McCusker's men all the way from Manchester to Chipping Warden. And I watched them fill a can full of gas at one of the freeway services on the way. When I realized what they were going to do, I immediately called 999 and, yes, it was before the fire started, but not by more than five or ten minutes. And a good job too or you'd all be toast this morning."

"It was a ring of fire — a wall of flames," Tony said, "but set back, away from the house. The fire officer said he's seen nothing like it before. Meant to scare me, I suppose, rather than kill me. And it's bloody worked too, I can tell you. Margaret is in a real state."

I could believe it. So would I have been.

"Where in Manchester does Margaret's sister live?" I asked.

"Eh?"

"Margaret told me that her sister lives in Manchester. Which part?"

"Somewhere called Didsbury. South of the city center. Why?"

"No reason."

I doubted that Margaret's sister had given McCusker the information about the Molson twins on purpose. It was probably just a good story to tell at some local social gathering when she'd had a few too many glasses of wine. But Billy McCusker had known all too well how to exploit the knowledge for his own ends.

"Are you going to the police about us?" Tony asked.

"Do you want me to?"

There was a lengthy pause.

"No," he said, sounding like he was almost in tears. "What I really want is for you all to go away and leave me in peace."

"Retire, then," I said. "Quit as a jockey. Do it now. Today. Then McCusker will have no further use for you. And, even if the BHA did take away your jockey's license, it wouldn't matter because you'd not be race-riding anymore."

"But I don't want to retire yet," he said pitifully. "I reckon I've got a few more seasons left in me."

"Then McCusker isn't going to go away. Not unless you help me do something about him."

"Like what?" he said dryly. "You've seen what the man's like. I'm telling you, if he tells me to lose a race again, I'll bloody lose it. Next time it won't be just a scare, he'll burn the house down with us inside it."

I couldn't argue with him.

I believed it too. In fact, I was quite surprised he hadn't done it this time.

Chico was already in the kitchen when I went through to make myself some coffee.

"Don't you ever sleep?" I asked.

"It's nine o'clock. I should be at work."

"Won't the juvenile delinquents miss you?"

"Nah, they won't even notice. Good old Scottish granny." He grinned at me. "I'm off all week, thanks to her."

"Well, I hope you get to sleep more than you did last night. And keep your hands off me from now on, my hip's really sore this morning."

I rubbed it.

"You shouldn't wander round the place in

bare feet, then. You gave me quite a fright, driftin' about the place like a bleedin' ghost."

"Not as much of a fright as you gave me," I assured him.

He laughed. "I'm off for a run round the village. You don't need me for a bit, do you?"

"No, that's fine," I said. "We'll decide what to do next when you get back."

"Right," he said. "I'll be about forty minutes."

He departed just as Marina returned from having taken Saskia to school.

"Everything OK?" I asked her.

"So-so," she replied, screwing up her face. "Paula's still not speaking to me."

"Give her time," I said.

Rosie came over and snuggled up to Marina's leg, wagging her tail with enthusiasm. Marina tickled her behind her ears.

"When can we all go home? Charles is lovely, but he nearly drove me nuts yesterday. And I want my own things, my own bath and my own kitchen."

"I'll see what I can do."

I went back to the study and called D.C.I. Watkinson's number without much expectation that he'd answer. But I was wrong.

"Detective Chief Inspector Watkinson."

"Hello, Chief Inspector," I said with levity. "This is Sid Halley."

"I shouldn't be talking to you," he replied.

"As you've said before, but you are. Have you seen the report of a fire last night in Chipping Warden?"

"Not our patch," he said. "Chipping Warden is in Northamptonshire. We're Thames Valley."

"Billy McCusker doesn't take much notice of police force boundaries, and Chipping Warden is only just down the road."

"Maybe," he said, "but it's over the county boundary."

"Well, ask your Northamptonshire colleagues for the report. It will make for interesting reading. Tell them that Billy Mc-Cusker's heavies were the men with the gasoline."

"How do you know?" he asked.

"Because I followed them all the way from his house in Manchester, and I watched them fill the jerry can they used at the Hilton Park services on the M6. And I have the photos to prove it."

"My, you have been busy."

"What did you expect?" I asked. "Someone has to do it, and your lot don't seem to be doing much other than arresting the innocent. And that reminds me, who was it that made a complaint against me?"

"I can't tell you that."

"Can't or won't?" I said, echoing what Sir Richard Stewart had said to me all that time ago.

"Can't," the chief inspector replied. "Even if I knew who it was, and I don't, that sort of information is confidential to protect the identity of any children involved."

"How about protecting the identity of those incorrectly accused?" I said. "The law in this country seems stacked against me at the moment."

"You and me both," he said. "Have you any idea how hard it is to get a conviction these days?"

"Is that meant to make me feel better?" I said. "Because it doesn't. When can I move back into my own house?"

"What do you mean?"

"My bail conditions are that I cannot knowingly go within two miles of Annabel Gaucin, but my house is only a mile from hers. And it's not as if there's anything I could do to her at one-mile distance that I couldn't do at two."

"So where are you now?"

"At my ex-father-in-law's place. It's three miles from the Gaucin household."

"Didn't you mention that when you were released?"

"Yes," I said, "but the custody sergeant, in his own inimitable way, said it was tough luck, and I'd have to find somewhere else to live. He didn't seem to like me very much. Kept calling me scum."

"Custody sergeants can be like that," he said. "I'll have a word with Superintendent Ingram to see if we can amend the conditions."

"Thank you."

"Anything else?" he asked, clearly indicating that our conversation was over.

"Yes," I said. "Find out about that fire."

But what good would that do? If they could convict McCusker's men of setting it, which I doubted, they'd hardly be sent down for a decent stretch, if at all. No one was killed or injured, and there was no substantial damage to property.

And even if McCusker himself was convicted of conspiracy to commit arson, he'd get nothing more than a slap on the wrist. And stepping forward as a witness for the prosecution was hardly likely to endear me to him.

I had to find a bigger battle to win, one that would end the war.

The telephone records arrived in the mail

from Terry Glenn at the Metropolitan Police.

There was also a brief note from Terry, stating that the cell number I'd given him was registered to a pay-as-you-go SIM card, and even though he was able to send me the calls list, there was no official record linking any particular individual to the number.

The records showed that someone, presumably McCusker, had used that cell phone quite extensively, with several dozen outgoing calls listed over the past six months. Sadly, they didn't show details of his incoming ones.

If he used this number for incoming calls as well, as he had done for the information tips from Robert Price, then the outgoing calls list might not give me the full roll of the jockeys he had corrupted as I had hoped.

I scanned through the numbers, looking for any that I recognized, but none appeared familiar. Sadly, I didn't have my own extensive contacts list close at hand to compare them with. I'd have to wait for the police to return my cell phone or computer in order to do that.

I glanced through McCusker's home-phone list. Again there were dozens of calls, but, as before, there was no number that shouted out to me in recognition. I thought it unlikely that he would carry on any suspicious business on his home number anyway because it would surely be far too easy to trace.

Unfortunately, McCusker was no mug, and I was confident that he'd have used the untraceable pay-as-you-go phone for his nefarious goings-on, probably rerouting calls through various SIM cards just as he'd done when he'd called me.

And that reminded me, I needed to get a new SIM card from the telephone shop in Banbury to replace the one cut up the previous night.

I stuffed the number lists into my pocket and went looking for Chico.

"Good run?" I asked, finding him in the kitchen.

"Yeah," he said. "Nice change to have fresh air to breathe rather than the usual diesel fumes of North London. So what's on the agenda for today."

"Banbury for new SIM cards," I said. "I'll get a few, just in case."

"Then what?"

"I wish I knew," I said. "I feel so lost without my phone and computer."

"Have you picked up your voice mail messages using Charles's landline?"

"No," I said slowly. "Good point."

I went back to the study and Chico followed.

In all, there were fifteen, mostly old, messages on my voice mail, but, thankfully, not one from Queen Mary's Hospital, demanding my presence on their operating table.

Five of the messages were abusive, calling me a pervert or a pedophile. Charming, I thought, and wondered what sort of person takes the trouble to call someone's phone to leave such a message.

Six other calls were from so-called friends or acquaintances who said they didn't believe a word of what was said in the papers or on the television, and they wanted to make sure that I knew that. But they also asked questions like *Is it true?* or *Is Saskia all right?* So maybe they did believe what they read or heard after all.

But it was the other four messages that were the most interesting.

The first was from our Irish friend, and I played it out on the speakerphone on Charles's desk for Chico to hear.

"Well, Mr. Halley, now you know what it feels like to be banged up in jail." The sound of his voice, even in a recording, sent shivers down my back. "Remember that, and, in future, do as I tell you."

The message had been left at half past six on Thursday evening, the same day that I'd been released on bail. He'd probably been watching the six o'clock news on the television.

"He sounds a bit like he looks," Chico said, "all brawn and no brain."

"Don't underestimate his intelligence," I said. "He's no fool or he would still be in jail for Darren Paisley's murder."

"Who's Darren Paisley?" Chico asked.

"Someone McCusker murdered in Belfast in the nineties. Nailed him to a floor and left him to die of thirst."

"How delightful," Chico said. "Remind me always to carry a pair of pliers."

One of the messages was from Peter Medicos, left on Sunday afternoon, again demanding that I tell him who I'd spoken to about Sir Richard Stewart's suspicions. "Are they jockeys?" Peter said in a rather pompous tone that implied he didn't think much of mere jockeys. "You must tell me for the good of racing so we can seek out the guilty parties and punish them."

I suppose I couldn't blame him for trying; after all, it was his job. I just didn't care much for his tone.

For the good of racing.

That's what Sir Richard had said to me at least twice, and now Peter Medicos was saying the same. It seemed to be a mantra at the BHA.

What actually would be for the good of racing?

Would the revelation that a dozen or more top jockeys had conspired to fix races be the best thing? Or would it be better if the whole saga remained secret and life went on as before with the betting public in happy ignorance of any corruption?

Only if it didn't happen again.

Only if there were no more races where the result was determined not by equine performance but by threats and fears, menaces and coercion, terror and intimidation.

Only if Billy McCusker was stopped once and for all.

One of the other two messages was also from him, left late the previous evening, and clearly after I had managed to evade his goons in the alley behind the Fortune Cookie restaurant.

"Now, you listen to me, Mr. Halley," he said furiously. "If you think that coming after me is wise, I suggest you think again. If I see or hear of you snooping round me ever again, your little girl will end up raped, murdered and fed to the pigs. Do you understand?" He was almost shouting with rage.

"Maybe he was leaving that message when I was watching him in the study," Chico said. "He was bloody angry then, I tell you."

Maybe he had been.

Would I have still followed the Toyota down the M6 if I'd known the content of the message beforehand? Would I have told D.C.I. Watkinson that McCusker's men had set the fire at the Molsons' house? Was anything worth putting Saskia in such danger? Pigs eating her! It didn't bear thinking about.

I thought about getting the police superintendent to listen to the message. Maybe he'd then believe me about Billy McCusker being behind everything.

But, there again, maybe he wouldn't.

The caller hadn't given his name, and he'd withheld his number. Sure, the message was a clear threat against Saskia, but how could I actually prove that McCusker had made it? He would deny it. And even if it could be proved with voice-recognition software, a minor conviction for threatening behavior would hardly get rid of him for long.

And the superintendent was probably still obsessed with that damn photograph of the girls in the bath.

Perhaps it was best not to stir that particular pot again.

But was doing nothing really a viable alternative? Never mind the good of racing, how about the good of my family? Could it survive intact if we lived continually in the shadow of an Irish terrorist? Was it not better to rid ourselves of this monster now? And permanently?

Maybe so, but not at any price.

I was not in the market for a Pyrrhic victory.

The final message on my voice mail was short and to the point and had been left only at ten o'clock that morning.

"Sid, it's Angus," said a male voice out of the speaker. "It's on again. This Friday at Aintree, in the two-mile handicap hurdle, after the Topham Trophy. Don't tell anyone I told you."

"Who's Angus?" Chico asked.

"Angus Drummond," I said, "one of the jockeys who's been intimidated into fixing races. McCusker burned down part of his parents' farm and threatened to burn the rest if he didn't play ball."

"And what's on again?"

"I presume it's another race in the series where McCusker has fixed the whole race, deciding the winner before the start, one on which he will bet heavily on the Tote. It would follow the pattern of the others. All of them have been late in the afternoon on a big-race day. The system needs a big betting crowd to make it worthwhile, and there are few bigger betting days than at Aintree on the day before the Grand National. The Liverpool locals put on their best clothes and flock to the course in their thousands, utilizing every available gaudy stretched limo in the northwest of England. They love to drink and gamble, in that order. It's a sight to see."

"I'll look forward to it," Chico said. "But what do we do before then?"

"Try and apply pressure," I said.

"To whom?"

"The jockeys."

26

I knew from experience that trying to speak with jockeys when they were at the races was not ideal. For a start, they were there working, and, often with multiple rides in the day, they didn't have the time to stand around and chat. Also, there was nowhere particularly private on a racetrack to talk about race fixing without others seeing or even hearing the conversation.

And I didn't fancy discussing such matters on the telephone.

Consequently, Chico and I decided to visit them at their homes in the evening, starting with Robert Price at seven p.m. on Monday.

"I think you'd better stay in the car," I said to Chico. "I'll call you in if I need you, but he might talk more freely if I'm on my own."

"Right you are, squire," Chico said. "I'll catch up on some winks." He reclined the seat and closed his eyes.

As before, Judy Hammond opened the door of their farm cottage, just outside the village of Lambourn, but she wasn't as welcoming as on my last visit.

"Oh God," she said. "What do you want?"

"Is Robert here?" I asked.

"He's in the bath. He had a fall at Huntingdon this afternoon, and the horse kicked him."

I remembered such moments all too well. Fallen horses often kicked outwards as they tried to shift their bulk on the ground in order to regain their feet. If the jockey were unlucky enough to be within range, he'd get hit. It wasn't as if the horses were kicking him on purpose, but that didn't diminish the damage and the bruising.

"I need to speak with him," I said. "It's urgent."

"Everything's always bloody urgent. You'd better come in."

I stepped inside and waited in the tiny hallway while Judy went up the narrow wooden stairs to consult.

"He'll be down in a minute," Judy said. "Do you want a cup of tea?"

"No thanks," I said. It didn't seem right to accept their hospitality when I was about to apply the thumbscrews.

Robert came down the stairs in a thin blue

paisley dressing gown, wincing every time he put his left foot down.

"Bad?" I asked.

"Bloody nag kicked me. I've got a nice horseshoe-shaped bruise on the inside of my left thigh. But it could have been worse. At least it missed my bollocks."

"Nothing broken?"

"No, luckily not. It would have buggered my knee."

Yes, I thought, and kneecaps were notoriously difficult things to fix. Billy McCusker had told me so.

"Will you be stood down?" I asked.

"I hope not," he said. "I'll have to pass the doctor tomorrow at Exeter, but I should be all right in the morning. Nothing a few codeine and a good night's sleep won't fix. Come on, let's go outside."

We stepped out through the front door and stood on the path. It wasn't exactly a cold night, but it was a bit sharp for dressing gown and slippers. I reckoned he didn't want to be overheard by Judy.

"So what do you want?" he asked. "I don't suppose this is a social call."

"No," I said. "Are you at Aintree this week?"

"I certainly am. I'm riding Summer Nights in the National, for a start."

"And are you riding Maine Visit in the two-mile handicap hurdle on Friday?"

He didn't say anything.

"He'll start favorite, I reckon."

He still said nothing.

"Have you been told to lose?" I asked.

Again he said nothing.

"Come on, Robert," I said, "yes or no?"

"Yes," he said quietly.

"When were you told?"

"This morning, before I went to Huntingdon. I got a phone call."

"And are you going to lose?" I asked pointedly.

"What do you think?" he said. "While McCusker's got that video of me accepting that cash, I've not got a leg to stand on. Of course I'm going to bloody lose."

"How about if I threatened to tell the BHA Security Service that you had stopped the horse."

"You wouldn't."

"Try me."

"Then I'd fall off on Thursday and break something so I that I couldn't ride on Friday."

"Then you'd also miss the ride on Summer Nights, and rides on Grand National favorites don't come along too often. I assume you're not planning to fix that race as well."

"You bastard," he said with feeling.

"You could always explain away the video by saying that you'd sold something on the Internet and you were simply receiving the cash for it."

"Don't be bloody stupid," Robert said. "Don't you think I've thought of that? Mc-Cusker would simply produce some fall guy who'd happily get warned off by saying it was him in the video giving me money for information or for stopping one. There's no need for *beyond reasonable doubt* at the BHA, you know, they convict on the balance of probability."

He was right, and we both knew it.

"So will you tell them?" he asked. There was a degree of pleading in his voice.

"That depends," I said. "Would you try to win if all the others were trying to win as well?"

"You're living in cloud-cuckoo-land if you think you can get the other jocks to agree to that. If they're anything like me, they'll be absolutely bloody terrified of winning because of the consequences."

"But the consequences of losing are hardly slight either. The BHA would take away your licenses, and then you'd all lose your livelihoods."

"Maybe," he said, "but McCusker can take more than your license and your livelihood. He can take your life as well."

Didn't I know it?

"Any luck?" Chico asked as I got back into the Range Rover.

"Not really," I said. "Everyone is so frightened."

"Perhaps we should be too," he said with a wan smile. "Where to now?"

"David Potter's place in Upper Lambourn."

"Hello, Sid," said David with resignation. "I sort of knew I hadn't seen the last of you."

"David, this is Chico," I said. "He works for me. Can we come in?"

"It's not very tidy."

"I'm sure you can find us a couple of clean cups for some coffee."

He gave me a look that had a touch of panic about it. "I'll try."

Not very tidy was a major understatement. It was only two and a half weeks since I'd last been in David's kitchen, but the transformation was dramatic. Whereas, then, the place had been spotless, it was now a mess — a true humdinger of a mess. Every inch of flat surface was stacked high with un-washed crockery, half-eaten takeaways and empty cans of beer.

"Joyce left me," David said by way of explanation, "just after you were here last time."

I remembered his wife fussing around us cleaning everything in sight. I looked at the piles of dirty dishes and decomposing food. I reckoned that David hadn't felt the urge to clean anything since her departure.

"I'm sorry," I said.

"Yeah," he mused, "so am I, really. We argued about money. It is always about money. I spend too much — always have — and more than I'm earning these days. Joyce reckons I'd be better off on welfare than spending my days at the tracks, hoping to pick up spare rides. She's probably right, but I can't give it up, can I? It's like a drug. I only feel alive when I'm riding in races."

I knew how he felt. For me, it had been exactly the same, but retirement had been forced onto *me*.

"How old are you now, David?"

"Thirty-seven."

"You'll have to give it up soon. And all this junk food can't be doing much for your riding weight. To say nothing of the beer."

He stood looking at the chaos. "Perhaps

411

you're right."

"Are you going to Aintree this week?" Chico asked, clearly bored with David's domestic arrangements.

"I sure am," David replied with enthusiasm. "I never miss the National meeting. And I've got seven rides already booked — that's if they all run. It's bonanza time." He smiled broadly and rubbed his hands together.

"Is one of those rides in the two-mile handicap hurdle on Friday, after the Topham Chase?" I asked.

David's smile instantly disappeared. He said nothing.

"Is it, David?" I pressed.

"Maybe."

"Which horse?"

He shook his head and said nothing.

"And have you been told by the Irishman to lose."

Again nothing.

"Would you like me to ask my friend Chico here to twist your arm a little?" I smiled. "Just enough so your shoulder dislocates?" I tried to put as much menace into my voice as I could muster.

"I'm not afraid of you, Sid Halley," David said brazenly. "I've known you for too long, and I know what you're like. You won't hurt me. But the Irishman would." He paused and took a couple of deep breaths to calm himself. "I now wish I'd never told you anything."

"How is your mother?" I asked.

"She's fine," he said. "And I intend that she should stay that way."

"So you will lose the race on purpose?"

He looked me straight in the eyes and then he nodded slightly. "Unless I'm told I'm riding the one that has to win."

"When are you told that?" I asked.

"The day before," he said.

"And you always do as you're told?"

"Yup," he said with a sigh. "For my old mum's sake."

I could see that there was nothing I could say or do to convince him otherwise. As he had said, he knew what I was like.

"I think we'd better go," I said.

"Don't you want that coffee?"

I looked again at the mess, and the green-and-yellow mold that was beginning to grow on what looked to me like the remains of an onion bhaji.

"No thanks, David," I said. "We're fine. And I hope Joyce comes back soon."

"Yeah," he replied with a sigh, "so do I."

"Who next?" said Chico when we were back

413

in the car.

"I had thought of paying Tony Molson another visit," I said, "but I doubt that he'll speak to me."

"Do we need to persuade him?"

"I honestly think we'll be wasting our time. He as good as told me he'd do whatever McCusker wants. No, let's go home. From what Angus Drummond said in that voice mail message, and after our encounters with David Potter and Robert Price, I think it's safe to say that the betting coup is definitely on for Friday. We can look up the entries for the race on the *Racing Post* website, but we'll have to wait for the twenty-four-hour declarations on Thursday to find out the actual runners and their jockeys. Then we'll decide."

"So what do we do until then?" Chico asked.

"Keep safe."

"We could always go on another trip up north," Chico said with excitement. "What d'yer say?"

"What for?"

"What for! To keep watch on McCusker, of course. But, this time, I reckon we should steer clear of the local pubs. But anythin's better than sittin' round, twiddlin' our bleedin' thumbs, all week at the Admiral's house. For a start, we could go and check out that Liverpool bookie — you know, the one from Uttoxeter."

"Barry Montagu," I said.

"That's the one. Provided he got out of Uttoxeter alive with all those punters after him." He laughed at the memory.

"OK. How about we go up on Wednesday, ready for the start of the three-day Aintree meeting on Thursday? And we'll spend some time Wednesday afternoon checking out Barry Montagu."

"Right you are," Chico said cheerfully.

"Although God knows where we'll stay," I said. "I reckon everywhere will be fully booked by now."

"You'll manage somethin'," Chico said confidently. "You're Sid Halley."

"I cannot spend another day here," Marina said to me when we arrived back just after midnight. She was standing in our bedroom in her dressing gown with her hands on her hips, and she was annoyed. "If it's not Charles, it's Mrs. Cross."

"What about them?" I asked gently, trying to take the heat out of the situation.

"They're both driving me completely crazy. Charles is a complete nuisance who hovers round the place, watching everything

I do, as if he'd never seen a woman work before, and Mrs. Cross won't stop talking to me. I've been trying to edit a paper, but there's no Wi-Fi here, so every time I need to use the Internet I have to borrow the cable in Charles's study, and I'm obviously completely in his way, although he doesn't actually *do* anything. And the Internet is so slow, even worse than at home. It took me half an hour just to download a paper on the post-translational modification statistics of glycoproteins. I ask you!"

It was no good asking me, I thought. It would take me more than half an hour just to spell it.

"Do you want me to have a word with Charles?" I asked.

"No," she said angrily. "I want to go home."

"So do I, but what can I do? I've asked the police to vary their bail conditions, but, until they do, I can't go home. You can, if you want, but I can't. It's up to you. Perhaps you could go home to work during the day."

"Yes," she said. "I'll do that tomorrow. Even the bloody cell phones don't work here properly."

I made the mistake of trying to explain. "The signal is very intermittent because we're on the wrong side of the hill. You have to be patient. They generally work, in the end."

She gave me an angry stare that I took to mean that her patience was completely exhausted and that now was past the time for excuses.

She was clearly not a happy bunny, and her body language towards me was hostile, almost aggressive.

Sadly, therefore, there was no repeat of the previous night's sexual delights. Instead, Marina climbed into bed, turned her back towards me and went straight to sleep.

Why did I think it was unfair for me to shoulder the blame for Charles and his broadband failures?

I found Chico asleep in a kitchen armchair when I went downstairs to make tea at seven o'clock on Tuesday morning. He was fully dressed.

"Forget to go to bed?" I asked as he stirred, woken by the sound of me getting mugs out of the cupboard in spite of my best effort to keep quiet.

"Someone has to stand watch when you're upstairs screwin' your missus," he said with a mischievous laugh. Little did he know.

"Want some tea?" I asked.

"Ta." He stood up and stretched. "Come

on, Rosie, time you and I went outside." Rosie just opened an eye and looked at him without moving. Her bed in front of the AGA was clearly much too comfortable. "Bloody useless guard dog."

I gave him his tea and took a steaming mug up to Marina.

"Feeling any better this morning?" I asked, sitting on the edge of the bed.

"Yeah. Sorry about that. Must be the wrong time of the month. I'm always a bit cross just before my period starts."

I sighed. She wasn't pregnant this time, then. But I hadn't really expected her to be, not with all the stress of the past three weeks and the consequent lack of sexual activity. Ah well, we'd just have go on trying again next month, as we had done each month for the past six years.

I took my tea down to the study and switched on Charles's computer. I had tried to explain to him that it didn't need to be switched off every night, but he knew better.

"It surely needs to rest," he'd said. "All that thinking must make it tired."

I'd thought he was joking, but he wasn't.

In his day, technology meant an Aldis lamp flashing Morse code between warships or shortwave radio communication using a

Marconi transmitter. And even though he had owned a computer for many years, its finer points had mostly passed him by. He was always asking me what my e-mail *number* was, as if it was a telephone system, which would then change if I moved from one location to another.

Eventually, Charles's computer finished its booting-up procedure, and I was able to look at the card for Friday's two-mile handicap hurdle at Aintree on the *Racing Post* website.

There were twenty-eight horses entered for the race, although over half of those would almost certainly not be declared to run. Most horses were entered for more than one race within a few days, and some for two or more races on the same day at different racetracks. One horse of the twenty-eight, Transfer Fee, was entered in six different races, one on Thursday, three on Friday and two on Saturday, but he would run in only one of them at most.

Between now and the declaration-to-run deadline on Thursday morning, there would be frantic telephone calls between the trainers as each tried to find out which horses were actually going to run and in which races. They were all hoping to give their horses the best chance to win and would avoid a particular race if a highly rated rival was definitely going to be in it.

Of the twenty-eight entrants in the Aintree two-mile handicap hurdle on Friday, twenty-one were entered in other races within a day or two either side of it, leaving only seven that were entered for this race alone. But even that did not guarantee that any of the seven would actually run.

Ten of the twenty-eight had names of jockeys next to them, but everyone knew that at this stage they were speculative. Names would often be added by the jockeys' agents simply to advertise the fact that their jockeys would be at that racetrack on that day.

The actual rider for each horse had to be declared by one o'clock on the day before the race, ready to be printed overnight in the official race program and in the newspapers, but even that was subject to change in the event of illness or injury.

The final confirmation of who would ride each horse was made by the trainer at least forty-five minutes before the race was due to start, but there could still be a late change if the declared jockey was subsequently injured due to falling in an earlier race.

In truth, no one could be certain who would ride a particular horse until the jockey appeared from the Weighing Room wearing the owner's silks, and even then the rules did allow for a substitution to be made if the jockey was prevented from riding before coming under starter's orders.

All of this made it impossible for me to be sure which jockeys, or even how many, would actually be riding in the race at Aintree in three days' time.

The ten allocated jockeys included Robert Price on Maine Visit, but there were no horses yet with David Potter's or Angus Drummond's names next to them.

There was, however, one other jockey of interest listed.

Jimmy Guernsey was down to ride a horse called Staplegun.

27

"So who the hell is this Jimmy Guernsey anyway?" Chico asked as I went through the details with him.

"I believe he's McCusker's man in the jockeys' changing room. He's definitely involved somehow. He certainly knows Billy McCusker by name, and he knew in advance which horse was due to win at Sandown in one of the fixed races."

"So you think he knows which horse will win on Friday?"

"I'm sure he will by the time the race starts," I said, "even if he doesn't already."

"Then why don't we pay this Guernsey fellow a little visit and ask him, all gentle-like, for the info?"

"Just what I was thinking, but we need to be careful. I don't want Guernsey bleating to McCusker that we've been to see him asking questions."

"How are we going to stop him doing

that?" Chico asked.

"By making him more frightened of us than he is of McCusker."

"And how, pray, are we going to do that?"

"I'm working on it."

According to the *Directory of the Turf* website, Jimmy Guernsey lived in the village of Blewbury in South Oxfordshire, but even with the Range Rover's satnav it took Chico and me nearly half an hour to find his house, which was outside the village on Didcot Road some distance from where the destination was marked on the electronic map.

We drove past a few times, having a good look at the large, white-painted bungalow with its red-tiled roof. It was set back from the road behind a hedge that had just a hint of green from the first new shoots of the year.

There were two cars parked in the driveway, a silver Mercedes and a small red hatchback.

"What do you think?" Chico asked.

"I think there's somebody in."

"Full-frontal approach or stealth?"

"Full-frontal, I reckon, especially if there's more than one person in the house."

"Agreed," said Chico. "Although I might

hang round outside while you go in and do business."

"Oh, thanks," I said sarcastically. "Why is it always me who has to do the hard bit?"

"Because you're the boss," he said with a grin.

I drove halfway through the gate and stopped, blocking the two parked cars.

"Nice call," Chico said. "No one can get in neither."

We both climbed out, and I went and rang the front-door bell while Chico leaned nonchalantly on the Range Rover's hood.

Jimmy Guernsey opened the door and took in the scene.

"What the hell are you doing here?" he demanded angrily. "And move that bloody vehicle. It's blocking my gate."

"So it is," I said calmly, but making no effort towards moving it. "May I come in?"

"No."

"I think it would be best," I said.

"Oh, you do, do you? Well, I think it would be best if you get off my property. Right now, before I call the police."

"The police," I echoed. "That could be interesting."

For the first time, he was unsure. "Why would it be interesting?"

"You could explain to them why you

fraudulently fix horse races."

"I don't know what you're talking about," he said belligerently. But he was worried, I could hear it in his voice.

"I think you do," I said. "Now, do you want to let me in and talk about it or shall I go straight to the racing authorities and lay the evidence before them?"

For a moment I thought he was going to bluff it out and tell me to get lost, but he hesitated, and then opened the door wide for me to go in.

"Who's that?" he asked, nodding towards Chico.

"My assistant." I resisted the temptation to say that he was also my hired muscle.

I followed Jimmy into the house, through an open-plan living room to a study beyond, where he sat down on a chair behind his desk, offering me another to the side.

"Now, what's all this nonsense?" he asked more confidently.

"Are we alone?" I asked.

"Chrissie's outside with the horses." He waved a hand towards a couple of stables I could see through the study window.

"Staplegun," I said.

"What about him?" The worried timbre was back in his voice.

"Will he win on Friday at Aintree in the

two-mile handicap hurdle?"

He stared at me in a manner that I took to be total disbelief. His breathing had noticeably shallowed, and it had increased in frequency. He was scared.

"Come on, Jimmy," I said, "don't be shy. Will Staplegun win on Friday?"

He still said nothing.

"You're in trouble, young Mr. Guernsey, and make no mistake. I think they call it being stuck between a rock and a hard place. Billy McCusker on one side and the BHA and the law on the other. Grisly death or disqualification and ruin. Not a happy choice."

His shoulders drooped a little.

"Nice house," I said, looking around me. "A few stables and a couple of acres, is it? Or maybe more?"

No answer.

"Got a mortgage, have you? Not easy to keep up the payments without a job, I'm sure. And no jockey's license would mean no job. Maybe a prison sentence too. Do you think you'd ever work in racing again?"

Still nothing.

"How about Chrissie? Does she know about all those races?"

Jimmy put his hands up to his head, one on either side, and squeezed his temples as if he was stopping his head from exploding.

I went on. "Not just Red Rosette at Sandown and Martian Man at Newbury, but Fallacy Boy at Ascot, and the others as well. I know about them all. I have statements from the other jockeys, and they all say the same thing — Jimmy knew, Jimmy is the enforcer, Jimmy is McCusker's man in the changing room."

It wasn't all true. I didn't have the statements, and no one had mentioned Jimmy. But there was enough truth for him to believe it all.

"And now Staplegun," I said. "Will he win on Friday?"

Jimmy slowly shook his head. "Probably not."

"So what will win?" I asked.

"I don't know."

I looked at him and wondered if he was telling me the truth.

"When will you know?"

"On Thursday, after the declarations close."

"How do you find out?"

"I receive a call."

"From McCusker?"

He nodded. "He just says the name of the horse that must win."

Now I knew for certain that Jimmy Guernsey was *in* on everything.

"So what do I do?" he said forlornly, holding his head in his hands with his elbows resting on the desk. "I'm finished, one way or the other."

"Not necessarily," I said.

His head came up a fraction.

"There might be a way out."

"How?" He sounded as if he didn't believe it.

"First, you tell me why."

He sighed — a great big sigh that had all the weight of his troubles behind it.

"Money, I suppose," he said. "It started about three years ago. I was riding one at Chepstow, and he calls me and offers me a grand in cash to lose. A grand! That was five times what I'd get if I won the damn thing. And no tax too."

"So did you agree?" I asked.

"No, I didn't. I told him to get lost. I rode in the race and finished second — never had a chance to win it, but I was trying. Next thing I know, a thousand in cash arrives in the mail just like that."

"No note?"

"No, nothing. Just twenty nice, new, crisp fifties in a padded envelope, wrapped inside cooking foil."

"So what happens next?" I asked.

"He calls me again and offers me another grand to lose at Newbury."

"And you agreed?"

"What do you think?" he said, almost with a smile. "Money for old rope, especially when I didn't think I had a chance anyway."

"And the money arrived?"

"Sure did, just as before. But then it got serious. He rang again and told me to lose on Wine Society in the Champion Hurdle. He was the favorite, and . . ." He tailed off.

"So?" I said encouragingly.

"I don't often get rides as good as that. Winning the Champion Hurdle is what all jockeys dream of."

I knew. It was one of the few major races I'd never won and I still regretted it.

"So what did you do?" I asked.

"I told him that it was not possible for me to lose on Wine Society. He was the best horse in the race by a streak. But he said he'd recorded our conversation the last time and he'd give the recording to the racing authorities if I won."

"So you lost?"

"Yes. Blundered through the downhill hurdle simply by not asking old Society to jump, then I took a pull, then we failed to make up the ground on the hill to the finish. Easy, really."

"And he paid you?"

"Yeah. Two grand that time. But it cost me the ride on the best horse I've ever sat on. I was jocked off for the Aintree Hurdle the following month."

"So was it worth it?"

"Not really," he said. "I'd have loved to win the Champion Hurdle, but there's still time."

I raised my eyebrows at him. There would be no time if I took this to the BHA, and he knew it.

"So how come you became McCusker's man in the changing rooms?"

"Because he went on paying me," Jimmy said. "I went on stopping a few for him, one a month or so, but then he had the idea to fix the whole race. He laughed about it. Thought it was a great joke. I told him he was bloody crazy and that I didn't want to go on, but he wouldn't take no for an answer. Easy, he said it would be, and everyone has his price, either money or threats. And it was easy — bloody easy — with my help."

Jimmy smiled at me.

I felt sure that he was actually proud of his achievement.

"So you fix every other horse in the race except the one you want to win?"

"Not quite every horse," he said. "It's not necessary. The top six or seven in the betting is usually enough."

"And that's what you're planning to do again on Friday?"

He nodded. "Assuming the right horses run."

"Right," I said. "If you want to get out of this mess with your jockey's license intact, then you'll have to do exactly as I tell you."

"How do I know you won't go to the authorities anyway?"

"You don't, but what choice have you got? And if you let on to McCusker that I've been here or what I want you to do, then all bets are off. And, what's more, I'll tell him it was your idea in the first place. Do you understand? No contact with McCusker whatsoever. No calls, no texts, nothing other than his call to you on Thursday with the selected winner."

He nodded. "But what if he calls me otherwise?"

"Tell him everything is fine."

He nodded again.

Then I explained to him exactly what he was going to do.

He didn't like it.

"You're crazy," he said. "He'll bloody kill you, and me."

Not if I bloody kill him first, I thought.

"So do we have a deal?" I asked.

"Yeah, I suppose so. As you said, I haven't got much choice. But why are you doing all this?"

"Because I want to be rid of McCusker once and for all, and this is the only way I know of getting him out into the open, of provoking him into trying something stupid."

"You could get hurt. Or worse."

"I'm well aware of that."

"So why don't you just take what you have to the BHA and let them deal with him?"

It was a good question, but I believed that McCusker would then come after me anyway. And perhaps I wanted to be more in control of the timing.

Or maybe it was because I had some mad idea of preventing the exposure of such widespread corruption within the Sport of Kings, something that would potentially damage, beyond repair, its reputation amongst the betting public.

Maybe I was doing it for the good of racing.

"Everything OK?" Chico asked as I climbed back into the Range Rover.

"I hope so," I said and told him in outline

what I'd arranged to happen.

"You are bloody mad," Chico said with enthusiasm. "But I love it."

28

Chico and I left for Liverpool on Wednesday, late morning. This time, we did take overnight bags as I had found us a couple of rooms in the Park Hotel quite close to the track, thanks to a late cancellation and inflated prices.

Tuesday evening at Charles's house had not exactly been a barrel of laughs.

Marina had spent the day at our home working, but she hadn't felt very comfortable there on her own, not with a bunch of pyromaniacs still on the loose, to say nothing of McCusker himself.

For some reason, Saskia had not had a good day at school, and she was grumpy too, especially when we all wouldn't spend the whole evening playing sardines. There are only so many places to hide, even in a big house, and we had surely exhausted them all by now.

Charles was also on edge, partly, I discovered, for having found Chico asleep in the kitchen the previous morning.

"I can't understand why he won't sleep in the bed Mrs. Cross has made up for him in the old butler's room," he'd complained to me.

"He's standing watch," I'd said. But far from that reassuring Charles, it had made him even more nervous and jumpy.

We had clearly all outstayed our welcome, but there was little I could do.

"We'll be gone just as soon as I can get us out," I'd said to him, but it had done little to improve his humor.

Even Mrs. Cross was living up to her name. She'd been waiting for me as Chico and I had arrived back from seeing Jimmy Guernsey. "That wretched dog of yours stole my best beef. I left it on the kitchen table for only a second. And it was for the Admiral's supper."

The wretched dog in question wagged her tail and seemed to be the only member of the household who was content. Who wouldn't be, with filet steak in their tummy?

"Only a few more days, I promise," I'd said to Marina. "I have a plan that should bring everything to a conclusion this week."

"Is it dangerous?" she'd asked.

"No more dangerous than riding a bad

jumper in the Grand National."

It hadn't cheered her much, and with good reason — both could get you killed.

Chico drove while I used a replacement SIM card to make some calls. I removed McCusker's cell telephone records from my pocket and starting working through the list of numbers, all of which were for other cell phones beginning with 07.

I wasn't sure what I should say to anyone who answered. It was a bit difficult to ask directly to whom I was speaking, so I decided simply to ask for Geoff. My plan was that when someone said that he wasn't Geoff and I must have the wrong number, I would read out the correct number and then ask who he was.

However, it didn't quite work out like that.

The first three numbers on the list clearly no longer existed, as I simply heard a computer-generated voice saying that the number was not recognized. Perhaps they were pay-as-you-go SIM cards that had since been thrown away or cut up, as Chico had done to mine.

I put a pencil line through those.

The next one was at least a current, active number, as dialing it produced a ringing tone. But then another computer-generated voice told me that the person I was trying to call was unavailable, please try later.

The sixth number I called connected me to a real live person, but whoever it was hung up as soon as I asked for Geoff. I didn't even know if it had been a man or a woman as they had said nothing, not even when answering.

The same occurred with numbers seven, eight and nine. Only one real voice answered in my first fifteen calls, and whoever it was refused to say who he was after my wrong-number trick.

I got bored and put my phone down. I'd try again later.

"Are you OK driving?" I asked Chico as we went around the north of Birmingham on the freeway.

"I'm fine," he said. "Why?"

"I thought you might be tired, that's all, with all these sleepless nights you've been having."

"It worries me that there'll be no one there keeping watch tonight."

Yes, I thought, that was worrying me a bit too. I'd even considered asking Marina if she and Saskia would like to come with us, but that might have been even more danger-ous, to say nothing of missing three days of school. If things were different, they could have gone to stay with Tim and Paula Gaucin, but, under the present circumstances, that might be awkward.

I'd had a quiet word with Charles about ensuring everything was locked up, and he'd given me a strange, sideways glance. The shotgun, I'd thought. There was no way I would stop him having it loaded and ready, short of taking it away from him altogether, and I had no intention of doing that. I just hoped he wouldn't shoot someone by mistake.

Marina also hadn't been very happy when we'd left Aynsford. She had hugged me tightly and told me to be careful in much the same way that Jenny, my first wife, had done early on in our marriage whenever I went off to the races to ride.

But if I'd been too careful when I was riding, I wouldn't have been such a good jockey. Winning was the important thing, and sometimes risks had to be taken in order to win. Kicking hard and asking a horse to stand back and take off early at a fence could gain lengths in the air over a rival, whereas taking ahold and putting in an extra stride may have been safer but was much slower.

Safety and winning didn't often go together.

Not that I was advocating taking undue risks.

Reckless jockeys might occasionally win races that no one else would have, but they also spent long periods laid up with injuries that saner riders might avoid.

Now, in my battle with McCusker, I had to make an assessment of the risks and behave accordingly. If I was not prepared to get hurt, then I should have stayed in bed. I had to do just enough to provoke him into showing himself without driving him to completely irrational behavior that I'd be unable to predict.

I had no intention of being nailed to a floor to die of thirst.

Chico and I checked into our rooms at the Park Hotel and then went in search of Barry Montagu, bookmaker of Liverpool, he who had been offering higher than prudent prices on Black Peppercorn at Uttoxeter the previous Sunday.

According to the Internet, Barry Montagu, as well as manning his pitch at various northern racetracks, also had a single betting shop in the Liverpool district of Bootle, close by the Liverpool docks.

As we drove along Stanley Road, past the Strand Shopping Centre, it seemed impossible to believe that this urban landscape was once a holiday bathing resort for the wealthy Liverpool merchants of the early nineteenth century, eager to immerse themselves into the healing waters of the River Mersey. That was before the coming of the trains, the building of the docks and the industrialization of the whole region.

Bootle had flourished until the opening of a new container terminal just to the north in Seaforth had rendered most of the Bootle docks redundant, pushing up local unemployment and forcing the neighborhood into decline.

However, Barry Montagu's wasn't the only betting shop on Stanley Road. There was a whole range, including independents and all the national chains. To my eye, there appeared to be more betting shops than any other type. Clearly, a worsening of the area's economic fortunes hadn't deterred Bootle residents from their gambling.

We found a parking space around the corner from the shop.

"We'd better not be too long," Chico said, "or we'll find it up on bricks when we get back." He laughed at his little joke, a joke that once had had more than a ring of truth about it. "What are we lookin' for, exactly?"

"I'd like to know if Barry Montagu is a

front for McCusker or is part of the Honest Joe Bullen chain. The man you bet with at Uttoxeter clearly had insider knowledge that Black Peppercorn was due to lose the race, but, for all we know, that might have come from a different source."

Gone were the days when, like pubs, the holder of the gambling license had to be written above the main door, but it still remained a requirement of the law that the license be displayed in a prominent position within the premises.

Business was surprisingly brisk for three o'clock on a Wednesday afternoon, with seven hopeful punters standing around either watching the live video feeds from the horse and dog tracks or playing on the fixed-odds electronic casino machines in the corner.

Chico went unerringly to the counter and started to chat up the girl standing behind it while I drifted around the periphery looking at the racing pages of the newspapers that were pinned to the walls. Much was being made of the upcoming Aintree meeting just a couple of miles down the road, with posters offering a free ten-pound bet on the Grand National itself — provided, of course, you opened an account and made an initial bet of fifty pounds.

It was certainly a hard sell.

Perversely, there was one small, dog-eared poster from Gamblers Anonymous tucked away behind the entrance that gave advice and a telephone number to anyone who felt they were becoming addicted and needed help. It seemed to me to be like putting up a Vegetarian Society leaflet in an abattoir.

I was edging my way towards the framed license summary on the wall beneath the bank of television screens when Chico suddenly turned towards me and started for the door, nodding furiously for me to follow. I needed no second invitation.

Outside, we ran down the road and around the corner to the Range Rover that was, thankfully, still in possession of its full set of wheels and tires.

"What was all that about?" I asked as I drove away.

"I am chattin' to the bird, all happy-like — you know, tellin' her how nice her hair is and so on. Then I asks if she's lookin' forward to the Grand National meetin'. Yes, she says, very excited because she's goin' up to the track on Friday to help with the pitch as they're expectin' a bumper day.

"So I asks her why are they expectin' a bumper day, and she says she doesn't know, but that was what Mr. Wilson told her. So I asks her who is Mr. Wilson, and she says he's the boss, and she points towards the back office. I looks behind her at the mirror, but it's one of those mirrors with slots in it that you can only really see through one way. But the guy in the office must have been lookin' out 'cos he opens the door and tells her to stop talkin', and if I wants to make a bet, to make it and move away from the counter."

He stopped to draw breath.

"But why did we have to leave so suddenly?"

"Because there's another man in the office, wearin' a black suit. I sees him when the door was open, and I'm sure he's one of the men I clocked in McCusker's study last Sunday night, one of the three who'd tried to beat you up behind the Chinese restaurant."

"Did he recognize you?" I asked.

"No, I don't think so, he wasn't really lookin'. But he sure as hell would have recognized you, that's why I wanted you out of there, and pronto."

"Good thinking," I said. "We don't want to show our hand until Friday. But at least it's confirmed our suspicions that the name Barry Montagu is just another front for Billy McCusker and his cronies."

We went back to the hotel, and while Chico chatted up the girl behind the bar, I spent a frustrating hour calling more of the numbers on McCusker's phone record. For most, either there was no ringing tone with the number not recognized or nobody answered. Of the handful of live people at the other end, not one was prepared to tell me who he was, being very wary right from the start.

I sat down with a pen and paper and made a list of those numbers that McCusker had called more than once. After a while, the numbers appeared to blur together, and I was beginning to make mistakes from tiredness. However, by then there was a pattern emerging, with the same numbers appearing regularly together, just a few days ahead of each of the fixed races.

They must be the jockeys, I thought. But why won't they answer?

I searched for Robert Price's cell number, which I knew, but I couldn't find it anywhere on the list. So I called him.

"Hi, Robert, it's Sid."

"Oh." He sounded far from enthusiastic. "What do you want?"

"Sorry to call so late, but when you said on Monday that McCusker had called you to tell you to lose on Maine Visit, what

444

phone did he ring you on?"

"Why?"

"I'm just interested," I said.

There was a pause, and I could tell that he didn't want to tell me.

"Come on, Robert," I said, "which phone?"

He sighed. "He called me on his special phone. Same as always, these days."

"What special phone?" I asked.

"A cheap, old-fashioned phone that he gave me about a year ago. It's only for his calls. No one else has the number."

"What does he say when he calls you?"

"He just says the name of a horse that I've been engaged to ride."

"Nothing else?"

"No, just the name. That's how I know I have to stop it. He says the name twice and then hangs up."

No wonder I couldn't get anyone to talk to me.

"What's the phone's number?" I asked.

"I've got no idea."

"Doesn't it tell you on the phone?" I asked.

"No. I can't even access the menu. It's all password-protected, and I don't have the password."

There had to be some way of getting the

number.

"Are you at home?" I asked.

"Yes."

"Use the phone to call your home number and then dial 1471. That should give you the number."

There was a short pause until he came back on the line.

"No good," he said. "It tells me I've no credit. Incoming calls only."

Why had I imagined it would be so easy?

Thursday morning dawned bright and sunny, the perfect start to the Grand National meeting, when all eyes in the steeplechasing world would be turned towards Aintree. These three days, together with the four of the Cheltenham Festival in March, were the pinnacle of jump racing in Britain, culminating with the Grand National itself on Saturday afternoon.

Thursday may have been the first day of the meeting, with smaller crowds expected than on Friday and Saturday, but there was still quite a buzz of excitement at breakfast in the Park Hotel dining room, with eager punters, heads down, busily studying the form in their copies of the *Racing Post,* each of them trying to spot a winner for later in the day.

Chico and I, meanwhile, were much more interested in the ten o'clock deadline for the declarations for the two-mile handicap hurdle on the following afternoon, and I had my cell at hand, hoping for a text from Jimmy Guernsey.

It arrived at twenty past ten, and it was just one word long.

Geophysicist.

29

Twelve of the twenty-eight entrants had declared to run, with Geophysicist halfway down the weights at a hundred and fifty-seven pounds, six fewer than Maine Visit, the mount of Robert Price.

Staplegun had also been declared to run with, as expected, Jimmy Guernsey engaged to ride him. In fact, all five of the jockeys I had spoken to were in the declarations, with David Potter down to pilot Geophysicist.

So David had indeed been chosen to ride the one selected to win, and he always did as he was told. He'd said so, for his old mum's sake.

"Do you think Jimmy can fix it?" Chico asked.

"I don't know," I said. "We'll have to wait and see."

Chico and I walked down the road to the racetrack, paying our way in at the Aintree turnstiles like the thousands of others around us.

To me, there was something truly magical about the Grand National meeting. Historically, it had been held at the end of March, but it was now a firm fixture in April, sometimes varying back and forth a week to accommodate the vagaries of the Christian calendar's calculation of Easter.

In the last twenty years or so, the prize money throughout the meeting has increased considerably due to sponsorship, and the supporting races, those in the lead-up to the Grand National, now attracted the cream of British steeplechasers. And the crowds certainly came to watch them.

Chico and I made our way separately through the throng to the viewing steps outside the Weighing Room.

"Hello, Sid," said a Northern Irish voice behind me.

Chico, standing a few yards away, looked concerned.

"Hi, Paddy," I said, all smiles. Chico relaxed.

"I'm surprised to see you here, Sid," Paddy said seriously, "what with all your troubles."

"And what troubles are those?" I asked.

"You know, that kiddie stuff."

"It's all a pack of lies. I assure you, I wouldn't be here if there was any truth in it. It's all a setup orchestrated by our West Belfast friend."

"He's no bloody friend of mine," Paddy said, looking swiftly around him to check that McCusker wasn't standing there, listening to our conversation. "Tell me you haven't been upsetting him."

"Not much," I said.

Not as much as I hoped to upset him the following afternoon.

"Steer clear of him," Paddy warned me once again. "He's dangerous."

But steering clear of danger wasn't something that came easily to me. Here I was, aiming straight for it, not so much poking the proverbial hornets' nest, more like sticking my hand inside and ripping out the guts. I just had to ensure it was my non-stingable hand that I used.

Which reminded me, I should give Queen Mary's Hospital my new cell phone number.

"So what's going to win the National?" I asked Paddy, changing the subject.

"Summer Nights has a good chance, I reckon," he said, "as long as that idiot Bob Price doesn't stand him off like he did at Ascot. I ask you. Jocks these days aren't like we were — no bloody idea how to set a horse for a fence. Don't you wish you were still riding? We could show them a thing or two, eh?"

"We sure could, Paddy," I agreed with a smile.

I'd ridden in the Grand National a total of seven times, winning it once but falling on all six other occasions, twice at the first fence. But the victory was the only one I liked to remember. And how! It had been one of the best days of my life, ranking right up there alongside the birth of Saskia.

"I'm off to find myself a Guinness," Paddy said. "D'you fancy one?"

"No thanks," I said. "It's a bit early, even for you."

He laughed and moved off towards the bar beneath the grandstand in search of a pint of the black stuff.

I, meanwhile, needed a clear head.

"How are you gettin' on with them telephone numbers?" Chico was standing behind me on the steps as we watched the runners for the first race circle in the parade ring.

"It's hopeless," I said, turning slightly. "McCusker gave Robert Price an old-fashioned, non-smart cell that only he knows the number of. If everyone else on that list is the same, then none of them will speak to us."

"I could always have a go meself to be sure," Chico said in a broad Northern Irish accent.

I smiled. "You're welcome to try." I handed him the list of numbers that I'd made the previous evening, about half of which I had so far called without response.

I watched the first race from the top of the County Stand, finding a place alongside the railed-off area reserved for the VIPs from the Sefton Suite below. Chico stood in front and slightly to my left.

I'd been in the VIP suite once, a couple of years previously, for a lunch courtesy of the meeting's sponsor, but I clearly wasn't considered a VIP today. In fact, I received a number of disapproving glances, not least from Peter Medicos.

After the race was over and most of the VIPs had gone back down, he leaned over the metal railing towards where I was still standing.

"Halley," he shouted. "I want a word with you."

I bit my tongue. I'd not been referred to as simply "Halley" by anyone since before I'd first become champion jockey, although it had once been commonplace for stewards and other race officials to refer to jockeys in that manner. Thankfully, the world had moved on. At least I thought it had.

"Here?" I asked, moving towards him.

"No," he said. "There's a private room near the entrance to the Media Centre with *Officials Only* on the door. Meet me there after the next race." He turned abruptly and went down the stairs to the suite, no doubt for his dessert and coffee.

"Charmin'," said Chico. "He could at least have said please."

"Peter Medicos was in the police force for twenty-five years, so he's not in the habit of asking politely. He tells, not asks." I sighed. I still believed I needed Peter Medicos as an ally, not an enemy. "Are you coming down?"

"Nah, I'll stay here and get a tan." He turned his face towards the sun. "I'm not really interested in the horses, if I'm honest. I'll just sit here and try some more of those numbers."

"OK," I said. "See you here for the third."

"Right you are."

I left Chico, balancing the list on his knees and entering numbers into his cell phone, and went back down to the Weighing Room.

I knew Jimmy Guernsey had a ride in the

second race, and I positioned myself so that he would walk right past me on his way to the parade ring. I didn't need to give him any message, or receive one, but I wanted to let him know that I was there and to deter any jitters he may be having.

He saw me as soon as he exited the Weighing Room door, but, this time, he didn't break stride, simply jogging down the steps towards me.

"Get the text?" he said quietly as he went past.

"Yup," I said equally quietly.

There was almost a spring in his step, as if a great burden had been lifted from his shoulders. It wasn't over yet, I thought, but we were on the way.

I remained nearby the parade ring, watching the fifteen runners battle out a two-and-a-half-mile juvenile hurdle on the big television screen.

Jimmy finished a close third, which seemed to greatly please the broadly smiling lady owner who greeted her horse in the unsaddling enclosure as if he'd won by ten lengths.

Her smile was infectious and I found myself grinning back before I remembered my upcoming appointment with Peter Medicos. That was enough to take the smile off anyone's face, I thought, as I went in search of the *Officials Only* door.

Peter was there ahead of me.

I knocked and went in, feeling just like a miscreant schoolboy who has been sent to see the headmaster, having been caught cheating.

The room was quite small, about twelve feet by ten, with a table in the middle surrounded by six ubiquitous, stackable gray plastic chairs. It reminded me of the interview room at Oxford police station.

Peter's battered trilby sat on the table.

"Ah, there you are, Halley," he said, not offering me one of the chairs to sit down.

"Mr. Halley, please," I said pointedly, "or Sid." I smiled at him. "Now, Peter, what's all this about?"

"I thought you would already know that," he said with astonishment. "You're the one who was arrested for child abuse. Uttoxeter may be one thing, but I don't consider it proper that you are here at one of racing's great festivals. You're bringing our sport into disrepute."

"I am completely innocent," I said. "And I haven't even been charged. I have as much right to be here as you do. I paid good money to get in."

He didn't like me answering him back.

"That's as may be, but I still want you off this racetrack now."

The door of the room suddenly opened and Chico walked in, closing it behind him.

"Excuse me," said Peter to him over my shoulder, "this is a private area. Would you please leave?"

Chico ignored him, simply standing there. I could hear a telephone ringing in the silence.

"Answer the phone," Chico said.

"I beg your pardon," Peter said, clearly annoyed. "Now, get out, before I call the police," he almost shouted, but Chico didn't budge an inch.

The phone went on ringing.

"Answer it," Chico said again.

Peter put his hand into his pocket and retrieved a small gray telephone. The ringing was suddenly much louder.

"Answer it," Chico said once more while removing his own phone from his coat.

Peter looked uncertainly at the number readout on the screen, then he pushed a button and the ringing stopped.

"Hello," he said into the small gray telephone.

"Hello," said his voice from the speaker in Chico's phone a fraction of a second later.

We all stood there in silence.

"What's going on?" I asked.

"Mr. Medicos here," Chico said, "has one of Billy McCusker's special phones. The number is on that list of yours, and the records show he was called each time one of them races was fixed."

Peter Medicos made a move towards the door, but Chico took a step across, blocking his path.

"He's a black belt at judo," I said by way of warning. "May I suggest you sit down before he throws you down?"

Peter Medicos stared at me with a degree of loathing, but he didn't move.

"Sit down!" I barked at him, making him jump.

He slowly pulled a chair out from under the table and sat down on it.

"No wonder the bleedin' jockeys never get caught," Chico said, "the effin' game-keeper is one of the poachers."

"I don't know what you're talking about," Peter said, regaining his composure.

"So I'm up on the roof, callin' those numbers you gave me rather than watchin' the race. That's funny, I thinks to myself, I'm sure I can hear a phone start to ring just as I makes a call. So I stops the call, and the ringin' also stops. I tries it again, and the same thing happens. Three times I do it, just to be sure. The ring is comin' from that VIP area, so I goes up slightly above it so I can see and I calls the number once again, this time I lets it ring and ring. Hey, presto, I sees Mr. Medicos here take that phone out of his jacket and answer it."

"I have got to go," Peter said, standing up and reaching for his trilby. "I have duties to perform."

"You're not goin' anywhere, sunshine," Chico said, smacking the trilby off the table, "not unless it's a one-way trip to the slammer. So sit down before I makes you."

"And take that phone," I said.

Chico came around behind Peter and forcibly removed the phone before pushing him back down into the chair.

"You can't prove anything," he said.

"Are you sure about that?" I asked. "And anyway, I don't need to. I simply have to tell McCusker that it was *you* who told me that Geophysicist will win the two-mile handicap hurdle tomorrow afternoon because none of the other runners will be trying."

He went pale, and his shoulders drooped.

I wasn't sure if it was because he was surprised that I knew so much about the fix or because he could all too clearly envisage

458

what would happen to him if I carried out my threat. Maybe it was a bit of both.

"Now what?" Chico said. "We can hardly keep him here all afternoon. What is this place anyway?" He looked around him at the bare, windowless walls.

"Some sort of interview room," I said. "Perhaps the police use it occasionally. Or maybe it's used to sort out bookmaker disputes with punters, that sort of thing."

But I agreed with Chico, we could hardly keep Peter Medicos here all afternoon, and all night, right up until the time of the two-mile hurdle the following afternoon. The penalties for false imprisonment were harsh.

What I found difficult to understand, though, was how the head of the BHA Security Service, a retired chief superintendent of police, had become involved with a man like Billy McCusker. Maybe it was for money. But the BHA didn't pay that badly, and he must receive a police pension as well.

Or was there some other reason?

"What hold has McCusker got over you?" I asked him.

He looked up at me but said nothing.

"Has McCusker threatened you?"

"I don't know what you're talking about," he said. "Now, I have things to attend to." He again stood up, fully recovered from the shock of discovery.

"I thought I told you to sit down," Chico said, taking Peter's left arm and twisting it up his back before forcing him down in the chair.

"You can't treat me like this!" Peter said with barely controlled anger. "How dare you manhandle me! I'll have you in court for this."

"If you're ever in court, sunshine, it will be in the dock," Chico said. But was he right?

"You can't prove anything," Peter said again. "It is simply my word against yours, and who's going to believe someone arrested for child abuse over a chief superintendent?"

"But we have the telephone," I said, "and the records show that McCusker called you every time there was a fixed race."

"I'll deny ever seeing that cell phone before. I'll say it was yours." He was getting more confident by the second.

"Do you know that DNA is present in saliva?" I asked. I only knew myself because of a previous case where a DNA profile had been created from the saliva used to stick down an envelope.

"So what?" Peter said.

"When we talk little flecks of saliva are

projected from our mouths. Your DNA will be on the microphone of that cell."

"I'll say you made me answer a call on it." He was sure of himself now. "You have no proof whatsoever that I have any involvement in race fixing. I'm leaving."

He stood up once more and picked up his hat from the floor.

What should I do? I couldn't afford to let him tell McCusker that I knew about tomorrow's fix. It was a shame that Chico had revealed what he'd found out about the phone, and then I had compounded the error by divulging that I knew about the fix. But what was done was done. Now I had to deal with the situation as it was, not as I would have liked it to be.

"Did you kill Sir Richard Stewart?" I asked.

"No, of course not," he said dismissively.

"But it was murder, wasn't it?"

"I have no idea, but I think you'll find that the inquest will eventually return a verdict of suicide."

As may be, but I didn't believe it and nor did he.

Peter started to move around the table, and I was at a loss to know what to do to stop him.

"Why are you more frightened of Mc-

Cusker than you are of me going to the police or the BHA? You might say it's my word against yours, but there are two of us saying the same thing. Are you sure no one will believe us? Can you take the risk?"

He stopped and turned to face me.

"Nothing you can say or do will make me admit to any wrongdoing."

"I'm not asking you to admit to anything," I said. "In fact, I don't really care if you are found out or not. But I do care passionately about my life and my family, and I'm fed up with being used and abused by that man."

"You and me both," he said.

"So what hold does he have over you?"

He almost laughed. "I'm not going to tell you that, then you'd have the same hold." The laughter died in his throat.

So there was something. He wasn't McCusker's man by choice.

At least that was some good news.

"The phone, please," he said, holding out his right hand towards me.

I was not keen to give it back. But if McCusker called him on it and Peter didn't answer, McCusker was sure to realize that something was amiss.

I handed the phone over to him.

"Do nothing," I said. "If I find out from

462

our Irish friend that he is aware, ahead of time, that I know about tomorrow's fix, then I will tell him that it was you who told me. And, trust me, he would believe it."

"I have absolutely no intention of telling that Irishman anything."

Could I believe him?

Did I have any choice?

30

In contrast to Thursday's bright skies and balmy temperatures, Friday was wet and miserable, with an Atlantic weather front moving in from the west, and the mercury was on the slide.

The conditions seemed to mirror my own mood, but it did nothing to dampen the enthusiasm of the huge number of the local girls who had turned out in all their finery, ignoring the rain and the cold, and wearing skimpy chiffon dresses that left very little to the imagination.

Aintree on the day before the Grand National must be the only place in the world where thousands of "ladies" would turn up in open-toed, extremely high-heeled sandals to splash their way through the puddles from Champagne Bar to grandstand and then back to Champagne Bar.

"Cor blimey," Chico said, utterly transfixed, "have you seen that one." He pointed at one particular young woman who was teetering along on stiletto heels that must have been at least six inches high. "She'll fall and break her ankle."

But she didn't, helped along to the racetrack entrance by a young man in a shiny gray suit, polished shoes and a skinny tie.

Chico and I followed them in, expecting her to tumble at any moment, but she made it to the nearest bar and leaned against the counter. We, meanwhile, dragged our eyes away from her amply displayed cleavage and made our way once again to the Weighing Room steps.

"Do you think standin' here is sensible?" Chico asked. "Those goons from last week must be here to put the money on Geophysicist. Maybe even McCusker himself. You're very much out in the open."

"You go and check out the betting ring," I said to him. "Look out for Barry Montagu and Mr. Wilson, and that girl you chatted up at the betting shop. I need to stay here until I get final confirmation from Jimmy Guernsey. I'll see you on the County Stand roof for the first."

Chico slipped away while I scanned the faces in front of me for anyone familiar, especially anyone familiar from an alleyway behind a Chinese restaurant.

I spotted Jimmy walking in from the direction of the jockeys' parking lot, carrying a small holdall slung over his right shoulder. He spotted me at the same instant and made a slight detour in his route to the Weighing Room in order to walk right past me. He didn't say anything; he just put up the thumb on his left hand as he went by.

So the fix was unfixed.

Now all we had to do was wait for the fallout, provided of course that Peter Medicos or one of the jockeys hadn't bleated everything to McCusker.

I would find that out soon enough.

"We're on," I said to Chico, joining him on the County Stand roof to watch the first race in a fine drizzle.

"Good," he said. "I spotted that bird from the bookie's. But I thought it was better if she didn't see me, so I kept away from her pitch."

"You will have to go and look just before the two-mile hurdle, but it will be too late by then for them to change anything."

"Is it worth havin' a bet in that race?"

"You can, if you like, but I wouldn't put your money on Geophysicist."

"Are you sure it won't win?"

"Not if Jimmy Guernsey has managed to

do what we agreed," I said.

"And what is that, exactly?"

"McCusker believes that Geophysicist will win because all the other jockeys have been told to lose. If things have gone according to plan, Jimmy has told each one of the jockeys, individually and in confidence, that things have changed, and they are now riding the horse selected to win. All except David Potter, who rides Geophysicist. He's been told he has to lose."

"Won't they work it out?"

"They're all so frightened of getting caught that they won't even talk to each other about it. They just do what McCusker or Jimmy Guernsey tells them without question, out of fear. So they will all be trying like crazy to win — all of them, that is, except the very one that McCusker will be expecting to win."

He laughed. "Now, that's what I call a fix. But are you sure it's wise to antagonize him like this?"

"Are you having second thoughts?" I asked.

"Slightly," he said. "There's no one at home protectin' your wife and kid."

I'd been thinking of that too.

"They're perfectly safe at the moment," I said, "because McCusker and his merry men will all be here. But I agree we need to make a beeline for Oxfordshire as soon as the race is over."

"But why are you so keen to stick a spanner in his works?"

"I suppose I want him to realize that he can't go on dictating how races will be run. Maybe it's just a battle of wills between us. He's an irresistible force pushing against my immovable object. One of us will have to concede, and I'm determined it will be him."

"It's a dangerous game," Chico said.

Yes, I thought, bloody dangerous.

The afternoon seemed to drag by, but, eventually, it was nearing the time for the two-mile handicap hurdle.

I stood on the ground floor of the grandstand and watched as the predicted returns for each horse changed on the screen above the Tote counter.

Maine Visit was the favorite, showing a return of three pounds and ten pence for a one-pound stake.

Geophysicist was fourth favorite on the Tote, with a predicted return of six pounds, equivalent to a starting price of five-to-one.

I went out to where the lines of bookmakers' pitches were busily taking money from the swarm of eager punters.

I scanned the nearest of the boards. Geophysicist was mostly quoted at six-to-one or thirteen-to-two, with a few even offering seven-to-one.

I smiled. McCusker's scam was running as he would expect, with his chosen winner showing a lower predicted return on the Tote than the bookmakers' prices would suggest was normal. That meant that Mc-Cusker and his cronies must be betting heavily on Geophysicist on the Tote, using cash, with no resulting inconvenient record of their unusual betting activity.

Peter Medicos had been as good as his word. No warning had been given.

I made my way up to the roof to watch the race, the excitement of the moment making my heart beat a little faster than usual.

Chico was there ahead of me.

"Barry Montagu's pitch was doin' extremely brisk business," he said. "They were offerin' better-than-average odds on all the nags except, you've guessed it, Geophysicist, whose price was marginally worse."

I smiled.

"And Honest Joe Bullen's pitch was just the same," he said. "Absolutely heavin' with eager punters."

McCusker was trying to have his cake and eat it. Gambling heavily on the "sure" winner on the Tote while, at the same time, raking in the money on the other runners by offering slightly higher odds than the other bookmakers, confident in the knowledge that he wouldn't have to pay out.

I just hoped that Jimmy Guernsey really had done the business with the other jocks and that McCusker was about to receive a financial bloody nose, as well as a shock to his system.

I looked down towards the two-mile start, where the twelve runners were walking in a circle, having their girths tightened by the assistant starter and getting ready for the race. I wondered if there would be any banter between the jockeys or whether they were all too nervous about fulfilling their predetermined roles.

I assumed that in addition to David Potter on Geophysicist, Jimmy Guernsey wouldn't actually be trying too hard either. But I thought it was going to be quite entertaining with the other ten all believing that they were riding the horse that was meant to win.

And so it transpired.

The race was initially run at a slow pace, and the field was still tightly bunched as the horses passed the grandstands for the first time. But the pace began to pick up as they straightened up for the three hurdles in the back stretch.

By the time the runners swung left-handed around the last bend, the race was on in earnest, with most of the twelve still in contention.

There are three hurdles in the final straight, and the field began to string out slightly coming to the first of them, the less able horses being incapable of keeping up with the breakneck pace.

I could only imagine with amusement how some of the jockeys must feel if they had been expecting the other runners to fall back, leaving them alone to win. Panic came to mind.

Seven of them jumped the final flight abreast, and the crowd cheered appreciatively as the favorite, Maine Visit, ridden by Robert Price, won by a head in a blanket finish of six horses, with all the jockeys in serious danger of receiving riding bans for excessive use of their whips.

Geophysicist finished just three lengths behind the winner but in ninth place. Jimmy Guernsey's mount was tenth, a further two lengths in the rear.

"Bloody marvelous," said Chico. "Now what?"

"Home, James," I said. "There's nothing more to be gained from staying here."

We skipped down the stairs from the County Stand roof towards the exits and ran straight into Billy McCusker and his three Shankill Road Volunteers.

I am not sure who was the more surprised, but it was clear who was the more angry, and I was very grateful for the presence, about ten yards away, of a pair of large uniformed Merseyside policemen on the lookout for pickpockets amongst the bustling crowd.

"Halley," McCusker said, having dropped his supercilious use of the *Mr.* "Is this your doing?"

"Is what my doing?" I asked, trying to keep a smile off my face.

"I promise you," he said with real menace, his dark eyes appearing even more sunken under his protruding brow than in the photographs, "if I find out that you are responsible, I'll make sure you fry."

His words sent fresh shivers down my spine, and I edged a little closer to the policemen.

McCusker then turned and walked away, followed by his three burly bodyguards. Chico and I stood and watched them go until they disappeared amongst the crowd.

"If Jimmy Guernsey has any sense," I said, laughing, "he'll hide in the Weighing Room all night."

"Come on," Chico said, pulling at my coat sleeve, "let's get goin' before that friendly foursome decides to come back."

We hurried back to the hotel to collect the Range Rover and then set off south back to Oxfordshire.

"Do you think he'll come after us immediately?" Chico asked when we were safely on the freeway.

"Judging by how quickly he sent his boys to put a ring of fire round Tony Molson's place, I wouldn't be at all surprised if he wasn't already on the road behind us."

I pressed my right foot slightly harder on the gas pedal and broke the speed limit all the way down the M6 to Birmingham.

"What are we goin' to do?" Chico asked.

"Be vigilant," I said. "All hands on deck, and prepare to repel boarders."

I had called D.C.I. Watkinson as we had left the Park Hotel, leaving a message that asked him to call back urgently, and he did so as we neared Aynsford.

"What's the problem?" he asked.

"I may have poked that hornets' nest," I said, "and I might need some help with the fallout."

"Would that be a Mr. McCusker–type hornets' nest?" he asked.

"Precisely so," I said.

"And what sort of help are you wanting?"

"A police guard on my home."

"Mmm," he said. "When for?"

"Tonight," I said. "And maybe tomorrow as well."

"We don't have that sort of manpower."

"You had enough to place a policeman outside after I got arrested."

"He would have been there to prevent you removing any potential evidence from the property before our searches were complete."

And, all this time, I'd thought it had been for the protection of my home from over-zealous members of the press.

"Well, I need a policeman stationed there tonight because I firmly believe that McCusker or his cronies will attempt to gain entry or, worse, burn down the property. They as much as said so to me this afternoon."

"Do you have witnesses to that conversation?"

"Yes," I said. "Chico Barnes was with me."

There was a silence from the other end of the line, and I was worried that the chief inspector might think it would be better to get a conviction for arson after the event than for conspiracy to commit arson before it.

"I also have a witness to *this* conversation. And if you let my house burn down in order to try to get him for arson, I will sue the police for negligence."

"Mr. Halley, how is it that you have an uncanny knack of knowing what I'm thinking?"

"Well, you can stop thinking it and give me a police guard. Especially as I can't legally be there. Have you had any luck on that front?"

"No, sorry," he said. "It will have to wait for you to surrender to your bail at Oxford next week."

"By next week I may not have a house."

"OK, OK," he said, "I get the message. I'll see what I can do."

"Then do it fast," I said. "They may already be on their way."

"I'll ask uniform to route a patrol car round that way regularly throughout the evening and night, although it's Friday, and they'll be pretty busy in Banbury town center with the nightclub revelers."

It wasn't much, but I suppose it was better than nothing.

Marina, Saskia and Rosie were overjoyed to see us back at Aynsford in one piece, and Charles was pretty relieved too. He looked desperately tired, as if he hadn't slept for two nights.

"How have things been here?" I asked Marina quietly.

"Fine, I suppose. Charles has been good at making sure that all the doors are locked all the time, and he keeps us cheerful with stories of how nothing could be as bad as being up against the Chinese on the Yangtze." She rolled her eyes, and I laughed. "But I do wish he wouldn't wander round the house with that bloody shotgun under his arm. He frightens Saskia."

"I'll have a word with him."

"How about you?" Marina asked. "Did you get done what you wanted?"

"You might say that," I said. "I managed to unfix the race that McCusker had fixed. I'm afraid it made him rather mad."

"Will he come after you?" She was worried.

"I expect so. That's partly why I did it. I need to get him out in the open, to show himself."

"So Charles can shoot him with his shot-gun?"

"Or I can. I think it's the only way of bringing all this to a finish. Otherwise, we'll never get rid of him. It's a dangerous tactic, but you should be safe here. And I've arranged for the police to patrol regularly past the house."

"It's us I'm more concerned about than the house," she said, putting an arm around my waist.

"We'll all be fine," I said.

Silly thing to say, really.

31

"Do you really think he'll come tonight?" Chico asked.

"I think he may come to our house in Nutwell," I said, "but I don't think he knows we're staying here in Aynsford — at least I hope he doesn't. He's shown before that he's impulsive and does things very quickly. He managed to arrange for Saskia to be kidnapped from school in just one day, and he attacked the Molsons' house the same night that Tony rode Black Peppercorn to win against his orders. Yes, I think it's quite likely he'll come tonight."

"Then we shouldn't be here. We should be guardin' your place, and bugger the bail conditions."

"I agree."

Marina was far from happy, especially when I told her that there was no way I was taking her with me.

"You and Saskia have got to stay here," I

said firmly. "It is much safer for you here than it is at home. Charles will stay here too."

But I might take his shotgun, I thought.

It was about eight o'clock when Chico and I took up our position in the dog kennel, sitting in the caged run on garden chairs with Charles's loaded shotgun on my knees.

It was beginning to get dark, but, thankfully, the rain had stopped, so we could sit out in the open. The view from the kennel was up the driveway towards the gate, and covered the whole front of the house and part of the road beyond.

I was happy to sit there, quietly waiting for things to develop, but Chico had itchy feet and insisted on going on a reconnaissance tour around the property every ten to fifteen minutes or so to check that no one was approaching from the rear over the garden fence.

After about an hour and a half, I had a wander around too, eager to stretch my legs. For the umpteenth time, I checked the cartridges in the gun and the spares in my pocket. I wondered if I would use them. It would undoubtedly get me into trouble, as it was Charles who held the shotgun license, not me. But surely acting in self-defense included using all means at one's disposal.

I went back to sitting in the dog kennel, waiting and watching, as the evening turned into night.

Chico and I had done plenty of stakeouts during the ten years or so we had worked together as a team, often at various racetracks, endlessly waiting for the bad guys to turn up. And we had learned to be patient.

I sat for a while longer and then went for another stroll around the property. So much for the police, I said to myself. I hadn't seen the promised patrol car pass by once throughout the whole evening.

At about eleven-thirty, Chico's phone rang loudly in the still night air.

"Oops," he said, extracting it from his pocket. "Sorry."

He answered, and I thought it would be his little blonde number, or some other female interest, but, instead, he held the phone out to me.

"Hello," I said with trepidation.

"Is that Sid Halley?" I could hardly understand what was being said, as the person at the other end was mumbling.

"Yes," I replied. "Sid Halley speaking."

"I told him where you are," came the mumbled reply.

"Sorry," I said. "Who is this?"

"Peter," said the mumbler. "Peter Medicos."

"How did you get this number?"

"It was on the phone." It was still difficult to hear what he was saying.

"Peter, are you all right?" I asked.

"I will be," he mumbled. "At least I hope I will be. McCusker's men . . ." He tailed off.

"Beat you up," I said, finishing his sentence.

"Yes. He wanted to know where you were. He said he'd tried to phone you several times, but you'd gone into hiding. I told him I didn't know where, but he wouldn't take that for an answer. In the end, I told him you were staying with Admiral Roland at Aynsford."

I could feel the panic rising in my throat.

"When did you tell him that?" I asked in trepidation.

"Hours ago. I couldn't move for ages. Quite apart from my face, I fear one of them might have ruptured my spleen."

I remembered the beating I had received in the Towcester racetrack parking lot and how I hadn't been able to function for a while afterwards. McCusker's men certainly knew where to punch for maximum effect.

"How many hours ago?" I asked with

increasing alarm.

"I don't rightly know. Lots. I'm sorry."

It was under three hours' drive from Aintree to Aynsford.

"Peter, get yourself to the hospital as quickly as possible," I said. "And thank you."

At least he had called. He hadn't needed to.

I hung up. And immediately tried to call Charles's number, but there was just a continuous tone on the line. Unobtainable.

Oh God!

"Come on," I shouted urgently at Chico. "We're in the wrong damn place."

The Range Rover fairly tore up the tarmac between Nutwell and Aynsford, reaching speeds in excess of seventy miles per hour on the winding, single-lane road.

"Stealth or full-frontal?" Chico said as we swayed sideways around a bend.

"I don't think we have time for stealth," I said. "Charles's phone is out. They must be there already. Call the police, and the fire department. Do it now."

He pressed the buttons, hanging on to the grab handles for dear life as I swerved around yet another bend.

"No effin' signal," he said. "We're too

close to the hill."

"Keep trying," I shouted at him. "It usually works, in the end."

The black Toyota Land Cruiser was parked in the road outside the gate to Charles's house. Both Chico and I saw it together.

"Stop," Chico shouted. "I'll deal with that."

I braked sharply to a halt, and he climbed out, unfolding his penknife.

I left him there and gunned the Range Rover's engine, racing down the long driveway towards the house.

I suppose I should have really waited for Chico. Odds of two against four were hardly sensible for an attack, in the first place. To have reduced it to one against four was plain careless. But all I could think about was McCusker's threat to rape, murder and then feed Saskia to the pigs.

He was a man who didn't make empty threats. I knew he would do what he said. That's why I was desperate to get to Saskia as soon as possible and before Billy McCusker could.

I swung the Range Rover around the corner towards the front door and the glassed-in porch, the headlights lighting up the scene. There was a man, all dressed in black, standing in the middle of the driveway, and he was pointing at me.

A star appeared in the windshield just above my head. A second joined it. And then another.

It took me an instant to realize that they were bullet holes. The man wasn't just pointing at me; he was aiming a gun and firing. I flung myself over and down to my left, across the central console, and stamped hard on the accelerator, pointing the Range Rover straight at him.

I both heard and felt the impact.

I sat up and braked hard, but the wheels skidded over the loose gravel and I plowed right on, straight into the wall of Charles's garage.

The air bag deployed with a bang, saving me from hitting the steering wheel, but the crash had been a fairly low-speed affair, and I was uninjured.

I scrambled out through the driver's door and went to look around the front. The man in black must have been collected up by the front bumper and carried forward, as he now lay squashed between the vehicle and the garage wall, his bloodied head clearly visible in the glow of the left-hand headlight, which had amazingly survived the impact.

The man, however, appeared not to have

been so lucky.

The odds had improved suddenly. Now it was one against three, and would be two against three when Chico arrived.

I grabbed the shotgun off the backseat and made my way gingerly towards the glassed-in porch and the front door, balancing the double barrels in my opened plastic palm.

The house was in complete darkness, and silent.

Charles habitually left the light switched on at the far corner of the porch, but even that was now off and dark.

Where were McCusker and his other two men?

They must have heard me arrive, so were they waiting for me to walk through the front door and straight into a hail of lead?

And where were Marina, Saskia and Charles? And how about Rosie? Why wasn't she barking?

And where were the police and fire department? Had Chico even managed to call them yet?

So many questions raced through my head, and so many fears with them.

I stepped onto the porch through the open door, the only sound in my ears being that of my own heart thumping away at fifteen or twenty to the dozen.

I knew I had to go in.

Hurry up, Chico.

Perhaps I could have waited for the police to turn up, if indeed they were coming, but I just *knew* I had to go in.

This had to be settled between McCusker and me and settled now.

The heavy oak front door proper was also wide open, with pitch-blackness beyond: no light from the alarm keypad near the door, no glow from the phone charger on the hall table. The power had been cut, along with the phone line.

I went through the doorway at knee level, crouching down and silently pulling my legs beneath me like a Cossack, the shotgun cradled in my lap.

There was no hail of lead, just silence.

Where were they?

I stood upright and moved quickly in the darkness towards the kitchen, but I didn't get there because I tripped over something lying on the floor in the middle of the hall, tumbling headlong and sending the shotgun flying out of my grasp and clattering across the flagstones.

Bugger, I thought. So much for stealth.

On my knees, I reached back to see what had tripped me.

It was Charles. I could tell from the velvet-and-silk smoking jacket he was wearing. And he was lying on his back, not moving.

Oh God!

I fumbled, one-handed, trying to find his wrist.

Thankfully, there was a pulse, but it was weak and fast.

I rolled him over onto his front and placed him as best I could in the recovery position, although it was difficult to tell exactly in the dark.

I listened, straining to hear any sound.

There was nothing, other than the slight wheeze of Charles's breathing.

Where was McCusker? Was he inside the house or outside?

I scrambled forward, still on my knees, searching for the shotgun. There was just about enough light coming in from outside for me to determine in which direction lay the door to the kitchen.

After what seemed like an age, I found the gun, nestling under a console table, and retrieved it.

Now, then, you bastard, where are you?

I said it to myself rather than out loud.

I stood up and went into the kitchen, searching for any slight variation in the darkness that might indicate a person's face or hand.

I was scared. Very scared.

I'd been lucky not to be hit by one of the bullets that had come through the Range Rover windshield. Would I be so lucky again? I'd been shot once before, in the stomach. The resulting damage had nearly killed me, and it still gave me trouble more than fourteen years later.

So I had no particular wish to repeat the experience.

I went through the kitchen into the laundry room, but that too was empty.

Had they already seized Marina and Saskia and then departed? If so, why had one of their number been standing in the drive when I arrived? And how about their vehicle? It had still been there on the road outside the gate. I'd seen it.

They must be still here. And so must Saskia and Marina. But where?

And where the hell was Chico? Had he yet managed to call the police?

There was a creak above my head. Charles's old floorboards were at it again, and someone was definitely moving about upstairs. Was it Marina and Saskia or someone else more unwelcome?

I retraced my path back through the kitchen towards the hallway, my eyes now better adjusted to the darkness.

There were more creaks from above.

What should I do? Did I go up the stairs or wait for them down here?

My mouth was dry, and my heart went on thumping away fortissimo, almost as if it would burst out through my ribs. I felt sick with fear, but forced myself forward towards the staircase.

I had to find Marina and Saskia.

That was my job. To keep them safe.

Oh God! I had put them in too much danger. Was it all about to end in disaster?

Stop it! I told myself. Pull yourself together. Don't disintegrate now. There is work still to be done.

I put a foot on the bottom step and went up, standing only on the very edges to avoid the creaky bits in the middle.

As I neared the top, I lay down on the stairs so just my head popped up over the landing — along with the shotgun, of course, which I held one-handed.

The landing was very dark, and I strained my eyes to see any movement.

Come on, you bastards, I said to myself, where are you?

Keeping as low as possible, I went slowly along the landing towards the guest room where Marina and I had been staying, keeping my feet right next to the wall to avoid the creaking floorboards.

Once again, maybe for the hundredth time, I checked that the safety catch on the shotgun was set at off so that it was ready to fire.

I crept forward, listening out for any telltale sounds of movement.

Where were they?

My tongue felt huge, and it stuck to the roof of my mouth. My breathing was fast and shallow, and my heart went on thumping.

I pushed open the door to the guest room with the barrels of the shotgun, the hinges emitting a tiny squeak that sounded much too loud in the stillness.

I stepped through the doorway, my finger twitching on the trigger.

Nothing.

I moved farther into the room, swinging the door closed to check that no one was hiding behind it.

There wasn't.

Where were they?

I leaned down and looked under the bed.

Zilch.

Suddenly, I heard footsteps running along the landing.

I leaped out of the room in time to see

shadowy figures running towards the stairs, three men clearly silhouetted against the lighter rectangle of the window beyond.

I dropped to one knee, swung the shotgun and discharged both barrels, great flashes extending from each in the darkness.

The noise was unbelievable, the reports bouncing back at me off the walls and ceiling.

I had aimed low, but I couldn't be certain if I'd hit anyone. The three had been on the stairs before I'd fired. Perhaps I'd been too slow. I couldn't hear any cries of pain, but I probably wouldn't have heard them anyway over the dreadful ringing in my ears.

I urgently scrabbled in my coat pocket for the spare cartridges, spilling them both out onto the floor in my haste.

Dammit. Why did I have just one hand when I desperately needed two?

I had to put the gun down to search around with my fingers for the shells, all the time worrying that McCusker was getting away, and maybe getting away with Saskia, although I was sure she hadn't been with the men on the landing or I wouldn't have fired.

At last I found the cartridges and managed to fumble them into the chambers. I snapped the gun closed and released the safety catch.

Now what?

I edged towards the stairs.

There was no one lying there wounded or dying. I must have missed.

But then I noticed some droplets on the wooden treads, each one glistening slightly in the meager light from outside.

Blood splatter.

I smiled. I hoped it was McCusker's.

My joy, however, was short-lived.

Gasoline! I could smell gasoline!

I rushed down the stairs and over to the front door, glancing briefly around it and onto the glassed-in porch.

The whole floor was awash with liquid, and the smell of gas was almost overwhelming. And I could hear someone pouring more of the damn stuff at the far end.

I daren't shoot, as the flash from the barrels would surely ignite the fumes.

I withdrew my head, slammed the heavy door closed and went swiftly to the window.

Against the light from the still-illuminated Range Rover, I could see a figure holding a jerry can, lifting it high to pour its last contents in a line across the gravel from the porch door. As I watched, he put down the can and then lit a rag with a cigarette lighter, holding it out in front of him.

It didn't take much of a genius to realize what he was about to do.

I fired at him through the glass, both barrels.

He staggered and fell. Another one down.

To my horror, a second man then stepped forward from the shadows. He picked up the burning rag, and I could see by its light that this was McCusker himself, his high cheekbones and protruding brow clearly visible in the glow.

I broke open the gun, ejecting the empty cases, but I had nothing to replace them with. Charles had had only four shells in the box, and I'd fired them all.

Why had I used both barrels?

I watched helplessly as McCusker moved a few steps closer to the porch before tossing the rag towards the open doorway.

What had Chico said about starting fires with gas? *Effin' stupid. Only a bloody fool sets a fire with gasoline. It's far too explosive.*

As if in slow motion, the flaming rag arced through the opening, igniting the air-and-gasoline-vapor mixture inside the porch long before it reached the liquid on the floor.

The porch exploded.

I instinctively ducked down as a huge fireball burst through the glass walls and roof of the porch, sending razor-sharp shards in every direction, the shock of the explosion also breaking the remaining panes in the window above my head.

When I stood up, the view in front of me was like a vision conjured up by the Devil.

Everything seemed to be on fire, covered in burning gasoline that had been thrown out by the blast.

Everything, including Billy McCusker, who danced around in a deadly jig with flames consuming his clothes, his face and his hair as he tried to beat them out with his burning hands.

Suddenly, the place was awash with blue flashing lights as a firetruck pulled up abruptly in the driveway behind my burning Range Rover.

I stood there transfixed, watching through the broken window, as a burly fireman in a big yellow helmet threw a blanket over Mc-Cusker and then knocked him to the ground with a rugby tackle, rolling him over and over on the gravel until all the flames were extinguished.

I watched as the fireman stood up, leaving McCusker lying in a heap under the still-smoldering blanket. Was he dead? I wondered. Probably, I thought. He'd been on fire like a human torch. But stuntmen do it every day and they survive. But they have full-cover fireproof suits, while McCusker had had nothing at all on his face and head. Even if he survived, he would be dreadfully burned.

Either way, dead or alive, it was over.

He had sown the wind, and now he had reaped the whirlwind.

Meanwhile, other firefighters were already connecting hoses to the firetruck, and they would soon have the rest of the flames out.

What I really wanted now was an ambulance for Charles and a search party to find Marina and Saskia.

32

The following Monday, I ended up back in the same interview room at Oxford police station with Detective Superintendent Ingram, together with his sidekick, Sergeant Fleet, Detective Chief Inspector Watkinson and Maggie Jennings, my solicitor.

Although this time, it seemed, I wasn't under arrest, and I'd not been required to wait for hours beforehand in cell number 5. But I was still being interviewed under caution. Everything I said would be taken down and may be used in evidence.

"Now, Mr. Halley," said the superintendent, "can you tell us everything that occurred at Aynsford last Friday night."

As before, Maggie Jennings didn't want me to tell them anything. If it had been up to her, I'd have replied "No comment" to every question. But I'd had enough of doing that.

Now it was time to put the record straight.

So I told the policemen everything that I could remember from the moment Chico and I arrived back at Aynsford from Aintree.

"You admit that you willfully disregarded your bail conditions by going to your house?" asked the superintendent.

"Yes," I said.

He made a note on his pad while Maggie Jennings pursed her lips in disapproval.

"And you took Admiral Roland's shotgun with you in spite of you not holding a license for it?"

"Yes," I said again, and he made another note. Maggie Jennings snorted.

"Are you aware that discharging a shotgun at somebody is an extremely serious matter?"

"So is trying to burn down a house with people inside it," I replied. "And, by the way, how are McCusker and his Volunteers?"

"McCusker has been transferred to the special burns unit at Stoke Mandeville Hospital. He's alive, but only just, and the prognosis is not good for his survival. The man you hit with your Range Rover, Luke Walker, was probably luckier. He was killed outright by the collision and pronounced dead at the scene."

"And the other two?"

"Both of the men you shot will live," he said, "although one of them, Andrew Hebborn, may lose his arm, such was the extent of the damage caused."

I suppose I had instinctively shot straight at the flaming rag rather than at the man actually holding it. Now he might lose his arm.

Join the club.

"How about the other one?" I asked.

"The other man, Shane Duffy, was peppered by some shot in his left calf and knee, but there was only soft tissue damage with a minor loss of blood. Very sore, I'm sure, but he'll make a full recovery. He is now under arrest. He was tackled by Mr. Barnes while trying to fetch their vehicle."

I nodded. Chico had told me about it later that night in his own unique manner.

"So there I am, comin' down the drive, and this geezer is walkin' towards me, limpin'-like and swearin' blue murder. Cor blimey, you should have heard him, effin' this and blindin' the other, and not a good word for you, Sid, I can tell you. But he's so preoccupied with himself that he doesn't even notice me until I've chucked him over my shoulder and put him in a stranglehold."

"What took you so bloody long?" I'd

asked him.

"First, I has to puncture the tires on their Toyota, like, then I tries to make the calls, but there's still no effin' signal on me bleedin' phone, is there? Had to almost break into someone's place to get a landline to call the cops and the fire department. No one would bloody answer their doors."

I didn't blame them. I wouldn't have either.

"Is there anything else you'd like to tell us?" the superintendent asked, bringing my thoughts back to the present.

"Yes," I said. "As a matter of fact, there is."

Against Maggie Jennings's better judgment, I went through everything that had happened in the preceding four weeks in chronological order.

Well, almost everything. I didn't say anything about Tony and Margaret Molson being kidnappers, not only of Saskia from her school but also of Pierre Beaudin's twin sons from the clinic in Montparnasse.

I also decided not to apprise them of the finer details of the race fixing, and especially not the names of the jockeys involved. Nor did I tell them of Chico's uncovering of Peter Medicos as McCusker's inside man at the BHA. I had decided that that information was something I should keep to myself.

For the good of racing.

As I walked out of the police station at six-thirty, I thought back to what had happened since the explosion.

Charles was still in intensive care, the doctors being worryingly noncommittal about his chances of survival.

He had been severely beaten around the face and head, one blow being of sufficient force to fracture his skull and cause a hemorrhage in the brain. A team of surgeons had operated on him throughout Friday night in order to remove a portion of his skull to relieve the pressure in his head.

The doctors had became more optimistic as time had moved on and there had been no further deterioration in his condition, but it was still touch and go as to whether he'd have severe amnesia, permanent brain damage or even if he'd wake up at all.

Marina and Saskia, together with Rosie, had been hiding in the house all the time, in Saskia's favorite "sardines" hiding place, high up in the eaves, through a removable access panel in one of the old servants' bedrooms.

It had taken quite a while for me to find them, even with the help of a fireman and a powerful flashlight. I had continually shouted their names, and, eventually, Marina had deemed it safe to emerge.

She clung to me like a limpet and told me how terrified she'd been — first, when all the lights had suddenly gone out, and then later, even worse, when she'd heard the shots being fired and the sound of the explosion. She had tried to phone for help, but the landline had been cut, and there was no signal on her cell. Charles had sent her up to hide with Saskia while he had chosen to stay downstairs to protect them. Rosie, it seemed, had crawled in with them and had refused to budge.

I had been determined to bring matters to a head between McCusker and me, but even I hadn't foreseen the collateral damage it would cause. Quite apart from what had happened to Charles, one man had died, and McCusker himself was in critical condition and not expected to survive, with third-degree burns over forty percent of his body.

In addition, the house at Aynsford had been badly damaged by the explosion, to say nothing of our Range Rover and Charles's old Mercedes, neither of which would cruise the open road again.

The Admiral recovered consciousness four

days after being attacked and confounded all the doctors by the pace of his recovery. Far from there being any loss of memory, Charles could recall everything right up until the moment he had been struck on the head by McCusker's baseball bat.

Marina and I went to see him in the hospital as soon as we were allowed.

"The ruddy doctors won't let me get up," he said when we arrived. "Some bloody nonsense about me possibly feeling dizzy if I stand."

I laughed. There was no permanent brain damage there, then, but his poor face was swollen and bruised, and he sported a humdinger of a pair of black eyes. There was also a line of stitching stretching halfway across his scalp where the surgeons had been busy.

"You poor thing," Marina said, stroking the back of his hand.

"Can you tell us what happened?" I said.

"Those awful Irishmen wanted to know where Marina and little Saskia were hiding," he said, "but I wouldn't tell them. They also demanded to know where you were too, Sid. They were quite frantic. Two of them held me by the arms while the others hit me in the face and in the stomach." He rubbed his tummy. "Jolly hard too, let me tell you. But I was damned if I was going to tell them anything."

He smiled, and Marina squeezed his hand and kissed him on the cheek. Charles had clearly been elevated from "complete nuisance" to "dashing hero" in her eyes, and with good reason.

A week after Charles regained consciousness, I returned once again to Oxford police station, where I was officially released from my police bail and reunited with my laptop computer, cell phone and passport, although the same custody sergeant as before was not in the slightest apologetic as he handed them back to me.

But at least he hadn't described me as *scum* like he had the last time.

I could now legally return to my home, even though I'd been openly staying there for the past ten days.

Not having a car was a real bore. I'd already ordered a replacement Range Rover from the dealer, but it would take three weeks to arrive.

My insurance, I discovered, did not cover the cost of an interim rental car in the event of a complete write-off. "It only allows for a replacement car during the repair period," the woman from the insurance company had said unhelpfully. "If yours can't be repaired, then I'm afraid it doesn't apply."

Marina, in one of her "greener" moments, had suggested that we should try living without a car for the three weeks. "It will make us appreciate it all the more when it does come," she'd said, all self-righteously, before swiftly organizing a lift to school and back for Saskia with the mother of another girl in the village.

I, personally, thought it was a damn silly idea. Did Marina have any idea how difficult it was to get from Nutwell to Oxford and back again on public transport? Especially as it hadn't stopped raining for a week.

I dodged another heavy shower as I walked through the city center towards the railway station.

I know that I'd been hoping for rain, but not this much.

Detective Chief Inspector Watkinson was the first person to call me on my newly recovered phone as I waited on the platform for a flood-delayed train to Banbury.

"There are a couple of things I thought you'd be interested to know," he said. "First, Billy McCusker died this morning. He had too much of his skin burned away to survive. Apparently, he did well to last as long as he did, but it seems it was inevitable. According to the doctor I spoke to, skin is needed as a barrier to keep fluids in the body, and McCusker had lost so much of his that the fluids simply evaporated away faster than they could replace them. He died of multiple organ failure brought on by severe dehydration."

He had, effectively, died of thirst.

Just as Darren Paisley had in Belfast, nailed to the floor.

"And the second thing?" I asked.

"More copies of those indecent photos were found by Greater Manchester Police when they searched McCusker's house. Even Superintendent Ingram is now convinced you were the victim of a malicious frame-up, and he's even gone so far as to issue a press release to that effect."

That was a relief, I thought, provided people would believe it. In my experience, folk always wanted to imagine the worst of their fellow man, whatever the actual facts might indicate.

"So who was it that complained to you in the first place?" I asked.

"No complaint was made directly to the police," he said. "But I understand three were made to social services."

"Who from?" I asked again.

"It wasn't so much the complaints that

got you into trouble, it was the pictures found in the shed, and that one on your cell phone."

"But those pictures would never have been found without the complaints having been made first. That's why I'd like to know who made them."

"Does it really matter?" he said.

Did it? I supposed not. Whoever had complained would have been forced to do so by McCusker. Did it really matter who they were?

"Do you know?" I asked.

"No way," he said with a laugh. "I'd need a court order to find out, and, even then, they probably wouldn't tell me. Social services are more secretive than MI6. Nothing gets said unless it's in the best interest of the children."

The best interest of the children.

Saskia was still nervous going to bed, and she liked to go to sleep with the light on in her bedroom. But, overall, she had come through the experience pretty unscathed and was now making grand plans for the imminent arrival of her very own red setter puppy.

Marina and I had made our peace with Tim and Paula Gaucin, even though I suspected that Annabel wouldn't be coming for another sleepover anytime soon, if ever.

"Oh yes, one more thing," said the chief inspector. "I see from my newspaper this morning that Peter Medicos has resigned as head of racing security."

"Yes," I said, "so I've heard."

"One of my ex-colleagues who now works for Greater Manchester Police told me that they found some compromising pictures of him in a safe in McCusker's house. Naked in bed with another man, it seems. Could that have had anything to do with his resignation?"

"I have no idea," I lied. "Didn't he say to the press that he wanted to spend more time with his wife?"

He laughed. "Oh yeah! That's what they always say when someone leaves under a cloud. Especially in those circumstances. Nudge nudge. Wink wink. Say no more!"

But I had little doubt that he had been the victim of a setup, and that the pictures had been created solely for the purpose of blackmail and control. I rather hoped they would remain out of the papers.

In spite of everything, I believed that Peter Medicos was fundamentally a good man. Otherwise, he wouldn't have made that phone call, and I would have been still waiting in the dog kennel at Nutwell while Mc-

Cusker took out his fearful revenge on my family two miles away at Aynsford.

"Perhaps you should apply for his job," I said. "The BHA seem to like appointing ex-policemen as head of their Security Service."

"Not me," he said. "I don't know enough about horses or racing. But how about you? I would have thought that you'd have been the perfect candidate."

Now, there was a thought.

The phone buzzed in my hand.

"Sorry, I've got another call coming in," I said.

"OK. Take it. We'll speak again soon."

The chief inspector hung up, and I answered the second call.

It was from Harold Bryant at Queen Mary's Hospital.

"Sid," he said excitedly. "We've got you a hand."

ABOUT THE AUTHOR

Felix Francis, a graduate of London University, spent seventeen years teaching A-level physics before taking on an active role in the writing career of his father, Dick Francis. He has assisted with the research of many of the Dick Francis novels, including *Shattered, Under Orders*, and *Twice Shy*, which drew on Felix's experiences as a physics teacher and as an international marksman. He is coauthor with his father of the *New York Times* bestsellers *Dead Heat, Silks, Even Money*, and *Crossfire*, and the author of *Dick Francis's Bloodline* and *Dick Francis's Gamble.* He lives in England.